A SEAL'S OATH

By Cora Seton

Author's Note

A SEAL's Oath is the first volume in the SEALs of Chance Creek series, set in the fictional town of Chance Creek, Montana. To find out more about Boone, Clay, Jericho and Walker, look for the rest of the books in the series, including:

A SEAL's Vow
A SEAL's Pledge
A SEAL's Consent

Also, don't miss Cora Seton's other Chance Creek series, the Cowboys of Chance Creek and the Heroes of Chance Creek

The Cowboys of Chance Creek Series:
The Cowboy Inherits a Bride (Volume 0)
The Cowboy's E-Mail Order Bride (Volume 1)
The Cowboy Wins a Bride (Volume 2)
The Cowboy Imports a Bride (Volume 3)
The Cowgirl Ropes a Billionaire (Volume 4)
The Sheriff Catches a Bride (Volume 5)
The Cowboy Lassos a Bride (Volume 6)
The Cowboy Rescues a Bride (Volume 7)
The Cowboy Earns a Bride (Volume 8)
The Cowboy's Christmas Bride (Volume 9)

The Heroes of Chance Creek Series:

The Navy SEAL's E-Mail Order Bride (Volume 1)
The Soldier's E-Mail Order Bride (Volume 2)
The Marine's E-Mail Order Bride (Volume 3)
The Navy SEAL's Christmas Bride (Volume 4)
The Airman's E-Mail Order Bride (Volume 5)

Visit Cora's website at www.coraseton.com
Find Cora on Facebook at facebook.com/CoraSeton
Sign up for my newsletter HERE.
www.coraseton.com/sign-up-for-my-newsletter

CHAPTER ONE

★

N AVY SEAL BOONE Rudman should have been concentrating on the pile of paperwork in front of him. Instead he was brooding over a woman he hadn't seen in thirteen years. If he'd been alone, he would have pulled up Riley Eaton's photograph on his laptop, but three other men ringed the table in the small office he occupied at the Naval Amphibious Base at Little Creek, Virginia, so instead he mentally ran over the information he'd found out about her on the Internet. Riley lived in Boston, where she'd gone to school. She'd graduated with a fine arts degree, something which confused Boone; she'd never talked about wanting to study art when they were young. She worked at a vitamin manufacturer, which made no sense at all. And why was she living in a city, when Riley had only ever come alive when she'd visited Chance Creek, Montana, every summer as a child?

Too many questions. Questions he should know the answer to, since Riley had once been such an integral part of his life. If only he hadn't been such a fool,

Boone knew she still would be. Still a friend at least, or maybe much, much more. Pride had kept him from finding out.

He was done with pride.

He reached for his laptop, ready to pull up her photograph, whether he was alone or not, but stopped when it chimed to announce a video call. For one crazy second, Boone wondered if his thoughts had conjured Riley up, but he quickly shook away that ridiculous notion.

Probably his parents wondering once again why he wasn't coming home when he left the Navy. He'd explained time and again the plans he'd made, but they couldn't comprehend why he wouldn't take the job his father had found him at a local ranch.

"Working with horses," his dad had said the last time they talked. "What more do you want?"

It was tempting. Boone had always loved horses. But he had something else in mind. Something his parents found difficult to comprehend. The laptop chimed again.

"You going to get that?" Jericho Cook said, looking up from his work. Blond, blue-eyed, and six-foot-one inches of muscle, he looked out of place hunched over his paperwork. He and the other two men sitting at the table were three of Boone's most trusted buddies and members of his strike team. Like him, they were far more at home jumping out of airplanes, infiltrating terrorist organizations and negotiating their way through disaster areas than sitting on their asses filling out forms.

But paperwork caught up to everyone at some point.

He wouldn't have to do it much longer, though. Boone was due to separate from the Navy in less than a month. The others were due to leave soon after. They'd joined up together—egging each other on when they turned eighteen over their parents' objections. They'd survived the brutal process of becoming Navy SEALs together, too, adamant that they'd never leave each other behind. They'd served together whenever they could. Now, thirteen years later, they'd transitioned back to civilian life together as well.

The computer chimed a third time and his mind finally registered the name on the screen. Boone slapped a hand on the table to get the others' attention.

"It's him!"

"Him, who?" Jericho asked.

"Martin Fulsom, from the Fulsom Foundation. He's calling me!"

"Are you sure?" Clay Pickett shifted his chair over to where he could see. He was an inch or two shorter than Jericho, with dark hair and a wiry build that concealed a perpetual source of energy. Even now Clay's foot was tapping as he worked.

Boone understood his confusion. Why would Martin Fulsom, who must have a legion of secretaries and assistants at his command, call him personally?

"It says Martin Fulsom."

"Holy shit. Answer it," Jericho said. He shifted his chair over, too. Walker Norton, the final member of their little group, stood up silently and moved behind the others. Walker had dark hair and dark eyes that hinted at his Native American ancestry. Unlike the others, he'd taken the time to get his schooling and become an officer. As Lieutenant, he was the highest ranked. He was also the tallest of the group, with a heavy muscular frame that could move faster than most gave him credit for. He was quiet, though. So quiet that those who didn't know him tended to write him off. They did so at their own peril.

Boone stifled an oath at the tremor that ran through him as he reached out to accept the call, but it wasn't every day you got to meet your hero face to face. Martin Fulsom wasn't a Navy SEAL. He wasn't in the military at all. He'd once been an oil man, and had amassed a fortune in the industry before he'd learned about global warming and had a change of heart. For the last decade he'd spearheaded a movement to prevent carbon dioxide particulates from exceeding the disastrous level of 450 ppm. He'd backed his foundation with his entire fortune, invested it in green technology and used his earnings to fund projects around the world aimed at helping him reach his goal. Fulsom was a force of nature, with an oversized personality to match his incredible wealth. Boone liked his can-do attitude and his refusal to mince words when the situation called for plain speaking.

Boone clicked *Accept* and his screen resolved into an image of a man seated at a large wooden desk. He was gray-haired but virile, with large hands and an impressively large watch. Beside him stood a middle aged woman in a severely tailored black suit, who handed him pieces of paper one at a time, waited for him to sign them and took them back, placing them in various folders she cradled in her arm.

"Boone!" The man's hearty voice was almost too much for the laptop's speakers. "Good to finally meet you. This is an impressive proposal you have here."

Boone swallowed. It was true. Martin Fulsom—one of the greatest innovators of their time—had actually called *him*. "It's good to meet you, too, Mr. Fulsom," he managed to say.

"Call me Martin," Fulsom boomed. "Everybody does. Like I said, it's a hell of a proposal. To build a fully operational sustainable community in less than six months? That take guts. Can you deliver?"

"Yes, sir." Boone was confident he could. He'd studied this stuff for years. Dreamed about it, debated it, played with the numbers and particulars until he could speak with confidence about every aspect of the community he wanted to build. He and his friends had gained a greater working knowledge of the fallout from climate change than any of them had gone looking for when they joined the Navy SEALs. They'd realized most of the conflicts that spawned the missions they took on were caused in one way or the other by struggles over resources, usually exacerbated by climate conditions. When rains didn't come and crops failed, unrest was sure to follow. Next came partisan politics, rebellions, coups and more. It didn't take a genius to see that climate change and scarcity of resources would be two prongs spearheading trouble around the world for decades to come.

"And you'll start with four families, building up to ten within that time frame?"

Boone blinked. Families? "Actually, sir..." He'd said nothing about families. Four *men*, building up to ten. That's what he had written in his proposal.

"This is brilliant. Too brilliant." Fulsom's direct gaze caught his own. "You see, we were going to launch a community of our own, but when I saw your proposal, I said, 'This man has already done the hard work; why reinvent the wheel? I can't think of anyone better to lead such a project than someone like Boone Rudman.'"

Boone stifled a grin. This was going better than he could have dreamed. "Thank you, sir."

Fulsom leaned forward. "The thing is, Boone, you have to do it right."

"Of course, sir, but about—"

"It has to be airtight. You have to prove you're sustainable. You have to prove your food systems are self-perpetuating, that you have a strategy to deal with waste, that you have contingency plans. What you've written here?" He held up Boone's proposal package. "It's genius. Genius. But the real question is—who's going to give a shit about it?"

"Well, hell—" Fulsom's abrupt change of tone startled Boone into defensiveness. He knew about the man's legendary high-octane personality, but he hadn't been prepared for this kind of bait and switch. "You yourself just said—"

Fulsom waved the application at him. "I love this stuff. It makes me hard. But the American public? That's a totally different matter. They don't find this shit sexy. It's not enough to jerk me off, Boone. We're trying to turn on the whole world."

"O-okay." Shit. Fulsom was going to turn him down after all. Boone gripped the arms of his chair, waiting for the axe to fall.

"So the question is, how do we make the world care about your community? And not just care about it—be so damn obsessed with it they can't think about anything else?" He didn't wait for an answer. "I'll tell you how. We're going to give you your own reality television show. Think of it. The whole world watching you go from ground zero to full-on sustainable community. Rooting for you. Cheering when you triumph. Crying when you fail. A worldwide audience fully engaged with you and your followers."

"That's an interesting idea," Boone said slowly. It was an insane idea. There was no way anyone would spend their time watching him dig garden beds and install photovoltaic panels. He couldn't think of anything less exciting to watch on television. And he didn't have followers. He had three like-minded friends who'd signed on to work with him. Friends who even now were bristling at this characterization of their roles. "Like I said, Mr. Fulsom, each of the *equal* participants in the community have pledged to document our progress. We'll take lots of photos and post them with our entries on a daily blog."

"Blogs are for losers." Fulsom leaned forward. "Come on, Boone. Don't you want to change the world?"

"Yes, I do." Anger curled within him. He was serious about these issues. Deadly serious. Why was Fulsom making a mockery of him? You couldn't win any kind of war with reality television, and Boone approached his sustainable community as if he was waging a war—a war on waste, a war on the future pain and suffering of the entire planet.

"I get it. You think I'm nuts," Fulsom said. "You think I've finally blown my lid. Well, I haven't. I'm a free-thinker, Boone, not a crazy man. I know how to get the message across to the masses. Always have. And I've always been criticized for it, too. Who cares? You know what I care about? This world. The people on it. The plants and animals and atmosphere. The whole grand, beautiful spectacle that we're currently dragging down into the muck of overconsumption. That's what I care about. What about you?"

"I care about it, too, but I don't want—"

"You don't want to be made a fool of. Fair enough. You're afraid of exposing yourself to scrutiny. You're afraid you'll fuck up on television. Well guess what? You're right; you will fuck up. But the audience is going to love you so much by that time, that if you cry, they'll cry with you. And when you triumph—and you *will* triumph—they'll feel as ecstatic as if they'd done it all themselves. Along the way they'll learn more about solar power, wind power, sustainable agriculture and all the rest of it than we could ever force-feed them through documentaries or classes. You watch, Boone. We're going to do something magical."

Boone stared at him. Fulsom was persuasive, he'd give him that. "About the families, sir."

"Families are non-negotiable." Fulsom set the application down and gazed at Boone, then each of his friends in turn. "You men are pioneers, but pioneers are a yawn-fest until they bring their wives to the frontier. Throw in women, and goddamn, that's interesting! Women talk. They complain. They'll take your plans for sustainability and kick them to the curb unless you make them easy to use and satisfying. What's more, women are a hell of a lot more interesting than men. Sex, Boone. Sex sells cars and we're going to use it to sell sustainability, too. Are you with me?"

"I…" Boone didn't know what to say. Use sex to sell sustainability? "I don't think—"

"Of course you're with me. A handsome Navy SEAL like you has to have a girl. You do, don't you? Have a girl?"

"A girl?" Had he been reduced to parroting everything Fulsom said? Boone tried to pull himself together. He definitely did not have a *girl*. He dated when he had time, but he kept things light. He'd never felt it was fair to enter a more serious relationship as long as he was throwing himself into danger on a daily basis. He'd always figured he'd settle down when he left the service and he was looking forward to finally having the time to meet a potential mate. God knew his parents were all too ready for grandkids. They talked about it all the time.

"A woman, a fiancée. Maybe you already have a wife?" Fulsom looked hopeful and his secretary nodded at Boone, as if telling him to say yes.

"Well...."

He was about to say no, but the secretary shook her head rapidly and made a slicing motion across her neck. Since she hadn't engaged in the conversation at all previously, Boone decided he'd better take her signals seriously. He'd gotten some of his best intel in the field just this way. A subtle nod from a veiled woman, or a pointed finger just protruding from a burka had saved his neck more than once. Women were crafty when it counted.

"I'm almost married," he blurted. His grip on the arms of his chair tightened. None of this was going like he'd planned. Jericho and Clay turned to stare at him like he'd lost his mind. Behind him Walker chuckled. "I mean—"

"Excellent! Can't wait to meet your better half. What about the rest of you?" Fulsom waved them off before anyone else could speak. "Never mind. Julie here will get all that information from you later. As long as you've got a girl, Boone, everything's going to be all right. The fearless leader has to have a woman by his side. It gives him that sense of humanity our viewers crave." Julie nodded like she'd heard this many times before.

Boone's heart sunk even further. Fearless leader?

Fulsom didn't understand his relationship with the others at all. Walker was his superior officer, for God's sake. Still, Fulsom was waiting for his answer, with a shrewd look in his eyes that told Boone he wasn't fooled at all by his hasty words. Their funding would slip away unless he convinced Fulsom that he was dedicated to the project—as Fulsom wanted it to be done.

"I understand completely," Boone said, although he didn't understand at all. His project was about sustainability. It wasn't some human-interest story. "I'm with you one hundred percent."

"Then I've got a shitload of cash to send your way. Don't let me down."

"I won't." He felt rather than heard the others shifting, biting back their protests.

Fulsom leaned so close his head nearly filled the screen. "We'll start filming June first and I look forward to meeting your fiancée when I arrive. Understand? Not a girlfriend, not a weekend fling—a fiancée. I want weddings, Boone." He looked over the four of them again. "Four weddings. Yours will kick off the series. I can see it now; an empty stretch of land. Two modern pioneers in love. A country parson performing the ceremony. The bride holding a bouquet of wildflowers the groom picked just minutes before. Their first night together in a lonely tent. Magic, Boone. That's prime time magic. *Surviving on the Land* meets *The First Six Months*."

Boone nodded, swallowing hard. He'd seen those

television shows. The first tracked modern-day mountain men as they pitted themselves against crazy weather
conditions in extreme locations. The second followed
two newlyweds for six months, and documented their
every move, embrace, and lovers' quarrel as they settled
into married life. He didn't relish the idea of starring in
any show remotely like those.

Besides, June first was barely two months away.
He'd only get out of the Navy at the end of April. They
hadn't even found a property to build on yet.

"There'll be four of you men to start," Fulsom went
on. "That means we need four women for episode one;
your fiancée and three other hopeful single ladies. Let
the viewers do the math, am I right? They'll start pairing
you off even before we do. We'll add other community
members as we go. Six more men and six more women
ought to do it, don't you think?"

"Yes, sir." This was getting worse by the minute.

"Now, I've given you a hell of a shock today. I get
that. So let me throw you a bone. I've just closed on the
perfect piece of property for your community. Fifteen
hundred acres of usable land with creeks, forest, pasture
and several buildings. I'm going to give it to you free
and clear to use for the duration of the series. If—and
only if—you meet your goals, I'll sign it over to you
lock, stock and barrel at the end of the last show."

Boone sat up. That was a hell of a bone. "Where is
it?"

"Little town called Chance Creek, Montana. I believe you've heard of it?" Fulsom laughed at his

reaction. Even Walker was startled. Chance Creek? They'd grown up there. Their families still lived there.

They were going home.

Chills marched up and down his spine and Boone wondered if his friends felt the same way. He'd hardly even let himself dream about that possibility. None of them came from wealthy families and none of them would inherit land. He'd figured they'd go where it was cheapest, and ranches around Chance Creek didn't come cheap. Not these days. Like everywhere else, the town had seen a slump during the last recession, but now prices were up again and he'd heard from his folks that developers were circling, talking about expanding the town. Boone couldn't picture that.

"Let me see here. I believe it's called… Westfield," Fulsom said. Julie nodded, confirming his words. "Hasn't been inhabited for over a decade. A local caretaker has been keeping an eye on it, but there hasn't been cattle on it for at least that long. The heir to the property lives in Europe now. Must have finally decided he wasn't ever going to take up ranching. When he put it on the market, I snapped it up real quick."

Westfield.

Boone sat back even as his friends shifted behind him again. Westfield was a hell of a property—owned by the Eaton family for as long as anyone could re-member. He couldn't believe it wasn't a working ranch anymore. But if the old folks were gone, he guessed that made sense. They must have passed away not long after he had left Chance Creek. They wouldn't have broken up the property, so Russ Eaton would have inherited and Russ wasn't much for ranching. Neither was his younger brother, Michael. As far as Boone knew, Russ hadn't married, which left Michael's daughter the only possible candidate to run the place.

Riley Eaton.

Was it a coincidence that had brought her to mind just moments before Fulsom's call, or something more?

Coincidence, Boone decided, even as the more impulsive side of him declared it Fate.

A grin tugged at his mouth as he remembered Riley as she used to be, the tomboy who tagged along after him every summer when they were kids. Riley lived for vacations on her grandparents' ranch. Her mother would send her off each year dressed up for the journey, and the minute Riley reached Chance Creek she'd wad up those fancy clothes and spend the rest of the summer in jeans, boots and an old Stetson passed down from her grandma. Boone and his friends hired on at Westfield most summers to earn some spending money. Riley stuck to them like glue, learning as much as she could about riding and ranching from them. When she was little, she used to cry when August ended and she had to go back home. As she grew older, she hid her feelings better, but Boone knew she'd always adored the ranch. It wasn't surprising, given her home life. Even when he was young, he'd heard the gossip and knew things were rough back in Chicago.

As much as he and the others had complained about being saddled with a follower like Riley, she'd earned their grudging respect as the years went on. Riley never complained, never wavered in her loyalty to them, and as many times as they left her behind, she was always ready to try again to convince them to let her join them in their exploits.

"It's a crime," he'd once heard his mother say to a friend on the phone. "Neither mother nor father has any time for her at all. No wonder she'll put up with anything those boys dish out. I worry for her."

Boone understood now what his mother was afraid of, but at the time he'd shrugged it off and over the years Riley had become a good friend. Sometimes when they were alone fishing, or riding, or just hanging out on her grandparents' porch, Boone would find himself telling her things he'd never told anyone else. As far as he knew, she'd never betrayed a confidence.

Riley was the one who dubbed Boone, Clay, Jericho and Walker the Four Horsemen of the Apocalypse, a nickname that had stuck all these years. When they'd become obsessed with the idea of being Navy SEALs, Riley had even tried to keep up with the same training regimen they'd adopted.

Boone wished he could say they'd always treated Riley as well as she treated them, but that wasn't the truth of it. One of his most shameful memories centered around the slim girl with the long brown braids. Things had become complicated once he and his friends began to date. They had far less time for Riley, who was two years younger and still a kid in their eyes, and she'd withdrawn when she realized their girlfriends didn't want her around. She still hung out when they worked at Westfield, though, and was old enough to be a real help with the work. Some of Boone's best memories were of early mornings mucking out stables with Riley. They didn't talk much, just worked side by side until the job was done. From time to time they walked out to a spot on the ranch where the land fell away and they could see the mountains in the distance. Boone had never quantified how he felt during those times. Now he realized what a fool he'd been.

He hadn't given a thought to how his girlfriends affected her or what it would be like for Riley when they left for the Navy. He'd been too young. Too utterly self-absorbed.

That same year he'd had his first serious relationship, with a girl named Melissa Resnick. Curvy, flirty and oh-so-feminine, she'd slipped into his heart by slipping into his bed on Valentine's Day. By the time Riley came to town again that last summer, he and Melissa were seldom apart. Of all the girls the Horsemen had dated, Melissa was the least tolerant of Riley's presence, and one day when they'd all gone to a local swimming hole, she'd huffed in exasperation when the younger girl came along.

"It's like you've got a sidekick," she told Boone in everyone's hearing. "Good ol' Tagalong Riley."

Clay, Jericho, and Walker, who'd always treated Riley like a little sister, thought it was funny. They had their own girlfriends to impress, and the name had stuck. Boone knew he should put a stop to it, but the lure of Melissa's body was still too strong and he knew if he took Riley's side he'd lose his access to it.

Riley had held her head up high that day and she'd stayed at the swimming hole, a move that Boone knew must have cost her, but each repetition of the nickname that summer seemed to heap pain onto her shoulders, until she caved in on herself and walked with her head down.

The worst was the night before he and the Horsemen left to join the Navy. He hadn't seen Riley for several days, whereas he couldn't seem to shake Melissa for a minute. He should have felt flattered, but instead it had irritated him. More and more often, he had found himself wishing for Riley's calm company, but she'd stopped coming to help him.

Because everyone else seemed to expect it, he'd attended the hoe-down in town sponsored by the rodeo that last night. Melissa clung to him like a burr. Riley was nowhere to be found. Boone accepted every drink he was offered and was well on his way to being three sheets to the wind when Melissa excused herself to the ladies' room at about ten. Boone remained with the other Horsemen and their dates, and he could only stare when Riley appeared in front of him. For once she'd left her Stetson at home, her hair was loose from its braids, and she wore makeup and a mini skirt that left miles of leg between its hem and her dress cowboy boots.

Every nerve in his body had come to full alert and Boone had understood in that moment what he'd failed to realize all that summer. Riley had grown up. At sixteen, she was a woman. A beautiful woman who understood him far better than Melissa could hope to. He'd had a fleeting sense of lost time and missed opportunities before Clay had whistled. "Hell, Tagalong, you've gone and gotten yourself a pair of breasts."

"You better watch out dressed up like that; some guy will think you want more than you bargained for," Jericho said.

Walker's normally grave expression had grown even more grim.

Riley had ignored them all. She'd squared her shoulders, looked Boone in the eye and said, "Will you dance with me?"

Shame flooded Boone every time he thought back to that moment.

Riley had paid him a thousand kindnesses over the years, listened to some of his most intimate thoughts and fears, never judged him, made fun of him or cut him down the way his other friends sometimes did. She'd always been there for him, and all she'd asked for was one dance.

He should have said yes.

It wasn't the shake of Walker's head, or Clay and Jericho's laughter that stopped him. It was Melissa, who had returned in time to hear Riley's question, and answered for him.

"No one wants to dance with a Tagalong. Go on home."

Riley had waited one more moment—then fled.

Boone rarely thought about Melissa after he'd left

Chance Creek and when he did it was to wonder what he'd ever found compelling in her. He thought about Riley far too often. He tried to remember the good times—teaching her to ride, shoot, trap and fish. The conversations and lazy days in the sun when they were kids. The intimacy that had grown up between them without him ever realizing it.

Instead, he thought of that moment—that awful, shameful moment when she'd begged him with her eyes to say yes, to throw her pride that single bone.

And he'd kept silent.

"Have you heard of the place?" Fulsom broke into his thoughts and Boone blinked. He'd been so far away it took a moment to come back. Finally, he nodded.

"I have." He cleared his throat to get the huskiness out of it. "Mighty fine ranch." He couldn't fathom why it hadn't passed down to Riley. Losing it must have broken her heart.

Again.

"So my people tell me. Heck of a fight to get it, too. Had a competitor, a rabid developer named Montague." Fulsom shook his head. "But that gave me a perfect setup."

"What do you mean?" Boone's thoughts were still with the girl he'd once known. The woman who'd haunted him all these years. He forced himself to pay attention to Fulsom instead.

Fulsom clicked his keyboard and an image sprung up onscreen. "Take a look."

Letting his memories go, Boone tried to make sense

of what he was seeing. Some kind of map—an architect's rendering of a planned development.

"What is that?" Clay demanded.

"Wait—that's Westfield." Jericho leaned over Boone's shoulder to get a better look.

"Almost right." Fulsom nodded. "Those are the plans for Westfield Commons, a community of seventy luxury homes."

Blood ran cold in Boone's veins as Walker elbowed his way between them and peered at the screen. "Luxury homes? On Westfield? You can't do that!"

"I don't want to. But Montague does. He's frothing at the mouth to bulldoze that ranch and sell it piece by piece. The big, bad developer versus the environmentalists. This show is going to write itself." He fixed his gaze on Boone. "And if you fail, the last episode will show his bulldozers closing in."

"But it's our land; you just said so," Boone protested.

"As long as you meet your goals by December first. Ten committed couples—every couple married by the time the show ends. Ten homes whose energy requirements are one-tenth the normal usage for an American home. Six months' worth of food produced on site stockpiled to last the inhabitants through the winter. And three children."

"Children? Where do we get those?" Boone couldn't keep up. He hadn't promised anything like that. All he'd said in his proposal was that they'd build a community.

"The old-fashioned way. You make them. No cheating; children conceived before the show starts don't count."

"Jesus." Fulsom had lost his mind. He was taking the stakes and raising them to outrageous heights... which was exactly the way to create a prime-time hit, Boone realized.

"It takes nine months to have a child," Jericho pointed out dryly.

"I didn't say they needed to be born. Pregnant bellies are better than squalling babies. Like I said, sex sells, boys. Let's give our viewers proof you and your wives are getting it on."

Boone had had enough. "That's ridiculous, Fulsom. You're—"

"You know what's ridiculous?" Fulsom leaned forward again, suddenly grim. "Famine. Poverty. Violence. War. And yet it never stops, does it? You said you wanted to do something about it. Here's your chance. You're leaving the Navy, for God's sake. Don't tell me you didn't plan to meet a woman, settle down and raise some kids. So I've put a rush on the matter. Sue me."

He had a point. But still—

"I could sell the land to Montague today," Fulsom said. "Pocket the money and get back to sorting out hydrogen fuel cells." He waited a beat. When Boone shook his head, Fulsom smiled in triumph. "Gotta go, boys. Julie, here, will get you all sorted out. Good luck to you on this fabulous venture. Remember—we're going to change the world together."

"Wait—"

Fulsom stood up and walked off screen.

Boone stared as Julie sat down in his place. By the time she had walked them through the particulars of the funding process, and when and how to take possession of the land, Boone's temples were throbbing. He cut the call after Julie promised to send a packet of information, reluctantly pushed his chair back from the table and faced the three men who were to be his partners in this venture.

"Married?" Clay demanded. "No one said anything about getting married!"

"I know."

"And kids? Three out of ten of us men will have to get their wives pregnant. That means all of us will have to be trying just to beat the odds," Jericho said.

"I know."

Walker just looked at him and shook his head.

"I get it! None of us planned for anything like this." Boone stood up. "But none of us thought we had a shot of moving back to Chance Creek, either—or getting our message out to the whole country." When no one answered, he went on. "Are you saying you're out?"

"Hell, I don't know," Jericho said, pacing around the room. "I could stomach anything except that marriage part. I've never seen myself as a family man."

"I don't mind getting hitched," Clay said. "And I want kids. But I want to choose where and when to do it. And Fulsom's setting us up to fail in front of a national audience. If that Montague guy gets the ranch and builds a subdivision on it, everyone in town is going to hate us—and our families."

"So what do we do?" Boone challenged him.

"Not much choice," Walker said. "If we don't sign on, Fulsom will sell to Montague anyway."

"Exactly. The only shot we have of saving that ranch is to agree to his demands," Boone said. He shoved his hands in his pockets, unsure what to do. He couldn't see himself married in two months, let alone trying to have a child with a woman he hadn't even met yet, but giving up—Boone hated to think about it. After all, it wouldn't be the first time they'd done unexpected things to accomplish a mission.

Jericho paced back. "But his demands are—"

"Insane. I know that." Boone knew he was losing them. "He's right, though; a sustainable community made only of men doesn't mean shit. A community that's actually going to sustain itself—to carry on into the future, generation after generation—has to include women and eventually kids. Otherwise we're just playing."

"Fulsom's the one who's playing. Playing with our lives. He can't demand we marry someone for the sake of his ratings," Jericho said.

"Actually, he can," Clay said. "He's the one with the cash."

"We'll find cash somewhere else—"

"It's more than cash," Boone reminded Jericho. "It's publicity. If we build a community and no one knows about it, what good is it? We went to Fulsom because we wanted him to do just what he's done—find a way to make everyone talk about sustainability."

"By marrying us off one by one?" Jericho stared at each of them in turn. "Are you serious? We just spent the last thirteen years of our lives fighting for our country—"

"And now we're going to fight for it in a whole new way. By getting married. On television. And knocking up our wives—while the whole damn world watches," Boone said.

No one spoke for a minute.

"I sure as hell hope they won't film that part, Chief," Clay said with a quick grin, using the moniker Boone had gained in the SEALs as second in command of his platoon.

"They wouldn't want to film your hairy ass, anyway," Jericho said.

Clay shoved him. Jericho elbowed him away.

"Enough." Walker's single word settled all of them down. They were used to listening to their lieutenant. Walker turned to Boone. "You think this will actually do any good?"

Boone shrugged. "Remember Yemen. Remember what's coming. We swore we'd do what it takes to make a difference." It was a low blow bringing up that disaster, but it was what had gotten them started down this path and he wanted to remind them of it.

"I remember Yemen every day," Jericho said, all trace of clowning around gone.

"So do I." Clay sighed. "Hell, I'm ready for a family anyway. I'm in. I don't know how I'll find a wife, though. Ain't had any luck so far."

"I'll find you one," Boone told him.

"Thanks, Chief." Clay gave him an ironic salute.

Jericho walked away. Came back again. "Damn it. I'm in, too. Under protest, though. Something this serious shouldn't be a game. You find me a wife, too, Chief, but I'll divorce her when the six months are up if I don't like her."

"Wait until Fulsom's given us the deed to the ranch, then do what you like," Boone said. "But if I'm picking your bride, give her a chance."

"Sure, Chief."

Boone didn't trust that answer, but Jericho had agreed to Fulsom's terms and that's all that mattered for now. He looked to Walker. It was crucial that the man get on board. Walker stared back at him, his gaze unfathomable. Boone knew there was trouble in his past. Lots of trouble. The man avoided women whenever he could.

Finally Walker gave him a curt nod. "Find me one, too. Don't screw it up."

Boone let out the breath he was holding. Despite the events of the past hour, a surge of anticipation warmed him from within.

They were going to do it.

And he was going to get hitched.

Was Riley the marrying kind?

RILEY EATON TOOK a sip of her green tea and summoned a smile for the friends who'd gathered on the tiny balcony of her apartment in Boston. Her thoughts were far away, though, tangled in a memory of a hot Montana afternoon when she was only ten. She'd crouched on the bank of Pittance Creek watching Boone Rudman wade through the knee-deep waters, fishing for minnows with a net. Riley had followed Boone everywhere back then, but she knew to stay out of the water and not scare his bait away.

"Mom said marriage is a trap set by men for unsuspecting women," she'd told him, quoting what she'd heard her mother say to a friend over the phone.

"You'd better watch out then," he'd said, poised to scoop up a handful of little fish.

"I won't get caught. Someone's got to want to catch you before that happens."

Boone had straightened, his net trailing in the water. She'd never forgotten the way he'd looked at her—all earnest concern.

"Maybe I'll catch you."

"Why?" She'd been genuinely curious. Getting overlooked was something she'd already grown used to.

"For my wife. If I ever want one. You'll never see me coming." He'd lifted his chin as if she'd argue the point. But Riley had thought it over and knew he was right.

She'd nodded. "You are pretty sneaky."

Riley had never forgotten that conversation, but Boone had and like everyone else he'd overlooked her when the time counted.

Story of her life.

Riley shook off the maudlin thoughts. She couldn't be a good hostess if she was wrapped up in her troubles. Time enough for them when her friends had gone.

She took another sip of her tea and hoped they wouldn't notice the tremor in her hands. She couldn't believe seven years had passed since she'd graduated from Boston College with the women who relaxed on the cheap folding chairs around her. Back then she'd thought she'd always have these women by her side, but now these yearly reunions were the only time she saw them. They were all firmly ensconced in careers that consumed their time and energy. It was hard enough to stay afloat these days, let alone get ahead in the world—or have time to take a break.

Gone were the carefree years when they thought nothing of losing whole weekends to trying out a new art medium, or picking up a new instrument. Once she'd been fearless, throwing paint on the canvas, guided only by her moods. She'd experimented day after day, laughed at the disasters and gloried in the triumphs that took shape under her brushes from time to time. Now she rarely even sketched, and what she produced seemed inane. If she wanted to express the truth of her situation through her art, she'd paint pigeons and gum stuck to the sidewalk. But she wasn't honest anymore.

For much of the past five years she'd been married to her job as a commercial artist at a vitamin distributor, joined to it twenty-four seven through her cell phone and Internet connection. Those years studying art seemed like a dream now; the one time in her life she'd felt like she'd truly belonged somewhere. She had no idea how she'd thought she'd earn a living with a fine arts degree, though. She supposed she hadn't thought much about the future back then. Now she felt trapped by it.

Especially after the week she'd had.

She set her cup down and twisted her hands together, trying to stop the shaking. It had started on Wednesday when she'd been called into her boss's office and handed a pink slip and a box in which to pack up her things.

"Downsizing. It's nothing personal," he'd told her.

She didn't know how she'd kept her feet as she'd made her way out of the building. She wasn't the only one riding the elevator down to street level with her belongings in her hands, but that was cold comfort. It had been hard enough to find this job. She had no idea where to start looking for another.

She'd held in her shock and panic that night and all the next day until Nadia from the adoption agency knocked on her door for their scheduled home visit at precisely two pm. She'd managed to answer Nadia's questions calmly and carefully, until the woman put down her pen.

"Tell me about your job, Riley. How will you as a single mother balance work and home life with a child?"

Riley had opened her mouth to speak, but no answer had come out. She'd reached for her cup of tea, but only managed to spill it on the cream colored skirt she'd chosen carefully for the occasion. As Nadia rushed to help her mop up, the truth had spilled from Riley's lips.

"I've just been downsized. I'm sorry; I'll get a new job right away. This doesn't have to change anything, does it?"

Nadia had been sympathetic but firm. "This is why we hesitate to place children with single parents, Riley. Children require stability. We can continue the interview and I'll weigh all the information in our judgement, but until you can prove you have a stable job, I'm afraid you won't qualify for a child."

"That will take years," Riley had almost cried, but she'd bitten back the words. What good would it do to say them aloud? As a girl, she'd dreamed she'd have children with Boone someday. When she'd grown up, she'd thought she'd find someone else. Hadn't she waited long enough to start her family?

"Riley? Are you all right?" Savannah Edwards asked, bringing her back to the present.

"Of course." She had to be. There was no other option but to soldier on. She needed to get a new job. A better job. She needed to excel at it and put the time in to make herself indispensable. Then, in a few years, she could try again to adopt.

"Are you sure?" A tall blonde with hazel eyes, Savannah had been Riley's best friend back in school, and Riley had always had a hard time fooling her. Savannah had been a music major and Riley could have listened to her play forever. She was the first person Riley had met since her grandparents passed away who seemed to care about her wholeheartedly. Riley's parents had been too busy arguing with each other all through her childhood to have much time left over to think about her. They split up within weeks after she left for college. Each remarried before the year was out and both started new families soon after. Riley felt like the odd man out when she visited them on holidays. More than eighteen years older than her half-siblings, she didn't seem to belong anywhere now.

"I'm great now that you three are here." She wouldn't confess the setback that had just befallen her. It was still too raw to process and she didn't want to bring the others down when they'd only just arrived. She wasn't the only one who had it tough. Savannah should have been a concert pianist, but when she broke her wrist in a car accident several years after graduation, she had to give up her aspirations. Instead, she had gone to work as an assistant at a prominent tech company in Silicon Valley and was still there.

"What's on tap for the weekend?" Nora Ridgeway asked as she scooped her long, wavy, dark hair into a messy updo and secured it with a clip. She'd flown in from Baltimore where she taught English in an inner-city high school. Riley had been shocked to see the dark smudges under her eyes. Nora looked thin. Too thin. Riley wondered what secrets she was hiding behind her upbeat tone.

"I hope it's a whole lot of nothing," Avery Lightfoot said, her auburn curls glinting in the sun. Avery lived in Nashville and worked in the marketing department of one of the largest food distribution companies in North America. She'd studied acting in school, but she'd never been discovered the way she'd once hoped to be. For a brief time she'd created an original video series that she'd posted online, but the advertising revenue she'd generated hadn't added up to much and soon her money had run out. Now she created short videos to market low-carb products to yoga moms. Riley's heart ached for her friend. She sounded as tired as Nora looked.

In fact, everyone looked like they needed a pick-me-up after dealing with flights and taxis, and Riley headed inside to get refreshments. She wished she'd been able to drive to the airport and pick them up. Who could afford a car, though? Even when she'd had a job, Riley found it hard to keep up with her rent, medical insurance and monthly bills, and budget enough for the childcare she'd need when she adopted. Thank God it had been her turn to host their gathering this year. She couldn't have gotten on a plane after the news she'd just received.

When she thought back to her college days she realized her belief in a golden future had really been a pipe dream. Some of her classmates were doing fine. But most of them were struggling to keep their heads above water, just like her. A few had given up and moved back in with their parents.

When she got back to the balcony with a tray of snacks, she saw Savannah pluck a dog-eared copy of *Pride and Prejudice* out of a small basket that sat next to the door. Riley had been reading it in the mornings before work this week as she drank her coffee—until she'd been let go. A little escapism helped start her day off on the right foot.

"Am I the only one who'd trade my life for one of Austen's characters' in a heartbeat?" Savannah asked, flipping through the pages.

"You want to live in Regency England? And be some man's property?" Nora asked sharply.

"Of course not. I don't want the class conflict or the snobbery or the outdated rules. But I want the beauty of their lives. I want the music and the literature. I want afternoon visits and balls that last all night. Why don't we do those things anymore?"

"Who has time for that?" Riley certainly hadn't when she was working. Now she'd have to spend every waking moment finding a new job.

"I haven't played the piano in ages," Savannah went on. "I mean, it's not like I'm all that good anymore—"

"Are you kidding? You've always been fantastic," Nora said.

"What about romance? I'd kill for a real romance. One that means something," Avery said.

"What about Dan?" Savannah asked.

"I broke up with him three weeks ago. He told me he wasn't ready for a serious relationship. The man's thirty-one. If he's not ready now, when will he be?"

"That's tough." Riley understood what Avery meant. She hadn't had a date in a year; not since Marc Hepstein had told her he didn't consider her marriage material. She should have dumped him long before.

It wasn't like she hadn't been warned. His older sister had taken her aside once and spelled it out for her:

"Every boy needs to sow his wild oats. You're his shiksa fling. You'll see; you won't get a wedding ring from him. Marc will marry a nice Jewish girl in the end."

Riley wished she'd paid attention to the warning, but of course she hadn't. She had a history of dangling after men who were unavailable.

Shiksa fling.

Just a step up from Tagalong Riley.

Riley pushed down the old insecurities that threatened to take hold of her and tried not to give in to her pain over her lost chance to adopt. When Marc had broken up with her, it had been a wake-up call. She'd realized if she waited for a man to love her, she might never experience the joy of raising a child. She'd also realized she hadn't loved Marc enough to spend a life with him. She'd been settling, and she was better than that.

She'd started the adoption process.

Now she'd have to start all over again.

"It wasn't as hard to leave him as you might think." Avery took a sip of her tea. "It's not just Dan. I feel like breaking up with my life. I had a heart once. I know I did. I used to feel—alive."

"Me, too," Nora said softly.

"I thought I'd be married by now," Savannah said, "but I haven't had a boyfriend in months. And I hate my job. I mean, I really hate it!" Riley couldn't remember ever seeing calm, poised Savannah like this.

"So do I," Avery said, her words gushing forth as if a dam had broken. "Especially since I have two of them now. I got back in debt when my car broke down and I needed to buy a new one. Now I can't seem to get ahead."

"I don't have any job at all," Riley confessed. "I've been downsized." She closed her eyes. She hadn't meant to say that.

"Oh my goodness, Riley," Avery said. "What are you going to do?"

"I don't know. Paint?" She laughed dully. She couldn't tell them the worst of it. She was afraid if she talked about her failed attempt to adopt she'd lose control of her emotions altogether. "Can you imagine a life in which we could actually pursue our dreams?"

"No," Avery said flatly. "After what happened last time, I'm so afraid if I try to act again, I'll just make a fool of myself."

Savannah nodded vigorously, tears glinting in her eyes. "I'm afraid to play," she confessed. "I sit down at my piano and then I get up again without touching the keys. What if my talent was all a dream? What if I was fooling myself and I was never anything special at all? My wrist healed years ago, but I can't make myself go for it like I once did. I'm too scared."

"What about you, Nora? Do you ever write these days?" Riley asked gently when Nora remained quiet. When they were younger, Nora talked all the time about wanting to write a novel, but she hadn't mentioned it in ages. Riley had assumed it was because she loved teaching, but she looked as burnt out as the rest of them. Riley knew she worked in an area of Baltimore that resembled a war zone.

Her friend didn't answer, but a tear traced down her cheek.

"Nora, what is it?" Savannah dropped the book and came to crouch by her chair.

"It's one of my students." Nora kept her voice steady even as another tear followed the tracks of the first. "At least I think it is."

"What do you mean?" Riley realized they'd all pulled closer to each other, leaning forward in mutual support and feeling. Dread crept into her throat at Nora's words. She'd known instinctively something was wrong in her friend's life for quite some time, but despite her questions, Nora's e-mails and texts never revealed a thing.

"I've been getting threats. On my phone," Nora said, plucking at a piece of lint on her skirt.

"Someone's texting threats?" Savannah sounded aghast.

"And calling. He has my home number, too."

"What did he say?" Avery asked.

"Did he threaten to hurt you?" Riley demanded. After a moment, Nora nodded.

"To kill you?" Avery whispered.

Nora nodded again. "And more."

Savannah's expression hardened. "More?"

Nora looked up. "He threatened to rape me. He said I'd like it. He got... really graphic."

The four of them stared at each other in shocked silence.

"You can't go back," Savannah said. "Nora, you can't go back there. I don't care how important your work is, that's too much."

"What did the police say?" Riley's hands were shaking again. Rage and shock battled inside of her, but anger won out. Who would dare threaten her friend?

"What did the school's administration say?" Avery demanded.

"That threats happen all the time. That I should change my phone numbers. That the people who make the threats usually don't act on them."

"Usually?" Riley was horrified.

"What are you going to do?" Savannah said.

"What am I supposed to do? I can't quit." Nora seemed to sink into herself. "I changed my number, but it's happening again. I've got nothing saved. I managed to pay off my student loans, but then my mom got sick… I'm broke."

No one answered. They knew Nora's family hadn't had much money, and she'd taken on debt to get her degree. Riley figured she'd probably used every penny she might have saved to pay it off again. Then her mother had contracted cancer and had gone through several expensive procedures before she passed away.

"Is this really what it's come to?" Avery asked finally. "Our work consumes us, or it overwhelms us, or it threatens us with bodily harm and we just keep going?"

"And what happened to love? True love?" Savannah's voice was raw. "Look at us! We're intelligent, caring, attractive women. And we're all single! None of us even dating. What about kids? I thought I'd be a mother."

"So did I," Riley whispered.

"Who can afford children?" Nora said fiercely. "I thought teaching would be enough. I thought my students would care—" She broke off and Riley's heart squeezed at Nora's misery.

"I've got some savings, but I'll eat through them fast if I don't get another job," Riley said slowly. "I want to leave Boston so badly. I want fresh air and a big, blue sky. But there aren't any jobs in the country." Memories of just such a sky flooded her mind. What she'd give for a vacation at her uncle's ranch in Chance Creek, Montana. In fact, she'd love to go there and never come back. It had been so long since she'd managed to stop by and spend a weekend at Westfield, it made her ache to think of the carefree weeks she spent there every summer as a child. The smell of hay and horses and sunshine on old buildings, the way her grandparents used to let her loose on the ranch to run and play and ride as hard as she wanted to. Their unconditional love. There were few rules at Westfield and those existed purely for the sake of practicality and safety. *Don't spook the horses. Clean and put away tools after you use them. Be home at mealtimes and help with the dishes.*

Away from her parents' arguing, Riley had blossomed, and the skills she'd learned from the other kids in town—especially the Four Horsemen of the Apocalypse—had taught her pride and self-confidence. They were rough and tumble boys and they rarely slowed down to her speed, but as long as she kept up to them, they included her in their fun.

Clay Pickett, Jericho Cook, Walker Norton—they'd treated her like a sister. For an only child, it was a dream come true. But it was Boone who'd become a true friend, and her first crush.

And then had broken her heart.

"I keep wondering if it will always be like this," Avery said, interrupting her thoughts. "If I'll always have to struggle to get by. If I'll never have a house of my own—or a husband or family."

"You'll have a family," Riley assured her, then bit her lip. Who was she to reassure Avery? She could never seem to shake her bad luck—with men, with work, with anything. But out of all the things that had happened to her, nothing left her cringing with humiliation like the memory of the time she'd asked Boone to dance.

She'd been such a child. No one like Boone would have looked twice at her, no matter how friendly he'd been over the years. She could still hear Melissa's sneering words—*No one wants to dance with a Tagalong. Go on home*—and the laughter that followed her when she fled the dance.

She'd returned to Chicago that last summer thinking her heart would never mend, and time had just begun to heal it when her grandparents passed away one after the other in quick succession that winter. Riley had been devastated; doubly so when she left for college the following year and her parents split. It was as if a tidal wave had washed away her childhood in one blow. After that, her parents sold their home and caretakers watched over the ranch. Uncle Russ, who'd inherited it, had found he made a better financier than a cowboy. With his career taking off, he'd moved to Europe soon after.

At his farewell dinner, one of the few occasions she'd seen her parents in the same room since they'd divorced, he'd stood up and raised a glass. "To Riley. You're the only one who loves Westfield now, and I want you to think of it as yours. One day in the future it will be, you know. While I'm away, I hope you'll treat it as your own home. Visit as long as you like. Bring your friends. Enjoy the ranch. My parents would have wanted that." He'd taken her aside later and presented her with a key. His trust in her and his promises had warmed her heart. If she'd own Westfield one day she could stand anything, she'd told herself that night. It was the one thing that had sustained her through life's repeated blows.

"I wish I could run away from my life, even for a little while. Six months would do it," Savannah said, breaking into her thoughts. "If I could clear my mind of everything that has happened in the past few years I know I could make a fresh start."

Riley knew just what she meant. She'd often wished the same thing, but she didn't only want to run away from her life; she wanted to run straight back into her past to a time when her grandparents were still alive.

Things had been so simple then.

Until she'd fallen for Boone.

She hadn't seen Uncle Russ since he'd moved away, although she wrote to him a couple of times a year, and received polite, if remote, answers in turn. She had the feeling Russ had found the home of his heart in Munich. She wondered if he'd ever come back to Montana.

In the intervening years she'd visited Westfield whenever she could, more frequently as the sting of Boone's betrayal faded, although in reality that meant a long weekend every three or four months, rather than the expansive summer vacations she'd imagined when she'd received the key. It wasn't quite the same without her grandparents and her old friends, without Boone and the Horsemen, but she still loved the country, and Westfield Manor was the stuff of dreams. Even the name evoked happy memories and she blessed the ancestor whose flight of fancy had bestowed such a distinguished title on a Montana ranch house. She'd always wondered if she'd stumble across Boone someday, home for leave, but their visits had never coincided. Still, whenever she drove into Chance Creek, her heart rate kicked up a notch and she couldn't help scanning the streets for his familiar face.

"I wish I could run away from my dirty dishes and laundry," Avery said. Riley knew she was attempting to lighten the mood. "I spend my weekends taking care of all my possessions. I bet Jane Austen didn't do laundry."

"In those days servants did it," Nora said, swiping her arm over her cheek to wipe away the traces of her tears. "Maybe we should get servants, too, while we're dreaming."

"Maybe we should, if it means we could concentrate on the things we love," Savannah said.

"Like that's possible. Look at us—we're stuck, all of us. There's no way out." The waver in Nora's voice betrayed her fierceness.

"There has to be," Avery exclaimed.

"How?"

Riley wished she had the answer. She hated seeing the pain and disillusionment on her friends' faces. And she was terrified of having to start over herself.

"What if… what if we lived together?" Savannah said slowly. "I mean, wouldn't that be better than how things are now? If we pooled our resources and figured out how to make them stretch? None of us would have to work so hard."

"I thought you had a good job," Nora said, a little bitterly.

"On paper. The cost of living in Silicon Valley is outrageous, though. You'd be surprised how little is left over when I pay my bills. And inside, I feel… like I'm dying."

A silence stretched out between them. Riley knew just what Savannah meant. At first grown-up life had seemed exciting. Now it felt like she was slipping into a pool of quicksand that she'd never be able to escape. Maybe it would be different if they joined forces. If they pooled their money, they could do all kinds of things.

For the first time in months she felt a hint of possibility.

"We could move where the cost of living is cheaper and get a house together." Savannah warmed to her theme. "With a garden, maybe. We could work part time and share the bills."

"For six months? What good would that do? We'd run through what little money we have and be harder to employ afterward," Nora said.

"How much longer are you willing to wait before you try for the life you actually want, rather than the life that keeps you afloat one more day?" Savannah asked her. "I have to try to be a real pianist. Life isn't worth living if I don't give it a shot. That means practicing for hours every day. I can't do that and work a regular job, too."

"I've had an idea for a screenplay," Avery confessed. "I think it's really good. Six months would be plenty of time for me to write it. Then I could go back to work while I shop it around."

"If I had six months I would paint all day until I had enough canvasses to put on a show. Maybe that would be the start and end of my career as an artist, but at least I'd have done it once," Riley said.

"A house costs money," Nora said.

"Not always," Riley said slowly as an idea took hold in her head. "What about Westfield?" After all, it hadn't been inhabited in years. "Uncle Russ always said I should bring my friends and stay there."

"Long term?" Avery asked.

"Six months would be fine. Russ hasn't set foot in it

in over a decade."

"You want us to move to Montana and freeload for six months?" Nora asked.

"I want us to move to Montana and take six months to jumpstart our lives. We'll practice following our passions. We'll brainstorm ideas together for how to make money from them. Who knows? Maybe together we'll come up with a plan that will work."

"Sounds good to me," Avery said.

"I don't know," Nora said. "Do you really think it's work that's kept you from writing or playing or painting? Because if you can't do it now, chances are you won't be able to do it at Westfield either. You'll busy up your days with errands and visits and sightseeing and all that. Wait and see."

"Not if we swore an oath to work on our projects every day," Savannah said.

"Like the oaths you used to swear to do your homework on time? Or not to drink on Saturday night? Or to stop crank-calling the guy who dumped you junior year?"

Savannah flushed. "I was a child back then—"

"I just feel that if we take six months off, we'll end up worse off than when we started."

Savannah leaned forward. "Come on. Six whole months to write. Aren't you dying to try it?" When Nora hesitated, Savannah pounced on her. "I knew it! You want to as badly as we do."

"Of course I want to," Nora said. "But it won't work. None of you will stay at home and hone your craft."

A smile tugged at Savannah's lips. "What if we couldn't leave?"

"Are you going to chain us to the house?"

"No. I'm going to take away your clothes. Your modern clothes," she clarified when the others stared at her. "You're right; we could easily be tempted to treat the time like a vacation, especially with us all together. But if we only have Regency clothes to wear, we'll be stuck because we'll be too embarrassed to go into town. We'll take a six-month long Jane Austen vacation from our lives." She sat back and folded her arms over her chest.

"I love it," Riley said. "Keep talking."

"We'll create a Regency life, as if we'd stepped into one of her novels. A beautiful life, with time for music and literature and poetry and walks. Westfield is rural, right? No one will be there to see us. If we pattern our days after the way Jane's characters spent theirs, we'd have plenty of time for creative pursuits."

Nora rolled her eyes. "What about the neighbors? What about groceries and dental appointments?"

"Westfield is set back from the road." Riley thought it through. "Savannah's right; we could go for long stretches without seeing anyone. We could have things delivered, probably."

"I'm in," Avery said. "I'll swear to live a Regency life for six months. I'll swear it on penalty of… death."

"The penalty is embarrassment," Savannah said. "If we leave early, we have to travel home in our Regency clothes. I know I'm in. I'd gladly live a Jane Austen life for six months."

"If I get to wear Regency dresses and bonnets, I'm in too," Riley said. What was the alternative? Stay here and mourn the child she'd never have?

"Are you serious?" Nora asked. "Where do we even get those things?"

"We have a seamstress make them, or we sew them ourselves," Avery said. "Come on, Nora. Don't pretend you haven't always wanted to."

The others nodded. After all, it was their mutual love of Jane Austen movies that had brought them together in the first place. Two days into their freshman year at Boston College, Savannah had marched through the halls of their dorm announcing a Jane Austen film festival in her room that night. Riley, Nora and Avery had shown up for it, and the rest was history.

"It'll force us to carry out our plan the way we intend to," Savannah told her. "If we can't leave the ranch, there will be no distractions. Every morning when we put on our clothes we'll be recommitting to our vow to devote six months to our creative pursuits. Think about it, Nora. Six whole months to write."

"Besides, we were so good together back in college," Riley said. "We inspired each other. Why couldn't we do that again?"

"But what will we live on?"

"We'll each liquidate our possessions," Savannah said. "Think about how little most people had in Jane Austen's time. It'll be like when Eleanor and Marianne have to move to a cottage in *Sense and Sensibility* with their mother and little sister. We'll make a shoestring budget and stick to it for food and supplies. If we don't go anywhere, we won't spend any money, right?"

"That's right," Avery said. "Remember what Mrs. John Dashwood said in that novel. 'What on earth can four women want for more than that?—They will live so cheap! Their housekeeping will be nothing at all. They will have no carriage, no horses, and hardly any servants; they will keep no company, and can have no expenses of any kind! Only conceive how comfortable they will be!'"

"We certainly won't have any horses or carriages." Savannah laughed.

"But we will be comfortable, and during the time we're together we can brainstorm what to do next," Riley said. "No one leaves Westfield until we all have a working plan."

"With four of us to split the chores of running the house, it'll be easy," Avery said. "We'll have hours and hours to devote to our craft every day."

Nora hesitated. "You know this is crazy, right?"

"But it's exactly the right kind of crazy," Riley said. "You have to join us, Nora."

Nora shook her head, but just when Riley thought she'd refuse, she shrugged. "Oh, okay. What the hell? I'll do it." Riley's heart soared. "But when our six months are up, I'll be broke," Nora went on. "I'll be homeless, too. I don't see how anything will have improved."

"Everything will have improved," Savannah told her. "I promise. Together we can do anything."

Riley smiled at their old rallying-cry from college. "So, we're going to do it? You'll all come to Westfield with me? And wear funny dresses?"

"And bonnets," Avery said. "Don't forget the bonnets."

"I'm in," Savannah said, sticking out her hand.

"I'm in," Avery said, putting hers down on top of it.

"I guess I'm in," Nora said, and added hers to the pile.

"Well, I'm definitely in." Riley slapped hers down on top of the rest.

Westfield. She was going back to Westfield.

Things were looking up.

CHAPTER TWO

★

"REMEMBER, I WANT a blonde," Clay said as Boone shouldered his duffel bag and took a last look around the room he'd inhabited while on base. "And she needs to like walks on the beach in the moonlight, fine dining—and opera. If she doesn't like opera, she's out."

Boone rolled his eyes. There'd been weeks of this patter now. He'd done his best to ignore it, but couldn't blame his friends for exacting their revenge. He was lucky all three of them hadn't turned tail and run after the fiasco with Fulsom. Between the man's demands regarding marriage and his emphasis on Boone being the leader, he'd nearly driven Clay and the others away. Luckily his friends had a sense of humor, and as Clay said, they were all of an age to think about settling down.

"Mine's got to be a redhead," Jericho said, stepping aside as Boone headed for the door. "And remember, she's got to be a registered masseuse and speak at least three foreign languages. Oh, and ninja skills. She's got to have mad ninja skills."

Boone turned to Walker. "What about you? Got any requests?"

The large man surveyed him, his dark eyes lacking any sign of humor. "Good at fishing," he said.

"Fine," Boone clapped him on the back. "I'll find you a fisherwoman."

Walker snorted. Boone knew what he meant; the man didn't think he could pull any of this off. Well, that was fair, considering Boone didn't think Walker would actually make it to Chance Creek. His commanding officer had always been the wild card in this operation. Boone had his suspicions that someday Walker—a man deeply jaded when it came to human beings—would cross the border into Canada and disappear in the boreal forest of the Great White North. Walker supported Boone's sustainable vision, but he didn't believe they would succeed in their mission. "Humans are humans," he said whenever Boone pressed him. "They don't change."

Boone had long since backed off of trying to persuade him otherwise. Walker had gone along with things this far; he couldn't ask for more. All he could do was hope Walker would surprise him. His quiet confidence and unerring instinct for finding a path through dangerous territory made the perfect counterpoint to Boone's tendency to fast decisions and overconfidence. There was a reason Walker was LT and Boone only Chief, and Boone had never begrudged his friend the higher rank.

"How are you going to find these women?" Clay

asked, not for the first time.

"Don't you worry about it. I'll find them." The truth was Boone didn't have the slightest idea. They didn't need just any women; they needed a special breed who wouldn't mind primitive conditions, hard work and a separation from modern conveniences. The girls they'd grown up with in their rural town were no strangers to hard work and many of them would make fine ranch wives, but would the ones who'd stuck around Chance Creek be interested in a sustainable community?

He couldn't answer that.

As for Riley, her phone number and Boston address was tucked into his wallet, but he still hadn't called her. The time never seemed right. There was always something to do—or someone around. He'd told himself he'd make contact with her once he reached Westfield.

Maybe.

The truth was, every time he reached for the phone, Boone found a reason to postpone the call. He didn't know what Riley's reaction would be when she realized it was him on the other end of the line. He wasn't sure he wanted to know.

What if she hated him? What if he'd taken too long to apologize?

"What if we don't like the ones you find?" Jericho asked.

"Then I'll find you another one," Boone said, focusing on the present. He'd fielded all these questions before.

"What if I don't like that one, either?"

Boone reached his breaking point. "This isn't about personal happiness. You heard Fulsom; we're going to save the world. So you'll man up and marry whoever I match you with, got it? You need to be engaged in the next couple of months."

His friends exchanged a glance. "Yes, sir, Chief, sir." Jericho snapped him an ironic salute. "But respectfully, sir, find your own wife first. Let's see if you're any good at this."

Boone bit back an acid retort, snapped his own ironic salute and headed for the door. He paused when he reached it and turned back to face the others. "We're really doing it, aren't we?"

"Of course we are. We swore an oath, didn't we?" Clay said. The others sobered, remembering the circumstances of that promise.

Boone nodded. He'd always remember Yemen— and Francine Heller. If he could do one small thing to set the world on a better course, he'd give it his all.

As a Navy SEAL he'd put his life on the line.

Now he'd put his heart on the line, if that's what it took.

"See you soon."

As he strode through the naval base, Boone's heart lifted. He'd loved his military career, but he couldn't wait to start the next phase of his life. The real fight was yet to come. The next seven months would challenge him in every way, but he wasn't afraid. He was exhilarated.

He couldn't fail.

As Riley directed the taxi to park in front of the stone steps leading to Westfield Manor, she sighed with something like contentment. The last month had been busy as she wrapped up her life in Boston, disposed of most of her things, and prepared to move to Montana. "It isn't Pemberley, but it's as close as we'll find in Chance Creek." Her heart was still sore from her missed chance to adopt, but knowing she'd spend at least the next six months with three of her closest friends and get to paint each and every day had lifted her spirits.

"It's beautiful," Savannah said from the back seat. "Look at it! It's even better in real life than in the photographs."

"Westfield's sat empty for a long time. I know I'm not the only one who will be glad you've come to live here," their driver said. Riley had been surprised when she'd climbed into the taxi and found Alan Higgens behind the wheel. She hadn't known him well from her visits to Chance Creek, but she'd recognized him all the same.

Riley bit back a smile. Westfield was beautiful, even in the waning light of an early May evening. With its stone exterior, it presented a proud façade worthy of Jane Austen's Regency England. As the shadows deepened, the warm stone exterior mellowed in the failing light until the large home looked like it had been part of the landscape forever. She didn't care that it perched on a rise of ground on an expansive ranch in Montana. It would do wonderfully. "Wait until you see it in daylight."

"I don't need to wait. Savannah's right, it is gorgeous," Avery said.

"More than gorgeous—three floors! It's stunning, Riley!" Savannah said.

"But so remote." Nora peered at the landscape as if she was looking out at the snowy steppes of Russia.

"It's the country. Come on; let's go see!" Riley paid Alan and climbed out of the taxi. Savannah and Avery quickly followed, while Nora trailed along more slowly. Alan helped them retrieve the baggage they'd brought: two suitcases a piece. They'd sold everything else.

Riley couldn't believe how freeing it had been to watch her worldly possessions disappear one by one. Knowing everything she owned fit in the two large bags meant there was nothing to distract her from the future she'd chosen. On the other hand it was terrifying to see how little was left in her bank account at the end of the exercise. They each had shifted an equal amount into a communal account from which all their expenses and their allowances would be drawn. She'd have just enough at the end of six months to put down a deposit on an apartment. She hoped she managed to sell a painting or two along the way.

"Good luck," Alan called as he got back into the taxi.

"Thank you!" Riley waved, but couldn't wait a moment longer to go inside. She trooped up the steps with the others and fumbled with the key for a few long minutes until Avery took out her cell phone and used a flashlight app to help her see in the dim light. When the key finally turned in the lock, Riley threw the door open and a waft of stale, warm air washed over them, but while the house smelled musty, it didn't stink of rot. Encouraged, she stepped inside, switched on the entryway lights, and a reverent chill washed over her as she took in the front parlor to the left side of the central hall and the great room to the right.

"It's perfect," Savannah breathed, coming into the house behind her. "I feel like it's true, like I just stepped into *Pride and Prejudice*."

Riley turned on more lights, thankful that Uncle Russ hadn't shut off the electricity in his long absence. She knew the caretakers came through periodically and opened windows to let in fresh air. An older couple who lived in town, they cleaned and dusted and kept an eye on things. She'd left a message on their voicemail to alert them to her coming and was pleased to see Westfield in such great shape, even if they hadn't responded.

Avery pushed forward. "I say we change right now—before we do anything else. We need to do this right. We're committing to six months at Westfield pursuing our passions no matter what. Let's draw a line in the sand that allows for no going back."

"How do we do that?" Riley was curious. Avery always had fun ideas.

"We only brought Regency clothes with us, right?"

The others nodded. Savannah enthusiastically. Nora not so much.

"So we change into them and burn the clothes we're wearing now. I saw a beautiful stone fireplace outside.

We can do it there. Everything from the twentieth century goes."

"Definitely," Savannah said without hesitation. "Let's do it!"

"It sounds great," Riley echoed. They all looked at Nora.

Nora heaved a sigh that lifted her shoulders. "Fine. Except for my laptop."

"Well, of course not our laptops," Savannah said.

Riley bit back a smile; they'd already sorted out what technology they'd keep and what they'd ban. They'd decided to share one phone, with each having access to it for a half-hour a day. They'd take turns carrying it for emergency communications and had passed the number on to their families, with strict instructions not to abuse it.

They'd decided to keep their laptops, but not spend money on an Internet connection. If they needed to look something up, they could do it on the phone. That would keep their productivity high and their distractions low.

They'd banned television and, since it was summertime, electric lights—except for this first night. They decided to devote two hours every morning to chores. During this time, they'd wear what they called their servant clothes—gowns made of tougher material patterned after the kind of clothes the help would have worn, and they'd do their best to keep energy consumption to a minimum. As soon as they were done, they'd don their prettier gowns and live a life of art and refinement the rest of the day.

Still, their lives would be rustic by modern standards and she wondered if Nora would be able to go the distance with them. The more the others had delved into their Jane Austen fantasy, the more Nora had pulled back. Riley thought she felt guilty for abandoning her students so close to the end of the year, but during the few weeks she'd returned to class after their get-together in Boston, the threats had continued until Nora had found it hard to sleep.

"Let's go upstairs and choose our bedrooms," Riley said and led the way up the grand staircase that hugged the right wall of the central hall. Seven steps led to a small landing graced by a delicate table with an empty vase on it. The stairs continued up in the opposite direction and seven more steps brought them to a hall on the second floor.

"There are six bedrooms on this floor," Riley explained. "Four corner bedrooms and two middle ones. My grandparents rehabbed everything and now each of them has its own bathroom."

"That must have been a huge project in a house this old," Savannah said.

"My grandmother came from old money and she spent most of it redecorating. She insisted the house be updated so she could entertain. I still can't believe neither my father nor Uncle Russ want to live here, but Dad's a Chicago man through and through, and Russ loves Munich. I don't think he'll ever leave." She led the way down the hall that encircled the stairwell at the center of the house, and opened door after door to the bedrooms that ringed it. There were four identical corner bedrooms. Each of them held a canopy bed, although the canopies and drapes had all been stowed away. Antiques filled out the rooms so that each one had a distinct style.

"They're so lovely," Savannah said.

"You should see the servants' quarters," Riley said, suppressing a smile. She'd never told them this secret. She led the way to the stairs again and continued up to the top floor of the house. When she flung open the first bedroom door, all her friends gasped.

"The servants lived like this?" Avery stepped inside the room and spun around. Riley knew what she meant; it was even more beautiful than the ones on the second floor with its sloped ceiling, king-sized bed, large dormer windows and lovely antique furnishings.

"The servants were long gone when my grandmother renovated the attics. She put the family up here and gave the guests the second story."

"You can barely tell." Avery ran her hand over the tall wooden dresser in one corner. "It looks just like the rest of the house."

"It was a work of love." Nostalgia for the days when her grandparents were alive washed over Riley. Her grandmother had been such an artist in her own way, with the house as her canvas. Would she approve of what Riley was doing? Riley thought so.

"You're so lucky this will all be yours someday," Avery said.

"Emphasis on someday," she told them. "I used to think Russ would pass it on to me when I grew up. It's clear now that he's going to hang onto it until he dies. I can't begrudge him that, but Westfield won't really be mine until I'm eighty. Russ is tough as nails."

"At least we have it now," Savannah told her. "I'm going to enjoy every minute of our six months, and I think we should copy your grandmother and take the rooms on this floor, even if it means running up and down an extra flight of stairs. I feel like I'll be able to see the whole world from these windows in the day-time."

"Who gets what room?" Avery asked.

"I'll take this one," Savannah said. "Jane herself could have been comfortable here."

"They're all pretty much the same," Riley said. "Everyone choose one and get changed."

Changing into Regency clothing wasn't the work of a moment or two, but Riley didn't care. Happy in her new room, she fiddled with the complicated outfit, glad for the electric light for the moment. They'd discussed their clothing carefully back when they'd sorted out the details of their new lives on her balcony in Boston. As a pledge of commitment to their plan to create a life worthy of Jane Austen, they'd decided they would each have a wardrobe similar to that of a moderately wealthy woman in the early 1800s. Part of the beauty of Jane Austen's era was that people cared for their possessions. Things were too expensive to replace easily when everything had to be made by hand. Avery had taken charge of their clothing, with several of her friends pitching in to help make the outfits. Riley was surprised by how reasonably priced they were, but Avery had told her she'd salvaged much of the material from thrift stores and discount fabric outlets. Her friends, who helped out with costumes for local theater companies, were all too glad to have the opportunity to work on the period pieces. For the sake of ease—and hygiene— they'd chosen to part ways with Regency fashion in the items they'd wear closest to their skin. They'd all found it funny back in college when they'd learned that Regency ladies didn't wear bloomers, or even knickers or panties of any kind. Faced with emulating them, Riley had decided to wear modern thigh high stockings and panties. She figured the others would do something similar. She pulled the stockings on, tugged a chemise over her head, stepped into her petticoat, and realized she needed help with her stays—a kind of old-fashioned corset that laced up from behind.

She headed for the door, but stopped for a moment to take in the fact that she was really here. She couldn't wait to wake up tomorrow morning in this beautiful room. It faced the rear of the house. From this direction she would be able to see a long way in the daylight, including most of the outbuildings on the ranch and the pastures beyond them situated a fair distance away. That distance between the house and the barns was one of the more impractical aspects of the ranch, but the Eaton who built Westfield obviously still longed for the England he'd left behind. The family legend said he'd come to America in the second half of the 1800s because he saw little chance of improving his fortune in England. He'd ventured west, taken in the possibilities of Montana, and settled down right here. He must have done well for himself to build a house like this one. Riley surveyed her new room with satisfaction. It was so peaceful here at Westfield. So serene and beautiful.

Avery, whose front bedroom shared a wall with hers, knocked on her door. "I need help." She, too, was dressed only in her stockings and chemise. Her stays dangled from her hand.

"Me, too." Riley let her in and they took turns helping each other into the unfamiliar items of clothing. Once they were corseted, they each pulled their gowns over their heads, then did up each other's fastenings. "How do I look?" Riley asked Avery when they were both finished.

"Beautiful. I mean it, Riley; you're absolutely stunning. How about me?"

"Ten years younger for a start."

It was true, Riley thought as they both faced the old-fashioned mirror that stood in one corner of her room. While the dresses emphasized their womanly attributes, there was something about their old-fashioned cut that was downright innocent. She'd gladly let the past few years fall away, but she wasn't sure how she felt about how *female* the dresses were. At the office she'd dressed to emphasize her professionalism. There was nothing professional about the way she looked now.

"It might have been better if we'd worn our work

dresses."

Riley knew what Avery meant, but she'd known instinctively that none of the women would choose them for this occasion, even if they were lighting a fire outdoors. She was right. When they all met up downstairs again, all four of them had chosen pretty dresses more suitable for playing piano or painting watercolors than lighting fires.

"We'll have to be careful," Avery warned. "Remember what we said about replacing these."

They'd agreed to keep to the kind of budget that would have maintained a family that was upper class but not overly rich in Jane Austen's time. The idea was that the kind of economy practised by Jane herself would keep them from spending too much of their savings. They needed money left over when their six months were up.

As darkness settled over Westfield, Riley carefully built up a fire in the outdoor fireplace positioned in one of the formal gardens to the side of the house and stood back when the flames caught. "Ready?" She lifted the bundle of clothing she'd worn when she arrived.

"I'm ready," Savannah said happily.

"Me, too." Avery held out her bundle as well.

"I guess so," Nora sighed. They tossed their modern clothing onto the fire. For a moment Riley was afraid they'd smothered the flames and the fire had gone out. She worried what the bad omen might mean for their project, but before she could overthink it, flames began to lick the edges of their clothes and soon they all had to step back as the fire surged into a blaze.

"Do we have water handy?" Nora asked.

"Yes, but the fire is already subsiding," Savannah said.

Riley was relieved. She looked around the circle of her friends over the flames. "We're really doing this."

"We are," Savannah said.

"We're crazy, but we are," Nora said, shaking her head.

"There's no going back now," Avery agreed.

A glow of pride filled Riley—they'd pulled this off. They'd actually quit their unfulfilling jobs and embarked on an adventure. She was filled with love for the friends who were going to help her live out a fantasy she'd always held dear. Why should life be hard and ugly and filled with plastic trash? Why couldn't it contain long walks, good literature, excellent conversation and—

"Hey!"

All of them jumped as a male voice pierced the air. "Hey! What the hell are you doing?"

"Who is that?" Avery asked. She peered into the darkness. Riley did too but she couldn't see anything past the glow of the flames.

When a man finally appeared at the edge of the circle of firelight, Riley's breath caught in her throat. He was tall, his broad shoulders straining a T-shirt across a muscled chest, his jeans encasing long legs that covered the ground in powerful strides. There was something aristocratic about the strong lines of his face as he glared at them, shadows and light from the fire playing across his features. Something hotter than hell.

Something... familiar.

"Boone!"

Shock propelled her forward and before she knew it she was running to meet him like she used to when they were teenagers. Boone. Her best friend—

She stumbled to a halt as she came to her senses. Boone hadn't been her friend at the end. He'd watched Melissa humiliate her, and then he'd left town without ever looking back.

"He'd make a fine Mr. Darcy," she heard Avery murmur behind her.

Avery was right—he would. If she hadn't known him, she would have been intimidated by his muscular build and aggressive stance. Instead she was filled with a yearning to go to him—to touch him and see if he was real.

"What is this? Who said you could trespass on my property?" Boone demanded.

"Y—your property?" Surprise tore the words from her throat. Riley realized he hadn't recognized her. "This isn't your property. It's my property!" That might not technically be true, but it would have to stand in for a long explanation of the present state of things. Her friends stiffened and exchanged glances. Riley's throat ached as unbidden memories crowded in on her. Boone represented a time in her life she'd lost forever, and she missed those easy, happy days.

She missed *him*—the Boone who'd been her best friend, her first crush, not the self-absorbed boy who'd turned his back on her.

"Like hell—Riley? What are you doing here?" His voice changed abruptly and his gaze raked her from head to toe, making her all too aware of her Regency gown with its tight bodice and straight skirts. From his vantage point he'd have a spectacular view of her cleavage. She squashed the urge to cover it up.

"I live here." She grabbed his arm and propelled him away from the fire. She didn't want to have this awkward reunion with an audience. "What the hell are you doing here?" she hissed.

"Riley? Who is that?" Nora called after her as she led Boone into the shadows.

"Hang on—it's family business."

Boone let her move him out of the circle of firelight, still staring down at a point somewhat lower than her chin. "You can't live here—"

"Of course I can," Riley said in a low voice. "Uncle Russ said I could."

He dug in his heels and tugged her to a stop. "I live here now. I'm funded by the Fulsom Foundation. You know—the people who bought the ranch from Russ more than a month ago?"

Riley let go of him and fell back a step. "Bought the ranch—" She fought for comprehension. Bought the ranch? Had Russ... sold it?

Riley opened her mouth. Closed it again. She couldn't seem to form words. If Boone was telling the truth, then Westfield was gone from her forever. "No. That doesn't make any sense. Russ said he'd leave it to me. He told me—"

Boone stepped closer, his face a mask of concern. "Like I said, he put the ranch up for sale and the Fulsom Foundation bought it. They gave it to me. Why are you dressed like that? Are you in a play?" His proximity only confused her more.

Bought it…uncle…put it on the market… Riley's head swam. This couldn't be happening. "Russ sold Westfield?" she said again. Her bodice was too tight. She couldn't breathe.

"Didn't you know?" Boone peered at her with concern. "Riley, what's going on?"

"I don't know." Lightheaded, she put out a hand and Boone took it, steadying her. Riley leaned into his touch, unable to make sense of any of it. How could Russ have sold Westfield without her knowing? Wouldn't he have told her?

She shut her eyes, realizing how long it had been since he'd written to her at all. His last e-mail had been far more formal than usual, wishing her well but communicating little else. Had he changed his mind about leaving the ranch to her—and been too afraid to admit it?

Riley thought she'd be sick.

How could she survive without Westfield to sustain her? And what about her friends? She'd just convinced them to quit their jobs and upend their lives.

She fought to pull herself together. "Russ promised Westfield to me."

Boone's eyes widened. "You have a contract?"

"No." Of course they didn't. They were family. "You don't understand—"

"You're right; I don't. Russ put it up for sale and Fulsom bought it fair and square. I figured something had happened to your uncle and he needed the money. How could you not know?"

"He... he didn't say a word. I sent him a note to let him know I was moving in—" She broke off, horrified at the mistake she'd made by not waiting for an answer, but she'd always used Westfield as she pleased, just like Russ had told her to do. What would she tell her friends?

Boone waited for her to go on. Traces of the teen-ager she'd known remained, but there were sides to him she could only guess at now. She knew he'd spent nearly thirteen years in the Navy—most of it as a SEAL. She shivered to think what he was capable of. He looked... formidable.

"I was... We were... going to spend six months here."

He cast his gaze over her Regency clothes. "How do these come into it?" He touched her dress.

Heat flared into her cheeks and she was grateful for the darkness. "You wouldn't understand. We swore an oath." She couldn't put it into words. Not while Boone was staring at her like that, light and shadow from the fire playing over his face. Interest kindled in his eyes at her words. And something more. Something that stirred up old desires she'd sworn were long gone.

"What kind of oath?"

She had to answer him. He owned the land she was standing on. The house she meant to live in. Her legacy. Riley hung her head, unwilling to meet his eye. "That we would leave our lives behind for six months. Quit our jobs, give up our apartments, sell our furniture and get rid of everything that doesn't belong in a Regency world."

"Why?"

She finally looked at him. "Because we need a change. We wanted something different, something better. Boone, what do I tell my friends?"

"Jesus, Riley—you've gotten yourself in a fix. We'll have to figure out what to do with you." He shifted even closer, until even in the low light she could make out all his features. How could he be so familiar and so different all at the same time? Boone's nearness made it hard to think. Memories swirled in her mind, competing with the facts about her present situation she needed to keep straight.

"We?" She peered into the darkness behind him. Who else was with him?

He smiled for the first time. "The Horsemen will join me soon. We still stick together. We'll build down near the barns."

The Four Horsemen of the Apocalypse had taken Westfield from her? Riley didn't know whether to laugh or cry. Or scream. Screaming sounded good right about now. They'd taken her self-respect from her once upon a time, hadn't they? Why shouldn't they steal Westfield, too? "Build what?"

It was Boone's turn to look uncertain. "A community."

Disbelief reared its head again. "You're developing Westfield?" Over her dead body.

"No, I'm not developing Westfield. You know me better than that."

She could breathe again. "Thank God. I guess even you couldn't go that far."

A change came over him. "Even me…?"

She didn't answer his unspoken question. He knew what he'd done. She wouldn't shower fresh humiliation over herself by confessing how much he'd hurt her when they were young. That was water far under the bridge. Besides, she had to secure her friends a home until they figured out what to do next. Riley stiffened her spine. "Are you using the manor? If not, why can't we? We'll pay a fair rent." If they were able to; they hadn't figured rent into their budget at all.

"How did you even get into the house?"

"I've had a key to Westfield since I was eighteen. Russ told me to use it whenever and however I wished. He liked it when I stayed here—which I've done tons of times." An exaggeration, but he wouldn't know that.

"So you thought nothing of moving your friends in without his knowledge?"

"I sent him a note, and like I said, he encouraged me to have friends over and stay as long as I wanted. I'm the only one who uses the house."

Boone studied her for a long moment. "Maybe we can work something out. We both landed here at the same time. That's a hell of a coincidence."

"So?" The way he was looking at her made her uneasy. Once she'd known Boone so well. Now she knew so little about him.

"Maybe Fate put us here together."

Fate? She couldn't quite make out his expression, but his tone had gone almost… gentle. She hadn't expected that. "What exactly are you doing here again?"

"We're trying to build a model sustainable community that can be reproduced throughout the world. Clay, Jericho and Walker will join me shortly and we'll recruit other like-minded people who want to live lightly on the land."

Riley's jaw dropped open. "You're building a *commune* at Westfield?"

BOONE STIFFENED. COMMUNE was a word he detested. It reeked of hippies and weed, good intentions gone awry due to megalomania, group sex and apathy. "I'm not building a commune. I'm building a community. There's a difference." It was important she understand that. Without meaning to, his gaze fell again to where Riley's tight bodice strained to hold her breasts in check, breasts that were all too distracting, even in the low, uneven light cast by the distant fire. Her dress was cinched tight with a sash underneath them and a long skirt fell from there straight to the ground, hiding all the rest of her curves. He could guess at them, though, something his body had registered even though his mind was scrambling to keep up with the situation. As much as he'd hoped to see her again, he'd never dreamed he'd find Riley at Westfield. Not after Russ had sold it. He couldn't believe she had no idea it didn't belong to her family anymore—or that she'd brought three friends to live here in a house she didn't own. He didn't envy her the explanation she'd need to give them in another minute or two.

But before that happened he needed to know more about Riley. An idea was beginning to percolate in his mind, an idea both intriguing and somewhat shady. The minute he'd seen Riley, a part of his brain had locked on target, and he'd felt something vastly more powerful than curiosity about an old friend. It was as if she'd reached into his chest and taken hold of his heart. Now he wanted to be close to her. He wanted to talk to her. He was willing to do what it took to keep her here long enough to get to know her again.

"I'm up here, sailor." Her flat tone bordered on anger.

"Sorry." But he wasn't sorry and she had to know it. Her cleavage was so prettily displayed it would be impossible to ignore.

"You could at least pretend not to ogle me."

"I don't think I could." He braced himself for an angry answer, but she only stared at him impassively, leaving him wishing he hadn't tried to joke with her. Riley deserved better than that. His old shame washed over him, but it was tempered by her presence. God, he'd missed Riley. He hadn't realized how much until faced with her again.

"It's good to see you." He meant it. She'd grown up into a beautiful woman, but her cautious manner told him she was still the Riley he knew, and he was grateful for that. A woman as lovely as her could have become vain and shallow, but not his Riley.

She made a face he couldn't decipher. "Look, I don't want to disappoint my friends. Would it make any difference if I told you we're trying to live up to a set of ideals, too?"

She didn't have to convince him to let her stay, but he used her question to buy time, wanting to discover the lay of the land before he said yes. "By dressing up?"

She frowned and once again Boone regretted his words. Riley often had surprising ideas, but she always had a reason for what she did.

"By paying homage to an era when beauty meant something. When people respected literature, poetry, art and spending time—real time—with their family and friends."

"I'm not sure I understand." He glanced over at the other three women still standing by the fire. They looked straight out of a movie poster for some period drama he'd automatically pass over. "Jane Austen," he said suddenly. "Oh, God. Don't tell me. *Pride and Prejudice.*"

"What's wrong with *Pride and Prejudice?*"

His grandmother liked that movie and she'd forced him to watch half of it once. "Are you acting it out or something?"

"No."

"Then what are you doing?"

"Forget it," Riley said. "You wouldn't understand."

"Give me a chance." He shifted closer again. There was something magnetic about Riley that pulled him in. He wanted to touch her. Was her skin as soft as it looked?

"Haven't you ever felt like modern life is just so... empty?" she said. "We work, work, work so we can spend, spend, spend on all kinds of crap we don't even need. Do you know how much junk I threw out when I gave up my apartment? And don't even get me started on how much I spent on eating out since I was in the office sixty hours a week and didn't have time to shop or cook!"

Riley drew a breath and Boone could only stare at her as she continued her tirade, a female version of the rant he'd spewed himself on countless occasions. So she did care about the state of the world. He was surprised how much that gratified him—and turned him on. Who would have guessed this woman he hadn't seen in thirteen years could come to the same conclusions about life as he had? He knew his memories were just that—memories. It defied the odds that Riley could still be the kind of soulmate she once had promised to be, but if she shared a passion for his causes, too, it would be a miracle.

"What happened to friendship?" Riley was saying when he tuned into her words again. "What happened to long afternoons poring over a good novel or a great work of art? What happened to an honest exchange of opinions between educated people who respect each other? What's wrong with tending a garden or creating a beautiful home? Did you know that a well-to-do woman in Jane Austen's time would have had seven or eight dresses?"

Caught off guard by her sudden question, it took Boone a minute to answer. In truth he'd been too absorbed in examining her face—so sweetly familiar and so different, too. Her eyes reflected the light of the far-off fire. "Uh… no, I didn't know that."

"Seven or eight," she repeated. "How many outfits did I have before I came here?"

"I… don't know." Boone didn't often find himself at a loss for words, but the more he thought about it, the more he was sure of one thing. An extraordinary coincidence had placed him and Riley in the same place at the same time. He'd be a fool not to seize the opportunity with both hands.

"Forty-six. At least! I counted them! That doesn't even include all the outfits I gave away a few months ago because they were too out of fashion."

"Okay." Distracted, Boone wasn't sure where she was headed with this, but he didn't really care, either. He could listen to her as long as she cared to talk.

She lifted her hands in exasperation. "Think about it. Think about what I could do if I didn't have to worry about what I was going to wear each day." She tugged at her dress, a gown of soft material with a light background that was dotted with flowers. "This is my morning dress. I have two of them. Two! For the next six months that's the only choice I'll have. Wear this one or the other one. How simple is that?"

Boone's attention snapped back into focus. He knew exactly what she was talking about now. "Simplicity. You're into simple living?" He couldn't believe his luck.

"Not simple living. Beautiful living!"

"But you just said about the dresses—"

"Two morning dresses, one walking dress, one promenade gown, one riding habit"—she ticked them off on her fingers as Boone's bewilderment grew—"and…well, we decided against getting evening gowns, ball gowns, and court attire since we intend to stay home for the most part."

"Yeah, I doubt you'll need a ball gown in Chance Creek." He waited for her to laugh, but she didn't. Maybe they weren't as compatible as he'd thought.

"I suppose not. It was tempting, though," she said after a moment's hesitation.

Boone lifted a hand to rub the back of his neck. This was not how he thought his first night at Westfield would go. He'd spent the last few hours walking around the ranch and taking in the contours of the land. Deciding on a building site had been easy. The rest was harder. "So you're going to wear a bunch of impractical outfits and do what—sit around and read all day?" His disappointment made him angry. He wanted Riley to be a match, but ball gowns had no place in the world he was building, and if she was fixated on them, they wouldn't get far.

"What are you going to do in your *sustainable community*?" She made the term sound like a dirty word.

"Create a home, tend a garden, produce my own food, generate my own power, make a community that can sustain itself without input from the outside world."

"We're going to do most of that, too," Riley said. "We'll tend the manor"—she waved a hand at the house behind them—"garden, cook, and pursue our passions while sticking to a budget that most people couldn't live on. That will give us a chance to paint, play instruments, write and act; all the things that increase beauty in the world."

"The world doesn't need beauty," Boone said, suddenly exasperated. "The world needs practical solutions to its problems."

A heavy silence greeted this pronouncement.

"Go on back to your commune, Boone. Forget you ever saw me here. We'll leave first thing in the morning." She turned away, but not before he saw the sheen of tears in her eyes. His gut tightened and he grabbed her hand instinctively. He wasn't ready to lose her again.

"Come on, Riley." He felt like he'd kicked a puppy, but good intentions and pretty dresses weren't going to solve anything. The world needed people who weren't afraid to get their hands dirty and work on its problems. He'd made a promise to dedicate his life to finding some of those answers. She should, too.

He assessed her again. She was intelligent. Caring. She was here in his own backyard. Practically in his arms.

He could teach her to care about sustainability the way he'd taught her to ride and hunt.

He knew he didn't want to watch her walk away again.

Boone told himself it was because he had an impossible deadline, and he'd already figured out how to coerce Riley into marrying him. It was only practical to make use of an opportunity put right in front of him. Any man would do the same.

The truth was, practicality had little to do with it.

Faced with Riley again, he ached to take the opportunity she'd once offered him. From the moment he'd seen her, she'd taken his breath away, captivating him from the curve of her cheek to the swell of her breasts under that ridiculous gown, to the way the breeze caught at the tendrils of her hair and sent them dancing. She was so much more beautiful standing in front of him than she'd been in her photograph. So much more… alive. He wanted to get inside her head and know what she was thinking—know if they could still connect the way they once had.

Most of all, he wanted to share his life with a woman who mattered to him, and no one he'd met in the last thirteen years had ever mattered the way Riley once had.

She tugged at his hand, trying to break free.

"Uh-uh." Boone didn't let go. "We're not done here."

The night he'd watched Riley walk away he'd made the biggest mistake of his life.

Now he'd been given a second chance. He'd taken a

leap of faith many times in his career. Time to leap again.

"Why aren't we? Done, I mean," she demanded.

"Because I need a wife and you need a home. We're going to make a deal."

RILEY WASN'T SURE she'd heard Boone right. "You need a... wife?"

"That's right. And I'm looking at her."

Riley swallowed in a suddenly dry throat. Boone had lost his mind. Maybe he didn't even own Westfield. Maybe he'd gotten a brain injury during one of his missions. Was he packing a gun somewhere on that long, lean frame?

"I don't understand."

"It's a simple trade. You can stay at Westfield—for free—as long as you agree to marry me."

"Why would you want to do that?"

Boone's quick grin transformed him from formidable to sexy as hell. "Because I can't think of any woman I'd rather marry."

Her body responded to that smile with a rush of desire, but Riley clamped down on her overactive libido. He had to be pulling her leg. She wished she understood what kind of twisted joke he thought he was playing. "What is this all about, Boone?"

He held his hands out in a placating gesture. "I get it. This is pretty strange. Confession time. Fulsom—the man funding us—wants our community to be realistic. A bunch of single men won't do the trick. We need couples. Families. I'm supposed to set the tone." Boone waved the details away like they weren't important, but a muscle twitched in his jaw. Riley remembered that tic.

Boone was keeping something back.

"Who's going to care if you're married or single?"

"The audience watching our reality television show."

Riley blinked. "You're going to be on TV?"

"That's right. That's how Fulsom is going to help us increase awareness about sustainable living."

"You're nuts if you think I'm going to marry you." He hadn't bothered to contact her since the day he'd left Chance Creek. He'd stood by and watched her crash and burn in front of all his friends. If it weren't for infrequent updates passed along via gossip, she wouldn't even have known he was still alive.

"More like desperate," he confessed. "I'm in a jam, too, Riley. I didn't know about the marriage part until it was too late. Come on, let's help each other out. Think of it as a temporary solution with a possibility of permanence. If it doesn't work out we can divorce when it's over. But I hope it doesn't come to that."

Riley couldn't keep up. How could Boone leap from recognizing her to wanting to marry in less than a few minutes? She understood he needed to for his sustainable community thingy with Fulsom, but still, wasn't that jumping the gun?

"From June through November—that's all I'm asking. Just until the show wraps up."

November? She'd already planned to stay at least through October. Was that a coincidence, too? Or was

Boone right—was Fate at play here?

"Listen," he went on. "You just told me you sold everything, gave up your apartments, your jobs. I could boot you all out of here right now. Are you going to let your friends go homeless?"

His jab hit a target and Riley winced. She'd do just about anything not to let her friends down. But marriage—to a man she hadn't seen in years? To… Boone? That wasn't a good idea, fake or not. "Don't you have a girlfriend?"

"I just got out of the Navy, remember? Haven't had much time to date."

"You said the Fulsom Foundation owns this place," Riley tried. "So you don't actually own—"

"The house is mine to offer. Or to take away." He leaned closer. "Did you really sell everything?"

"Everything a woman in Regency times wouldn't have. We thought we'd found a way to step out of the rat race for a minute." She explained about her friends. "Can you blame us for wanting something different?"

"What about you?"

"Me?" She hesitated to tell him too much about herself. "I just want to be part of a bigger conversation about life. About what's beautiful, what's wonderful, what's meant to be treasured. I want to slow down and think about things rather than rushing from job to job, filling my days with meaningless work."

"Musician, actor, writer. Didn't you get a degree?"

"Yes. Bachelor of Fine Arts. I'm a painter," she said. That was a side of herself she hadn't shared with the

Horsemen—or even Boone.

He didn't seem surprised, though.

"If you stayed at Westfield with me, you'd have all the time you wanted to paint."

"Would I? I'd expect you to think it was as much a waste of time as reading."

"I never said reading was a waste of time."

"Didn't you?"

Boone frowned. "I didn't mean to. Sustainable living isn't just a hobby of mine. It goes deeper than that. I can get... single-minded."

Riley knew all about the ways Boone could focus on something to the exclusion of everything else. It had been frustrating at times when they were kids and she'd felt he'd forgotten about her while tinkering with an engine or doing his chores. But when he'd focused exclusively on her—those had been the most breathtaking moments of her life.

"I've overwhelmed you. Don't feel like you have to make up your mind tonight," he went on. "Let's talk about it again tomorrow." He slid his hands over her arms and for a brief, heart-pounding moment she thought he might kiss her. When he didn't, she couldn't fathom why she felt disappointed. Hadn't she learned anything over the years?

"This feels like a setup—like someone's going to jump out and tell me I've been tricked on camera." She pulled away from him.

"No tricks, Riley. I couldn't be more serious about this."

If it was anyone else, she wouldn't have believed him, but even though Boone had hurt her feelings badly, he'd never once lied to her. "It takes more than a day to know if you want to marry someone."

His gaze held hers. "We were good friends once, you and me. We could make this work. I know you've had a shock—" He glanced at her friends still grouped around the fire. "But you love Westfield, I know you do. If you help me, you can stay."

"Boone—"

"Think about it for twenty-four hours. I'll pick you up at eight tomorrow night. We'll go on a date. Maybe it'll be fun." With a wicked smile, he caught her wrist and pressed a kiss into her palm. "If you ask me to dance, I'll say yes this time, Riley Eaton." Riley gasped and tried to pull away, but he merely pressed her hand to his chest. She could feel his heart thumping, a strangely intimate sensation.

She snatched back her hand. Her palm tingled from the contact with his shirt. Boone gave her a salute and turned to stride off into the shadows.

Riley held still a long time before returning to her friends, still clustered around the fire.

"Who was that? What did he say?" Savannah asked.

Riley had no idea how to answer her.

CHAPTER THREE

★

BOONE'S MIND WAS reeling as he picked his way through the dark along the rutted dirt track that wound down the hill to the cluster of outbuildings. The last thing he'd expected when he'd charged up that hill to see who'd set the fire was to find Riley—and propose to her. Maybe he should have waited and wooed her first, but a courtship could go wrong in all kinds of ways. He needed a wife. Riley wanted Westfield. And he hadn't felt this interested in a woman in a long time.

Why chance it?

He could probably have strong-armed her into agreeing to the marriage idea tonight, but that would be winning the battle in order to lose the war. One glance at her told him she must have her choice of men these days. He had to make his offer too good to turn down—and then use the time he'd gained with her to see if they could connect enough to make their marriage real. Boone was prepared to do whatever it took to satisfy Fulsom, and if he only had to marry he could have suffered through a fake relationship in order to fulfill that requirement. But Fulsom wanted pregnancies and that was a whole other matter. Boone refused to bring children into the world unless he loved their mother.

Could he love Riley? The question nearly made him stumble, but he recovered his footing quickly, and the answer came just as fast.

Yes.

He'd loved her once, in his way. He'd never put it into words when they were young. Back then she was simply part of his existence. Someone he took for granted until those last few minutes before he lost her for good.

He wouldn't make that mistake again.

This time around he'd get to know all about her and hope the connection that had once wound between them could tighten into the kind of relationship that stood the test of time.

He didn't know how to convince Riley to give him a chance, though. Her whole demeanor told him she hadn't forgotten or forgiven what he'd done when they were teens. He had to turn things around before she dug in her heels. Maybe if he talked to her about his interests he could prove he wasn't the thoughtless teenager he once was. It seemed like they'd taken different paths to reach similar conclusions. She might talk about beauty while he talked about sustainability, but in the end they had in common the desire to improve the world. When she learned what he was doing, wouldn't she become interested in sustainability—and him—too?

Giving her too much time to think it over wouldn't be smart. First thing tomorrow he'd head back up to the house, take her on a tour of the ranch and explain his intentions for the place. Something about him had attracted her to him when they were young. He hoped like hell he still possessed that quality. He'd emphasize the community aspects of his plan and the way everyone involved would work together to build a harmonious whole. She craved beauty, so he'd give her beauty. He'd show her the way the spare lines of his houses and communal buildings wouldn't block the view of the natural world that surrounded them. He'd talk about the cycle of life they would tap into and the way they would emulate it in their planting, reaping and replenishing of their gardens, and the closed-loop systems they'd put in place to harvest natural energy to fuel their homes.

He'd gamble on the possibility she was as lonely as he'd been these past few years. Fulsom was right—he was ready to settle down. Did Riley want a partner, too?

Did she want kids?

He did.

Suddenly uncomfortable, Boone pulled his phone out of his pocket and called Jericho, who picked up on the third ring.

"You at the ranch?" Jericho asked by way of greeting.

"I've already surveyed it and found a home site."

"That was fast."

"You want to hear about fast, check this out. I

found a wife, too."

"You're shitting me." Jericho chuckled. "Even you couldn't pull that off."

"Well, my ring's not on her finger, but it will be soon."

"You must have pulled out the charm."

"Something like that. It's Riley."

After a pause, Jericho dredged the name up from his memory. "Tagalong Riley?"

Anger gripped Boone. "Call her that again—*ever*—and you and I will part ways. Got it?"

"Fuck, man. Yeah—I got it."

Boone didn't care if Jericho thought he'd lost his mind. That nickname ceased to exist now.

"She didn't know her uncle sold the ranch," he went on, "so she arrived here with some friends today to stay at the house. Apparently Russ has been gone a long time and she comes and goes as she pleases. Or she used to, anyhow."

"Shit. What'd you tell her?"

"That if she wants to stay she has to marry me."

Jericho chuckled. "You've got balls. You'd better watch your back, man. I wouldn't want a pissed-off Riley on my tail. Remember the time she hit Walker with a two-by-four?"

He'd forgotten that. It was an accident—mostly. Walker had a way of getting under Riley's skin. He'd been the only one of them who tried to watch out for her and she didn't like being reminded she was younger and less experienced than them. "She's not pissed off.

She's… intrigued." More like stunned and horrified, but Jericho didn't need to know that.

"You think she'll go for it?"

Boone hesitated. He should have known Jericho would ask difficult questions. "Maybe. There's something else. She's into all that *Pride and Prejudice* crap now."

"Heck, if she's got two X chromosomes, that's a given."

"I'm not sure that's true."

"Well, it's true for a lot of them. Just how into it is she?" Boone heard the creak of a desk chair. Jericho must be doing paperwork again.

"As in, she dresses like one of them—one of those women in the movies."

"Like—all the time?" Jericho sounded alarmed.

"As far as I can tell. She and her friends were all dolled up like that when I met up with them. She said they'd sworn an oath to live a beautiful life for six months. Something about taking time off from the real world to rediscover the things they're passionate about."

"An oath, huh? Well, I guess it could be worse. They could have decided to rob banks." Boone heard a tick, tick, tick sound, Jericho's pen tapping against his desk. Boone wished the others were here already. One day on the ground had brought too many complications for him to deal with alone. "I know you hung around with her more than I did, but do you really like Riley enough to marry her?"

Another hard question. "I think so," Boone said.

"I'm... attracted to her." This was an uncomfortable conversation. "She's still Riley. Beyond that, I've got to spend time with her to answer your question."

"It's hard to picture her grown up enough to be a wife. She looked pretty hot that last night before we left town, though."

"Yeah." Boone's answer was short. He didn't like Jericho thinking about her that way. And he didn't like remembering how that night had turned out.

A silence. "We were shitheads to her at the end," Jericho said.

"You got that right. I don't know if she'll forgive us, either."

"We were pretty young. She'll take that into consideration."

"I hope so." Boone reached the outbuildings and began to build a fire in the old fire pit several dozen yards from the bunkhouse. He needed to eat and he was a long way from ready to sleep.

"Do you think she's into you?" Jericho asked after a pause.

"I don't know," Boone said. "She kept her distance. She has friends," he added as an afterthought.

"Interesting. So what's your first move?"

"I'm going to take her on a date."

"You're a brave man, Chief."

"Either that or very, very stupid."

"OUT WITH IT," Savannah said. "Who on earth was that man?"

"That was our landlord," Riley finally said, struggling to process everything that had happened in the last few minutes. For one thing, she needed to present this new development to her friends in a way that wouldn't send them running for the hills. For another, she had to sort through her feelings for Boone. Their conversation had been so strange she didn't know what to believe.

Had she really just gotten her first proposal?

What a proposal it was. Trading marriage for a chance to stay at Westfield? That was ridiculous.

Except it was Boone making the offer.

She had to at least think it over.

She'd read and heard enough about Martin Fulsom to know the demands he'd made of Boone weren't that unusual. No one else would tie their donations to a requirement like marriage, but Fulsom was larger than life, brash and a media darling. He thought nothing of pulling outrageous stunts himself. He'd do whatever it took to get his television show top ratings.

What was Boone getting himself into?

"That's your uncle?" Nora asked. They crowded around her as the fire burned down.

"No. That's definitely not my uncle—that's Boone Rudman. He's a friend of mine from a long time ago." Riley was still in shock that he was here at Westfield at all, let alone the owner of the ranch.

"Boone? The guy you've told us about? The Navy SEAL? The one who embarrassed you in front of everyone?" Savannah exchanged a look with the others.

"I thought your uncle owned the ranch," Nora persisted.

"He decided to sell it recently. I didn't want to worry you. Boone bought it, so it's all right." She wished that was true.

"I don't understand," Nora said. "If Russ doesn't own Westfield, what are we doing here?"

"We can still live here, can't we?" Avery asked worriedly.

"I thought you were supposed to inherit Westfield," Savannah said.

"I was. Things have changed, but Boone said we could stay until December." As long as she married him. Russ's betrayal blindsided her again. It was cruel to promise that she'd inherit Westfield if he didn't intend to follow through. Losing the ranch was like losing her grandparents all over.

"Will we have to pay rent?" Avery asked.

"You should have told us," Savannah said.

"I know, I know. It was really unexpected."

"Why was he so angry at first? Didn't you tell him we were coming today?" Nora pressed.

"He… got the date wrong," Riley improvised. "He thought we were kids up to mischief." She was relieved when the others seemed to accept this.

"What's it like to see him again after all these years?" Savannah asked.

"It's… awkward," Riley said.

"Lieutenant Rudman. It has a ring to it," Avery said.

"I don't know what his rank is," Riley said.

"Lieutenant will do just fine," Avery declared. "It

sounds very Jane Austen-y. Is he single?"

"Yes." Riley bit her lip. She had to give them some indication of what was to come. "He... asked me out."

"Really?"

"What'd you say?"

The questions came from all sides.

The fire was quickly dying down to ashes. Riley moved closer to it, suddenly chilled. "I said yes."

The others exchanged a glance again. Riley couldn't tell if they were surprised or dismayed. Or both.

"Good for you," Avery managed to say.

"Are you sure that's wise?" Savannah asked.

"No. I'm not sure of that at all," Riley told her.

"That's because it isn't wise," Nora said. "But it's probably inevitable."

"He'll make a good Darcy for your Elizabeth," Avery broke in, obviously trying to avert an argument. "Maybe he has a friend."

"He does. In fact, several of them are coming to live here, too." Riley brightened at being able to provide this information. She didn't want to go down the rabbit hole Nora had opened up. Maybe she was right; maybe it was inevitable she'd try again with Boone, even after he'd hurt her, but she didn't need someone else to point it out. "When we were kids I called them the Four Horsemen of the Apocalypse. But they're all grown up now."

"Are they military men, too? I do so love a man in uniform." Avery batted her eyelashes.

"Down, Kitty," Nora said, referencing the Jane Austen novel they all knew so well. "You know how much trouble military men can be."

"And how exciting," Avery said.

"Well, I think things are looking up." Savannah put her hands on her hips. "Let's put out this fire and go back inside. We can plan what we'll tackle tomorrow. Except for you, Riley." A mischievous smile lit her face. "We know exactly who you're going to tackle."

The others laughed appreciatively, but Riley could only smile wanly as she watched Nora pour the bucket of water they'd brought with them over the fire. If only they knew the price she was going to pay for their happiness.

Not that she was going to marry Boone. That was ridiculous.

But as she watched Avery, Nora and Savannah link arms and head indoors, she knew she was well on her way to being caught. She couldn't bear to disappoint her friends—especially knowing the precarious positions they'd put themselves in to join her here.

Maybe she'd have to marry him after all.

BOONE KNOCKED ON the front door of Westfield Manor at seven-thirty the next morning. He'd wanted to come earlier, but he figured the women might sleep in if they'd traveled a long way the day before. When no one answered, he knocked again, louder this time.

He was about to knock a third time when the door swung open suddenly, revealing a disheveled Riley in an old-fashioned nightgown which somehow managed to cover everything and reveal far too much all at the same time. Boone hadn't expected Riley would continue her Regency masquerade into the night and he had to bite back a smile at the picture she presented.

Her white cotton gown buttoned up nearly to her chin and the matching white cap trailed silly pink ribbons down over her shoulders. Her hair was tucked up into it, and she looked young and vulnerable somehow. Her eyes widened as she took him in. She nearly shut the door in his face, but he stuck his foot between it and the frame, thankful for the thick leather of his boot.

"Morning," he said, doffing his cowboy hat. When he'd stopped by his parents' house on the way to Westfield yesterday he'd found it hanging in his bedroom where he'd left it. It still fit.

While his parents had hoped he'd stay with them, he'd felt the need to camp on the land. It had never occurred to him to stay in the manor—the large, old house strayed too far from his ideal of sustainable. He could have slept in the bunkhouse, even though the bunks were long gone, but Boone wanted a connection to the ground on which he'd build his community and he'd slept in a tent instead.

He'd stayed up half the night planning for this meeting—and daydreaming about Riley. It didn't take much to leap from thinking about marrying her to what would come next. Yesterday, his body had reacted to her like he hadn't seen a woman in months and last night, alone in his tent, Riley consumed his thoughts, no matter how practical he'd tried to be.

The more he'd thought about Riley, the more he'd wondered how he'd ever let so many years pass before trying to see her. He wished he had time to get to know her over a period of months. To pursue a relationship in the normal way.

Fulsom wasn't going to give him that luxury.

Somewhere before dawn Boone realized he was making things far too complicated. He felt like some unwritten rule dictated he'd need six months to decide whether he wanted to marry Riley. But that wasn't true. The minute he'd seen her, something had clicked in his brain and he'd known she was the one for him.

Now he just had to let himself fall in love.

As the sun rose, he'd allowed himself to spin a fantasy of life with Riley. He'd imagined marrying her. Making a home with her. Working with her.

Making love to her.

It wasn't long before that particular daydream got away from him and when he could think clearly again, Boone had admitted to himself that falling for Riley wasn't going to be difficult.

Getting her to fall for him might prove more problematic, though.

"Go away," Riley said. "It's the middle of the freaking night." She tried to shut the door again, but Boone muscled it open.

"The sun has been up for over two hours. Time to rise and shine."

"What are you so cheerful about?"

"Getting to see you again." It was true; there wasn't anywhere he'd rather be than right here. "I'm glad you came to Westfield."

"Glad enough to let me stay?"

"Of course. If you'll marry me."

"Boone." Even disapproving, she looked so delicious in her old-fashioned getup.

"Riley."

"Are you really serious about that?"

"You have no idea." He was afraid she'd close the door, so he steered the conversation to safer ground. "You four can have the manor and the two acres around it, including the gardens out back. The Horsemen and I won't touch them. In fact, we won't trespass without your invitation."

Riley relaxed a little. "Okay."

"Feel free to wander the rest of the ranch, of course; just be careful of our gardens and installations. If you want to learn more about our solar power system or anything else, just ask. I'd love to show them to you once they're up and running."

Riley nodded. "We'll be careful." She bit her lip and he had the feeling she was remembering that Russ had sold the place out from under her. Time to distract her again.

"My sustainable community will be off-grid. How about we get the manor off the grid, too?"

"That would be… interesting," Riley said. She stifled a yawn. "Could you maybe come back later? Like, when I'm dressed?"

"I'd prefer to talk now. I'm kind of enjoying this," he said.

Riley rolled her eyes, but color bloomed in her cheeks, and Boone's pulse two-stepped in his veins. Without thinking, he leaned in closer, intent on stealing a kiss. Riley didn't pull away. Instead, she watched him come toward her, and even lifted her chin as if to meet him halfway.

"Riley? What's going on?" a voice called.

They sprang apart. Boone looked past Riley to see an ethereal blonde come down the stairs. A possible match for Clay, he thought.

"It's our landlord." Riley smoothed her dress. A blush tinged her cheeks.

"This early?" Another woman descended the stairs. A brunette. Boone paired her with Walker in his mind; she looked nearly as serious as he pretended to be. When a redhead joined the group, pattering down the steps so quickly her white nightgown billowed around her, he had to bite back a smile. Jericho would be pleased.

"Just had a few things to say. Riley, can you introduce me?"

"This is Savannah," she said, indicating the blonde.

"Good morning, Lieutenant," Savannah said with a little curtsy. "It's a beautiful day, isn't it?"

"It sure is. But I'm not a lieutenant," Boone said. "I enlisted in the Navy straight out of high school and—"

"We appreciate you letting us stay at the manor, *Lieutenant*," the redhead interrupted. "I'm Avery, by the way. It's a shame you aren't wearing your uniform, you know."

"I'm happy to have you here." What was with the lieutenant bit?

"We're very happy to be here, Lieutenant. And we'll take care of the house as if it was our own," the brunette said.

"Because it should be," Riley added. "This is Nora, by the way. She's a teacher."

Boone forged ahead. "First things first. I'm not a lieutenant. I'm a non-commissioned officer and—"

"But lieutenant sounds so romantic," Avery said. "They're always lieutenants in Jane Austen novels."

"That's not even true," Nora said. "There's Colonel Brandon, Captain Wentworth…"

"Are you a colonel or a captain?" Savannah asked Boone.

"No, but—"

"See, he's a lieutenant," Avery said.

"Of course, Jane Austen would have pronounced it lef-tenant, being British and all," Nora pointed out.

"I'm damn well not a lef-anything," Boone growled.

"That's okay, we're not British." Avery shrugged. "Lieutenant it is."

Boone gave up. "I was explaining to Riley that I want you all to feel at home here. Three friends will be joining me soon. Until then, please let me know how I can help make Westfield comfortable."

"Lieutenant Rudman's building a commune down by the barn," Riley added sweetly.

"*Community*. A sustainable community." If he thought he'd have the upper hand by coming early, he'd definitely been mistaken.

"When are your friends arriving?" Avery asked.

"A couple of weeks."

"Weeks?" She sounded disappointed.

"Avery." Nora looked reproving.

"That's a long time. It's not like I can head into town on Friday night and go to a bar dressed like this," Avery said.

Boone suppressed a smile. He'd like to see that.

"We're not here to meet men," Nora said.

"Maybe you aren't."

"We swore an oath, remember?"

"There'll be plenty of men to choose from in my community," Boone interjected. He could handle them screwing up his rank if they'd agree to marry his friends. "Maybe you'll find your Mr. Darcy there. Come on down whenever you get lonely. You can take your pick."

Nora's eyebrows shot up. "Sounds like you're running a brothel as well as a commune down there."

Riley laughed. "Community," she corrected just as Boone did the same. "Lieutenant Rudman is running a brothel and a *community*." He shot her a dark look. She batted her eyelashes at him.

"No brothels. Just hard working men who'd maybe like to find a partner. A real partner," he emphasized. "All the men joining me have served their country for years. They've put their lives on the line more often than you've taken out the trash. They're coming here because they believe in our goals and want to make this world a better place. They don't deserve your mockery."

Riley sobered. So did her friends.

"I didn't mean to mock anyone," Avery said, plucking at her nightgown as if suddenly conscious of it.

Boone relaxed. "That's okay. I guess we'll all have to figure out how to get along. Who says a bunch of SEALs and a pack of Austenites can't be friends?"

Savannah broke into a sudden smile. "Austenites. I like that. And I for one am glad there'll be a militia stationed close by, just like there was in *Pride and Prejudice*. Men in uniform are so delightful."

Militia? Boone decided it wasn't worth trying to sort that one out.

"Bossy, more like it," Riley said.

"Direct," Boone corrected her. "We know what we like and we go after it." He held Riley's gaze a moment. "I'd better get going. Riley, want to come with me? I could tell you about my plans."

"Not now. We have chores to do and I want to paint today. That's the reason we're here, after all. I'll be ready at eight o'clock tonight."

Unhappy with the brushoff, Boone leaned closer. "I'd like you to come with me now."

"I said no." She folded her arms over her chest.

Boone wanted to press the matter, but he had a feeling it would backfire. "Fine. Eight o'clock. I'm happy to have met you all," he said to the others, touching the brim of his hat. "I hope you enjoy your stay at West-field." He couldn't help adding, "However long it might be."

RILEY CLOSED THE door behind him and faced her friends, seething at that last non-subtle hint Boone had tossed her way. *However long it might be.* She didn't need reminding it was her decision that would determine the length of their stay, or that Russ had sold her ranch out from under her. She'd sent her uncle an e-mail last night with the subject line, "You SOLD Westfield???" She'd check for an answer as soon as she could.

"You are in trouble," Savannah told her. "You've got no defenses that'll stand up to that."

"Boone's definitely not brushing you off now," Nora agreed.

Avery spoke up. "Are his friends anything like him?"

"If they are, I want one," Savannah said. "You're so lucky, Riley."

"I don't know about lucky. If I give him any encouragement, he'll have us out of these dresses and down there living on grubs and mushrooms."

"I wouldn't mind getting out of my dress with a man like that, but I'll skip the grubs and mushrooms, thank you very much. Can't wait to hear all about your date tonight." Avery hugged Riley impulsively. "At least he didn't mention rent. Are you sure he won't charge us any? Because I'm not sure we can afford it."

The others waited to hear her answer. Again, she wondered if she should confess it all, but one look at the hollows under Nora's eyes convinced her not to.

What if Nora decided she should go back to Baltimore? She'd nearly bailed on them twice before everything was settled. Only multiple phone calls from the rest of them had kept her on course.

"Boone keeps his promises," she said, evading the question.

"Terrific. So what should we do?" Savannah asked. "I'm not going to be able to go back to sleep."

"Let's get to work. We'll pretend Boone doesn't even exist." Riley lifted her chin and turned toward the stairs.

"Lieutenant Rudman," Avery corrected her. "In Regency times, it didn't do to be too familiar with strange men."

She was far more right than she knew, Riley thought. Familiarity with Boone in the past hadn't ended well for her. If she was smart she'd gather her friends and leave the ranch now, no matter how much she wanted to stay and get to know Boone all over again. They could book a hotel room and have a spa weekend instead.

And then what, Riley wondered. None of them had homes to return to anymore.

They couldn't leave without a plan, and all of them needed a break, which meant she'd better string Boone along for a few days, at least, until she'd had time to think.

Meanwhile, she needed to act normally. "First things first," Riley said briskly. "Let's unpack our things, and then we'll go through the house and make a list of anything else we'll need. Those supplies we ordered will be delivered this morning. If anything's missing, we can place a new order later today. We'll start with a little breakfast after we're dressed. Working clothes for now." Her friends' faces echoed the same mixture of excitement and trepidation she felt. "Everyone ready?"

"We burned our regular clothes," Avery said. "There's no going back now."

"Group hug?" Savannah said.

The group hug ritual had stood them in good stead for years and they fell into it willingly. Even Nora lightened up as they swayed together, laughing and shrieking until it became more of a rugby scrum.

"What would Jane think?" Avery cried.

"She'd think we should get busy with our new lives," Savannah said. "Let's go!"

CHAPTER FOUR

★

B OONE STOOD ON the gently sloping hillside that would soon become the heart of his community. It faced the larger hill upon which Westfield stood. He should have been thinking about his plans, but instead he gazed at the manor.

He wished he hadn't beat such a hasty retreat. It had only taken moments in Riley's presence for his entire body to be aware of her proximity. The tomboy had been replaced with a curvy, delicious woman who still knew how to push his buttons. He was intrigued by the idea of getting to know her again. The years would have changed Riley—matured her. What were her passions—besides Jane Austen? Did she still ride like the wind?

What made her laugh?

He pulled a ball of twine from his pocket, reached down to pick up one of the stakes he'd brought and pushed it into the ground. He used a tape measure to mark the distance and planted another stake eight feet away. He kept working until he'd marked out a rectangle and affixed twine to the stakes.

When he was finished, Boone moved on to make another rectangle, and another. He toiled under the rising sun until he'd marked out ten of them. Stepping back to survey his handiwork, Boone frowned. He didn't like the position of the last one. He undid his work and started over, his mind drifting back to Riley.

He wondered what she did at the vitamin company. She'd gone to school to study painting, but that wasn't a very useful degree. She'd said nothing about exhibiting her work. Was she still an artist?

He thought back to the sketches she'd sometimes made. Quick little pencil pictures she'd crumple up or pocket if he showed them any attention. He'd never really thought about them. They were just a habit she had, like Jericho tapping his pencil or Clay cracking his knuckles when they were teens.

Were there other things she'd hidden from him? He didn't like that idea. It struck at the heart of his memories of his childhood to think that he hadn't known Riley as well as he thought. It occurred to him that she'd done a good job of hiding something else back then. Unless her desire to dance with him that last evening had come out of nowhere, she'd liked him—maybe for a long time—and he'd never guessed.

He'd have to pay more attention to Riley this time around, Boone told himself. He couldn't be the same self-absorbed teenager that had trampled on her feelings. Not if he wanted her to agree to marry him.

It was time to get to know Riley all over again.

And he looked forward to the task.

"WHAT IS HE doing now?" Savannah asked when she caught Riley gazing out the window toward an area where Boone was marking out rectangles with stakes. They'd finished their chores and had come downstairs after changing out of their work clothes into prettier dresses in preparation for their first afternoon of art, music and writing. Riley had made Avery give her their cell phone for a minute so she could check her messages, even if it wasn't her time yet. There was still no word from Russ.

"The same as before. Do you think he's planning a garden? Maybe those are vegetable beds."

"If they were, why wouldn't they be lined up?" Savannah peered down the hill. "We need binoculars."

"Put it on the list," Avery said, coming to join them. "Those are way too wide for vegetable beds. You couldn't reach across to weed them."

"Maybe he's sending a message to the mother ship," Nora said.

"If a flying saucer comes and sucks him up I'm going right back to California," Savannah said.

"Wait a minute," Riley said, her stomach sinking. "Housing! That's got to be some kind of housing he's planning down there!" He'd said he was going to build by the outbuildings.

"The rectangles are too small. Those aren't even big enough to be trailers!" Savannah protested.

"Tiny trailers?" Nora asked.

"Tiny houses?" Avery said, brightening. "Like the ones on TV. Those are so cute!"

"Tiny houses wouldn't be so bad," Savannah said.

"Are you kidding? They'd be awful!" Riley said. "He's ruining Westfield!"

"It could be like a village. Villages are cute," Avery said.

"He's not building a village! He's building a bloody trailer park! On my land!"

"It's not really your land anymore, though, is it?" Savannah said. "So before you fly off the handle, let's go ask him. Maybe it's not as bad as it seems."

"We'll go for our first Jane Austen walk," Nora added. "It'll be fun."

If Nora was the one rallying her, she was really in trouble, Riley thought as they made for the front door again.

"Wait. We ought to be wearing our bonnets," Savannah said. "No Regency woman would go outside without her bonnet."

Since bonnets were a new item of clothing for everyone, it took some minutes for them to put them on and adjust them to their satisfaction.

"I wish I could wear my spencer, too, but it's too warm," Savannah said, tying a bow in the wide ribbons of her pale blue bonnet that nicely complemented the blue of her dress.

"I know. Me, too," Avery said. Hers was a rich brown.

"Focus, before he gets too far into whatever it is he's doing down there," Riley said, although she knew what they meant. Spencer jackets looked so cute with their gowns. She'd chosen a straw bonnet that would go well with all of her dresses. It was made so that she could swap out ribbons to match her outfits. Today her ribbon was moss green. Nora's bonnet was a deep burgundy echoed in the pattern of her dress. It set off her dark hair and pretty face.

They set off and despite her concerns, Riley had to smile at the picture they made. The four of them looked like the Bennett sisters as they walked together, their long straight dresses flapping a little and wrapping around their legs. The breeze teased the strings of their bonnets, too. All in all they looked lovely, she thought. Lovely and far more innocent than they really were.

If Boone was building houses he'd find out just how innocent she wasn't.

The sunshine and fresh air soothed Riley's frazzled nerves. She took a couple of deep breaths, drinking in Westfield's familiar scents. It lacked the tang of livestock it used to have, and she wondered if Boone meant to buy horses. She couldn't imagine the Horsemen without them. As kids those boys practically lived in the saddle. She had, too, but she'd never been as skilled as they were. Boone had been fearless in the rodeo. Jericho, too.

Westfield seemed empty without the herds moving among the pastures and her grandparents and their hired hands working the spread. Boone hadn't mentioned anything about cattle, however. How were the people in his commune going to keep themselves afloat?

Boone noticed them when they were still some distance away and straightened from his work. He watched them approach, his expression inscrutable, but Riley felt a little thrill under his gaze. A thrill she tried to ignore.

Unsuccessfully.

"Didn't expect to see you again so soon, ladies."

"What are you doing?" Riley asked without preamble.

"We're curious," Savannah added quickly, as if trying to soften Riley's attack.

"Glad you came to ask. I'm staking out housing units for my community. I want to get a feel for how they'll look."

"Why are they so small?" Avery asked. She walked over to survey one of the staked-out perimeters.

"And why are they all facing the same way?" Savannah chimed in.

"I'm positioning the widest part of the buildings to face south." Boone's gesture described an arc over the sky like the path of the sun. "That way they make the best use of available sunshine. Their roofs will be pitched carefully to block the sun during the height of summer, and let it in all winter long. We'll make sure to capture that solar gain by using materials that can hold the heat and radiate it back..." He trailed off and shrugged. "You get the picture."

"But why are they so tiny?" Avery asked again.

"That makes them easier to heat. You four are going to bankrupt yourselves heating that monstrosity up there this winter." He nodded toward Westfield. "We'll spend pennies to keep warm down here."

"We won't bankrupt ourselves," Riley snapped. They'd be long gone by Christmas, after all, a thought that gave her an uncomfortable pang. This time when she left Westfield, she wouldn't be coming back. "Besides, there's a fireplace in every room. If we were staying here, we could burn wood all winter long."

"You're kidding, right?" When she didn't answer he went on. "From what I remember, those old fireplaces haven't been converted to any kind of efficient wood-burning stoves, right?"

"They're original," she said stiffly.

"Which means most of the heat you'd generate by burning wood would go straight up the chimney, along with all the pollutants. You'd roast within three feet of the fires and freeze everywhere else, and meanwhile you'll burn up trees and release their carbon dioxide!"

"I don't care about the trees. I care about the way you're ruining Westfield!"

"You've put your houses right in the line of sight from the manor," Savannah interceded. "It really changes the view."

"The view's the last thing on my mind," Boone said, an edge to his voice that surprised Riley.

"Boone—"

"I surveyed the ranch and this is the best location for our community. It's crucial we do this right. The houses go here."

Riley burned at the injustice of it. This is the way it would be from now on; Boone would call the shots and control the ranch that should have been hers. She hadn't even had time to process the hurt and pain of losing it. "You won't even talk about it?"

"Is that what you came here to do? Talk? Or are you here to dictate to me?" When she couldn't find an answer, he chuckled. "Thought so. I only take orders from my superior officers, Riley."

"This isn't a game!"

"You're exactly right; this is not a game." Once again it was the Navy SEAL in him talking, not the boy she'd once known. "You don't know where I've been, Riley. You don't know why I'm doing this. I swore an oath…"

They all waited for him to continue, but he didn't. Riley saw the strain in every line of his face, though. Something had happened to Boone while he was away.

Well, things had happened to her, too.

Boone sighed. "Look, take any war or insurrection or rebellion or terrorist act and trace it back—all the way back—and you'll find the same thing. At its heart the fight is over resources. Who has them. Who doesn't. Right?"

The others nodded. Riley pinched her lips together. None of them needed a history lesson from Mr. Navy SEAL.

"Our population is growing, our weather is getting unpredictable. Global warming, climate change, whatever you want to call it. It's making things worse. What I want to do is show Americans they can live a good life while consuming far fewer resources than they do today."

"By shoving them into tiny little houses like animals in their cages?" Riley said. She actually agreed with everything Boone had said so far, but she'd be damned if she'd admit it.

"By creating functional, private residences grouped in a community setting that maximizes efficiency, minimizes cost and brings a sense of wellbeing to all its inhabitants."

"I'm an inhabitant of Westfield and my wellbeing will be shot to hell if you build here."

Boone's expression hardened. "I'd do a lot for you, Riley, but saving the world takes precedence over your sensibilities."

Riley sputtered, but couldn't come up with a response. She whirled around. "Let's go." She didn't wait to see if her friends would follow. She marched off back up the hill, fighting against her skirts as she climbed. She was fighting tears, too. Some part of her had thought she'd been important to Boone after all, since he seemed so set on marrying her. What a joke. All he wanted was his damn funding so he could tear Westfield to pieces and ruin her past.

"Riley, it will be all right." Avery panted as she caught up to her.

"How could it possibly be all right?"

"I don't know, but it will."

Riley halted and Avery nearly tripped over her. "Look at him down there," Riley said. "So smug. So... righteous. He's going to save the world, huh? And to hell with us?"

"He's passionate about his cause, that's all."

Riley stared at Boone as he returned to his stakes and twine. Savannah and Nora caught up and gathered around her.

"Westfield was supposed to be mine!" The emotions she'd managed to hold at bay overnight finally crashed down around her. She blinked furiously to stave off the tears that threatened to fall. "I've loved this place my entire life. It isn't fair."

"Why did your uncle sell it so suddenly? Did he tell you?" Nora wanted to know.

"No," she said truthfully. "I didn't know until it was done. Why would he do that?" It was the question that haunted her. She'd had no reason to doubt his word—until now.

"If he'd promised it to you, he was probably ashamed of himself for changing his mind," Savannah said.

"It was a good thing Boone's the one who ended up with it. Can you imagine if Russ had sold it to a stranger? We wouldn't have had anywhere to go," Avery said.

Her words made Riley feel even more alone. They didn't know Boone would kick them out unless she married him. She wiped away her tears. He might have ruined everything for her, but she'd be damned if she let him steal the time her friends needed away from the world.

"Boone should understand he's changing a place you love," Nora said to Riley. "He should have more respect."

"Maybe you should go talk to him again and tell him how you feel. You might be able to persuade him," Savannah said hopefully.

"Maybe." But she doubted it. Boone had already shown how far he was willing to go to make his plans work. "I'll talk to him tonight."

"Come and eat," Avery urged her. "Then it'll be time to paint."

"Go on ahead. I need a minute."

She watched her friends turn toward the house again. Regaining her composure, Riley realized she had to make a decision. If she accepted Boone's offer and traded a fake marriage for free lodging at Westfield for her friends, she would have to accept that he was going to change the ranch. If she couldn't do that, she needed to confess everything to her friends and plan to move on—and know that Boone would still change the ranch after she left.

Two things kept her from wanting to choose the second path. One was the fear that without Westfield, there'd be no Jane Austen experiment. She wanted the chance to devote time to her painting, but more so she wanted Nora to be safe, Savannah to resume her career as a pianist, and Avery to get the chance to write that screenplay she was so excited about. If they had to go somewhere else and pay rent, they wouldn't have time for those things. They'd be right back to square one.

The other reason was far more complicated. It was a mixture of things, really. Nostalgia for the ranch—it would be hard to leave it again. A feeling that if she remained she could mitigate the damage Boone did. Curiosity about his plans. As much as she hated to admit it, she sympathised with his cause and wondered how he'd pull it off. Curiosity about Boone, too. For all she hated the way he'd treated her at the end, she also remembered all the good times they'd had when they were young, and she had to admit a strong chemistry popped and fizzed between them now. She couldn't help wondering where that might go.

She watched Boone toil at the building site. If she was being honest, her body responded to him every time she saw him. That kiss he'd pressed into her palm still made her skin tingle.

As if sensing her gaze, he turned to look up the hill at her and touched his finger to his hat in the same half-mocking, half-acknowledging way he'd always done. Riley crossed her arms and stared back down. After a minute, he shrugged and went back to work, but Riley didn't move. Should she stay or should she go?

She couldn't decide.

When Boone looked over his shoulder at her a minute later, and again a few minutes after that, she realized her steady gaze was getting to him. A smile tugged at the corners of her mouth. She'd made him nervous.

Good. The SEAL was too damn cocky.

She kept her position until Boone nonchalantly set down his twine and stakes and walked away. She wasn't fooled. When he didn't return, it confirmed she'd won.

Boone had a weakness, after all.

But as she trudged up the hill toward the manor, she realized what an empty victory it was. Boone still owned Westfield.

And she didn't want to leave.

CHAPTER FIVE

★

ONCE MORE BOONE crouched over the fire he'd lit in the rough, stone-lined circle some distance from the bunkhouse. Irritation tensed his muscles as he cooked a quick meal. Since breakfast, he'd done another quick survey of the ranch, settled on a housing site, staked out a number of imaginary houses and photographed the slope and other features of the ranch, then sent the images to Jericho, Clay and Walker. Jericho and Clay both sent back detailed responses about the pros and cons of his choice, along with lists of questions about the ranch they wanted answered. Walker had responded with his usual brevity: "Good."

All in all, it was a fine day's work and he should have felt energized by the progress he'd made. Instead, he was as jumpy as a bronco with a burr under its saddle. When he'd left the manor this morning, he'd thought he had the upper hand in the situation. But when Riley had come marching down the hill like an avenging angel it had all gone to hell. It hadn't occurred to him she'd object to the location of his houses. The truth was, he hadn't given a second thought to the manor when he'd set up his plans. That old-fashioned monstrosity was superfluous to the community he was building.

It wasn't to Riley, though.

Now he didn't know what to do. After she'd stood up on that hillside and watched him work for a while, he'd felt like ants were crawling over his skin. He didn't understand it. He'd kept his cool in all kinds of situations under the scrutiny of men far more dangerous than that bonnet-wearing Austenite. But this was Riley. He cared what she thought.

When he'd stood back and pictured the cluster of houses he'd designed, for the first time he saw the way it would look from the manor.

A slash of ugly industrial buildings across what once had been a pastoral view.

Boone swore again in memory of the revelation. He was drawn to steel and glass structures and he'd been enamored of the designs he'd cribbed from online plans. The idea was to reclaim shipping containers and trick them out with scrap metal and glass. It worked from a sustainability standpoint—reuse, repurpose and all that.

It would look like ass here at Westfield.

It infuriated him Riley could lay bare his inadequacies with just a few words and a judgmental glare. He'd worked hard to consider every angle when he designed his community.

Except beauty.

Boone's shoulders slumped. What if he'd missed

other things? What if he failed—he who had one of the best records for successful missions in the SEALs? What if Montague destroyed Westfield?

This was all a huge mistake.

Still, it wasn't fair to fault him for not spending time on luxuries like beauty. He was trying to set an example for the rest of the world to follow. Beauty as an abstract notion was all well and good, but too often the pursuit of it was an excuse to spend money on things that never should have been manufactured in the first place.

He remembered Riley talking about all the outfits she'd owned. He'd bet she and her friends had rented storage containers to stuff with all the things they hadn't brought with them to Westfield. The bathrooms in the manor were probably filled with makeup, hair products, perfumes and the like. She certainly had no right to judge him.

He and his friends needed women who found beauty in nature rather than artificial things. Who thought the face God gave them was good enough.

He frowned. Had Riley been wearing makeup when she confronted him? Had any of them?

He couldn't recall. He'd been far too busy… talking.

Boone shifted to dispel an uneasy feeling that trickled through his veins, sure that Jericho would have some comment on his bossiness. To hell with that. They had definitely been wearing makeup. And if he searched the house he'd find evidence to prove beyond a shadow of a doubt that their pledge to live like Jane Austen characters was frivolous and wasteful—nothing like his own goals.

But maybe he should look at those house plans again. Or better yet, let Clay do it.

Discouraged, he finished his simple dinner of soup, baked beans, and a couple of protein bars, and cleaned up after himself, the familiar motions and quiet surroundings working their magic on him. The sun was low in the sky. Soon it would be time to head up the hill and pick Riley up for their date, but if he didn't want to frighten her with his manly stink, he needed to rinse off after a long day's labor.

He grabbed a towel and a bar of soap from his bag, but instead of heading to the bunkhouse to shower, he set off the quarter mile to Pittance Creek, which ran through the property on its way to connect with Chance Creek.

As he strode past the stakes and twine he'd used earlier to designate possible housing sites, he couldn't help but glance up the hill across the way to the high ground Riley had stood on earlier when she'd folded her arms and watched him work, her displeasure all too clear even across that distance. No one was in sight. No doubt the women were eating a four-course dinner up there off of newly purchased plates.

He squared his shoulders and kept walking, refusing to bend to an urge to look back again. When he reached the creek, it gurgled and chuckled over rocks as it flowed through its curving banks and bit-by-bit, Boone's mind emptied of his troubles and filled with a kind of contentment he hadn't known in a long time. A memory bubbled up—another hot summer day when they were kids and Riley had decided to dam up the creek with a stone wall. She'd figured they could corral fish like they corralled horses. Boone had known it wouldn't work, but he struggled on gamely to move rocks under her command. He had no idea what had possessed him to become Riley's laborer that time when normally she was the one to carry out his orders. Maybe he'd instinctively known the balance of power between them was unfair and was trying to put it back somewhat to rights.

In any case, it was one of the happiest memories he had. The dam hadn't worked, but they'd goofed off and laughed throughout the afternoon. What he'd give for that kind of peace again.

Or at least to be alone with Riley for a couple of hours.

His body responded to that idea and with a growl of frustration, Boone stripped down, stepped into the shallow, icy water and bent down to splash himself. The sting of the cold spray felt good, but it wasn't enough to shake the vision of Riley in his arms. He'd need a full dousing in this cold water to accomplish that. He surveyed the creek, but didn't see a deeper pool.

He decided to head upstream.

RILEY STUMBLED DOWN a path from the manor she hadn't traversed since she was a teenager, so deeply lost in thought she barely noticed where she was going. She and her friends had spent the afternoon at their separate pursuits, but Riley had found it hard to concentrate on her sketches. She'd tried several versions of the landscape outside the windows, but she kept arguing with

Boone in her head and at one point she looked down to find she'd sketched him instead of the pastures and mountains. She'd ripped the drawing from her sketchbook and balled it up.

As the afternoon waned, her nervousness grew. Boone would want an answer when they met tonight, and she didn't know what to tell him. She wasn't sure what he wanted from her—or if it was worth it to enter a legal entanglement to secure the manor for a short time period.

On the other hand, the thought of leaving Westfield and giving up on their experiment was too awful to bear. When it had finally been her turn with the phone, her heart had raced when she'd seen there was an answer from Russ.

Riley,

I was out of town when your first e-mail came, so I couldn't warn you that I'd sold Westfield. I'm sorry you made the trip for nothing. I have exciting news, however: I'm finally getting married. I need to buy a fitting house for my wife and can no longer afford to carry Westfield while it sits idle.

Your parents report that you are happy with your life in the city. We'll both hold fond memories of Westfield as we move ahead, won't we?

I wish you luck in all your endeavors.

Uncle Russ

Riley had been so appalled at the message she'd had to leave the room and pace the kitchen until she'd regained her composure. How could he back away from a promise he'd made her without even missing a beat? Why did she figure so little in everyone else's thoughts? The three women who'd come to Westfield with her were the only ones alive who truly cared about her at all. Neither her mother nor her father had much to say when she'd informed them she was moving to Montana for six months.

Meanwhile, Savannah, who'd been thrilled to find Riley's grandmother's baby grand piano in the drawing room, had spent the whole afternoon practicing, despite the fact it needed to be tuned. Avery and Nora had each slipped away to their rooms and came down at dinnertime equally energized.

Riley was the only one who'd seemed to struggle. Sensing her discomfort, Avery suggested they try their hand at cooking over the large hearth fire to experience an authentic Regency meal. Nora had pointed out that by the late Regency, cooks would have had wood fired stoves on which to create their meals. Avery stole the cell phone and found an early Regency sketch that showed a very primitive hearth and grate affair. Their bickering and the difficulty of the task both worked to distract Riley, but not the way Avery had meant it to. It had taken forever to coax flames from the wood and they'd forgotten to open the flue, so they'd nearly choked themselves to death on the smoke that billowed throughout the kitchen before Savannah figured it out and fixed it.

Then Nora had managed to char the potato soup

she'd tried to prepare, while the bread Avery had made according to a camping recipe had turned out so doughy that none of them could stomach much of it. They'd choked down what they could of the meal, refusing to throw it out and start over. All of their brand new outfits reeked of smoke and the burned food proved so hard to clean up, they'd ended up leaving some of the dishes in the sink to soak overnight.

Savannah was the one who'd said, "Okay, let's all take a break. One hour to ourselves before we regroup. Riley, you'd better get ready for your date. Scatter!"

They'd scattered—the others to their rooms and she to walk this lonely trail she'd often traversed when she was younger. She needed the quiet offered by the woods before she faced her next challenge—Boone.

Still, even with all the day's ups and downs, it had been far more interesting than a workday back in Boston. If they didn't manage to kill themselves with their Austen experiments, she and her friends could have a wonderful time together. If only Boone wasn't set on spoiling it all.

A glint of sunlight on water caught her attention as she rounded a bend in the path. Pittance Creek—a small stream that flowed into the larger Chance Creek that gave the nearby town its name. There was far more than a pittance of water in it at this time of year. In fact, a pool had formed in a bend in the creek that was all too inviting. Suddenly aware that she was hot and sticky from her labors over the fire, Riley considered the flashing, bubbling creek before her. Maybe a quick dip was just the thing. Not that she cared what Boone thought of her, but it would be hard to have the upper hand if she was covered in grime and sweat. If she cleaned up she could return home and change into one of her nicer outfits without ruining it.

She glanced around to assure herself she was alone, glad that the creek was sheltered from the house by a strip of forest. No one was in sight. In fact, she could be alone on the Earth for all the signs of civilization she could see from here.

She had her bonnet off in an instant, but getting out of her dress was a struggle. By the time she'd accomplished it, she was warmer than ever. She was glad to be free of the chemise and petticoat, as well, and the slight breeze and late day sunshine felt liberating on her bare skin.

Plucking the hair pins from her bun, she let her hair swing loose. She couldn't remember the last time she'd gone skinny dipping. In her early twenties, maybe. She remembered how delicious it felt to bathe outdoors with nothing between her body and the water. She shrieked a little and then laughed as she stepped into the cool creek, but nothing could stop her from plunging in now. She ducked right under the water and came up splashing, delighted with the feel of it. Jane Austen probably never skinny dipped in her life.

She'd missed something wonderful.

If only she'd brought some soap and shampoo down here to rid her skin and hair of the smoky smell from the hearth fire. She ducked under the water again, swished her hair around, hoping that would do the trick, and came up for air.

"Hell—Riley?"

Riley shrieked at the masculine exclamation and whirled to find Boone not five feet away. Thigh deep in the swirling water, he was as naked—and as shocked—as she was.

"What are you doing here?" She clapped her arms over her chest and ducked down in the water, hoping he hadn't noticed that she wasn't wearing a bathing suit. Judging by the direction of his gaze, he'd noticed.

Judging by a certain other part of his anatomy, he liked what he saw.

Unlike her, Boone didn't rush to hide himself, just ambled into deeper water until it was up to his waist. She had to admire his poise. He apparently didn't possess an ounce of self-consciousness. She was glad he didn't, because it gave her time to examine the prime specimen of maleness in front of her. Boone naked was a spectacular sight.

He'd bulked up a lot over the years and his body bore scars whose origins she could only guess at. He was powerfully built, his muscles cut from hard work and training.

Despite the icy water surrounding her, heat traced through her cheeks and Riley forced herself to look Boone in the eye and keep her gaze there. "Well? You didn't answer my question."

He nodded slowly. "I suppose I'm here for the same reason you are."

"Can't you swim somewhere else?"

That sudden, devastating smile of his flashed across his face. "I don't think I should leave you here all alone. Haven't you ever heard of the buddy system?"

"I don't need a buddy. I'll be fine."

"Maybe I'm the one that needs watching then," he said conversationally.

"Don't think I'd save you if you were drowning." Did he know what a liar she was? She'd never thought of herself as the type of woman whose common sense would fly straight out the window when confronted with a hot body, but Boone was far more than a hot body. He always had been. As much as she'd wanted to paint him as the enemy today, it hadn't been his handsome face she'd fallen for as a teen. There were plenty of handsome faces around Chance Creek if that was what she'd wanted.

Instead she'd fallen for the way he was gentle with a colt, the way he could sit in silence beside you without making you feel alone, the way he did everything with a sure precision she'd never felt about anything in her life. The way he'd taken so much time to teach her all the things he'd thought were important. She'd thought about that over the years and realized how sweet it was he had done that. As a ten-year-old, Boone could hardly have found it fun to oversee an eight-year-old girl's riding lessons. As a thirteen-year-old, had he really wanted to teach an eleven-year-old girl to fish? He'd been so patient with her when they were alone.

So why had it been so easy for him to turn his back

and leave her in the end?

He took another step toward her. She stepped back, struggling to find footing on the rocky bottom of the stream. "Keep away from me."

"All right." He stopped and put his hands on his hips.

She couldn't help wondering what was happening below the water line. The look in his eye told her he knew exactly where her thoughts had gone.

Why didn't she turn away? Riley couldn't answer that. Maybe it was simply that Boone represented her ideal man. His body looked like a sculpture, all hard planes, light and shadow.

"Now what?" she demanded. She couldn't move while he stood there. Not without exposing herself. The thought sent a delicious throb through her veins that irritated her all the more. She could not be attracted to this man. Not when chances were he'd hurt her again.

"You tell me."

Riley's breath hitched. Was he coming on to her? "You should leave," she said again.

"Ah, you want another look."

So he knew she'd taken in all the contours and planes of his body when he'd first approached. How could she not?

"I couldn't care less about your appearance."

"You could leave," he suggested.

"So *you* can watch?"

"It would only be fair."

"Nothing about this is fair."

Boone's eyes narrowed and he took a step toward her. "Neither of us has to leave." He took another step. "I'll wash your back if you wash mine." His voice caressed her as he moved even closer. Before she knew it he was within touching distance. She found herself leaning toward him, wanting his hands on her skin.

But that was crazy. This was Boone. She couldn't trust him.

She needed to back away. Instead she moved closer as if he'd put her under a spell.

"You're so beautiful."

His whispered words pierced through the lustful haze that had enveloped her only a moment ago. He'd spurned her the last time she'd allowed herself to feel something for him. She wouldn't set herself up for that kind of treatment twice.

Riley lurched away, but her foot didn't find purchase on the rocky bottom. She slipped under the water altogether and came back up gasping and choking. As she scrambled to find the ground, she slipped under again. Two strong hands clamped around her arms and Boone pulled her to the surface, steadying her until she could stand.

She peered up at him through the runnels of water streaming from her hair, all too aware of her nakedness—and his—and read his intention in his eyes before he even began to move. Boone gave her plenty of time to pull back as he bent closer, but Riley could have no more turned away than arm-wrestled him for a victory. She wanted to know what he tasted like, and soon she found out, when he pressed his mouth to hers.

He tasted of fresh water, cool air and warm skin all in a heady mix that made her senses reel, and Riley forgot all about her reservations. She pressed her hands flat against his chest and leaned into his kiss, drinking it in as if she'd been craving its refreshment for hours. As his powerful arms circled her body, they made her feel slight and supple. She melted against him, knowing the contrast of her soft curves against his hard muscles would make her irresistible.

Boone's touch filled her with warmth, even as the cool water continued to rush around them. She wanted to be closer to him. She wrapped her arms around his neck and a wash of victory rushed through her when she felt the hardness of his arousal against her. Boone wanted her as much as she wanted him. As she pressed against him, Boone's grip on her tightened and his kiss deepened. She opened to his tongue, wanting badly to open to him in other ways. She fought against the urge, knowing she should hold back, but in the end her desires won out. The buoyancy of the water made it all too easy to lift her legs and wrap them around his waist, positioning the hard length of him right where her body wanted it most.

Boone groaned. His fingers pressed into her hips as he steadied her there.

The heat of him pressing against her made her ache with want. It had been so long since she'd been with a man and she'd never felt so hungry for one as she did for Boone now. She clung to him, unwilling to let him go.

Boone didn't seem inclined to let her go either. His kiss went on and on and his hands stroked over her body, exploring her—teasing her back to life.

When she finally broke the kiss, Riley buried her face against Boone's neck, not wanting time to move forward. She didn't want to face what came next. She became aware again of the rush of water around her body. What had she done? Made out with Boone in the middle of a creek? The man who'd left her so crushed once before it had taken ages to get over him?

She'd never gotten over him.

Clarity hit her like a splash of creek water. Some part of her heart had always belonged to Boone no matter what he'd done in the past. It was as unfair as losing the ranch to him.

But there was nothing she could do about it.

Boone rocked her gently against him and Riley knew if she didn't get down right now they'd do it right here in the creek. That sounded like heaven, but she reluctantly extricated herself from his embrace. She was wobbly on her feet and ached with an unmet desire that threatened to consume her. She didn't think she could meet his gaze, but when she did, she found him staring down at her with intense solicitude.

"Talk to me, Riley. Tell me you're okay." Boone reached out and tucked a dripping strand of her hair behind her ears.

She nodded, unable to find the words. "I'm okay," she finally managed to gasp out.

"We should probably go on a date or two before we try that again." In direct opposition to his words, he reached up to capture her chin and pull her close for another blazing kiss. Hunger blossomed inside her all over again. But she couldn't do this.

Riley pressed her palms against his chest and pushed. At first Boone resisted, but then he let her go and searched her face. "What's wrong?"

"That shouldn't have happened."

His hands dropped to her waist. "It definitely should have happened. Why did I take so long to come back and find you?"

She blinked. "You never wanted me."

"That's not true. The night you asked me to dance I wished I was with you instead of Melissa."

"Right." She didn't believe that.

"Listen, I was young. Melissa was… well, she was Melissa. Up until then I'd thought of you as a sister."

She burned with shame all over again. She wanted to cross her arms over her breasts and hide, but it was too late now.

"Then you showed up at the hoedown looking like an angel. Riley, you blew me away." He slid his hands over her hips. "I was an idiot. I was eighteen. I didn't know what to do, so I did nothing."

"That hurt." She didn't want to admit it, but the words refused to remain unsaid.

"You have no idea how sorry I am. But I'm here now and so are you. We've been given another chance."

"A chance at a fake marriage." She couldn't reconcile what Boone had just told her with what had happened all those years ago.

"I want a hell of a lot more than that from you." Boone tugged her close to meet him in a kiss that seared her all the way down to her soul. When he released her again, Riley stumbled before she found her footing. "I know a lot more about life than I once did. A friendship like the one we had doesn't come around very often. Why can't we have that again—and more?"

Riley's heart was nearly beating out of her chest. "It doesn't work that way. You can't go back and fix the past like that."

"Why not?"

"Because I don't trust you."

He drew in a breath. "Give me a chance, Riley."

Riley backed away. This was too much to take in all at once. Boone looked like he'd pursue her, but he let her go.

"I still want that date. We'll keep our clothes on this time. We have some talking to do."

"But—"

"Eight o'clock. Sharp."

He turned and stalked off through the water like some ancient Greek hero, his body mesmerizing as he moved. Left behind, Riley could only watch him leave. She had no idea what had just happened.

Or what she meant to do about it.

CHAPTER SIX

★

"SLOW DOWN," JERICHO said over the phone. "You skinny dipped with Riley? Was that your idea or hers?"

"It just happened. I wanted to wash up for my date." Boone stared out of the bunkhouse window at the manor on its rise of ground. The sun was low in the west, casting a soft glow on the ranch that made it almost look magical, which seemed possible after the experience he'd just had with Riley in the creek.

He'd never expected she'd let him kiss her like that, especially not after the way he'd treated her when they were young. He knew she hadn't meant to let him, either. They'd both been carried away.

Still, their actions said something for their chances together. Their attraction was mutual and once they'd been good friends. Couldn't that add up to a marriage?

Boone wasn't sure.

"Sounds like she wanted to wash up, too. So you crashed her bath and decided to go for it."

"That's not exactly how it happened." Boone ran a

hand over his still-damp hair. "She said she doesn't trust me. She probably thinks I did it on purpose. I'm supposed to pick her up in fifteen minutes and I need to figure out how to recover from this." He was afraid what happened next would determine the outcome of their relationship. If she turned away from him now, he'd have lost his chance.

Was he so concerned because of Fulsom's demands?

Boone didn't think so. Maybe he'd first come up with the plan to marry Riley because it was practical, but that had lasted only an instant. Now he simply wanted her.

He'd never reacted to a woman this way before—with such naked need after such a short period of time. He couldn't account for his feelings. But they were strong.

"She's mad because you caught her naked?"

"Because of how I treated her the night before we left." Boone jammed his free hand into his pocket and paced the empty bunkhouse he'd commandeered as his office. It was a rectangular building with white walls and a scarred wooden floor. One large empty room would have held bunks for the ranch hands in the past. A spare but functional bathroom with a shower stall opened off one end. A kitchen with appliances from the eighties by the look of them was visible through another door.

"It'll take time to patch things up after something like that," Jericho told him.

"So what do I do now?" Boone kicked a rusty metal

wastebasket and sent it flying. "She thinks I'm a first-class prick and I don't have time to change her mind; not with this deadline hanging over my head."

"Well, you can't bully her into falling in love with you. You have to make her want to be with you."

"How do I do that?"

Jericho made a sound that was half derision, half frustration. "Find out what she wants and give it to her."

"She wants a Jane Austen life." He paced back to the window. "And I'm trying to give it to her—but I have to keep Fulsom happy, too."

"Just listen to her. Ask questions. Find out what it is about Jane Austen she likes so much. See if it's something you can help with. Now get out there and get yourself a wife."

Boone chuckled. "All right."

"How's the ranch?"

"As good as we thought it'd be. We couldn't have chosen better for ourselves." He walked out of the bunkhouse. "Take a look." He switched to video mode and panned his phone in a wide circle so Jericho could take it all in.

"So Riley's up at the manor, and you're stuck down in Base Camp, huh?" Jericho said when Boone got back on the line.

"That's one way of putting it." *Base Camp.* He liked the name.

"Climb that mountain. We're counting on you."

"Will do," Boone said and hung up.

Fifteen minutes later, Boone strode up the hill toward the manor, determination coursing through his veins. He was a Navy SEAL. He'd faced plenty of tough situations. He shouldn't doubt his ability to prove to Riley they could make a go of this. He was worried Riley wouldn't even open the door when he knocked, though, and he dreaded the humiliation of having to shout through it at her, or worse—having to walk back down the hill like a jilted lover.

It didn't help to know he deserved it.

But the front door swung open as he approached and Riley waited for him just inside, her expression wary. She wore a fresh, pretty gown, with tiny flowers dotted over a white background and a funny little dark green jacket, too. It followed the contours of her bodice and ended just below her breasts. Her hair was caught up on top of her head and her straw bonnet was decorated with a wide green velvet ribbon around its crown.

"Miss Eaton." He decided to go along with the old-fashioned mood. He bowed slightly and offered her his hand. She was wearing white gloves. He'd never seen a woman wear gloves—except the winter kind.

"Lieutenant Rudman." She bobbed a curtsy and allowed him to take her hand. He raised it to his lips and kissed her gloved fingers, hoping she knew he was thinking of their kiss in the stream. She tried to tug her hand away. After a moment he let her go.

"I'm not a—" he started to say, but realized he was fighting a battle he'd never win. "Never mind."

"You haven't told me where we're going. I don't know if I'm suitably dressed."

Her formality told him she was feeling uncomfortable. He needed to re-establish the connection between them. "Are you ever suitably dressed?" He smiled to show he was joking and he was grateful when the corner of Riley's mouth turned up.

"Not these days," she admitted.

Savannah appeared in the hall behind Riley. "Lieutenant Rudman, I have to say I find it irregular that you'd offer to take my friend out for the evening without a proper chaperone." Her eyes glinted with fun.

"I only mean to walk the property with Miss Eaton," Boone assured her. "After all, what harm could come to her so near her home?" He raised his eyebrows at Riley, whose cheeks pinked slightly.

Maybe this Regency stuff wasn't so bad; it made flirting easy.

"All sorts of trouble could happen with you around, I think." Savannah smiled sweetly. "That's why I'm coming, too."

Boone's heart dropped. "You've got to be kidding!"

Savannah let out a peal of laughter. "Of course I'm kidding, but you should see your face. That was worth the price of admission."

Riley's lips twitched. Boone snorted. "Okay, you ladies have had your fun. Come on, Riley." He tugged her hand.

"That's Miss Eaton to you." But Riley came along with him willingly. That was something.

He led the way back down the hill toward the cluster of outbuildings. He'd thought about what Jericho had said and realized he was right; Boone couldn't bulldoze Riley into sharing his beliefs. He'd had years to build a worldview that made his current endeavor important. He had no idea what life experiences had led Riley to hers. It was up to him to find out.

He kept hold of her hand while they walked, and to his surprise she didn't tug away from him.

"It's a beautiful evening, isn't it?" he asked her.

"Ah, the weather. Always a safe topic. It is beautiful, though. I love the view from up here." Her gaze fell on the south-facing slope where he'd staked out the houses. "At least I used to."

"You'll still love the view when my community is built. I promise."

"Will they at least be pretty? The houses?" she clarified.

He wasn't going to answer that. The houses wouldn't be beautiful unless Clay could pull something out of his hat. "They'll be incredibly functional."

"That doesn't set my mind at ease."

He decided to steer the conversation to another topic. "You'll like the vegetable gardens when they're planted."

"Will you have flowers, too?"

"No, but they'll still look good. Rows of green growing things always do, don't you think?"

She shrugged. "I suppose. I like English cottage gardens, though. They have regimented shapes, but the flowers themselves are exuberant and spill over their borders."

"You'll have a garden up at the manor?" Jericho would be proud he was asking so many questions.

"We will. The bones are already there, but it'll need a lot of sprucing up."

"What about food? Will you grow any?"

She nodded. "As much as we possibly can. In Jane Austen's time, food wasn't shipped all over the world. They ate what was in season, and most of it came from their own village or property. I love that idea, and since we'll be here all summer…." She trailed off and Boone knew she was thinking of his ultimatum; she wouldn't be at Westfield this summer unless she married him.

"I love that idea, too." He squeezed her hand to emphasize their agreement and distract her from her concerns. Jericho would approve. "I think it's great that you're painting."

"Do you?"

He knew why she asked. "I do, if it's something you like."

"But painting is hardly practical," she pointed out.

"It's not unsustainable, at least," he countered. "If it keeps you busy you won't feel the need to rip out a kitchen you just renovated three years ago to install a brand new one, like so many people do. And you'll be too poor to buy a McMansion."

"So now you support the arts?" She didn't sound convinced. "What's your favorite style of painting?"

"I don't know. Never thought about it. I haven't

spent much time in museums this past decade." Beauty hadn't played much of a part in his days. That didn't mean he didn't notice it, however. It was the unexpected things that caught his eye: a sky-blue burka against a dusty desert landscape, a hawk soaring over a war-torn village.

A woman pacing beside him in a Regency gown.

She stopped. He did, too. "Look at this scene. It's perfect for a painting. A landscape with barns and pastures and mountains in the distance. Would you prefer it to be painted as it is in a faithful replica or would you like something more impressionistic? Or maybe you prefer pointillism? Or something more modern?"

Boone gathered his thoughts. "I'll tell you one thing. If some painter drew a green stripe and a red square and told me it was a ranch, I'd be pissed."

Riley laughed. "I have to admit I'd be pissed, too."

He relaxed. "I think I like realistic painting, but with the brush strokes showing. You know what I mean. Up close they don't look like much at all, but you take a few steps back and suddenly they're perfect?" He hoped she understood.

Riley nodded slowly, as if he'd surprised her by venturing an opinion at all. "Those are my favorite, too."

"Is that what you paint?"

"Sometimes."

They stood together for a moment. Then Boone tugged her forward. "I want to show you something."

"What?"

He didn't answer until they were standing among the staked out rectangles. He turned her to face the larger slope upon which the manor sat. "I picked this site for a couple of reasons. Like I said earlier, all the houses will face south, to make the most of the sun. The gardens are positioned to take advantage of it, too. Down here they'll be somewhat more sheltered than yours up top on that slope. That'll help extend the growing season. But there's another reason I established Base Camp here."

"What is it?" she asked when he didn't go on.

"The view." He gestured to the manor on top of the rise of ground in front of them. "I didn't think about it consciously, but it was in the back of my mind. That old house is as inefficient as they come. You couldn't pay me to live in it. But it looks good."

He turned to Riley and caught the most interesting expression in her eyes before she pinched her lips together and nodded. She'd been looking at him with something like… fondness. Maybe they were closer to understanding each other than he'd thought.

"I hope the view will be as pretty from up there when you're done." Her pert tone put an end to the rapport between them.

Boone didn't answer. He wanted to explain to her all the decisions that had influenced his choice of housing and the layout of the community. He wanted to go over the charts and graphs that showed energy efficiency and solar gain. Instead he simply said, "Yes." Because it would be pretty.

If it killed him.

This time Riley squeezed his hand. Two emotions flooded Boone simultaneously, almost shorting out his inner circuitry. One was pure pleasure that the fledgling connection between them was back.

The other was pure fear he'd let her down.

"I guess I can't wait to see it then," she said.

"I can't wait to show you," he lied. He'd call Clay tonight, the minute he brought Riley back home. They'd change something. Anything. Whatever it took to make the community meet Riley's expectations.

"What?" she said. "You look... worried."

"That's not worry," he said. "That's lust."

SAVED BY THE bonnet. Riley ducked her head to block Boone's view of her face. Since when did she blush so much? There was something about this Regency stuff that made her reactions to Boone's flirting over-the-top. She couldn't believe she'd pressed her naked body against this man less than two hours ago. He'd felt... wonderful.

"Really, Lieutenant Rudman. Maybe we need that chaperone after all," she managed to say.

"Are you ever going to get my rank right?"

"Never. Is this the whole date? A walk down the hill?" She wasn't going to discuss his lusts. Or her own.

"No, but I've got to grab something." He let go of her hand and jogged to the nearest outbuilding—the old bunkhouse. Boone let himself inside and reappeared a moment later with a backpack, shutting the door behind him. "If I'd been thinking, I would have scheduled the date earlier and invited you for dinner," he said when he caught up to her again. "But I didn't, and I know you've eaten already, so I only packed us a snack." He glanced at her feet. "Think you can handle a little walk in those shoes?"

"They're sturdier than they look." She was wearing a light pair of boots that looked similar to those a Regency woman would own but were actually a much more comfortable modern equivalent. Footwear was too important to stint on in Riley's opinion. She liked being active and didn't mean to be hampered by her clothes.

He led the way a little farther down the track and then began to cut across the fields. That was harder going, but Riley followed him gamely, lifting her skirts as she traversed the uneven ground. After some hesitation, she allowed him to hold her hand as they crossed the worst parts. It seemed silly to refuse after what they'd done. She liked the swish of fabric around her legs as she walked and the girlishness of the green ribbons floating down from her hat behind her.

Despite her better judgement, she enjoyed Boone's solicitude and the opportunities the walk afforded them for touching, too. When they came to a barbed wire fence, they turned and followed it until they reached a gate.

"Just a little farther," Boone said. Riley nodded. She knew where they were going, so she wasn't surprised when he stopped a few minutes later. "Here we are."

Riley understood why he'd chosen the place—an

old favorite of theirs when they wanted to picnic as kids. The ground fell away rapidly here and the Beartooth Mountains were clear in the distance. Boone opened his backpack and pulled out a blanket which he spread on the ground. He gestured for her to sit, and he sat next to her, taking out a bottle of wine and two glasses.

"Hold these." He handed her the two glasses, worked a corkscrew into the wine and popped the cork. When he'd poured the drinks, he put the bottle down, took back one of the glasses and lifted it. "To whatever happens next."

After a moment, she decided she could toast to that. "To whatever happens next." She took a sip and closed her eyes. It was good. So good. "I've never had this before."

"It's a private vintage," he explained. "I had it on hand for later. For when the community was up and running."

"Why did you open it tonight?" She was both honored and a little unnerved.

"Because you've always been my community."

"Right. Which is why—"

He cut her off, unwilling to let her make her accusations again. "I made a mistake, Riley. A huge mistake. I wish you'd been my girlfriend these past thirteen years. I've always regretted what I did." He stared at the vista before them.

She digested this in silence. "So what do Clay, Jericho and Walker think about you proposing to me?"

"I don't think any of them believe you'll have me."

"Are you sure it's not the other way around?"

"Positive. You made an impression on them too that last night."

"I remember," she said sourly. The Horsemen's laughter still echoed in her ears.

"Tell me about Jane Austen," Boone said suddenly. "What is it about the Regency era that calls to you?"

THE CHANGE OF topic left Riley scrambling to keep up. "I think it's the idea that there is enough time," she said. "When you watch a Jane Austen movie, you see grown women living these graceful, leisurely lives. They spend time together, they go for walks, they're creative. I mean, they were circumscribed by so many rules, none of us would truly like to live that way, but even though I was distracted today, my afternoon of painting felt... decadent."

"What distracted you?"

She glanced down. "The prospect of losing the ranch I thought would be my home."

"It could still be your home."

She turned to him. "Boone, I need you to tell me the truth. Don't play with me. Are you for real with this marriage thing?"

"Yes." He twined his fingers in hers. "I know this is a crazy situation for both of us, but why couldn't it work? I think we're better suited for a sudden marriage than most people, don't you?"

"Why?"

"Well, there's a hell of an attraction between us, for

one thing, but that's just a start. Don't you remember how good things used to be between us when we were kids? Or do you only remember the one time I was an ass."

"The one time?"

"Don't focus on the bad stuff, Riley."

"It's hard to look past it."

"Try. Not just for me—for both of us." He took a sip of his wine. The glass seemed too small for his large, capable hand. "Can I ask you another question?"

"Of course." She was all too aware of his fingers tangled in hers. They were callused from hard work. Strong.

"Do you ever think about having a family?"

She pulled back but he caught her hand and held on. After a brief struggle, she gave in. "Yes."

"How many kids do you want?"

"Two." She'd always wanted two. She wasn't sure why.

"Me, too."

This time she succeeded in pulling her hand away from his and got to her knees. "We can't have this conversation."

"Why not?" He put down his glass and scrambled to stand as she did.

"Because I want kids—badly. And unless something changes, I won't ever get to have them." Riley dusted off the skirts of her gown, but Boone didn't move. His tone was concerned when he spoke again.

"Is something wrong?"

"Oh… no, not like that," she rushed to say. "I mean, I tried to adopt, but it fell through because I lost my job. Without a real career, no adoption agency will consider giving me a child. When my time at Westfield is up, I'll have to start all over and work for several years before I can apply again. There's no guarantee it'll ever happen."

"You want a child badly enough to raise one on your own?" Boone asked.

She nodded. "Of course."

"Then let me give you one and let's raise it together."

She held up her hands to ward him off when he stepped nearer. "Jesus, Boone. Has anyone ever told you you're intense?"

"Yeah," Boone said ruefully, coming to a stop. "More than once. But I mean it, Riley. I'd have kids with you."

Riley searched for a way to throw him off. She wasn't at all ready for this conversation. Kids with Boone sounded… magnificent, especially if they made them the old-fashioned way. After everything they'd done today, her body was wide awake and hungry for more. She wanted him to touch her again. She wanted so much more.

"Are you going to have horses?" she asked to deflect him. "Or is that unsustainable?"

"That's not an answer."

"I'm not ready to talk about it."

He looked like he'd argue. Instead, he let her off the

hook. "We'll have horses. Bison, too."

"Bison?"

"I've been studying up on sustainable ranching practices, and there's already a herd nearby. Jake Matheson from the Double-Bar-K has a hand in it. We'll consult with him and get a small herd up and running. Bison are indigenous to Montana, so they don't have as big an impact on grazing land."

"I've missed the horses," Riley said. "I ride when I can, but it isn't the same."

He held out a hand to her again and she took it without thinking. She loved the way his fingers felt in hers. "If we marry, you'll have a horse of your own." He tugged her back down to sit beside him.

Riley wasn't ready to talk about marriage either, but she didn't protest. She arranged the folds of her dress around her and tried to think of something else to say.

"What drove you and the Horsemen so hard to enter the military? I could never get a real reason out of any of you."

Boone picked up his wine glass and played with it, but didn't drink. "The usual stuff. Wanted to serve our country. Wanted to do something meaningful. I always liked being active. I couldn't see spending the rest of my life behind a desk. Neither could the others."

"You could have ranched."

"None of us had the money to do that. Our parents kept horses and let us ride, but you know none of us comes from a ranching family. Besides, I needed some adventure. A bigger purpose than just raising cattle."

"Did it turn out like you expected?"

"In some ways yes and in other ways no. I was smart enough to know I'd see things that would be hard to forget, and I was right, but it wasn't the things you might think. The blood and guts and all that." He looked down at her. "Sorry. Not too romantic."

"Maybe not, but it's true, isn't it? I'll take truth over romance." She glanced up to see a fond smile on his lips.

"Sometimes you say the damnedest things, Riley."

She thought he might kiss her again, but he didn't, and she was disappointed. "Anyway, it wasn't that, although no one can look on war and death and not be affected."

"What was it?"

"We kept seeing the same thing over and over again." He sat up straight and gestured with his hands. "People had built a life around a place—a system that worked. They'd figured out what to grow, what animals to keep, what businesses worked, what types of shelter and housing. And then something in their environment shifted and pretty soon all hell broke loose. It doesn't matter if you're talking about subsistence farming or city living. All lifestyles are built on the premise that things will stay the same. And guess what? They never do."

"Will your sustainable community be resistant to change?"

"Not resistant—flexible. The idea is to work with what you have rather than fight against it. And to convince people in the West that we might not need as much as we think we do."

"That makes sense." They sat so close together their legs touched. It felt natural when Boone turned and kissed her just as the sun kissed the top of the mountains to the west. His mouth was soft, searching. She met it hungrily, leaning into him as he slid an arm around her shoulders to support her. His cotton shirt was smooth under her hand, but the stubble on his jaw scratched her skin.

She knew she should pull away and leave this kiss chaste and pure—the gesture of a moment, nothing more. But she couldn't pull away. She wasn't through with Boone and he didn't seem to be through with her either. He pulled her tighter and deepened the kiss until she clung to him, breathless.

Suffused with warmth and craving, she fit herself into his arms, wanting nothing more than the kiss to go on and on. She could stay like this with Boone forever—

Riley tore herself from his arms again.

Wasn't that exactly what he wanted? Hadn't he already decided to marry her because he *needed* to?

Boone followed her, snatching another kiss, and another. "I know you want more time." He took her hand before she could scramble away. "I wish I had it to give to you, but I don't, so you'll have to trust me when I say it'll turn out all right. We can make a go of this; I know we can."

"I don't want a fake marriage."

"I don't either. Riley, there's something good between us. I know you feel it, too."

"It's not enough, Boone. You're asking me to share your life. I won't cheapen marriage by treating it like a game."

Boone drew back. She waited for him to speak, wondering if he was crafting an argument in his head he thought she couldn't refuse.

"You're right; Fulsom's rules have got me doing all kinds of things I wouldn't normally do," he said. "The thing is, if I don't have a wife on June first, we'll all lose. Fulsom will take Westfield back."

Riley drew in a shaky breath. So she'd lose her ranch all over again. "Can't you buy it from him?"

He hesitated. "No, I can't. I didn't want to say it before because I don't want that to be the reason you marry me, and I don't want you to feel like I'm forcing your hand, but it's the truth, Riley. Someone's got to marry me, or none of us will get Westfield."

Riley shifted and he let her go. Could she bear to lose the ranch?

Could she bear to marry a man who didn't love her—even for a little while?

As if he read her mind, Boone's expression softened and he touched her hand. "I wish I could do this the way you deserve. Down on one knee with a ring. Telling you I love you. I do love you for the past we've shared but you and I need to spend more time together before we know how we feel now. I hurt you. You don't trust me, but if you marry me, maybe we'll find out this thing between us can go the distance."

Riley didn't know how to answer. Marrying to secure a ranch went against everything she believed in. Part of her longed to believe Boone's assurances that they could make a life together, but she wasn't a child anymore and she couldn't be fooled. Boone wanted Westfield. He wanted his community. If she wanted the manor, she had to agree to his terms. There was no way a marriage based on such inequality could flourish.

Still, what was the alternative? Leave Chance Creek? Send Nora back to Baltimore? Let down Savannah and Avery, too?

Boone touched her wrist. "Six months to paint. Six months to be with your friends. A chance to save Westfield. If you want a baby, I'll give that to you too." His voice went husky as he reached up to cup her chin and brushed his mouth over hers. "I'll love you night and day until you're carrying my child."

A tide of longing washed over Riley—both for the love making, and the possible result. She shook her head. "I won't have a child if I don't love the father. That's different than adopting."

"Then give us the chance to fall in love."

Did he want to fall in love with her? She knew all too well she could love him. Riley took a deep breath, feeling like she stood on the edge of a precipice and Boone was urging her to jump. Fear and exhilaration made a heady mixture in her veins. And after all, she really didn't have a choice. "Okay," she said. "I'll marry you. On three conditions."

He pulled back. "Tell me." He watched her intently.

"One, you don't come between me and my friends. Two, we have a Regency wedding. And three, I call the shots about our relationship. No touching, no kissing, no nothing unless I say so."

A look came into Boone's eyes that made Riley bite her lip.

"Maybe you should choose to kiss me right now," he suggested.

That sounded like a good idea.

"We did just get engaged," he added conversationally.

Why not jump off the cliff and see where she'd land? Riley kissed him.

And couldn't seem to stop.

CHAPTER SEVEN

★

B OONE DID HIS best to stay in control, but when it
came to Riley that seemed impossible. With every
passing moment, he felt the years draining away until he
was as young and untried as he'd been before he'd ever
met Melissa. Riley understood him better than he
understood himself. Alone on this blanket in the middle
of Westfield, away from all the complications of their
lives, she shorted out the electric fence he'd built to
shield his heart and brought him face to face with
everything he wanted but was too afraid to admit he did.

He'd nearly lost all restraint when they'd stood in
the stream and he was all too close to losing it again
now. He kept waiting for Riley to pull back, but instead
she clung to him as if she couldn't bear to let him go.

He knew exactly how she felt.

He wasn't sure if he was lowering her to the ground,
or if she was the one tugging him down as they kissed
all the while. She'd wanted to call the shots, and he'd
meant to let her once he'd stolen a single kiss.

Now he didn't know what he was doing.

With Riley underneath him, her arms wrapped around his neck, the brush of her mouth over his unlocked every frustrated fantasy he'd concocted during his sleepless vigil the night before. He held out for what seemed like an eternity, but it might only have been moments before he gave in to his baser needs and slid his hands up her back to search for the opening to her dress. He found ties at the back of her neck and waist, but another garment underneath the first blocked his way even after he undid them. With a growl of frustration, he reared up and examined her gown.

Riley smiled a Cheshire cat smile as he hunted for a way past the defenses of her outfit. But Boone wasn't a Navy SEAL for nothing. He'd been trained to breach enemy strongholds, and a Jane Austen gown couldn't stand up to his determination. Still, the damn thing frustrated him at every turn.

When he couldn't find any way to access her breasts, he decided to hitch up her hem and try his luck from that angle.

"Having fun, sailor?" Riley asked, laughter all too clear in her voice.

"Don't worry. I'll have you out of there in a jiffy."

"Good luck."

Boone needed it. After a brief tussle with several layers of fabric he managed to reach her leg and discovered she wore thigh-high stockings, but above them her skin was bare. He skimmed his hands over her thighs and was rewarded when she gasped and leaned back, evidently enjoying his touch, but as he traced his fingers upwards, the fabric of her garments bunched over his arm and got in the way again.

With a grunt of exasperation, he shifted her skirts aside. Riley sighed in his arms as he continued to kiss her, but when his hand tangled in her petticoat, Boone got to his knees.

"What are you doing?" Riley asked as he bent over her and rolled up the hem of her dress, shift and petticoat like he would a sleeping bag to prepare it for storage.

"Trying to get this thing out of the way."

"You'll wrinkle my dress." She sat up and began to unroll his handiwork.

"I'm being careful." He batted her hands away and got to work again.

"This dress cost a bundle." She unrolled it as fast as he rolled it up.

"I'll buy you a new one." Boone started all over again.

"That's hardly sustainable," she said primly.

Boone groaned. "For God's sake, woman—get that thing off."

"I'm supposed to call the shots, remember?" She flipped out the skirts of her dress and dusted them off with her hands. Boone thought she meant to put an end to their fun, but the sly look she sent him from the corner of her eye raised his hopes all over again.

"You're going to be my wife," he said, advancing again. "Don't I get to see what I'm getting out of the deal?"

"I think you got an eyeful this afternoon."

"Yeah, I did. And I liked it. A lot." With a mock growl he bowled her over, kissed her and blew raspberries on her neck until she shrieked with laughter. He ducked down to make another attempt on her skirts.

"Boone—oh!" Riley gasped as he finally got them up to her waist, tugged down the tiny, silky panties she wore underneath and bent to explore.

Riley fell back and opened her legs, an invitation Boone didn't try to resist. Positioning himself between them, his hands lifting her hips, he got his first taste of her.

Heaven.

SHE SHOULD TELL him to stop. She should go back to the manor.

She would—in a minute.

Riley bit back a moan of pleasure as Boone languorously explored her with his mouth and tongue. She couldn't help moving against him in a rhythmic tilt of her hips, inviting him in further, almost begging him to make her his own.

She couldn't believe how much a little silly teasing had turned her on, but it was just this kind of playfulness she'd always wanted in a man, but never found.

She'd joked with Boone tons of times when they'd been children, but she'd never teased him in a flirtatious way.

She promised herself she would do it again soon.

For now all she could do was lie back and bask in

the sensations Boone was calling forth from her body. The rasp of his tongue over her most sensitive places had her bucking against him, wanting more. His hands gripped her hips, his fingers slid over her bottom, until she burned with a craving for something only Boone could give her.

Riley knew she should hold back—this was far too intimate an experience with a man she'd just gotten to know again—but somehow it felt so right. Every move that Boone made elicited its own exquisite response in her body. He played her with a virtuosity that stunned Riley. A touch here, a kiss there and she could only relinquish the control she'd thought she wanted and let Boone take them on a sensual journey she hoped would never end.

Riley didn't realize she was tugging Boone toward her until he lifted his head and questioned her with his eyes.

"I want…" she panted. "Boone—"

He moved over her body to cover her. He was still fully dressed. That didn't seem right. Riley's fingers tangled with his belt, until Boone covered her hand with his and undid it for her. She got his button undone and tugged down the zipper of his jeans. When she slid a hand inside his pants, Boone sucked in a breath.

He was so hard. So magnificent. Riley ached with a longing she could hardly define. It went beyond reason or rationality to a place that was ancient, instinctive—feral.

She helped him shuck off his pants and boxer briefs

and when he pressed himself against her, she gasped from the sheer pleasure of it.

"Riley. Protection? Is this safe?"

Safe? Hell, no this wasn't safe. She was flinging her heart at a man who'd trampled on it once before. That wasn't what he was asking, though, and Riley fought to untangle her thoughts. Protection?

"I'm clean," she gasped.

"Me, too." He pushed inside her just a little and Riley wanted to scream with impatience. It had been ages since she'd been with a man and her body wanted more—much, much more.

He pushed inside her so slowly it was like being propelled toward ecstasy in slow motion. She could tell how good it would feel when he filled her, but he was drawing the moment out until her nerves were on fire. One hand on her hip, the other bracing himself above her, Boone pushed in all the way, then began a slow retreat that was just as sensual. Riley whimpered, wanting him to speed up, but for all her talk about control, it was clear who had the upper hand.

"You are beautiful," he breathed. "So beautiful."

He was beautiful, too. She wished they'd managed to get the rest of their clothes off but it was too late to worry about any of that now. Boone picked up his pace and Riley closed her eyes.

Too late…

Too late—

"Boone!" She'd meant to say it loudly and stop him, but Boone was thrusting into her, every ounce of his concentration wrapped up in maintaining control, and her voice had come out a gasp. As he increased his pace again, he felt so good she didn't want to stop him.

She had to stop him, though. She wasn't—

Let me give you a child and we'll raise it together.

Without a job, you won't qualify to adopt.

Right and wrong tangled in Riley's mind with desire and hope. She wanted a child.

She wanted Boone.

She wanted—

Boone shifted and Riley arched back, her orgasm crashing over her hard and fast, the way Boone was making love to her. The sensation went on and on, and Riley could only ride the wave of ecstasy he'd called forth in her. Boone grunted out his own release, bucking against her until he shuddered and collapsed on top of her, pinning her to the earth.

As she panted for breath, her vision swimming from the intensity of her orgasm, Riley stared over his shoulder into the deep royal blue of the darkening sky, too dazed at first to take in what she had done. But as a star peeped through the velvet curtain of night, and she became all too aware of the lumps and bumps of the hard ground underneath the picnic blanket, remorse cut through her as sharp as a knife. She'd crossed a boundary she'd always held sacrosanct.

Shame stole her breath away as she searched for a rationalization. When Boone wrapped his arms around her as if he wouldn't let her go, Riley held still, afraid he could read the treachery in her thoughts. How could she have kept quiet knowing Boone had misinterpreted what she'd said? He'd thought she was using protection—the Pill. That she was safe.

But she wasn't safe. She had abandoned her pills long ago after Marc left her, angry at the universe who kept stealing her dreams. Why bother with birth control if no one wanted to touch her?

Boone had touched her. Had made love to her.

Had he made her pregnant, too?

BOONE THOUGHT IF he simply didn't move, he wouldn't have to face what he'd done. He'd railroaded right over Riley's wish to slow things down and build a relationship from scratch. He couldn't excuse himself, either. He'd wanted what he'd wanted—and he'd took it, barely slowing down enough to ask the most basic questions he should have asked a new partner.

He knew from his regular checkups he hadn't brought anything extra to the party and he trusted Riley when she'd said she was safe, too. Still, that was a discussion to have when their clothes were still on, before he was half inside her and long past stopping.

He had acted like a...

Teenager.

He stifled a groan. Had he killed this relationship before it even started? Judging by the way she'd arched against him, she'd enjoyed being with him, too, but now she was quiet underneath him. Far too quiet.

Reluctantly, Boone rolled off of her. Riley sat up, but didn't meet his eye. He hitched up his boxer briefs and jeans and fumbled with his belt. By the time he was done, Riley had smoothed down her skirts.

"Riley—" He didn't know what to say.

"I think—" She broke off. "Boone—"

"Hey, we're getting married, right?" he tried to joke. "I think it's allowed." He hoped she could see the humor in the situation, too, but Riley pinched her lips together. "Honey, I meant it when I said I wanted to give this a real go. You and me—" It was hard to keep going when she looked so miserable. "What's wrong?"

"I'm... not on the Pill," she confessed in a rush. "I'm sorry, Boone. I should have—"

Relief coursed through him, followed by a strange lift of... pride? Boone couldn't parse the feelings that cut through him like rip tides. She was sorry? That meant she wasn't angry at him. She wasn't on the Pill? That meant she could be pregnant already.

His parents would be pleased.

So would Fulsom. Although, wasn't he was supposed to wait until June?

He squashed those thoughts. Fuck Fulsom. He could care less what the man wanted. He hadn't done it for his parents, either.

His gaze raked Riley from head to toe.

He'd done it because Riley charged him up like no one else he'd ever met.

"It's okay." He wanted to lay her out and make love to her all over again. He felt like he'd stumbled off the map of the world into a whole new territory that had never been charted. He wanted to explore Riley, to find out everything there was to know.

She shook her head. "This isn't how it's supposed to be."

"Riley. Listen to me." He waited until she was looking him in the eye. "I don't intend to marry twice. Do you understand what I'm saying?"

After a long pause, she nodded.

"You're stuck with me. If we've made a child, it's stuck with me, too. I'm not going anywhere." He kissed her softly. "This dance is forever."

RILEY STOOD ON the manor's front porch and watched Boone stride away down the path into the darkness toward the outbuildings.

Engaged.

She was engaged to a man who made her breathless, confused and aggravated in turns. To a man who'd rocked her world—and just possibly gotten her pregnant.

Twenty-four hours ago she'd arrived at Westfield a free woman with a dream to build a better future. Now her dream had been caught up in Boone's and she had no idea what the future might hold.

They should have talked more. Instead, when Boone had gathered her to him, they'd made out like teenagers under the stars until she was so turned on she practically vibrated with need. Then he'd laid her down and they'd brought each other to completion again— while keeping safe this time.

Her cheeks burned at the thought of it. Letting

Boone take his time over her body and make her cry out as she came seemed all the more intimate the second time around. She'd taken her turn and teased him with her mouth until he'd come, too. She'd felt so powerful knowing she could bring him to such a vulnerable place. When they were done it had been hard to stop touching him.

She thought he felt the same way.

She had a hundred questions now that he was gone. Where would they live? Would he give her a ring? And what about Fulsom and his television show? Riley couldn't believe she hadn't asked about that.

She lingered on the front stoop, her mood too fragile to go inside and face her friends. Would she have to be on the show, too? Probably, she realized. She wanted to save Westfield, after all. She tried to picture the manor invaded by cameras and a film crew. She wouldn't be able to paint under those conditions. It would be hard for her friends to tend to their creative pursuits, also.

Speaking of which...

What would her friends say when they found out about her and Boone?

Riley knew she wasn't ready to tell them yet. She hoped Boone would understand that she needed some time before she announced her engagement. Wishing she could slip away and hide, she opened the manor's front door and found her friends gathered in the music room. Savannah was playing the piano softly, wincing whenever she sounded a sour note. Nora lounged on a sofa reading a novel. Avery was reading, too. She was seated on the opposite side of the sofa with her feet tucked underneath her and was studying a book on film techniques.

Savannah stopped playing. "How was your date?"

The others perked up, obviously ready for an interruption.

"Good," Riley said. The house still retained a burnt odor from their ill-fated dinner, but it was fading and the interval had soothed her friends' frazzled nerves. She cast about for something to say; something that would hint that she was beginning to fall for Boone, without revealing that she'd already agreed to marry him.

Or slept with him.

"Better than good, actually," she added.

"I wasn't sure you liked him all that much," Nora said, putting down her book.

Riley came to perch on one of the armchairs across from the sofa. "I had a major crush on him when I was sixteen."

"Before he brushed you off," Avery said.

"You never got over him, did you? Even if you said you did." Savannah snapped her music book shut and stood up.

"Is he a good kisser?" Avery almost sounded wistful. Savannah moved to a spot between her and Nora, and pushed Nora's feet aside so she could sit down.

"He is," Riley said. "Almost too good." Much too good.

"Is that possible?"

"It is. When I'm around him… I don't know." She twisted her hands together. "I thought I'd have grown out of what I used to feel, but…"

"But he's too damn sexy to fall out of lust with," Savannah said. "Ha! Riley's doing the landlord. Are we going to keep getting free rent?"

"I'm not doing him," she protested even though that's exactly what she was doing. A glance down at her rumpled dress told her she probably wasn't fooling anyone.

"Good, because you should keep your distance," Nora said.

"Why? It's a good thing, isn't it?" Avery said. "If she keeps our landlord happy, we'll get to stay."

"What if she doesn't keep him happy, though?" Nora retorted. "This is a recipe for disaster."

Would it set their minds at ease to know she was engaged to Boone? No, not under the circumstances. They'd want to know why she'd rushed into something like that and she couldn't give them an answer that made sense.

"I'm happy for you," Savannah said. "And we'll all do what we can to support your relationship with the handsome Boone Rudman. Right, ladies?"

"I guess so," Nora said.

"Of course," Avery said.

Riley figured she'd need all the help she could get.

CHAPTER EIGHT

★

D AWN WAS ALREADY lighting up the interior of his small tent and Boone had barely slept a wink. All night long he'd relived his mind-blowing evening with Riley, the way she'd opened to him like they were made for each other, the way his body felt when he'd pressed into her—and the way she'd held him like she couldn't get enough.

Now they were engaged, but he had a lot more work to do before the month was up. He knew Riley; she'd be full of doubt today—about herself and him. She'd especially second-guess making love to him without protection. Boone wasn't second guessing that at all.

He wanted to do it again.

He'd hated leaving her at the manor last night. In fact, he didn't want to be apart from her at all. He had no idea how a feeling like this could blaze up so brightly out of nowhere, but it was as intoxicating as the finest wine. He craved Riley. He wanted to see her now.

Was it too early?

Probably.

He'd be married within a month. Boone laced his fingers behind his head and stared up at the ceiling of the tent. Thinking about the ceremony, he almost groaned. Why had he agreed to a Regency wedding? Could he really make it through that while the whole world watched?

Would Fulsom let him?

He didn't know what Riley meant when she'd asked him to swear not to come between her and her friends, either. Would she help him recruit Nora, Avery and Savannah to join his community?

Or would she expect him to let her stay at the manor even after they were wed?

He didn't like that idea at all. Forget for a minute the need for her to live with him while the film crew was present; he didn't want to be without her more than strictly necessary. Once they were married he wanted to make love to Riley every night.

Hell, he wanted to make love to her now.

He sat up and scrubbed a hand over his face. How would she react when he told her about the goals they had to meet in six months? Would she commit to help him succeed?

One thing at a time. First he would solidify his relationship with Riley. Then he'd figure out how to deal with her friends. Then he'd make sure winning was never an issue.

And he'd make sure Riley never, ever knew about Montague's plans for the ranch should they fail. Once she found out that he intended to develop the land she loved, she wouldn't be able to think about anything else.

First things first, he needed to win over Riley's friends. He remembered the story she'd told him the previous night about the cooking fiasco at dinner. Maybe he could start there. If there was one thing he knew how to do, it was cook over a fire. If he could endear himself to Savannah, Avery and Nora, Riley would grow to trust him, wouldn't she?

With that settled, Boone lay back down and thought about the work ahead of him. He had expected to have some finagling to do with the county planning office, but Fulsom had already greased those tracks. It seemed like Fulsom was well-connected everywhere. That meant they'd be able to get started with building right on time. Meanwhile, Boone had begun to work on a governance document, patched together from ones he'd found on the Internet. It boggled the mind how many details there were to sort out, especially when what he was trying to obtain was freedom from the kind of re-strictions that bogged down so many lives. But people were complicated, which meant everything needed to be spelled out to prevent trouble down the road. He was supposed to spend the morning sorting it out, but after what had happened with Riley the night before, he had something far more pressing on his mind.

A short time later, Boone emerged from his tent and looked at the ten housing perimeters he'd staked out the day before. When he'd begun working on his sustaina-ble community, all the decisions he'd made around housing had been prompted by a desire to recycle materials already in use and to eschew society's conceptions of how a normal house had to look. He'd wanted his industrial-style boxes to proclaim to the world they were an antidote to consumption.

Now he realized that by doing so, he'd alienate the very people he wanted to convince.

He made a phone call and cancelled the delivery of the shipping containers he'd intended to use as frameworks for the houses. He was just about to call Clay to consult him on a new design when the clip-clop of hooves startled him from his reverie and Boone turned to see an incredible sight. Two high-stepping horses pulled a black, open carriage up the service road to the barns and outbuildings.

"Hello!" called a man in a dark, old-fashioned waistcoat and a powdered wig. He was seated high on a bench seat behind the horses. Boone blinked a few times, wondering if his sleepless night had just caught up to him, but the man remained. When the man brought the horses to a halt in front of him, Boone could only stare. He wore knee britches, socks, old-fashioned shoes and a patterned vest under his coat. A woman seated behind him in the carriage had on a getup similar to Riley and her friends—a long dress with a fitted bodice and straight skirts. Both looked to be in their sixties, with friendly, open faces. They looked amused at his surprise.

The man jumped down from the driver's seat. "I'm James Russell, and this divine creature is my wife, Maud. You must be Boone. We've heard all about you from your parents. When we found out you'd taken up residence just two miles down the road we had to come and see you for ourselves."

He strode forward and vigorously shook Boone's hand, then hurried back to help his wife from the carriage while the horses waited patiently. Her large stature made this an awkward task. "How was your journey?" James asked over his shoulder. "And are you really lately come from her majesty's navy?"

"From the U.S. Navy," Boone corrected him, utterly lost at sea. Did this strange person really know his parents? He couldn't picture that. "I believe we separated from the queen about 240 years ago."

The man ignored that. "What a fine thing it must be to ride the high seas on a sailing sloop. What stories you must have to tell."

Sailing sloop? The closest to that Boone had come was an aircraft carrier. Had these people simply decided to pretend they were two hundred years back in time, or had they lost their minds?

"Anyway, we've come to welcome you. We hear that there will be a whole contingent of naval men here before you're done. What an addition to the neighborhood!"

"And is there a Lady Rudman?" the woman—Maud—asked, finally safe on solid ground. She offered her hand and Boone shook it.

"No. Not yet."

"Ah, sounds as if one is pending, though," James said. "I smell a mystery. Who is she? Is she here?"

"Not here." Boone couldn't help sending a glance up to the manor house.

"At the manor, then? Well, this is a surprise."

"Don't tell me that the manor itself is to be occupied." Maud touched his arm. "There hasn't been a family at Westfield in years. Will the young lady in question be accompanied by her parents?"

"No. She's there already with her friends." Boone was beginning to regain his equilibrium. At first he'd suspected that Riley had sent these two theatrical individuals to bother him, but she'd barely been in Chance Creek for a day—that seemed too short a time to set up such an elaborate joke. He couldn't imagine how James and Maud knew his parents, although now that he thought about it, his mother had mentioned they'd been involved in some kind of historical re-enactment. But hadn't she spoken of the Civil War? The Russells weren't dressed for that.

"With friends! How modern," Maud remarked to her husband. "No chaperone at all?"

Boone hesitated. He could refuse to play along. He wasn't used to make believe. But the two people in front of him seemed harmless, and he had to give them credit for living their lives the way they wanted to. A lot of people were going to look at his community and think he'd gone off his rocker. Shouldn't he have a little patience for other people's eccentricities?

"No." Boone answered Maud's question gravely. "They are greatly in need of mature counsel, too. The things they get up to."

A glimmer of fun sparked in Maud's eye and he knew she appreciated that he was going along with the game. "We'll have to go see them right away. It's only neighborly," she said to Boone.

"We can come over any time the young ladies need help. Although I imagine you've already offered." James gave him a knowing grin.

"I'm pretty busy," Boone said, gesturing at the building site. "In fact, I meant to offer to show the young ladies around the area today, but I'm not going to be able to get away, and I don't think they'll like the look of my truck." He gestured to his rental pickup. "They did mention they were partial to horses. And I believe, madam," he turned to Maud, "that you and they must share a dressmaker."

"Really?" Maud said with surprise.

"Really."

"Well, if they're partial to horses, we must meet them right away," James said, exchanging a look with his wife. "We'll leave you to your work and go to visit up the hill. We hope you won't be a stranger, though."

"Of course not. Good to meet you."

James helped his wife back into the carriage and repositioned himself on the box seat. Boone waited until he clucked to the horses to get them started again before he headed back to work, a smile on his face. Riley was about to get the surprise of her life.

"WELL, THAT WENT a little better," Savannah said, looking at the remains of their breakfast on the table.

Riley nodded. "Most of it was pretty good." The bacon was fried to perfection, anyway. If the eggs were a little overdone and the toast downright charred, at least it was progress. They'd even remembered to put some washing-up water over the fire to heat while they cooked the meal, so they could do the dishes Regency style, too. "I suppose we could use our modern stove any time we care to make this easier, though," she pointed out, although she thought it was kind of fun to use the hearth.

"Why shouldn't we be as authentic as possible?" Avery said. "It'll make our six months that much more special."

"If we were going to be authentic, we'd need to ditch the refrigerator and the stove, and get a wood stove," Nora pointed out.

"And we'd have to hire a maid or two," Savannah added before they could start arguing again. "Because there'd be way too much work to do for just us."

"I guess we've got it good, don't we?" Avery said. "But I like cooking on the fire. I'm going to keep doing it."

"I like that we do our chores together. It's so much better than being alone in my apartment on a Saturday morning with a week's worth of cleaning and laundry to do," Savannah sighed.

"Let's get moving and get things done. I want to write," Nora suggested.

The rest agreed. "We'll see you two later," Avery said. She and Nora headed upstairs to give the bedrooms a once over. Riley led Savannah outside. Their task this morning was to make a plan for the garden.

"There's Boone," Savannah pointed out, gazing across the way where Boone was surveying his building site.

Riley bit her lip. She'd tossed and turned all night, her dreams so erotic they kept waking her up. Her subconscious had come up with any number of scenarios for them to act out together. She'd got up this morning as hot and bothered as she'd been when she went to bed.

She turned her back on Boone. "I'm sure we'll see him later. Let's start in the gardens. I'm looking forward to bringing those flower beds back to life, but I suppose we'd better prep the vegetable beds first."

"I think you're right."

Riley followed her around the back of the house, lifting the skirts of her work dress in her hand, and wondered when she'd see Boone again.

"I want to make the most of every minute this month," he'd said when they parted the night before. "I want you head over heels for me when we marry." A delicious thrill had zinged through her, but now she wondered if she'd lost her mind. She'd never felt so dizzy and wanton and hungry for a man. This couldn't be right.

Riley focused on the gardens. She preferred flowers to vegetables, but it was a beautiful day and the task of surveying the kitchen garden and tallying up a list of plants and seeds to buy was more compelling than she would have expected. Savannah had been almost a sister to her back in college. Getting the chance to work with her again was an unexpected joy.

"What are you thinking about?" Savannah asked, breaking off from sketching a garden plan.

"Nothing."

"You're smiling."

Damn it. Boone's body had slipped into her mind again. "I'm happy," Riley confessed. "I mean, I knew it would be great to do this, but it's turning out even better than I thought."

"Because of Boone?"

"Definitely not," she lied. "Because of you and Avery and Nora. I missed you."

"I missed you, too." Savannah came and gave her a hug. "I'm so glad you got us to do this. I don't think I could have stood my old life one more minute."

"You never told us what was wrong." Riley turned back to the garden.

"Because all that was wrong was boredom. Sheer boredom with my life, with my job—everything!"

Riley snatched another look at her friend. It was more than that. Savannah was far too clever to let herself be bored.

Secrets, she thought. Were they all hiding secrets from each other? "Well, you won't be bored here." She tried to sound upbeat.

They were interrupted by the scrape of an upstairs window being pushed open. "Riley! Savannah. You won't believe what's coming up the lane!" Avery called.

"Go around front. Quick!"

Riley and Savannah exchanged a glance, then picked up their skirts and hurried to follow her instructions. They were still on the path beside the house when the clip-clop of hooves penetrated the sound of their running feet. It wasn't just horses, though. There was a rattling sound that Riley knew she'd heard before but couldn't place for the life of her. She rushed around the corner of the house and nearly laughed out loud with astonishment.

"It's Sir John Middleton and Lady Jennings!" Savannah said in whispered awe as they joined Avery and Nora on the front porch. Riley nearly laughed again at the reference to the interfering but kindly neighbors in *Sense and Sensibility*, her second-favorite of Jane Austen's novels.

Avery was right; the inhabitants of the open carriage that had just pulled into the gravelled driveway in front of the manor did look much like the characters as they were depicted in a popular movie adaptation. He looked to be in his sixties, with an old-fashioned gentleman's wig covering his own hair. He was dressed from top to bottom in Regency-era clothing. His wife was well advanced into middle age, a large woman who wore a mob cap under her bonnet, and a dress like their own but made of far finer material.

"It's true!" the gentleman shouted jovially as he pulled the horses to a stop in front of them, the wheels of the carriage—was it a barouche, Riley wondered?—kicking up the gravel to either side. "Westfield is let at last and to a bevy of beautiful young women who will be just the thing to liven up the countryside!"

"Who on earth is that?" Savannah said in a low voice.

Riley shrugged. "I have no idea."

"We're so pleased to see you," the man called out. "More pleased than we can say. The name's Russell." He climbed down from the carriage and helped his wife down in turn. "James Russell. This is my wife, Maud."

She couldn't help smiling back at him. "So nice to meet you. I'm Riley Eaton. This is Savannah Edwards, Avery Lightfoot and Nora Ridgeway."

"Four young ladies living alone! Unchaperoned!" Maud turned to her husband. "It's unthinkable!" She turned back to Riley. "We shall have to step in and take you under our wings. No, no," she went on when Riley began to protest, "there's nothing else for it, or the whole neighborhood will be up in arms. Besides, we knew your grandparents, Riley. We shall introduce you as our friends and no one will say another word about your unusual situation." She looked them up and down as Riley began to wonder if the Russells were out of their minds. "Four young ladies, but not all that young, I'll daresay. And none of you are married yet?"

"No, we're not," Savannah broke in. "Are there any eligible beaux around?"

Avery looked enchanted with the whole situation. Nora seemed caught between bemusement and disbelief. Riley wanted to groan. They'd distinctly discussed this; they were not going to talk like Jane Austen characters, despite the Regency thing.

"There are," Maud exclaimed. "In fact, lately a regiment of marines has made their camp among us. Mark my word," she said to her husband, "that will set them all a-flutter."

"Nay, nay, you've got it all wrong," James said with good humor. "It's the Navy that's settled in for the duration—Navy SEALs, you know. Some kind of upstart regiment."

"They do not keep all together, though," Maud went on as Riley exchanged a look with Savannah at this pronouncement. A regiment of Navy SEALs? Did she mean Boone and his friends? "The main encampment is at Crescent Hall, to the south," Maud explained.

Crescent Hall? Riley hadn't thought about the place in years. "Aren't the Hall boys long gone?" They'd left when their father passed away and their uncle had taken over their family's ranch.

"They're back. All four of them. They spent years in the military before they inherited Crescent Hall and returned to Chance Creek. Now they all have wives and more military men have joined them to start a training camp."

"Wow." Things had really changed while she was gone.

"But you have your own contingent here at Westfield," Maud went on.

Nora nodded. "Lieutenant Rudman."

"The very same," Maud agreed. "As fine a specimen of manhood as I ever did see. Which of you shall he have for a bride, eh?" She leaned forward to inspect them each in turn. Riley wondered how Boone had greeted the pair of them. She stifled a chuckle.

"He informs us his friends shall be joining him soon enough. So there are soldiers and sailors enough for you all," James went on. "None of you shall be left out."

"I doubt Lieutenant Rudman's friends are looking for wives," Savannah said gaily. She obviously loved this turn of events. Riley still couldn't get over the fact that the Russells actually existed. She'd felt sure she and her friends were the only ones in the world who actually donned historical garb for their everyday lives—except the Amish, of course. Evidently she'd been wrong.

"On the contrary!" James said. "Rudman assured me he was well on his way to making a conquest quite close to home." He turned a quizzical eye on them. "So which one of you is it? Who will walk down the matrimonial aisle first?"

Riley felt her cheeks warm and to cover her confusion, she blurted, "Won't you come in for a cup of tea?"

"No, no," James said. "We hardly meant to stop at all. Just came to pay our good wishes, as it were."

"And to invite you to dinner tomorrow night at Coldfield Cottage," Maud said.

"And to entice you to take a drive through the country right now," James added. "You need to be acquainted with your surroundings, strangers that you are."

"Actually—" Riley started.

"Actually," Savannah said, cutting her off. "We'd

love to!"

"But our chores—"

"Our chores will wait for us. Who knows when I'll get another chance to ride in a barouche?" Savannah pushed past her.

With everyone else clamoring to go, too, Riley couldn't say no. "We won't fit, though."

"Sure we will," James said. "One of you will tuck alongside Maud. The other three will sit across the way. You'll be cozy as church mice. I have to drive, you see."

With a last glance over her shoulder at the house, Riley gave in. "Shouldn't we lock the door?"

"No one locks their doors," James said. "We're all friends here."

Riley climbed in with the others and took a seat between Savannah and Avery. Nora took the seat next to Maud, her normally stressed expression surprisingly full of humor. That was worth the price of entry, Riley thought. Nora needed cheering up.

"Everyone in? Hold on to your hats, ladies!" James clucked to the horses and they were off.

"HEY, IT'S ME," Boone said into his phone late that afternoon when Clay picked up. "Have some time to talk?" He'd called earlier, but Clay hadn't answered, so he'd spent a dull day sorting out the governing bylaws instead.

"Sure. I think the Navy's punishing me with paperwork now that I'm heading out."

"I can relate."

"What's up?"

"We need to put out a call for six more men to fill those spaces in our roster. Can you and Jericho get on it?" That wasn't exactly his reason for calling, but he'd start with something neutral first. He had a feeling he knew how Clay would react when he heard that Boone wanted to change the housing plans.

"Sure thing. We'll have them communicate with you, though. Boots on the ground and all that."

"Okay." He didn't look forward to vetting candidates.

"How's progress?"

"Good. I've been working on the governance document."

"Sounds like a good time."

"Not really."

"What's up? Is this about Riley? Jericho said she was there. He made it sound like you two were hot and heavy already."

Boone surveyed the slope with its rectangles. He still wasn't ready to get to the heart of the matter. "I guess."

"What's she like these days? Did she remember you right off?"

"Hell, yeah. Called us the Horsemen."

Clay chuckled. "Is she still pretty?"

Time to tell the truth. "Breathtaking. I asked her to marry me. She said yes."

"That was fast. So things are going well."

"There's a catch."

"There always is. Spill it."

"It has to do with Riley. She's here with friends and they dress like characters out of Jane Austen's books all the time. It should be stupid, but… it's not."

"Huh." The single word conveyed all too much.

"It's not because I'm soft on her either," Boone hurried to say. "The four of them swore an oath, like we did, except instead of trying to save the world, they're trying to…make it beautiful." He braced himself for scorn, but Clay surprised him.

"A noble cause. So what's the problem?"

Boone made a face. Noble cause? "It's our houses."

"What about 'em?" Clay's voice soured. He'd hated the container houses since the start, but Boone had browbeaten him into submission over them. He'd lectured Clay often and long about how their obsession with houses was what started Americans on the road to wastefulness.

"It all comes down to keeping up with the Joneses," he'd railed at Clay several times. "The only solution is to de-emphasize them altogether." In his head he saw the shipping containers as a good solution. He could get them all of a similar size and material to portray that everyone's home should be equal. They would constrain people's natural inclination toward excess.

"You know I think those houses are ugly," Clay went on.

"Riley won't like them either. We need a new plan. They need to look… good. Really good."

Silence greeted his proclamation until Clay started to laugh. "Well, halle-fucking-lujah! Give Riley a big, fat kiss for me. If I'd known it would take tits to change your mind I would have started cross-dressing."

"Very funny. She says we'd ruin the view."

"Damn straight you would."

"I still think the containers had a lot going for them, but I'm trying to be a good neighbor." Boone didn't like Clay's tone. "Think you're up to the challenge?"

"More than up to it. You'll be blown away, Chief. I promise."

"I'd better go," Boone said.

"Hold up now. You've forgotten the most important thing."

"What's that?"

"Have you scored me a woman yet? Is she blond?"

"Whatever."

"I want pictures. You said Riley had friends. Are they hot?"

"Good-bye, Clay."

"But—"

Boone cut the call. The Russells' carriage had just rolled up to the manor after having been gone for hours. It was time to go see Riley again.

"YOU MUST COME to dinner tomorrow," James said when they stopped in front of the manor. "Come at four. You'll find the walk splendid. We'll drive you home, of course."

"And pick you up, too, if you wish," Maud said. "They may not like the dust of the road on the hems of their dresses," she said to James.

"Nonsense, young ladies love to walk about," James said. "But say the word and prove me wrong; it makes no difference to me."

"We'll walk," Riley said firmly. She'd enjoyed the Russell's company, but she was ready for some peace and quiet and couldn't imagine she still wouldn't be at four o'clock tomorrow.

"Have you ordered your own carriage?" Maud asked.

"No—we don't have the means for that, I'm afraid," Riley said.

"Well, then you must think of me as your grooms-man. I will stop in daily to see what you require and drive you wherever you want to go," James said cheerfully.

"We couldn't do that," Avery said.

"We'll be fine on our own," Riley said. She wasn't sure if she could handle James on a daily basis.

"But you must! Otherwise I'll die from the lack of anything to do. You see, I am an old man who loves his horses more than anything."

"More than me," Maud affirmed gaily.

"Hush woman, not more than you, but more than anything else. I must drive them every day or they'll get as bored as I get. We can't do the same old circles around the neighborhood forever. You'll breathe new life into all of us."

"Until tomorrow then," Maud said, settled comfortably in the carriage.

"Until tomorrow," James agreed. "Four o'clock.

Don't forget!"

"Good-bye!" Maud cried as James clucked to the horses and they began to move away.

"Good-bye!" James called as the horses picked up their pace, circled around and headed back out the driveway in the direction they'd come.

"Somebody pinch me," Avery said. "Am I actually awake or was this whole day a dream?"

"If you're asleep, we're sharing a dream," Nora said. "The Russells are a little overbearing but you have to give them credit; they showed us just about everything."

"You're right." Riley's head was almost spinning with it all. The Russells had taken them by the grocery store, the doctor's office, several churches, although they recommended the Chance Creek Reformed, which Riley had attended when she visited as a girl, and then had driven them to two ranches to introduce them to other young people, as Maud termed them. To Riley's surprise, the citizens of Chance Creek didn't point or stare, although they did get some curious glances.

"They've gotten used to us," Maud confided to her at one point. "We heard about the barouche being for sale quite by accident two years ago when we attended a Regency get-together down in Wyoming. Until then we led quite modern lives between re-enactments. Once we got the barouche, however, we realized we couldn't bear to ride in it unless we looked the part. It got too tiring to change clothes all the time, so we threw over our modern lives in favor of the past. We've never looked back." She smiled at her pun.

Once Riley got over her self-consciousness, she enjoyed the excursion. At the Cruz ranch she was reintroduced to Ethan Cruz, who both ranched and ran a bed and breakfast with his wife, Autumn, a transplant from New York City. Riley had taken to Autumn right away.

Ethan had become a handsome man who obviously doted on his wife and baby girl. His sister, Claire, her husband, Jamie, and their baby made an appearance and were equally affable. Riley hadn't known either Ethan or Claire very well during her previous visits, but she enjoyed catching up with them. Before they left the ranch, Riley and the others also met the local sheriff, Cab Johnson, who lived in one of the cabins on the property with his wife, Rose. Rose apparently ran a jewelry store now. Riley remembered her as a vivacious, fun-loving girl. Her daughter was a tiny bundle of dark hair and blue eyes.

On their way off the ranch, James veered off up a dirt track to an area that had been planted as a vineyard. Riley didn't know anyone grew grapes in this part of Montana, but Rob and Morgan Matheson explained that the varieties they'd chosen to grow were bred to do well with this climate.

"We're still a few years from having a vintage, but we're getting there," Morgan said.

Riley couldn't believe the transformation Rob had gone through. He'd been quick with his fists and prone to playing practical jokes when they were younger. She'd always kept her distance from the rough boy. Now he had a passion for growing things she never would have guessed. Time did change people. She wondered if all her old acquaintances saw changes in her as well.

As if that wasn't enough people to meet, James insisted on driving them to Crescent Hall. The Hall brothers had each served in a different branch of the military during the last decade, but had come home to restore their family's ranch to its former glory. They were all married, too, as James pointed out, but Mason Hall, the oldest of the brothers, assured him that several new single recruits had already joined them to help out with the military-style training camp. "Dan Hemmins, who served with me, owns the business," Mason said. "His wife, Sarah, helps him out. She served in the Army. You'll have to come back soon and meet everyone else."

"I love your dresses," his wife, Regan, had said to Riley. "Jane Austen is one of my favorite authors. Where did you get them?"

They'd launched into a conversation about dressmakers, fashion, books and more, with the other Hall wives making an appearance. Regan had passed Riley a card with the name of a local seamstress on it. "She makes the most wonderful costumes for the Civil War re-enactments they do around here."

Finally James threw up his hands. "There's only so much of this a man can take," he said. "I'll be out with the horses when you're ready to go."

"I'll join you," Mason said.

Riley had thoroughly enjoyed getting reacquainted with the Halls and meeting their wives, but she'd been ready to go home by the time they were done and she still wasn't sure how the rest of the citizens of Chance Creek would treat them once they realized their Jane Austen attire was permanent. She'd figured she and her friends would spend the majority of their time on the ranch, but now she had a feeling they'd get visitors. Soon they'd be pulled into the social fabric of the community. She wasn't sure how she felt about that.

They waved to the Russells as the couple drove off.

"I'm exhausted and we didn't actually do any work today," Savannah said.

"Better start dinner," Riley said. They'd eaten lunch with the Cruzes but that had been hours ago.

"In a minute." Savannah stretched and rubbed her neck. Suddenly she stopped. "Boone's coming."

BOONE SET THE picnic basket he carried down onto the grass. "Afternoon, ladies. Hope you enjoyed your jaunt around town."

"We did," Savannah said with enthusiasm. "We met so many people."

"All our old friends have grown up, haven't they?" Riley said.

"I haven't had a chance to find that out. I will soon, though." Boone nudged the basket with his foot. "Figured you'd be hungry by now. I brought dinner."

"That was nice of you." Avery bent down to pick up the basket. "Come inside and join us."

Boone followed the women through the manor to a large, old-fashioned kitchen. It had been updated sometime in the last few decades with a decent electric stove and refrigerator, but there was no dishwasher and by the looks of things, the women were doing their best to keep use of the appliances to a minimum. He wondered why. "Dinner isn't anything special. Just what I had on hand."

Avery chuckled. "I'd be happy with a PB&J right about now."

"Your wish is my command." Boone opened the basket, which Avery had set on the table, and handed a sandwich to her. "PB&J's are just the appetizer, though." He made short work of starting a fire with the wood that was handy, opened a couple of cans of soup with the can opener he'd packed along, and looked around for a pot. Avery handed him the one they'd been using to cook over the fire. "Perfect. Thanks."

It wasn't long before the soup was bubbling. Meanwhile he handed out more of the sandwiches he'd made down at the bunkhouse. As the women ate, they became talkative, filling him in on the adventures of their day and all the people they'd met.

"I'll have to stop by and talk with Mason," he said. "I only bumped into him once the whole time I was with the SEALs."

"You wouldn't believe the transformation—all those boys. Well, they aren't boys anymore," Riley said, biting into her sandwich with relish.

"They weren't boys when they left."

"Sure they were. You were, too. I guess you don't stay innocent once you enlist, though." Perched on one of the dining room chairs, a sandwich in her hand, Riley looked so much like the teenager she'd once been it tugged at Boone's heart.

"Honey, if you think I was innocent when I left Chance Creek, you were thoroughly deluded."

He'd meant it as a joke, but Riley turned thoughtful and as much as he tried to draw her out, she didn't speak much more during the meal.

Afterward, he caught up to her outside when she went to hang the wet dishrags on the line. "What's up?"

"What do you mean?" She pinned up the damp squares one at a time.

"You know what I mean. Did I say something wrong?"

At first he thought she wouldn't answer. When she finally turned to him, her expression was guarded. "You said you weren't innocent when you left Chance Creek."

"So?"

"When you left, I lost my innocence, too. Not that way—" She shrugged. "My spiritual innocence, I guess. I lost my friends, my childhood, my self-respect. Soon after, I lost my grandparents, and then my family when my parents split up. Nothing was ever the same again."

For the first time it struck him how hard it must have been for her when he'd left town, and not just because he'd been an ass. "I'm sorry," he said simply. "I cared about you, but I wasn't there for you when you needed me."

He'd let her down. Boone wished he could go back and change that, but he couldn't. All he could do was try to make it up to her. "I'm going to be there for the rest of your life, though." He pulled her in for a kiss before she could protest. Words couldn't change the past and they couldn't convince her that the future would be better. He needed to tell her that with his body.

Judging by the way she sighed and kissed him back, Riley heard him loud and clear. It was a long time before they broke apart and when they did he wasn't the only one breathing hard.

"I can't wait to be with you again." He cupped her chin with both hands and raised her mouth to meet his.

"I wish I could be sensible around you."

"I'm glad you can't."

"I NEVER DREAMED we'd have Regency neighbors," Nora said the next day as they turned into the driveway that led to Coldfield Cottage. James had been right; the walk from Westfield was lovely, and while the hems of their gowns were a little dusty, as Maud had warned, the exercise had been just the ticket after a day spent on their creative pursuits. "Remember we said we'd see no one and never leave the ranch? That's not going quite as planned."

She didn't sound upset and Riley was grateful for that. As they'd prepared to leave for the Russell's place, she'd had the same thought. They'd have to guard their days carefully, or they wouldn't have time to paint, write or play music, after all.

She was already concerned about what would happen once Fulsom's film crews arrived. After dinner the previous night, she and Boone had gone for another walk and she'd asked him what to expect. He'd told her he wasn't sure. Before she could ask more questions, he'd distracted her with a whole lot more kissing, but at least they'd kept their clothes on this time. Riley knew a physical relationship wasn't enough to base a marriage on. She'd told Boone so and he hadn't pushed matters. By the time she'd gotten back to the manor again, though, she'd been so revved up she'd found it hard to sleep.

"That's a cottage?" Savannah said as they rounded a curve and a house came into view. Coldfield was a sprawling affair with a main white clapboard façade and two wings sprouting off of it. As they approached, Maud and James came out onto the front porch and waved them on.

"You're right on time," James boomed as they reached the steps. "Come in, come in. Where's that fellow of yours? He isn't with you?"

"Lieutenant Rudman is not our fellow," Savannah said tartly, jumping right into the game with relish.

"Oh, but he will be soon enough, eh?" James said. "I love a good guessing game. Which lovely lady has already snared his heart?"

Riley fought impatiently against a blush that threatened to stain her cheeks.

"No one's telling?" Maud examined them more closely and her gaze alighted on Riley. "Oh, I think I see the lay of the land," she said with a laugh. "Well, we wish you all the best, my dear. We've decided he's the best kind of man."

Before Riley could deny anything, hoof beats pierced the air and they all turned to see who was coming. Riley's mouth dropped open when Boone rode up on a huge black gelding. Where had he gotten that beauty? His movements as he dismounted called up all sorts of memories. Boone had always been at home in a saddle, and she'd been surprised that he'd given up the rodeo so easily as a teen to enlist in the Navy. Reins in hand, he walked toward the group assembled on the porch. "Where can I stow Behemoth?" he called up.

"In the stables around back," James said, hurrying down to meet him. "Wherever did you get this beast? A more beautiful example of horseflesh I never did see."

"I bought him today from Jamie Lassiter."

"Ah, Jamie. Good man," James said. "Are your stables up to snuff though? I've got an extra stall."

"The stables at Westfield are just fine," Boone said. "Good thing, too. I know all my men will want horses."

"Let's get him taken care of." James patted Behemoth's flank. "We'll meet you ladies inside."

Riley couldn't keep her eyes off of Boone. His jeans and white button-down cotton shirt showcased his wide shoulders and trim torso. She pictured undressing him and laying his clothing aside piece by piece, then spending a full night worshipping that wonderful body.

When a smile tugged at the corners of his mouth, she knew her face must have betrayed her thoughts. He nodded at her, and then each of the others, and turned to follow James to the stables as Maud led Riley and the others inside.

The cottage was furnished much like Westfield was with a mixture of antiques from several eras. "Dinner will be served in half an hour," Maud said. "Until then, let's gather in the parlor. Perhaps I could prevail on one of you ladies to play a piece or two on my piano to pass the time while we wait?"

Riley and the others exchanged looks. Maud seemed determined to run this evening according to Regency rules. "Savannah plays," Riley said.

"I'm horribly out of practice," Savannah protested.

"Nonsense, my dear, you're among friends," Maud said.

Riley noticed that Savannah's eyes lit up when she spotted the grand piano at one end of the parlor. She needed no more encouragement before she hurried over to the instrument and sat down. She'd been delighted to find the baby grand at Westfield, but the tuner wouldn't arrive for another few days, so Riley knew her endeavors at practicing hadn't been altogether satisfying.

Savannah sat down and let her fingers play over the keys. "Oh, it's wonderful," she exclaimed.

"Play something merry," Maud said.

"Okay." Savannah thought for a minute. "How about this?" She started to play a rather raucous march, and Maud laughed.

"Just the thing! We could almost dance to that."

"Bravo! Splendid!" James said, coming into the parlor with Boone trailing close behind.

Savannah stopped playing, but James would have

none of that. "Carry on, carry on." She started up again.

"We were just discussing dancing," Maud told him.

"Good exercise, dancing," James said. "Do you dance?" he asked Boone.

Boone made a face. "Only at gunpoint."

James roared with laughter and led Boone to sit on the couch next to Riley.

"Does anyone else play an instrument?" Maud asked. "I have it in mind to organize a musical evening here at Coldfield."

"I play guitar," Avery said.

"I play a little piano," Riley said. "Nothing like Savannah, though." She nodded at her friend who had switched to something light and lively she couldn't identify.

"I don't play anything," Nora said.

"How about you?" Maud fixed a challenging gaze on Boone.

"I know a little." He stood and crossed the room to the piano. Savannah immediately ceased playing again. Murmuring some words to her, Boone sat down next to her when she scooted over on the bench. Riley's heart contracted at the picture they presented, Savannah with a faint flush on her cheeks from the exertion of playing and Boone leaning in close to whisper in her ear.

"Perhaps we mistook the object of his affections after all," Maud observed to her husband. "Look at the attention he shows her."

Despite all her attempts to ignore it, jealousy simmered just below Riley's heart. When Boone stopped whispering and pulled back, Savannah laughed and both of them lifted their hands to the keys. Riley expected a silly version of chopsticks, so she was as surprised as anyone when the two began a complicated classical duet that took her breath away. The music—passionate and stirring—transported her, but the ugly feeling remained curled tightly in her gut. Savannah looked so right sitting next to Boone, and they were both smiling as they played, building up to a huge crescendo that had Riley's heart pounding.

She'd forgotten that Boone's mother had forced him to take music lessons for years. He had always claimed he hated it and he'd never touched the instrument in the summers when she was there. He must have been fonder of it than he'd admitted. Or else simply a good student.

Riley felt like she'd lost something precious before she'd even known she'd had it. How could Boone not sense a kind of kinship with Savannah that he didn't have with her? And how could he ignore Savannah's loveliness when he sat right next to her, their shoulders brushing and their hands intermingling on the piano?

She wished she'd paid more attention to her lessons when she was a child.

When the song concluded, everyone in the audience clapped and cheered, even Riley, although she felt like slipping out the front door and running for home. Surely now Boone would realize he'd picked the wrong woman. He escorted Savannah back to her seat and Maud gestured to Riley. "Your turn, my dear. Play for us."

The last thing Riley wanted to do was to compete with the stunning performance Savannah and Boone had just presented, but she knew she couldn't refuse. So she dutifully stood up, smoothed her skirts and made her way to the piano, trying to ignore the pit in her stomach. Thank goodness she had the perfect piece for just such an occasion. She'd do herself credit, even if she had just watched the beginning of the end of her relationship with Boone.

It was the same song Marianne played in the modern movie version of *Sense and Sensibility* the first time Captain Wentworth appears. Riley had tracked down the sheet music on the Internet years ago, learned the piece by heart and taught herself to sing it like the famous actress in the movie. It was simple, yet elegant, and while she was nowhere near as accomplished as Savannah and Boone—or the actress who performed it onscreen—when she opened her mouth to sing she was gratified to hear a startled gasp from her audience, and their silence as the piece went on told her she'd chosen wisely.

After the first few measures, the song drew her in as it always did and for a moment, she forgot the pain she'd felt watching Boone and Savannah together. Here in the Russells' parlor in the company of men and women dressed as they were, she felt as if she really had stepped back into the past and belonged there. Belonged here—singing for an appreciative audience the way Jane and her characters would have.

Something moved within her heart—as if ties that had held in her emotions for so many years loosened a little and allowed for healing. She hadn't realized how tensely she held herself in everyday life until she relaxed, knowing that the circle of people listening supported her.

When she finished the song, she paused, just like Marianne in the movie, and she understood for the first time why Marianne had done so. To hold onto the moment—the music and the feeling that accompanied it. To savor it.

When she finally looked up, she met Boone's gaze and what she saw there nearly overcame her. Pride and something that looked an awful lot like... love... shone back at her. Transfixed by such a startling turn of events, she didn't notice Maud bustling forward until the older woman hovered over her.

"That was marvelous. Play another one," Maud exhorted her.

"I'm sorry. That's the only one I know by heart." She stood up and made her way back to her seat, conscious of Boone's gaze tracking her the whole way.

CHAPTER NINE

★

BOONE ENJOYED THE dinner far more than he'd expected. He liked the Russells, but had expected to be put off by their lavish lifestyle. Instead, he'd been charmed by their sincere delight in entertaining Riley and her friends.

He was impressed by Savannah's prowess at the piano. Music lessons had been non-negotiable in his household and he had studied the instrument until a final ugly rebellion at sixteen ended them. He was accomplished, but Savannah was obviously an expert. He had a healthy respect for anyone who transcended mere capability and actually brought passion to their playing. He enjoyed sitting down to play a duet with her—one he couldn't believe he could still play after all this time.

It was obvious to him when Riley followed their performance that she feared she would come out the worse in a comparison with Savannah. As someone who'd struggled to become as competent as he was, he felt for her, so when she sat down and began to play he was relieved that she didn't stumble and stutter through the piece. The only thing worse than being forced to play unprepared was to watch someone else do so, red-faced with humiliation. He smiled and relaxed, happy for the chance to watch her.

Then she began to sing.

She might as well have punched him in the gut. Boone had no idea that Riley could sing. Every syllable of her song reached into him, tangled its hand into his basest emotions and twisted until he was no longer his own man. Each note threaded a new connection between the two of them he knew would never be severed. How could something as simple as a woman's voice create so much havoc in his heart?

The old-fashioned melody rose and fell, as did Riley's hands on the keyboard. There was something pure about her voice and about her manner, too. It heartened him. Surely a woman who could appreciate such simplicity would one day see that his plans for his community made sense.

He also had to acknowledge that the experience wouldn't be quite the same without the beautiful trappings. The song would have touched his heart no matter when or where he heard it, but the dress she wore, her elegant hairstyle, the room full of antiques framing her, all made the experience that much more special.

He wouldn't trade these few minutes of beauty for a working windmill, he realized. Someday his community's get-togethers would be just as memorable—he hoped—but this one would forever stand out as a special moment in time.

Everyone clapped heartily when Riley finished and she gave a little curtsy when she stood up from the instrument. When a woman Boone didn't recognize in a plain, dark blue gown and a voluminous white apron edged into the parlor and announced that dinner was served, his surprise was echoed on the others' faces.

"Thank you, Mrs. Wood," Maud said and stood up to usher them into the dining room. "Mrs. Wood cooks for us several days of the week," she explained. "She has a fine touch with pastry and chicken. I'm afraid I never quite became the cook I wanted to be. Plus it allows me more time to talk with our guests when I'm not stuck in the kitchen."

"That sounds like a wonderful arrangement," Avery said.

The dining room was large and formal, and Boone helped James hand the ladies into their chairs, appreciating for the first time in his life the formal gesture when it gave him the excuse to touch Riley briefly. He sat down between her and Savannah before Avery or Nora could slip into the seat.

"Tell us more about this community of yours," Maud said to Boone as Mrs. Wood set the food on the table. At least the Russells hadn't hired footmen and butlers too, he thought.

"I can sum it up by telling you the four guiding principles on which I'm founding it."

"Guiding principles! Imagine that," James said.

Boone prevented himself from rolling his eyes. James must have sensed he was getting too far into character. He cleared his throat a couple of times, took a drink of water and settled back to listen.

"I refer to the principles whenever I'm making a plan or a purchase, or even setting a goal. I ask myself, is this absolutely necessary?" He held up one finger. "Ninety percent of the time the answer to that question is no. Cutting out everything that isn't absolutely necessary could probably solve most of the world's environmental problems by itself." He held up another finger. "Can I accomplish this with less? I find if I put a little thought into my plans I can get by using far fewer resources than I would have if I rushed into them." Another finger went up. "How many people will this benefit? If it's only me, why am I doing it? If it's only a small group of people, like my family, again maybe it's time to reconsider. If it will truly benefit a lot of people, then it's more likely to be a good idea. And four." He held up another finger. "What will its impact be on the planet, both locally and globally?"

"So where does art, literature and music fit in?" Riley asked.

"I haven't really thought about them," Boone said. "Those aren't necessities—"

"They are to me."

"But they come long after things like food, shelter and clothing. My community is intended to show how few things we really need. You're talking about luxuries."

"That explains those little hovels you're building down by the barns. Who are you going to get to live in those boxes? No woman in her right mind would be caught dead in a cage like that!"

"Plenty of women will want to live in them." He frowned at her. She was going to be one of them. She had to know that.

"Name one!"

As the seconds ticked by, Riley surveyed him with an air of triumph. She knew she'd caught him. He couldn't name her—he'd promised to keep their engagement a secret. And he didn't have any other women lined up.

"You can't, can you?"

"Not at the moment," he was forced to concede. "But I will soon."

"Not if you keep calling art and literature luxuries."

Boone reached under the table, clamped his hand down on her knee and squeezed it through the delicate fabric of her dress. Riley inhaled sharply. "There are all sorts of benefits to sharing a small space with an interested man. I bet if you try you can imagine one or two of them." He slid his hand a fraction of an inch higher on her thigh, caressed her, and let go again.

"Sex isn't enough to keep people happy," she retorted. "It takes many things to make a well-rounded life."

"Not so many things that you require a mansion in which to store them."

Riley opened her mouth to answer, but Nora beat

her to it. "Riley doesn't need a mansion. She's the one who came up with rule number two. *Our* rule number two," she clarified when Boone frowned.

"What's *your* rule number two?"

"Only possess what a moderately well-off lady in Jane Austen's time would possess. Which turns out to be far less than what we're used to," Avery explained. "All four of us can live on what we each used to spend alone."

Once again the women had surprised him. "What are your other rules?"

"One," Riley said, holding up a finger just like he had. "Is it beautiful? Two, would a Regency lady of moderate means own it? Three, will it contribute to the enjoyment of the group? Four, does it uphold our commitment to Regency living?"

"Well, there you go," James said, unable to keep his peace any longer. "Now you and I will have to come up with principles, Maud, my dear. It seems to be all the rage this year."

"I already know our principles," she replied, passing him a platter of chicken. "One, is it fun? Two, will we enjoy ourselves? Three, will we laugh? And four, does it involve Champagne?"

"By heavens, you're right. Those sum us up quite tidily," her husband said.

Boone joined in the general laughter and knew he should be grateful to his hosts for defusing a tense situation, but the truth was he would have liked to talk more about Riley's stated principles. Once again he had the feeling they weren't so far apart, if only she would take a minute to discuss the matter.

"When are your friends arriving at Westfield?" Maud asked him.

"Within a couple of weeks," he said and noted the expressions of interest among the women around the table. Good, he wanted them to be interested.

"If the rest of your men are as handsome as you, they'll make quite a splash in Chance Creek." Maud raised her glass and took a sip of wine.

"We get first dibs, though." Avery bit her lip as color stained her cheeks. "I mean…" She busied herself with the salad tongs.

Boone flashed her a conspiratorial smile. He couldn't have asked for a better response. "I'm sure my men would be glad to give you first dibs." He'd match Clay, Jericho and Walker with them as soon as his friends arrived.

"That's enough. Just stop it." Riley, who'd taken a sip from her water glass, thumped it on the table.

"Stop what?" Boone asked.

"Stop trying to weasel your way in among my friends and make them fall in love with you."

He let the pause spin out before answering. "First of all, weaseling our way in is exactly what SEALs are trained to do. If we stopped, it would be detrimental to national security. Second, regardless of our skills, I don't think we're capable of making women fall in love— unless they want to."

"You have a slick answer for everything, don't you,

Lieutenant Rudman?"

"I'll always have an answer for you."

"Is it hot in here or is it me?" Maud said, fanning herself. "Summer is definitely on its way."

"It's only going to get hotter, too," Boone said with a wink at Riley. "This is Montana, after all."

Avery took up the topic of the weather and soon they were taking turns predicting what kind of summer they'd have.

Boone slid his hand under the table again and caught Riley's fingers in his. "Hey, are you all right?" he added in a low voice.

"It's one thing to get me involved in your problems, but don't you dare let your friends drag mine into this. They've waited for years for their chance to pursue their dreams. It's not fair of you to derail them," she said in a whisper.

"I would never do that."

She extricated her hand from his. "Prove it."

SEVERAL DAYS LATER, Riley bent over a huge cauldron of water she'd spent the previous hour heating over an outdoor fire, and gingerly tested it with a fingertip. "It's hot," she said to Nora and Avery, who had come to take a break and chat with her. They had fallen into a routine of working in the mornings, then changing their gowns, eating an early lunch outside when the weather was fair and turning to their creative pursuits in the afternoons. Maud and James had picked up on their schedule, and tried to hold off until after four for their almost daily visits. Riley found those long, unbroken afternoons a revelation. She had so much time to paint... and to walk... and ponder, even if far too much of her time had been taken up thinking about Boone.

He tended to appear in the evenings with a request for her company. Sometimes they hung out with her friends, sometimes they walked and watched the sunset. Once, when it rained, they'd played cards for hours at the bunkhouse. They'd been reserved the first night after the Russells' dinner party, but Boone had apologized for what he'd said about the arts, and Riley had forgiven him, though she still thought Boone ranked their creative pursuits far below the work he was doing down at Base Camp, as he called it. She understood why a man like Boone might think so after everything he'd seen during his time in the military, but it made it hard to trust that they could create a marriage that suited them equally.

Savannah, Avery and Nora got a censored version of her time with Boone. They thought she was doing a masterful job of making him woo her. The truth was, Boone was playing her like a fine violin.

His flirtation was subtle. A touch here, a smile there. He hadn't tried to make love to her again, and Riley wasn't ready to take the lead again. She found his new penchant for conversation more of an aphrodisiac than anything else he'd done so far. It was as if the years had fallen away and they were back to being kids, before hormones had made their friendship tricky. When she realized she wouldn't get more than a good-night kiss at the end of the evening, she relaxed, let loose her tight rein on her memories and enjoyed Boone's company more than she should.

They swapped stories about their lives in the past thirteen years, although she was sure he censored his with an iron hand. When she questioned him about the darker side of his missions, he just shook his head. "Some things should stay in the past," he told her. But he answered her other questions willingly and she built a portrait from the pieces he gave her that led her to believe Boone had served his country honorably—and that he'd been meant to be a SEAL.

She'd also come to realize something specific had happened to make sustainability such a priority with him. He'd referred to it a couple of times, but only obliquely. Riley wondered if he'd ever share that story fully. Sometimes she thought if he did she'd finally understand his singlemindedness on the topic.

"You're really going to hand wash our clothes?" Nora asked Riley, bringing her back to the present.

"It seems like an awful lot of work," Avery said.

"You're the one who inspired me with your cooking. I like learning about life during Jane's time. Why not try laundry the old-fashioned way? Besides, I'd have to lug it to town otherwise. Between the taxi ride and several hours at a laundromat, that sounds like way too many opportunities for someone to make fun of me."

"One of us would go with you, and James would give us a ride."

"James has given us rides all over the place. He's not

a taxi service." Riley wasn't sure she could express her real reason. She'd found that without a job, she experienced time differently. Her brain wasn't stuffed with a million details, so she had the luxury of curiosity. She'd begun to read *Pride and Prejudice* again in the evenings before bedtime and realized the book glossed over many details of Regency life, especially when it came to the way households were run. Jane Austen's contemporaries would have known how things were done, but Riley didn't, and when it came time to do the laundry, she'd decided to learn for herself.

"Don't you have your own chores to do?" Riley said when Avery and Nora lingered. As hard as it would be to hand wash the dresses and linens they'd worn this week, it would be harder to do it with the two of them staring at her.

"You're right. Good luck!" Avery curtsied, and headed toward the back of the house. Nora stayed. She'd been restless the last few days and Riley was worried about her.

"How did women do this in winter?"

"The exact same way, I suppose, but using the hearth inside."

"What a waste of time." Nora paced away, then came back. "Think about it, Riley, all those women over the years slaving over household chores rather than using their minds. What a complete and utter waste."

"When you think of how hard it was, it was valuable work, don't you think? Without them life would have been so uncomfortable."

"When has women's work ever been valued?" Nora flung back at her.

Riley's heart sank. She'd known this moment was coming. While the rest of them were enjoying their break from the twenty-first century, Nora was at loose ends. She'd been writing during the afternoons, but she never looked happy while she did it. Riley wondered if Nora still felt guilty for not completing the school year.

"I value your work."

"No, you don't! You persuaded me to give it up and come here."

"I persuaded you to escape from a job where someone wanted to kill you. How can you complain about that?"

"I loved that job! Why can't any of you understand that? I loved my job and some stupid kid ruined it for me. I was helping people! I was changing lives. I'm not doing that here. I'm just… playing dress up."

Riley, who had picked up the basket of their dirty clothing in order to carry it closer to the cauldron, dropped it again. "I'm doing a hell of a lot more than playing dress up! I can't speak for the others, but this past week has been amazing. I've reintroduced art into my life. I feel like I can breathe for the first time in years!"

"So where's all your art? You haven't finished a single piece."

Stung, Riley raised her voice. "We've only been here a week. This isn't a contest—it's a life. I value the silence and the hours free to experiment, and if it takes me time to finish a painting, that's all right."

"The thing is, time is all we've got here. Do you know how it feels to watch it tick away and know someone else is teaching my classes? I failed, Riley. I did the worst thing a teacher can do—I walked away."

Her words tripped Riley up, because there was a kernel of truth there; some of Nora's students might feel abandoned. But in a life-or-death situation like that, what was she supposed to do?

"I can't stand wasting my days like this," Nora went on.

Riley's sympathy fell away in tatters. She might be doing a lot of things, but she wasn't wasting her time here. "Are you saying writing is a waste of time? Or have you found out already that your literary pretensions were just that? Pretensions?"

She knew she'd gone too far the minute the words left her mouth. Nora stiffened, then whirled around and stalked off.

Riley went after her. "Nora, stop! Come on, I didn't mean that."

"Why not? It's probably true."

Nora kept going. Riley followed her. "If you've got writer's block, take the day off. The words will come, you'll see."

"It's not that easy."

"Nothing worth fighting for is easy. Look, it's a beautiful day. Why don't you go for a walk and clear your head? You are an amazing teacher and I know it was hard for you to leave your class behind, but I also know I love you too much to let you remain in danger. If writing turns out not to be your thing, you'll find another way. I know you will."

Nora stopped and faced her. After a moment, she nodded. "A walk. That's a good idea."

"Do you want company?" Riley followed her another few paces, glancing back at the cauldron of water.

"No. I need to be alone to sort this out."

"Okay." Riley let her go on ahead reluctantly. She'd never seen Nora look so defeated. She was afraid of what Nora would do next if she couldn't come to terms with life at Westfield.

They needed her, Riley realized. It took all four of them to make the perfect team, and she hoped that Nora knew how much they all loved her and wanted her here. It was so hard to see her once-vivacious friend become so cynical and unhappy. She'd hoped that a slower-paced existence on the ranch would soften Nora's sharp corners over time. Instead, the past week had whittled them into lethal points.

When Riley returned to the fire, still wondering what she could have said to make things better, she maneuvered the iron arm that hung the large cauldron over the flames to the side, wrapped rags around her hands, lifted the huge metal pot off and set it on the ground. She used a pitcher to transfer hot water from it into another large pot that was partially filled with cold water until the mix was right. She added biodegradable soap flakes to the water and picked up the first work dress in the pile. It was Savannah's and despite her care, it had several stains. Riley had researched old-fashioned cleaning methods, but she soon found the job to be hot and strenuous.

And wet.

She was glad that she wore one of her work dresses because soon she was soaked. She scrubbed diligently until she had gotten all the stains she could out of the first dress and dropped it on a towel she'd spread on the ground. She would rinse them all at once. She picked up the second dress, soaked it in the water and got to work on it. Thank God they'd used easy-to-wash modern cottons and Avery and her friends had taken care to pre-shrink the fabric. She doubted some of the finer dresses Jane Austen and her compatriots wore during the Regency could stand up to this treatment.

By the time she picked out the third work dress she was ready for a break, but her water was cooling and Riley knew she needed to keep going. Avery's dress had some particularly tough food stains and she knew the aprons would be worse. At least she could add bleach to the water for those. When she lifted a hand out of the water to push back a strand of hair, Riley noticed her knuckles were red. She needed rubber gloves. But Jane wouldn't have had rubber gloves.

She wouldn't have been doing her own laundry, either, Riley reasoned. Gloves it was.

"That looks like hot work."

Riley jumped and looked up to find Boone standing not five feet away.

"You scared me."

"I'm just about to head to the airport to pick up Clay and Jericho." He cocked his head. "Everything okay?"

"No. Not really." She pushed the dress she was cleaning into the water and stood up to ease her back.

"Your washing machine's broken?"

"It's non-existent. That's not the trouble, though. It's Nora. She's not happy here. I don't know if she'll stay." She shook her head. "I'm going to miss her like crazy if she goes."

"She's ready to pitch in the towel already? You've only been here a week."

"I know."

"Not everyone's cut out for simple living," Boone said.

"It isn't about simple living."

"What's it about?" He drifted closer, examining her pots of water and the pile of soapy clothes on the towel beside her.

"Teaching. Nora's a teacher. Or she was. She misses it."

"After a single week?" But Boone didn't look dismissive. He looked interested. "She must love it."

"I guess she does. I don't think I could last a week at her job." She explained the circumstances of Nora quitting. "I think she's good at what she does, though. I think it's eating her up to know that one bad egg ruined it for everyone."

"Sooner or later there'll be kids here to teach."

"I suppose so." Why did they always stray into such

dangerous territory? She knelt down again, plunged her hands into the water, found the dress she'd been washing and got back to work.

"Meanwhile, maybe she could teach locally. I never heard of a teacher getting a death threat here in Chance Creek."

"Maybe. I'll suggest that to her. But the idea was she'd write while she was here." She scrubbed a stubborn spot even harder.

Boone circled around behind her to watch. After a few moments, Riley looked over her shoulder at him. "Do you mind?"

"There are machines that do this, you know."

She rested her arms on the edge of the pot. "I know. We could have hauled all this into town. I didn't want to bother James."

"I mean hand-cranked washing machines."

"Would Jane Austen have had one?" she quipped.

"I think they came a little later in the century. I'm not sure, though. Want me to look it up? We should probably get one for Base Camp." He whipped a cell phone out of his pocket.

"No." Riley got back to work. She wanted him to leave. She was hot and sweaty and her hair was falling out of its bun and she had an overwhelming urge to drop the laundry, hurl herself into his arms and convince him to finally make love to her again.

Boone jabbed at his phone and she pressed her lips together. "I said no," she burst out when he didn't stop.

"Why not?"

"It's not my cell phone time." God, that sounded lame. She got back to work.

Boone lowered the phone. "You have a specific time for using cell phones?"

"We wanted to ban technology altogether, but there are some things we can't do without. We decided we each get a half-hour a day for phone calls and Internet access." When Boone chuckled her irritation grew. "What?"

"You guys are more hard core than we are."

Was that admiration she heard in his voice? "Don't you have to get to the airport?"

He checked his watch. "Yep, I'd better get going. Clay and Jericho will be happy to see you. Even happier to see your friends."

She stopped scrubbing. "They'd better steer clear of my friends."

Boone backed away. "You hook up with me. Your friends hook up with my friends. Everybody's happy, right?"

"You're sick in the head. Tell Clay and Jericho they're off limits."

"WHERE'S MY WIFE?" Clay asked as they waited at the baggage carousel at the Chance Creek Regional Airport. Boone had just finished detailing the events of the previous week.

"I've picked her out for you. Unfortunately Riley has drawn a pretty deep line in the sand and your future mate is on the other side."

"You'll have to sweet talk her into changing her mind," Jericho said. "After all, she'll be promising to obey you within the month, right?"

"I highly doubt that phrase will be in our marriage vows."

"What are her friends like?" Clay asked.

Boone kept his eyes on the moving belt. "Two of them are candidates. Savannah is musical and loves the life they're building here. Clay, I think she'll do for you. Avery is sweet and has aspirations to be an actress. She seems fun-loving and dedicated; I think she's a match for Jericho."

"What about the other one? You said there were three," Jericho pointed out.

"Nora?" Boone shook his head. "Sounds like she might fly the coop soon." He detailed the conversation he'd had with Riley that afternoon.

"Hand-washing the laundry? That's hard-core." Clay lunged suddenly and grabbed a bag. "This one's mine. There should be another one. Wait… there it is." He grabbed it, too.

"That's what I told Riley. It's uncanny the way these women have almost reproduced the same rules that we have—and downright aggravating they won't give up a couple of things that would put them right in line with us. We could join forces right now and just get on with it, but they're obsessed with these dresses and parties and art and music and…"

"…all the things that make life worth living?" Clay said.

Boone frowned. "Don't you start."

"You've got to lighten up a little, Boone." Jericho reached for a bag and picked it up off the carousel.

"Lighten up? I have to be married within the month. Then we need to hit the ground running when the cameras arrive. We don't have time to fool around with music and art."

"We can't work all the time." Jericho dropped his bag on the floor and held up his hands when Boone turned on him. "All I'm saying is that you've probably scared Riley off with that attitude. Why not give a little to get a little?"

"I don't want to operate on false pretenses."

"Hold on. Are you saying there's no room for fun in our community... ever?" Clay asked.

"Of course there is, but right now we need to focus, and even though Riley's agreed to marry me, she's shown no real interest in Base Camp. I think—" He broke off. "Wait a minute, that's Nora—right there. The one I said might fly the coop." He pointed across the terminal to where she was gazing at a monitor that showed arrivals and departures, her dark hair scooped up into a messy bun. She'd exchanged her Regency gown for a pair of jeans, knee-high leather boots and a cream-colored shirt. Boone could have sworn Riley had said they'd burned all their twenty-first century duds, but Nora must have kept a stash. Maybe she'd never meant to stay.

Boone couldn't let her leave. "Come on." He strode across the hall toward her. "Nora? Everything all right?"

Nora jumped, guilt glinting in her eyes when she took him in. "Boone, what are you doing here? Did Riley send you after me?"

"No. I'm here to pick up my friends. Clay Pickett, Jericho Cook, this is Nora Ridgeway. Nora's a teacher. Nora, meet Clay and Jericho. They grew up around here and served with me in the SEALs."

"Nice to meet you," Nora murmured. She sent a furtive glance toward the departures board.

"You catching a plane somewhere?" Clay set down his bags, shook her hand, and held onto it. Jericho waited for his turn, his hand half raised, but after a moment he let it fall again. Nora didn't notice.

"I... think so. You won't tell Riley you saw me here, will you? I need a head start." She extricated her hand from Clay's.

"Riley said you miss teaching a lot. Are you going back?"

She nodded. "I have to. I'm not used to being a quitter. I was helping those kids. Some of them, anyway."

"Sounds like it was a pretty rough situation, though." All Boone could think to do was delay Nora. He knew Riley would be devastated if her friend gave up on Westfield, and if Nora left, what would the others do? If Savannah and Avery quit, too, Riley would have no reason to stay on the ranch.

No reason to marry him, either.

"It was." Her indecision was all too clear. Boone wondered if he could capitalize on it, but Clay beat him to the punch.

"Aren't you going to miss your friends if you leave?" he asked.

Nora glanced back up at the monitor, but nodded. "Definitely. I missed them for years when we all lived in different places. No one else I know is quite like Riley and the others. I know they think I hold back a lot—that maybe I'm not as into the group thing as they are, but they're wrong."

"Maybe there's a compromise," Clay suggested. "What if you found a teaching job in Chance Creek?"

Nora bit her lip. "I've looked. There's nothing suitable. And what about the kids I left behind?"

"Won't they already have a new teacher? It seems pretty disruptive to change things a second time. I had a teacher go on maternity leave one year when I was a kid. It shook everything up when the new teacher came in. Then, just when we got used to her, the first one came back. Talk about confusion."

Boone had to hand it to him, Clay was thinking on his feet.

"Riley and the others are going to be pretty upset if you leave," Boone added. He touched her arm. "Maybe you should give Westfield another chance. What do you think? At least until you know for sure what you want to do next?"

He held his breath waiting for her answer. He had a feeling Clay was, too. His friend couldn't keep his eyes off of Nora. So much for pairing him with Savannah.

"Why do you care what I do?"

That was the Nora Boone recognized. He held his breath, wondering how Clay would react.

"For purely selfish reasons." Clay flashed her a thousand-watt smile. "I'm about to live in close quarters with three other guys. Cut me a break if I'm hungry for a glimpse of a pretty woman now and then."

Nora rolled her eyes, but a smile quirked her lips too. "Maybe you're right. It would be stupid to run away. I should at least talk to the others first."

"Don't be too hard on yourself. You're caught in a tough situation," Clay said softly. He took the suitcase from Nora's hand. "Come on, we'll take you home. You can use me as a sounding board. Maybe I can help."

"Thanks."

Boone breathed a sigh of relief as he picked up the bags that Clay had left behind. Jericho fell in beside him and they followed them out to his truck.

Disaster averted.

For now.

AS HARD AS the work had been, Riley felt a sense of real accomplishment when she stood back and gazed at a week's worth of their clothing and linens hanging on the long clothesline that stretched between two stout wooden posts in the side yard. Her hands were cramped and red, her work dress soaked, and her hair hung in damp tendrils around her face, but she'd done it.

She wondered if Nora was feeling any better. Riley certainly hoped so—nothing would be the same if she gave up and left.

She turned a suspicious eye toward the west where

some innocent looking white cumulous clouds had taken on a darker hue. If rain threatened, she'd have to move all the damp clothing inside and hang it down in the basement. They'd cleaned the space, but it was still dank and a little frightening. She didn't look forward to moving the heavy wet laundry and hoped the rain would hold off.

Something else caught her eye when she headed back to the fire and the heavy pots of water sitting near it. Puffs of dirt far off told her some vehicle was moving down the driveway toward her. Boone back from the airport. She didn't want any of the men to see her like this. Instead of tipping over the pots and cleaning up her mess, she hurried into the house and up the stairs to her room. She was struggling out of her wet dress when Savannah found her.

"Need help?" She asked with a laugh.

"Yes. Hurry!"

"Why?" She helped tug the dress over Riley's head.

Riley bit her lip. She didn't want to say, but Savannah went on. "Let me guess. Boone's coming?"

"I'm not doing this for Boone."

"Of course not."

Riley knew she wasn't fooling anyone. She appreciated that Savannah didn't tease her about it. She fetched the dress she wanted from the closet and Savannah helped pull it over her head. She did up the fastenings and patted Riley's shoulder. "Do your hair, quick. I'll run down and greet him."

"He's bringing friends home from the airport."

"More Navy SEALs? I'm on my way!"

CHAPTER TEN

★

"**N**OW, THAT'S A house. I'd forgotten how big Westfield is," Clay said when they pulled up in front of the manor.

"It's ridiculously inefficient," Boone reminded him. What was it about Westfield that sucked everyone in? He supposed it was the stone façade, its regal bearing perched atop the rise of ground, and the craftsmanship that had gone into building it.

"It's ridiculously beautiful, you mean," Nora said pertly. "You should see it inside," she added to Clay.

"I'd love to. It's got great lines. That stone work is amazing."

"I'd like to see it, too," Jericho put in.

"Do you know how much it will take to heat this house in a few months?" Boone said, stung by his friends' betrayal.

"I didn't say I wanted to move in," Jericho said. "I was just admiring…hello!"

Boone suppressed a smile at Jericho's reaction as Savannah burst out of the front door and skipped down the steps, her skirts swirling around her. He was zero for two as far as his matchmaking went, but that didn't matter, as long as each of his friends found a bride.

"That can't be Riley," Jericho said, leaning forward for a better look.

"That's Savannah," Nora answered before Boone could. "She's pretty, isn't she?"

Clay shrugged. "I prefer brunettes."

Boone decided to encourage his friends' interest in the manor, after all. "You two should check the place out. You'll see immediately what I mean about inefficiencies, though."

"Would you show me around?" Clay asked Nora. He opened his door, climbed out, and turned to hand her out of the cab.

"I'd be glad to. First I'd better change, though."

"Nora! Riley said you were out for a walk. What are you doing with Boone—and why are you dressed—" Savannah put her hands on her hips. "You ran away."

Nora nodded. "But I came back."

"Thank God." Savannah rushed to embrace her. Boone stepped away to give them some space. Clay and Jericho followed him.

"Is Savannah seeing someone?" Jericho asked, lowering his voice.

"As far as I know, she's fair game." Boone clapped him on the back. "Go for it." He saw Nora pull away from her friend and hurry toward the house. "Let's see about that tour."

Savannah waited for them. "Nora needs to change,

so why don't we go inside and have a cup of tea?" She led the way through the door toward the back of the house. When they reached the kitchen, they found Avery. Boone made the introductions. "Savannah, Avery, these are my good friends and fellow Navy SEALs, Clay Pickett and Jericho Cook. They've come to help me set up our sustainable community."

"Nice to meet you." Savannah curtsied prettily.

"Yes, nice to meet you." Avery smiled at both men coquettishly, but Boone could see the war had been lost already. Clay kept looking down the hall to see if Nora was coming back. Jericho had eyes for no one but Savannah.

"Nice to meet you, too," Clay said. He bowed over Avery's hand, then Savannah's.

Jericho took his turn, but it was Savannah's hand he lingered over. Boone saw Avery take that in and frown.

"I hope you two are more amenable to music and dancing than Boone is," Savannah said. "The Russells offered us a musical evening soon. I'm not sure Boone was interested."

"Who are the Russells?" Clay asked.

"Wait until you see them." Boone took in the affronted expressions on the ladies' faces and backtracked. "Nicest people you'll ever know, but they've been bitten by the Austen bug."

"I can't blame them. I have to admit it's tempting," Jericho said with a smile for Savannah. "I'd love to hear more about your plans."

"Me, too," Clay said.

That was all it took for Savannah and Avery to launch into a detailed description of their Regency lives. Boone was relieved when Riley appeared in the doorway. She'd changed out of her work dress into a simple but pretty gown he'd seen her in the week before. She'd fixed her hair, too, but her cheeks were flushed with exertion. She came to greet Clay and Jericho, executing the same little curtsy the others had. "Clay, Jericho. Good to see you again."

Boone saw the uncertainty in her eyes and he was glad when both of his friends greeted her warmly—without any teasing.

"Good to see you, too, Riley," Clay said and gave her a quick hug. "I was sorry to hear about your grandparents."

"Me, too," Jericho said. He embraced Riley, too, and she relaxed.

"It was hard when they went, but it's been a long time. I'm just glad I'm here."

"We're glad, too," Jericho said. His gaze slid to Savannah again.

"I'm also glad Boone isn't the only man on the property anymore. You don't know what we've had to put up with so far," Riley said, getting bolder.

"I can guess." Clay smiled. "Don't worry, honey. We'll protect you from the big, bad wolf here." He clapped a hand on Boone's shoulder. Boone shook him off. "Savannah's been telling me all about the musical evening that the Russells have suggested. Sounds like fun."

"We'll definitely attend," Jericho said.

"Everyone ready for tea?" Avery took the kettle off the hook where it had hung over the fire, filled a teapot and once the tea had steeped, she poured a cup for each of them.

Tea in the large kitchen was pleasant, but Boone doubted the women would want the fire going when the summer heated up. He suspected they'd go back to using their modern stove then. Still, it intrigued him they liked to experiment with old-fashioned techniques. Maybe the sustainable methods they used down at Base Camp would interest them, too.

When Nora returned, back in her Regency gown, Clay's face lit up and Boone caught the other women exchanging a surprised glance. Riley's lips pinched together and he could almost see her digging in her heels for a fight.

Time for a tactical retreat. He set his teacup down, even though he'd only taken a sip or two, and clapped Clay on the back. "We'd better go."

"But—"

"Both of you. We've got work to do."

"ALL I'M SAYING is I don't want to leave when our six months is up," Avery said late that afternoon as Nora took her turn with the cell phone.

"I know what you mean," Riley said as she gathered up her painting supplies. She'd had far more luck today and had actually applied paint to canvas now that she had a few sketches she liked. She loved the feel of her brushes in her hand and was happy with the results. Trying to recapture some of the confidence of her college days, she'd painted in thick, broad, curving strokes, bringing motion to a windswept landscape reminiscent of the one out their windows.

She wondered if it was time to break the news of her engagement to her friends. Maybe it was time for them to have a conversation about their long-term plans. She needed to warn them about Jericho and Clay, too, although she figured she might be too late.

"We'd need to find work if we wanted to stay," Nora said.

"I looked at job listings for Chance Creek when I had the phone, but there aren't many," Avery told her.

"I searched for teaching jobs yesterday," Nora said. "There's one for sixth grade, but that's not my favorite age."

Riley was heartened they were even having the discussion. If she was going to stay here with Boone, she dreaded the time when her friends moved on. "You never know what's really available," she told Nora. "Maybe you should go into town and let them know you're—"

She was interrupted by a whoop from Savannah, who was in the kitchen.

"Are you okay?" Nora called to her.

Savannah hurried into the parlor. "My cousin's getting married. She just got engaged and she's so excited! I've been telling her about our adventures here. She wants to know if she can come and have a Jane Austen wedding. What a hoot!" She bent over her phone and started tapping an answer.

"What a brilliant idea, you mean." Avery dropped the book she'd been reading. "Why couldn't we throw her a wedding here? That would be so much fun!"

"A wedding is a big deal," Nora said. "There's catering, flowers, seating arrangements—"

"We could do all that. Easy! Couldn't we, Riley? Would Boone mind?"

"I don't know. We could ask, I guess." Avery was right; it would be fun to throw a Regency wedding. They'd have plenty of practice after her wedding, which was coming up far sooner than she wanted to acknowledge.

"Ohmygod." Avery stood up. "Ohmygod, ohmygod! I know what we can do. Start a business! A Jane Austen wedding business! And a B&B. A Regency B&B! We'd run it from Westfield and we'd never have to leave!"

Nora looked to Riley. "I don't think Boone's going to let us stay here forever."

"But it's a great idea." Savannah lowered her phone. "We could charge top dollar for it, too."

"We're supposed to be taking a break from work, remember?" Nora said.

"We'll still take our break. We don't have to start the business right away," Avery said. "When's your cousin's wedding? Not for months, right?"

"I don't know." Savannah started to type again.

"We said we'd take six months off," Avery went on,

"but after that we need to earn a living. Why not run a B&B?"

"What would Boone say?" Savannah looked up from her phone.

Riley wasn't sure when she'd become his spokesman. "I don't know, except that it would have to be sustainable, and we'd definitely have to wait until the end of the year."

"Have to?" Savannah questioned.

Riley figured it was as good a time as any to clarify some things. "Base Camp is going to be center stage for a reality television series. I don't know much about it, but I do know they'll be filming for six months."

"What kind of television show?"

"When does it start?"

They flooded her with questions and she did her best to answer them.

"Will we be okay up here?" Nora asked.

"Yes." At least she thought so. Boone hadn't actually specified that, Riley realized. She understood that being on the show was part of the commitment she'd made when she agreed to marry him, but she had assumed her friends would be off limits. Was she wrong?

Riley stilled. The more she thought about it, the more she realized how little Boone had told her about the show. Had he been deliberately vague?

She'd better find out soon.

"Is it even possible to make the manor sustainable?" Nora asked. "It's a big place."

"Boone said he'd install solar panels and he talked about wind, too," Riley told her.

Savannah finished her message. "If we wanted to make a go of it, we'd make it super-exclusive. Word-of-mouth advertising and limited availability. If we were willing to stick to a budget, we could set things up so we worked one week out of every four, and spend the rest of the time on our own pursuits." The idea seemed to please her. "We'd charge a premium for weddings, spread the word about how exclusive it is, and we'd turn down more people than we'd accept."

Riley had to admire her business acumen. "Did you learn that in Silicon Valley?"

"It works the world over. People like to feel like they're getting something other people can't."

"I think Westfield's pretty special." Avery came to give Riley a hug. "Have I thanked you enough for bringing me here?"

"It's my pleasure." Riley's heart thumped with anticipation. If the plan worked, she wouldn't lose her friends after all. But what if the television show encompassed the manor, too?

Savannah's phone chimed. "It's Andrea." She read the message and her face fell. "Well, forget about holding her wedding; they've decided to put things on a fast track." She looked up with a rueful grin. "She wants to know if we can host it here on May twenty-second."

Avery gawked at her. "In two weeks?"

"That's not going to happen," Nora said.

Riley bit her lip, taking in their dejected expressions.

"The show won't have started by then," she said slowly. "I guess I could ask if you want me to." After all, it could be their only chance. Once the show started, her friends might not want to stay at Westfield.

"Would you?" Savannah said, brightening at once.

"Of course. Boone's coming over in a few hours." Riley went back to tidying her things, but she found it hard to concentrate.

What would Boone say to their request?

WHEN BOONE PICKED Riley up that evening, she was in a pensive mood. After walking all the way back down the hill and continuing on the path that led toward the creek, he gave up on small talk. Instead, he tugged her down to sit beside him on the riverbank. "What's wrong?"

"I keep remembering how it used to be when we were kids."

"What were you remembering?" He was distracted by a strand of hair that had escaped from her bonnet. He wanted to smooth it into place, but he was afraid to break her train of thought.

"How I spent so much time tagging after you and Clay and the others. I was so concerned with whether or not you liked me, I spent all my time doing the things you wanted to do rather than the things I liked to do."

He stilled. This conversation was going to be more serious than he'd expected. "We bossed you around a lot."

"Yes."

"I wish I'd treated you better."

"I learned a lot from you, too."

"I'm glad I did something right."

She leaned forward to trail a hand in the water. She wasn't looking at him. That told him he'd better proceed with care.

"Something else on your mind?"

"I'm not a little girl chasing a crush anymore. I'm a grown-up. I can't set everything aside for you."

He lifted her free hand into his lap and rubbed her fingers. "Is that what you think I'm asking you to do?"

"Isn't it?"

He gave that some consideration. He could see how she would think so. "Is this about something specific?" He stopped caressing her fingers, but kept her hand trapped in his.

"I came here to be with my friends, to take a break from the hustle and bustle of life, but the minute I got here you made demands of me and now in less than a month we're going to marry. What then? Will I have to work in your hydroponic garden all day while Savannah and the others live the life I was supposed to?"

"I guess I hoped you'd be at least a little bit interested in what I was doing."

"I could be," she said, "but it would be easier if I didn't feel I had to resist you all the time. Because you've forced me into this marriage, I can't relax and simply enjoy you. I feel like we're enemies."

"We're not enemies," he told her.

"But if you can strong-arm me into a wedding, you

can strong-arm me into anything. I can't help wondering what else you might have up your sleeve." She finally turned to face him.

Boone was uneasy. He still hadn't told her about Montague and the consequences to Westfield if he failed to meet the goals Fulsom had set. He needed to warn Riley about what was coming.

Not now, though. Her mood was far too fragile. She reminded him of a doe at the edge of the woods, pausing to sniff the air for danger. One wrong word and she'd flee.

"We'll have to compromise, like every husband and wife," he said carefully. "I won't keep you from your friends, though. I promise."

"So you'll let me spend my days at the manor?"

"Some of them—"

"But not my nights." It was a statement, not a question.

Of course he expected her to share his bed. Didn't she want that, too? His uneasiness grew. "I'll want you with me," he affirmed. He didn't want to compromise on that.

"Then it won't be the same. If I wake up in the middle of the night, I won't meet up with Savannah in the kitchen."

"No, you'll meet up with me."

"What good are you?" she said grumpily and pulled her hand away.

He smiled and took it back. "Let me show you."

RILEY DIDN'T MEAN to respond when Boone kissed her. Her concerns were serious. She'd realized that even if her friends stayed through the filming of the television show, it wouldn't be the same when she moved down to Boone's community. Everyone else would live at the manor. She'd live in a tiny house. There probably wouldn't be room to paint.

If only she didn't feel so torn between them. Every time she talked to Boone he told her more about his intentions and some of his plans were fascinating. She'd long heard of the idea of closed-cycle gardening, but had never seen someone actually put the theory into practice. Boone and the Horsemen had made such careful arrangements. It touched her to think that the four rowdy boys she'd known had grown up into men who cared so much about the world.

She felt hesitant every time she engaged with Boone about his ideas, however, because she knew if she got too involved with them, she could easily lose her chance to paint. She'd wanted something different when she came here—a kind of artistic idyll in which she didn't have to think or work so hard.

But Boone's kisses made her tingle all over and Riley couldn't help responding to him. The more his mouth moved over hers, the harder time she had remembering her grievances. What did she care where she lived as long as Boone would touch her the way he was doing now? His hands sliding over her skin felt so good.

"You've got too many clothes on," Boone said.

"So do you."

When his hands found the ties that bound up the back of her dress, Riley acquiesced with a look and Boone undid them. The more he fumbled, the more she wanted the dress gone. She got busy with the buttons of his shirt, and succeeded in almost unbuttoning all of them before Boone uttered an oath, gathered up her voluminous skirts and lifted her gown right up and over her head. He tossed it aside on the riverbank and took in her underthings.

"Our ancestors were sadists."

Riley chuckled. "It's all part of the fun."

"You have a strange definition of fun." But he got to work on her stays and chemise while Riley got the rest of his buttons undone and pushed the cotton shirt over his shoulders. His muscles were a work of art, each and every one of them bulging in high relief against his skin. Scars marred his chest and arms. Riley longed to know the history behind each one, but feared to hear Boone's stories at the same time. It was difficult to think of all the times he must have been in danger.

Boone extricated her from her stays. Riley's pulse beat double-time as he slid her chemise off and hooked his fingers under the band of the barely-there panties she wore underneath, the one non-Regency luxury she allowed herself. The skim of his finger as he pulled them down sent sensation thrilling through her veins. Riley wanted so much more from him. She tangled her hands in the waistband of his jeans, trying to undo the button and get them off. She couldn't wait to feel him in her hands. Just knowing he'd be inside of her soon made her ache with longing.

"You've been holding back. I thought maybe you wanted to wait for our wedding night," she teased him.

"To hell with that." Boone helped her free him from his clothes and when he stood in front of her, she couldn't help but drop to her knees to worship him.

"Riley—" His voice was a strangled moan as she took him into her mouth, reveling in the feel of his hardness. Feeling the girth of him made her blood throb. Soon he'd push inside of her. She loved that sensation more than anything else. Feeling her body yield to him—

But not yet.

First she had to give him the attention he was due.

She took her time exploring him with her mouth, tasting him, testing the texture of his skin with her tongue. The muscles in Boone's thighs flexed as he braced against her movements. He surrendered to her with his eyes closed, one hand tangled in her hair, guiding her head as she moved, caressing him and coaxing him to harden even more.

She could tell he was straining to stay in control, and she couldn't help experimenting with a few flicks of her tongue to see if she could force him over the brink. He caught her up and raised her to stand, too, despite her protestations, covering her mouth with his to stem the tide of her words. Kicking his clothes into place to create a kind of bed for them, he laid her down gently, never breaking off their kiss. Once she lay on her back, it was his turn to conquer her with his mouth. He explored every inch of her body, brushing his lips over her skin. When he played with her breasts, Riley found herself panting with need, but when he moved lower to bring his mouth to her sensitive core, she didn't think she could hold on much longer.

She whimpered and he was back at her side in an instant. "Tell me what you want."

"You, inside of me."

"Now?"

How could he tease her like this? "Right now!"

Boone chuckled. "You got it." But he paused again. "Should I use a condom?"

She didn't want him to, but prudence made her nod.

He dug one out of the pocket of his jeans and quickly sheathed himself.

When Boone straddled her, gave himself a few strokes in preparation and eased down to nudge against her, Riley moaned aloud. When he pushed inside an inch at a time, she thought she'd melt right into the ground.

Boone felt so good. She was content to let him make love to her, curious as to how he would set about it. As she'd hoped, he wasted no more time with foreplay. He pulled out and surged into her a second time, this time fast and hard, just the way she liked it. As his movements increased in tempo so did Riley's pleasure until she could have sworn that her skin was glowing with the beauty of the shared act.

As he plunged inside of her, Riley held on, blessing

the fates that had brought them together again. She might have gone through life never knowing this— bereft of Boone forever.

As Boone brought her to the precipice and pushed her over into a flood of heat and pulsing sensation, Riley realized that she didn't want to give Boone up, no matter what. Boone came with her, grunting as he pulsed inside her again, wrapping his arms around her and surrounding her until he became her whole world. When he finally stopped and fell on top of her, breathing as hard as she was, Riley bore his weight gladly.

She couldn't do without Boone.

Now she had to figure out how to get everything else she wanted, too.

"YOU'VE GONE QUIET again," Boone said as they lay on the banks of Pittance Creek and stared at the stars visible overhead between the trees that lined either side of the waterway.

"How do you feel about weddings?" Riley turned on her side. Boone loved the curve of her hip, the dip of her waist and the way her breasts spilled forward against the arm she was leaning on.

"If you're talking about our wedding, I'm all for it."

"I'm talking about one in particular, but not ours."

"Whose?"

"Savannah's cousin Andrea. She mentioned she'd like a Jane Austen wedding, and we thought it might be a good idea."

Boone sat up cross-legged. "You want to hold her

wedding here?"

"At the manor. The four of us could do a fantastic job, and we'd earn some money doing it, which wouldn't hurt. In fact, we wondered if we should make a business out of it."

"You'd turn Westfield into a wedding venue?"

"And a B&B. Down the line, when the show's over."

"I guess I don't see any harm in that. Although it's got to be sustainable."

"Of course. You and the Horsemen could help us. We'd run everything off solar and wind power; that would be part of our schtick. A sustainable Jane Austen B&B and wedding venue."

It was the first time he'd seen Riley get excited about the topic of sustainability, and he could finally see a way to pull the women into his community. If they took charge of running the manor sustainably, they would likely get interested in what his men were doing at Base Camp. He could assign Jericho and Clay to help Savannah and Nora get used to the equipment, and maybe speed along the romances that seemed possible to bloom between them.

"I like it," Boone said.

"There's just one problem."

"What's that?"

"Savannah's cousin wants to be married in two weeks."

"Two weeks?" Boone chuckled. "That doesn't give you much time."

"We can do it. The question is, will you let us?"

"Sure." He didn't see why not. In fact, it seemed like a good idea, because it had occurred to Boone they might have a problem he hadn't foreseen. Fulsom was eccentric, but not in a Jane Austen way. He wouldn't want period characters traipsing around his television show, and Boone didn't know how to persuade him it would be a good thing. That meant he'd need to get Riley out of her Regency clothes by June first. He'd promised her a Regency wedding, but maybe she'd be satisfied with throwing one for Savannah's cousin, instead.

He knelt down, ready to talk it over with her, just as Riley surged up onto her knees and flung her arms around his neck.

"Thank you! I knew you'd be reasonable! You won't regret it, I swear!"

Boone decided to put off the rest of the conversation until another day.

"HE SAID YES?" Avery grabbed Riley's hands and jumped up and down like a child.

"We can have the wedding here?" Savannah said, coming to join them in the front hall.

"And run the B&B?" Nora added, standing up from the sofa in the parlor.

Riley nodded. Boone had come up with as many suggestions as she had for how to bring their B&B and wedding venue in line with his sustainable community over the next few months. "He's going to draw up plans for increased solar and wind energy production and help us get the manor all wired up. As long as we run our ideas by him to figure out how to make them compatible with Base Camp, it's okay. We can have the wedding before filming starts and run the B&B after it ends."

"That's amazing! Now we can stay here indefinitely!" Avery couldn't keep still. "I want to shout it to the rooftops!"

"How about you, Nora? Are you on board?" Riley held her breath while she waited for her friend's answer.

"It isn't teaching, but it's a start," Nora said. "I really don't want to go back to Baltimore, but I have to do something useful."

"You'll have to do a lot of useful things if we're going to host weddings."

"How did you get Boone to agree to let us do this?" Savannah asked.

"And how much rent will we have to pay now that we're going to run a business on his property?" Nora chimed in.

"We didn't settle that, but I know he'll be fair." She felt a glow she'd missed ever since Boone had left Chance Creek all those years ago. After making love a second time, they'd thrown themselves into planning how the B&B could work. For the first time since they were teens, they were working together rather than getting in each other's way. Their ideas had tripped over each other, they came so fast, and the more they talked, the more excited she'd become—both about the B&B, and about making it sustainable.

Until now, sustainability had been a theory, too complicated for her to carry out in her own life. With Boone, she saw how she could master it, and that excited her. She would participate in one of the most important conversations of her time, not just read about it as a bystander.

Savannah smiled. "Riley Eaton, you seduced that cowboy, didn't you?"

"It was kind of mutual," she said.

"You're really sleeping with Boone?" Avery bounced again. "That's awesome!"

Even Nora looked amused. "I thought you two might be getting serious."

"Are you going to marry him? Can we throw your wedding, too?" Avery said.

"Don't get ahead of yourselves." But Riley couldn't help bite her lip, her secret nearly bursting out. Her upcoming marriage didn't seem like a farce anymore. She'd learned tonight that Boone was someone she could dream with—and that their dreams weren't so far apart after all.

"Are you engaged?" Savannah grabbed her hand and frowned when she saw Riley's ring finger was still bare.

Riley didn't know what to say. She was almost ready to tell them… but not quite.

She held up her hand and displayed her bare finger. "You'll be the first to know when there's a ring on it," she promised. "Is there anything left from dinner? I'm starving."

"Midnight snack!" Avery whooped and dashed toward the kitchen.

"We need to find her a man next," Nora said.

"What's Walker like?" Savannah asked Riley.

CHAPTER ELEVEN

★

"I'VE GOT SOME good news and some bad news," Boone said when Julie finally patched him through directly to Fulsom. He sat in the bunkhouse on a metal folding chair in front of his new desk—a large surface Clay had knocked together from scrap wood he'd found around the place. It was far more sturdy, functional—and cool—than any such thing had a right to be, but then that was Clay, a genius at carpentry. Fulsom stared back at him from the screen of his laptop.

"Good news?"

"We've got scores of responses to the ad from men wanting to participate in the project. After a preliminary look I can say with confidence we'll ramp up to ten easily during the course of the show."

"What about women?"

"I'm happy to announce my engagement. My wedding is set for June first—when we'll be filming the first episode. We have three other women interested in the project." Not a total lie. They were interested even if they weren't participating yet.

"You'll need more than that, but congratulations—you've made a good start. What's the bad news?"

"My fiancée and several of her friends are very interested in the Regency period."

Fulsom frowned, his patience obviously waning. "What does that have to do with me?"

"Before I committed to your show, she committed to a six month experiment living a Jane Austen-style Regency life."

"Jane Austen?" Fulsom scowled. "Are we talking *Pride and Prejudice*?"

"They're staying in the manor at Westfield—"

"In the middle of your sustainable community? Are you shitting me?"

Boone sighed. He'd known this wasn't going to go well. "It's not in the middle of the community. It's—"

"No. Absolutely not." Julie's arm appeared on the screen as she tried to hand Fulsom a piece of paperwork. He grabbed it from her, scrawled a signature and tossed it aside. Julie caught it just before it hit the floor. "And I want to know right now, are you serious about this project or not?"

"Sir, I—"

"I don't want to hear another goddamned word about Regency anything. Have I made myself clear? You get your people pointed in the same direction. Sustainable community or nothing. That's the way we'll play this. Got it?"

"Got it, sir."

Fulsom cut the call. Boone stared at the screen.

He'd known this would be Fulsom's answer, but he'd hoped he was wrong.

He was an idiot for thinking it could turn out any other way, though, and he dreaded the conversation he needed to have with Riley. Last night had been... amazing. There was no other word to describe it. The way she'd looked at him after they'd been together had rendered him speechless. And when she'd drawn him down again, ready for another round of lovemaking, it had been even better than the first time. He wasn't sure how that was possible.

Sweetest of all had been their walk back to Westfield. Finally on the same page, they couldn't talk fast enough to keep up with their ideas. By melding their visions, Boone instinctively knew he'd won her over to his cause.

She wanted to marry him.

Now he had to tell her to mothball her Regency life until the series was over?

She'd never agree to it. He'd lose her—and for what?

For the chance to get an important message out to the American public, he reminded himself.

Fulsom wasn't wrong; Riley's B&B confused the message. It would confuse viewers. Boone had seen enough reality television to know the recipe: simple message, simple storyline, lots of human interest. One big goal at the end.

Jane Austen didn't fit anywhere in that formula.

But how could he tell Riley?

"LAUNDRY DAY, I see?" Maud said several days later when Riley was just wringing out a dress and adding it to the stack of others in preparation for hanging them on the clothesline. She looked up to see both Maud and James had managed to sneak up on her. It was the second time she'd performed the arduous task, but she didn't mind it. The physical work left her mind free to wander, and she had so much to think about these days. She'd decided the trick was to do the laundry more frequently, so there was less to wash at one time.

Andrea had jumped at the chance to hold her wedding at Westfield. "She's waited five years for him to propose," Savannah said to explain her cousin's extremely short engagement. "She's afraid if she waits too long he'll change his mind again. That's why she wants to host it here. She knows it'll be unique and she won't be able to find a venue this last-minute in California." They were already working like crazy to be ready on time, but the truth was, Riley was excited, too. She was sure they could pull it off, and Savannah had dropped hints that Andrea's family was very well connected. The word-of-mouth advertising she and her friends might give them couldn't be beat.

Savannah had taken charge of the project and had written up huge to-do lists for each of them. Now every moment of their spare time was taken with wedding preparations, but although they'd shortened their afternoon creative hours, they'd made a promise to each other not to abandon them altogether. Riley had begun a new painting that really interested her. It was another

landscape, but it included the manor and the outbuildings. She was trying to contrast the manmade house and
barns with their natural setting. She was struggling
toward some kind of understanding she couldn't quite
grasp yet, but she was confident it would come. This
was what she'd missed about art.

"Looks like hard work," Maud went on, lifting her
skirts and coming closer. "You ladies need to hire help."

"We probably will in the future." Riley's hand drifted down to her abdomen. In a day or so she'd be able to
take a pregnancy test and it was hard to think of anything else. She didn't feel pregnant, but she wasn't sure
if she was supposed to feel anything this early on.

"I can't tell you how pleased I am that you four
have come to town. Westfield is a special place. It
deserves special treatment."

Riley nodded and plunged the last dress into the
scalding hot water. She'd already done the sheets, towels
and other household linens. She was getting faster at the
job.

"How are your preparations going for Savannah's
cousin's wedding?"

"There's still so much to do." Riley kept working.
"You should see our lists." She knew if she didn't start
on her own wedding plans soon, she'd never be ready
for June first, either.

"I came to make you an offer. I know you'll try to
refuse because you're so well-mannered, but I want you
to consider it carefully. I hope you'll indulge an old
woman."

"You're not old," Riley told her.

Maud waved that away. "Just listen. I'd like you to borrow Mrs. Wood for the duration of the wedding party's stay."

Riley sat back on her heels. "We couldn't do that. We can't afford—"

"I'll pay her wages. She'll simply report to you instead of me." Maud looked very satisfied with this idea, but Riley was already shaking her head.

"That's way too expensive. We couldn't possibly—"

"Nonsense, dear. You'll let Mrs. Wood help you and that's that. I insist."

Riley faced Maud with exasperation. "That's far too extravagant."

"You can't stop her. She's a very determined woman," James put in with a smile.

Maud tutted. "It would be downright mean of you to deprive Mrs. Wood of this opportunity. She loves to cook for a crowd. She heads up the food committee for the re-enactment group every year. She's a genius at cooking over an open hearth and she hardly gets a chance to do it. You have no idea how happy it would make her. I've explained to Mrs. Wood about Avery's interest in historical cooking and she's agreed to teach Avery all her little tricks when there's time."

"I've heard the Civil War re-enactments are a big thing in the summertime." Riley gave up. They needed a caterer, after all, and Mrs. Wood was a fantastic cook.

"You should see it. The whole thing was petering out about eight years ago and there was talk about shutting it down. Then we had a resurgence and now the club is bigger than ever. It's become an event everyone loves."

"I look forward to it."

"Back to the wedding," James said. "You'll need carriages and drivers. With livery. We've got just the thing."

"Oh, but—"

"I've been waiting for an occasion to pull our old covered buggy out of storage," he said. "I know a couple of young bucks who'd enjoy the work."

Riley's protests were all in vain. "I can't let you and Maud fund our entire venture," she finally exclaimed.

"My darling girl, someday I hope you'll understand how tiresome it is when you've amassed great wealth and no one will allow you to spend it on them. Why on earth did I work all these years if I'm not allowed to enjoy it?"

Riley had never seen the dear old man so serious. She stood up and hugged him impulsively. "I don't know what to do with you two."

"Enjoy us as much as we're enjoying you," Maud advised her. "And let my dear husband have some fun organizing things for you!"

"I can do that—as long as you agree to be guests of honor at the wedding!"

"WHAT'S EATING YOU?" Clay asked when he stumbled on Boone pacing the bunkhouse later that day.

Boone decided it was time to confess. "I think I

screwed up. Big time."

"Uh-oh. What'd you do?" Clay leaned against the desk he'd built for Boone. "It can't be that bad, can it?"

"Worse." Boone related his discussion with Fulsom.

Clay whistled. "Why haven't you said anything to Riley?"

"Because she's going to be upset. I told her she could have a Regency wedding. I said I wouldn't separate her from her friends. Now I have to tell her I was full of shit."

"At least they can hold Savannah's cousin's wedding. Filming won't start until a week later."

"I hope that cushions the blow a bit," Boone said. "But what if Riley calls everything off?"

"Maybe you two should move your wedding up and get it done before Fulsom comes. You could always do a second wedding for the show." He eyed Boone speculatively. "Should I be worried about the fact Riley still hasn't told her friends about your engagement?"

"I sure am," Boone said.

"I noticed she's not wearing a ring, either."

"I haven't bought it yet." Boone couldn't look Clay in the eye. "I was…" He'd been about to say afraid, but he didn't want to admit that. "I was worried that I'd jinx it somehow. Like if I bought the ring too soon it would mean it wouldn't happen."

"You're not usually superstitious."

"I've never wanted anything this much."

Clay rubbed the back of his neck. "Time to buy that ring, Boone. Time to tell her the truth, too. You can't mix marriage with lies, I know that much."

"What if she says no?" Boone asked.

"You'll have to find someone else."

"I can't do that."

Clay pushed away from the desk. "Then tell her it's only for six months, and we'll do everything we can to make it up to them later."

"I guess that's our only shot," Boone said.

But he didn't think it would work.

"THEY MAKE A good couple, don't you think?" Boone whispered into Riley's ear the following night. They were seated on a divan in the Russells' parlor watching Savannah play the piano and Jericho turn the pages for her. Jericho had already botched it once. Riley was beginning to suspect he didn't actually read music. But his interest in Savannah was plain to see and it worried her.

She'd wanted to warn her friends about the men, but she couldn't do that without telling them about her own engagement—and why she'd initially agreed to it. If they thought she was only marrying Boone to save Westfield, they'd have all kinds of objections. As much as they loved the manor and their plans for it, none of them would understand why she'd go so far to save it. They didn't understand her past and what it meant to her.

It was all so complicated. She loved Boone, even as she knew she had to protect herself from his tendency to rank Base Camp above her aspirations. It hurt to know that what was important to her came second in his book, but at the same time she could understand his position. If you believed you could alleviate future suffering, it made sense to focus on taking those steps. But wasn't there a balance?

"I'm not sure," she said to Boone. "I don't entirely trust Jericho's intentions."

"I think he intends to care about Savannah."

"But does he intend to care about what she cares about?" Riley asked.

She wanted her friends to fall in love with good, decent men. Jericho and Clay fit that bill. Still, they shared Boone's obsession. She didn't want Nora and Savannah to face the gut-wrenching choices she was having to make. Savannah had been spending every spare moment at the piano. Nora was back to working on her novel. If Clay or Jericho put an end to that, she'd be furious.

"He'd do his best," Boone said.

"I'm not sure that's good enough."

It wasn't entirely fair of her to say that. Boone had been trying to work out with her how to balance their competing interests, but she still couldn't shake the sense that Base Camp—and Fulsom's orders—would always come first. As they talked more about the show, Boone had begun to hint that it might take up most of her time. It had been a blow to realize she'd have to shelve her painting for another six months, especially when she was beginning to make progress. Still, if it meant she could hold onto Westfield and build a future here long term, she could handle that. What made it difficult was that Boone didn't have to give up anything. On the contrary, he always got what he wanted. She'd agreed to move down to Base Camp for the duration of the filming. She'd agreed to help out with his projects. She'd agreed to hold their wedding on camera. It was hard not to resent Boone when everything skewed his way.

The piece came to an end and everyone clapped. As a musical evening, the night had been a great success. The Russells had invited the Halls, too, and while their modern clothing made a contrast in the parlor, the musical members of that family had jumped right in to play, too. Regan turned out to be a whiz on the piano, while Storm had a wonderful singing voice, but Riley enjoyed most of all the rousing chant offered up by the Hall men, apparently a tame version of the ones they'd all learned in their various branches of the military during basic training.

The evening was filled with chatter and laughter and Riley wished she could enjoy it as much as everyone else was. She tried her best, leaving her hand clasped in Boone's as they listened to the '60s ballad Ella chose to sing.

She had begun to get excited about the wedding they were planning for Andrea, who had decided to come to Westfield several days early with all her bridesmaids and spend an extended weekend at the manor. She and her bridesmaids wanted a Jane Austen experience, and Savannah had gotten their measurements and had contacted Alice Reed, the local seamstress Regan had mentioned, who was excited to create several gowns for each participant.

Alice had stopped by that morning with sketches and examples of her work, and all of them had been stunned to see her beautiful creations. Riley and the rest had immediately commissioned her to make dresses for them for the wedding, too.

If she could hold out for six months, there'd be more weddings to plan, she reminded herself. There'd be plenty of time for painting, too. Things would get better. She had to be patient.

Later that evening, Colt Hall asked for the chance to drive a carriage, and James assented. When it was time to go, Colt sat on the barouche's high driver's seat with James. As Savannah, Nora and Avery climbed into their seats, Boone asked Riley, "Want to ride with me on Behemoth?"

"I'd have to sit side saddle."

"I think we can manage it." He lifted her up and sat behind her. Keeping Behemoth's pace at a slow walk and his arms around Riley, he directed the horse along the road by the light of the stars after the rest of the Halls drove off in their trucks and the carriage set out toward Westfield.

"You're quiet," Boone said.

"I'm okay."

"Good." He dropped a kiss on the top of her head. "You enjoyed the music?"

"And the company, and the food and… everything." It was too nice an evening to spoil it with her worries.

"So you think you can be content here?"

"I think so." She snuggled closer into his arms, wishing she could answer him unconditionally.

They rode along in peace for a while before Boone sighed.

"What is it?" Riley asked sleepily, the sway of the horse and the late hour combining to make her eyelids heavy.

"I have to tell you something. Something big."

His serious tone roused her a little. "What is it?"

"I love you. You know that, right?"

"Yes," Riley whispered. Despite everything, she felt utterly secure these days in the knowledge of how much Boone cared for her. It was evident in the way he touched her so reverently. The way he made sure of her pleasure before his own. He had even begun to give the arts a little more weight in his conversations.

"You know how important Base Camp is to me, too. Not because I'm out for glory, but because I truly want to help."

"Yes." She struggled to sit up, intent on giving him her full attention.

"I've never told you why."

"No," she agreed. "You haven't."

"I'd like to, if you're willing to listen."

"Do you really have to ask?"

For a moment the only sound was the clip-clop of Behemoth's hooves on the road. A light breeze touched her face, but otherwise the night was still and warm.

Riley wished Boone's words hadn't conjured such uneasiness in her, but she knew he wouldn't have brought up the topic if it weren't important.

"It was just over two years ago. My team was sent to Yemen. I haven't always gotten to serve with the Horsemen, but this time we were together. Good thing. I needed them."

Fear tightened Riley's gut even though Boone was safe here in Chance Creek with her. She hated the thought of him being in danger.

"Our job was to rescue four aid workers who'd been caught in the civil war that's been tearing up that country."

"I didn't realize it's been going on so long."

"It didn't make the news much back then, but believe me, things were bad. The workers were there to bring medical supplies for a civilian hospital. A battle broke out around them while they were en route, and they got stuck. They couldn't go forward and they couldn't go back. They had very little food. Even less water. They made a break from their car and holed up in a bombed-out building they thought was empty. It had been a school—and they found children hiding there, too."

"Oh, my God."

"They were able to communicate with us via satellite phone. The good news was they had a solar-charger for it and we were able to speak frequently. The bad news was we couldn't catch a break. Every time we thought we could get in to extract them, something went wrong."

"It sounds horrible." She could picture Boone pacing a room while he and the others tried to sort it out. She knew he'd have wanted to charge in and get those kids. What an awful kind of restraint he'd learned in his time with the SEALs.

"We talked with the aid workers for five days while they watched over and cared for the children with what little supplies they had. We tried to help keep up their morale as the situation got worse. We took turns." His voice was so bleak she wanted to hold him. Instead she kept still and let him talk.

"They took turns, too," he said. "Two of them keeping watch, one of them sleeping, one of them talking. My mark was Francine Heller. We talked for hours. Francine was sixty-eight. A hell of a woman. You would have liked her."

She closed her eyes against the sting of tears. *Would have liked*. Francine hadn't made it, then. "What did you talk about?"

"War. Love. Hate. Death. Life. Belief."

All the conversations she wanted to have with him. "What did she say?"

"That life was worth fighting for. That the West has to understand what's happening to the East. That things are changing—they're always changing—and somehow we have to learn to be more adaptable."

"She sounds wise."

"Yemen's civil war is about resources, Riley. At the end of the day it always comes down to that."

"Which is why you're building Base Camp." The rocking motion of Behemoth beneath her grounded her in a way she needed right now. There was so much suffering in the world. She was lucky—so very lucky—to be safe, warm, fed, clothed and in the arms of someone she loved. "What happened to Francine?"

Boone just shook his head, his chin grazing her hair. "I lost her, Riley. I lost all of them. I was on the phone with her when another strike took them out." His arms tightened around her. Riley's chest ached for those children, for Francine.

For them all.

"So when I'm too focused on my work, or when I demand things of you, I'm not trying to be an ass. I'm fighting for Francine in the only way I know how."

It was her turn to nod. She couldn't speak.

"There's something I haven't told you," he went on. "I should have been honest right from the start. I was... afraid... I'd lose you, too."

Riley could barely breathe. Whatever was coming would hurt. She knew that.

"It's about Fulsom. You know that in order to raise money for this project, he's arranged to document the entire process while we build our community. A film crew will arrive in a couple of weeks. After your guests leave," he hastened to add.

"Right." Behemoth kept walking and Riley wished the horse would stop. It was as if he was carrying her to some uncertain doom. She wanted to cling to things the way they were for just a few more minutes. But that was impossible.

"I talked to Fulsom about your plans for our Regency wedding. He said no."

"I… don't understand." But she did, only too well. Fulsom would win and she would lose—again.

"He won't sign over the deed to the ranch until the show is over. I don't call the shots here." He faltered. "Not even at the manor. The camera crew will be all over Westfield. You'll have to put an end to your Jane Austen life for the duration of the show. Your friends, too."

"Boone—you promised."

"I know. There's more."

"More?" She didn't think she could stand it.

"It's about the ranch. Fulsom has to drum up an audience, and let's face it, sustainability is pretty dry stuff. That's why he's forcing us to marry and film our weddings and that's why he's set a series of goals we have to meet in six months' time. If we fail—"

"You lose the ranch. I already know that."

"What you don't know is that he'll give it to John Montague, a developer who plans to knock down the manor and build seventy brand new luxury homes on the ranch."

"Let me down." She had to get away from Boone. From his words. From the image of destruction he'd planted in her brain. "Boone, let me down. Now."

"Riley—"

Riley jumped down from the horse, nearly stumbled, but caught herself. Behemoth sidestepped and Boone fought to control him. "Riley!"

She took off running. Maybe it wasn't dignified. Riley didn't care. She had to do something, because if Westfield was gone—

If Westfield was gone—

Riley ran faster, desperately needing to assure herself it was still there. She'd lost her grandparents. Lost the love they'd surrounded her with. Would she lose Westfield, too?

"Riley, if there was any other way, I'd never ask you—" Boone dismounted and followed her on foot. He touched her back and she wrenched herself away, stumbling to a stop.

She couldn't stand this. Why had God given her a heart when everything she loved kept getting ripped away?

"Do you want me to give up on Base Camp? Is that what you want? Because if it's the price of being with you, I'll do it."

She heard the desperation in his voice and it cut her to the quick, but what good was his offer if it meant Fulsom would turn the ranch over even sooner to Montague?

"It's only temporary," Boone went on. "As soon as the show is over, I'll marry you again. I'll wear whatever you want."

"How could you agree to his demands?" She finally found her voice again.

"I didn't have a choice. We won't lose. I swear to you, Riley—I will not let him take Westfield."

"What else are you hiding, Boone? Tell me everything." She'd never felt so utterly alone as she did now.

His hesitation terrified her. "Like I said, he's given us a set of goals."

"And they're impossible, is that it? He's stacked the deck too high against us?"

"No." He took her hand. "They're difficult, but not impossible. Fulsom wants ten couples. Ten married couples."

She tried to pull away, but he didn't let her go.

"We need to build ten sustainable houses that consume a tenth of the power a normal American house does. We can do that easily, Riley. That's right up my alley."

"What else?"

"We need to produce enough food on site to last us through the winter." He stopped. Riley scanned his face.

"That's it?"

"No," he said. "There need to be children, too. Pregnancies."

"Pregnancies." Her hand slipped to her belly and Riley thought she might be sick. Was that why Boone had made love to her so eagerly that first time—without using a condom? To meet Fulsom's conditions?

She backed away.

"Riley—"

"More than one?"

"Three."

"That's insane!" And it explained Clay and Jericho and their eagerness to get to know her friends.

Boone pursued her, Behemoth trailing behind him. "I never meant for it to be like this. At this point I'd pull out of the deal if I could, but it wouldn't do any good. The only way I can give you Westfield for keeps is to go through with it. And I need you by my side."

Riley shook her head. Boone was right; Fulsom had them in a trap. He'd get publicity for his cause, all right. Relationships, marriage, sex and babies? Wasn't that the fodder for all the popular shows on television? If he could only throw some zombies into the mix he'd probably top the charts.

"Talk to me, Riley. Tell me we can get through this."

"Stay away from me." Fulsom had taken over every aspect of her relationship with Boone—from the speed with which Boone had proposed to her, to the timing of having their first child. If she was pregnant, theirs would be one of the three pregnancies that saved Westfield from Montague.

If she was pregnant.

She picked up her skirts again and ran.

"Riley!" A few moments later, the clip clop of Behemoth's hooves told her Boone was following her. Riley didn't slow down and she didn't look back.

When she finally reached Westfield, breathless and exhausted, she slipped inside the manor and went straight up to her room. She had nothing more to say to anyone. The dreams she'd cherished of life at Westfield were well and truly gone.

CHAPTER TWELVE

★

"**T**HEY'RE STILL HERE," Jericho said the next morning when he, Boone and Clay gathered around the fire for an early breakfast.

Boone nodded. Telling Riley about Fulsom's rules was one of the hardest things he'd done. Watching her reaction when he'd done it was even worse. "I'll be surprised if they stay."

"It's shitty Fulsom won't change his mind."

"Well, he won't, so there's no use dwelling on it."

"Any new responses to our ad for other participants?" Jericho asked, obviously hoping to turn the conversation.

"More men," Boone said shortly. "I've weeded through all the ones we've gotten so far and have chosen some possible candidates. The first batch will arrive on Sunday. No women and no couples, though."

"We'll find them."

"I sure as hell hope so." Boone wasn't counting on it at this point.

They ate in silence for a minute. "I've finalized my

plans for the houses," Clay ventured.

"I'd like to see them," Jericho said.

Boone tried to muster up some enthusiasm, but all he could think about was Riley. What did she think of him now? Did she hate him for not being honest with her sooner?

Clay brought out a laptop and turned it on. Soon he pulled up a series of 3D images he'd generated.

"Those look like… hobbit houses," Jericho said.

"That's because they're constructed on similar principles. Riley and her friends don't want to look down on something ugly, so I thought… what if we integrate the houses into the landscape? Boone already had the idea of using passive solar gain to cut down on the need to heat or cool them. Digging them into the hillside allows us to use the principles of geothermal heat for even more efficiency. Instead of old-fashioned thatched roofs, we'll use cutting edge green roofs and blend the buildings into the landscape even more, while offering a renewable source of insulation. The front walls will have lots of windows to let in light and warmth in winter. Any exposed walls will be stuccoed for moisture resistance and even more passive solar gain. Most of the resources needed to build them can be found right on the ranch or within a short distance, and the end result will be a village—"

"—right out of a story book," Boone finished for him, distracted from his worries by the images. "Clay, that's something else."

"Wait'll you see what else I've got for you."

As he showed them floor plans and interior designs, Boone could only shake his head in wonder. Clay was born to do this job. Why had he spent so much time in the Navy instead of becoming an architect?

"We need to build one of these—fast," he interrupted as a seed of an idea took root inside him. "These houses might lure those women right down the hill. Maybe Riley won't mind so much—" Boone looked up when a truck turned onto the access road and trundled toward them. "Who's that?"

"It's Walker," Clay said in surprise.

All three of them stood up and went to meet him. Boone extended his hand to his friend when Walker parked and got out of the truck. "You should have called; we would have come and gotten you."

"Went home first."

Boone wondered if he meant to his mother's place out on the reservation, or his father's parents' place in town. Walker had bounced between them much of his childhood.

"Well, I'm glad you're here now."

"We were just talking about houses." Clay showed Walker his plans. Walker nodded.

"Looks good."

"We can't start until June first, though," Jericho reminded them. "Remember Fulsom's empty pasture?"

Boone's shoulders slumped. Jericho was right, which meant he couldn't entice Riley and her friends with the hobbit houses. He turned to Walker. "Wish I had a better welcome for you, but everything's fucked up."

Walker shrugged. "What else is new?"

RILEY HAD NEVER felt so conspicuous in her life as when she entered Thayer's Jewelers later that day. She'd been up most of the night trying to figure out a course of action that didn't end with her losing Boone, or her friends, or both.

At first she'd been so furious with Boone she'd wanted to cancel their engagement, but as she'd calmed down, she'd quickly realized it was Fulsom who infuriated her. As much as she wanted to lash out at Boone for ever agreeing to any of Fulsom's demands, she knew his commitment to Base Camp preceded his commitment to her, and if he didn't follow through, she'd lose Westfield forever.

Riley decided to be practical. She needed to persuade her friends to be patient for six months, win Westfield back and then create the life she wanted. She wouldn't think about her wedding—that hurt too much. She'd set her heart on a Regency affair, but after all, it was her pledge to Boone that would matter, not the clothes they wore.

She'd focus on Andrea's wedding instead. She'd put on her best gown and walked the two miles to Maud and James's house to ask for a lift into town. Maud had wholeheartedly endorsed the idea of going to see a wedding planner and recommended Mia Matheson, whose office was located within Rose's jewelry shop. Riley had met Mia when they were both younger, but hadn't spoken with her in years and she was pleased to find out the friendly girl had found her calling and opened her own business. She passed through the front door and spotted Rose Johnson serving a customer. Rose waved and Riley nodded to say she could wait, but it was only a moment before Mia appeared from the back of the store.

"Rose—oh, Riley! How are you? You look so lovely in that dress. Rose told me all about your visit to the Cruz ranch. I was so sorry I didn't get to see you."

Riley tried to summon a smile. "I've come because I need help organizing a wedding. Do you have some time?"

"Of course! Come on in. Who's getting married?"

"It's someone my friend Savannah knows." She explained all about the Jane Austen wedding and their need to show Andrea's guests a good time. "We're really under the gun. Do you think you could help us? We've made a good start, but there's still so much to do."

"Fast weddings are my specialty," Mia said. "It's all we seem to do in these parts."

Riley wondered if there was a story behind her private smile. "I'm so relieved to hear that. We've got a hundred guests coming and I have no idea how to find them accommodations on such short notice. We need a lot of help with decorations, too. The wedding will be Jane Austen-themed, of course." And she meant to do it right, in case this was the only one she got to throw.

"Of course! So the bride will arrive in a carriage?"

"The Russells' barouche," she confirmed.

"Perfect. What about catering?"

Riley explained about Mrs. Wood. "We'll need more help, though."

"Autumn Cruz for the wedding cake," Mia said. "She can help with side dishes, too. She's a whiz at this."

"Flowers? We need tons of flowers."

They went down the list that Riley and Savannah had built, and the longer Mia talked, the more Riley began to think it might all turn out after all.

"I've got Alice Reed working on costumes for the wedding party," Riley said, "but she'll need help, especially since we'll need table runners and decorations, too."

"That's easy. I'll rustle up all the women from the Cruz ranch and the Double-Bar-K. We're like an army when we get together."

"Thank you. I mean it, Mia."

"You're welcome!" Mia's eyes shone. "If I'm going to be your wedding planner, I need to have a Regency gown, too. By the time you're done every woman in town will have one, won't they?"

"Maybe so." Eventually. She didn't want to think about Fulsom's six-month moratorium on all things Austen.

"Don't you worry. Pulling together in an emergency is what we do best here in Chance Creek."

If she could only hire a wedding planner to fix the rest of her life.

Home again an hour later, Riley told the others she

had a headache and wanted to lie down. Upstairs, she locked herself into her en suite bathroom and pulled out the pregnancy test she'd bought while she was in town. It claimed to be accurate up to five days before a missed period. Riley had decided she couldn't wait another day to find out the truth. Her stomach was in knots and she wasn't sure what answer she wanted as she waited the three minutes for the results. She wished she could be unreservedly happy if the test was positive, but after everything that had happened she was afraid she'd never feel secure that Boone really wanted this child. She'd begun to wish she'd never heard of Martin Fulsom.

A minute passed, and then another, when she heard voices downstairs. Riley tried to make out who it was, but with two floors between them and several closed doors, she wasn't sure. It wasn't her friends, however. She distinctly heard the bass tones of at least one of the men. Her fears were confirmed a moment later when she heard heavy steps pound up the stairs. Riley panicked. The last thing she wanted was to be interrupted now.

When someone knocked peremptorily on her bedroom door, she bit back a frustrated groan, left the bathroom, and shut its door firmly behind her. She crossed her room. "Who is it?"

"Me. Can I come in?" Boone asked.

"What do you want?"

Boone opened the door before she could stop him. "Savannah said you weren't feeling well. Is everything all right?"

"I'm fine."

"I had to see you. Is this about Fulsom? I know I should have—"

"It's not about Fulsom." She bit her lip. "I just want to be alone."

"Don't give up on me. I know I fucked up—" Boone cupped her chin with his hands, as if he wanted to kiss her.

Riley pulled away. "It isn't that."

"Then what is it?" Boone came toward her again. Riley stepped back.

Boone's eyes narrowed. "Are you hiding something?"

"No!" How did he know to ask? Had she betrayed herself somehow? Riley panicked. She couldn't let him come any farther into the room.

When Boone took a step toward the bathroom, she blocked his way.

"Riley."

"It's nothing."

"It's something," he asserted grimly.

"Boone—"

He ducked around her, crossed the room and opened the door. When he spotted the pregnancy test stick resting on the cardboard packaging it had come in, he sucked in a breath.

"Are you...?"

Riley elbowed past him and snatched it up. She was the one who might be pregnant. Glancing down, she took in the minus sign and her stomach sank. "Guess not." She passed it to Boone. She wasn't prepared for the tears that filled her eyes.

Boone looked at the stick for a long moment, then put it down carefully and pulled her into his arms. "I'm sorry."

Riley didn't understand why she was crying, she hadn't wanted either of them to be forced into a pregnancy, but when Boone pulled her in tight, she buried her face into his neck. A minute later she backed away. "I'm being silly."

"No, you're not." His voice was rough. "We'll keep trying. I promise."

For the first time Riley looked up at him. Pain was etched clearly into the lines of his face. Had he wanted this pregnancy—for real?

"Tell me honestly," she demanded. "Are you sad for Base Camp?"

He shook his head. "I'm sad for us."

As SIX MEN climbed out of the airport shuttle and dropped their bags in the dirt outside the bunkhouse two days later, Boone felt another piece of the puzzle of their community fall into place. He saw them eyeing the twine outlines on the side of the hill and then turn to look at the manor sitting on top of its hill where Riley was pinning wash on the line. She'd been quiet since she'd gotten the results of her pregnancy test, but she'd remained at Westfield. Boone still wished they'd gotten a different result, but he was thankful that she'd used the opportunity to tell him she thought he might not want a child. They'd come to a deeper understanding of what they both felt and they'd decided to wait to try again until after they'd married.

"Good morning. Welcome to Base Camp," Boone called out to the new arrivals. Jericho and Clay fell into place beside him and the men came to stand in a line in front of them, almost as if they were back in the military.

Old habits died hard.

"I'm proud and honored that you men have decided to give our venture a shot. We're trying to change the world, one community at a time. You can be part of that." He went on to outline their plans and the roles they had for the men, all things he'd covered in his e-mails to them, but Boone knew that important information bore repeating.

"Any questions?" he asked at the end of his speech.

"Yeah—why is it called Base Camp?" a burly man named Curtis Lloyd asked.

Boone turned to point to the manor. "Because you aren't the only ones who can't keep their eyes off the summit. That is Westfield Manor. You'll see women coming and going in Regency outfits. Try not to get too distracted."

Everyone chuckled.

"I've got a question. Why did you make serving in the military a requirement for joining the team?" Greg Devon asked. He was a no-nonsense man with a shock of black hair whom Boone had already flagged as a great candidate for the community.

"You've had experience in tough situations, I can count on you to finish what you start, and last, but certainly not least, you know how to follow orders."

A couple of the men laughed. Greg fixed him with an intense stare. "This going to be a dictatorship?"

"They don't call him Chief for nothing," Jericho said.

"At first it will be a dictatorship," Boone said. "I'm willing to hear dissenting opinions, but I've put years into this plan. I won't change it on a whim."

"You really going to find us wives, Chief?" Angus McBride asked in a thick Scottish accent.

"I'm going to do my best. You ready to get hitched?"

"Sure thing, Chief."

He waited to see if anyone else had anything to say. "Okay, time for a tour." He led them toward the hillside. "These are where our houses will be. We can't break ground until filming starts, but we'll go over the plans with you and be as prepared as we can."

Murmurs of interest came from all sides.

"Here's where we'll have our main garden." Boone kept on moving. Despite his concerns about Riley, he was pleased with the way the morning passed. As he'd hoped, the men were curious, intelligent and asked good questions. He was also happy with the way his plans withstood the scrutiny of so many eyes. They'd spend the afternoon sorting supplies and going over the timeline of the project.

He lifted his eyes to the manor, as he did a thousand

times every day and wished Riley was with him. He knew he'd let her down and he wished there was something he could do to make up for it. Their wedding had been on his mind the past two days. Boone knew she was disappointed it would need to be modern, but as he glanced around Base Camp and recalled Fulsom's description of the empty field, an idea came to him. He'd been to several rustic western weddings in his time. Was it really so far a cry from that to a Regency theme?

Maybe not.

"ARE YOU EVER going to tell us what's wrong?" Nora asked as they set the table for dinner that night. They'd spent most of the afternoon on wedding plans, but had managed to squeak in an hour of creative time. Riley had continued to work on the painting she'd started, laying in lighter colors and details. She liked the structure of the scene, but something was missing. By the time she'd packed her things away again, she'd been thoroughly frustrated.

Avery looked up from her place by the fire where she was tending a stew. "Nora's right—you've been awfully quiet."

Savannah, preparing a salad at the counter, turned, too.

Time to fess up, Riley decided. She wasn't helping matters by delaying so long. "There is something on my mind." She tucked a napkin beside each plate. "You're not going to like it."

"You're leaving?" Avery said, straightening.

"No. Not that."

"I can deal with anything else."

Riley hoped the others felt the same way. "After the wedding, I'm afraid we'll have to put our plans on hold for a while." She explained all about Fulsom's decree that they would have to put aside their Regency outfits for the duration of the filming. "It'll last for six months. Then we can get back to our lives."

"We can't wear our gowns?" Savannah asked.

"No. We'll have to buy some modern things."

"Boone expects us to take part in the show? And he never asked?" To Riley's surprise it was Avery who asked the question, not Nora.

"He'd like us to."

"No," Savannah said. "I'm not going to do that. I know what reality TV is like and I don't want any part of it."

"Me, neither," Nora said. "Not in a million years."

When Riley turned to Avery, she shook her head, too. "That's an invasion of privacy. It would ruin Westfield for me."

"Then you don't have to do it." Riley began to lay out the forks and knives, fighting to keep calm. She hadn't expected anything more from them. Why should they lay their lives bare to television? They weren't in love with Boone.

Sometimes she wished she wasn't either.

"But you're going to?" Savannah came to her side. "Do you really want to do that?"

"I plan to." But the others were right; she didn't want to. She'd move down to Base Camp and stay there for the duration of the show. Like Savannah, she didn't want the manor tainted with those memories. "There's more you should know, though. About the men."

"What is it?" Savannah asked.

"The television show is set up like a contest." She explained all of Fulsom's terms, including the need for marriages and children. "Clay, Jericho and Walker all need to find wives. They'll probably want to try for children, too."

"How come Boone isn't doing that?" Nora asked. Understanding dawned on her face. "Is he doing that? Riley, what have you done?"

"I'm going to marry him," Riley confirmed. "June first will be my wedding day. You have to understand; Boone's an old friend. We know each other and we have chemistry. It's not like we just met."

"But if he's using you…" Avery said.

"He's not. If anything, I'm using him. If Boone and his friends fail, Fulsom will take back Westfield and give it to a developer. He'll carve up the ranch. It'll be gone forever. I can't let that happen."

"I can't believe you didn't tell us," Savannah said.

"I figured you'd react pretty much like you did," Riley said. "I understand, though. No hard feelings."

"We'll need to move out, won't we?" Nora said slowly. She caught Riley's eye and hurried to add, "Not because of Boone, because of Fulsom. If we stay on the ranch, his camera crews will try to pull us into the show."

"We'll have to look for a rental in town, I guess," Avery said, her disappointment plain.

"Which means we'll need to look for jobs. Just like I said at the outset," Nora said.

"It's only temporary."

"Maybe it's time for me to go back to teaching," Nora went on as if she hadn't heard Riley. "If there's nothing in Chance Creek, there might be in Billings."

"Maybe I should move back home," Savannah said. "My parents have a beautiful piano. Maybe if I took a part-time job they'd support me in trying to play seriously."

"No," Avery cried. "We've come so far; please don't ruin everything now!"

"We're not trying to ruin anything. Sometimes things don't work out… Where are you going?" Nora called after her.

Avery untied her apron and threw it on the table as she marched right out of the room. "I'm going to tell Lieutenant Boone Rudman what a colossal ass he is!"

CHAPTER THIRTEEN

⭐

"**N**OW WE'RE TALKING," Greg said. He dropped the ladle he'd been using to spoon soup into a mug and shaded his eyes with his hand.

Boone followed his gaze to see Avery striding down the path toward them, followed at a distance by Riley, Savannah and Nora. Their dresses rippled around them as they moved. They were coming fast. Boone straightened.

Another of the men whistled. "She's hot."

"She's pissed, you mean," Angus said, laying on his thick Scottish accent. "I think we're in trouble, lads."

"Goddamn you, Boone Rudman," Avery yelled as she marched right in among them, "you are a stupid, low-life, pond-scum-sucking, dirty old goddamn ass and I hate you!" She gave Boone a shove that actually managed to knock him off balance, mostly because he was surprised.

"Avery—"

Avery wasn't done. "You've ruined everything, you shitfucking butthead—you and your stupid band of merry frogmen. I hope you rot in hell!"

"Avery—"

"I've waited years for the chance to live with my friends and quit my asinine job so I could actually do something I loved and now you want to steal it all away from me?"

"I'm not stealing—"

"Nora's going to Billings to get a teaching job. Savannah's going to California because you're taking away her piano!"

It all became clear. "You told them," he said to Riley over Avery's head.

"That's right; Riley told us. Not you—you didn't have the balls to do it. And you—" Avery turned on Clay. "You've had the gall to pretend you liked Nora? Like hell! You want to use her to spawn your demon seed. And you—" She pointed an accusing finger at Jericho. "You thought you could sweet-talk Savannah all the way to the altar? Hanging's too good for you!"

Jericho froze like a deer caught in headlights. Clay opened his mouth to protest.

"But mostly it's you," Avery concluded, turning back to Boone. "You just… suck! I hope Riley finds a better man to marry. Someone like…" She scanned the crowd, caught sight of Walker for the first time, and fell silent.

"Okay," Boone said, wondering how in the hell to regain control of the situation, "let's all take it easy."

"She's right," Walker said.

Boone hadn't expected him to speak up. Walker had

been apprised of the situation, but since he hadn't spent any time at the manor, Boone didn't think he'd have an opinion. "It's not that simple," he tried again.

"It's simple."

Walker had everyone's attention, which riled Boone. This was his project—these were his men—

Walker raised an eyebrow and Boone bit back the words he'd been about to say. There he went again, all Chief, like Clay liked to say. It wasn't his place to dictate to anyone. Walker had the right to speak.

Walker let a moment pass, as was his way. By the time he continued, everyone was listening intently, but he spoke to Avery as if she was the only one there. "Sometimes there's compromise. Sometimes there's sacrifice."

"And you want us to sacrifice," Avery said, facing him. Boone couldn't help but appreciate the disparity between the lithe young woman in her pretty dress and the hardened warrior who towered over her.

Walker nodded. "We want you to sacrifice."

"You know how unfair that is?"

"I know."

Riley moved to stand beside Avery. "This is why I didn't want my friends involved," she said to Boone. She took Avery's arm. "Come on, let's go."

"You don't deserve her," Avery said to Boone, but let Riley drag her away. The women left as quickly as they'd come, and Boone watched them go, his heart heavy. This was exactly what he didn't want to happen.

"Now what do we do?" Jericho asked, his gaze on

Savannah's retreating back.

Boone just walked away.

RILEY DIDN'T THINK things could get any worse, but when her friends left in a taxi to go check out an apartment in town the following morning, the manor felt so empty without them she nearly broke down and cried. Instead, she forced herself to update all their to-do lists. There was still so much to do for the wedding she was overwhelmed. She hadn't even begun to plan hers. She simply didn't have the heart.

An hour later, Nora, Avery and Savannah arrived home again looking as glum as she felt.

"It was awful," Avery exclaimed. "The bedrooms were tiny. There was no yard. Everyone stared at us."

"What did you expect?" Nora snapped, but when she sat down on the couch, Riley saw tears in her eyes.

"It isn't going to be the same without you," Savannah said. "Nora won't tell us if she's going to stay in Chance Creek or go back to Baltimore."

"What about you?" Avery said to her. "I'm not convinced you won't make a run for California, either."

"I told you I was looking into renting a piano."

"We should focus on the wedding," Riley said. "Maybe—"

"I don't want to focus on the wedding," Avery said. "I want to focus on us. We came here to be together because we missed each other. We said that we valued friendship. Why are we being so quick to throw that away?"

"It's not our fault. It's the show," Savannah protested.

"And the way the men tried to play us," Nora said. "I can't believe Clay flirted with me when all he really wants is a fake wife."

A knock on the door interrupted them and Riley was relieved to go and answer it, but when she found Clay and Jericho waiting on the other side she nearly shut it again.

"Can we come in?" Jericho asked.

"Why? No one here is going to marry you," Savannah said, appearing by Riley's side. Nora and Avery followed close behind her.

"I understand that." He didn't look happy. Riley knew Jericho well enough to guess that the whole situation made him uncomfortable. He was an easygoing guy. She doubted he'd thought much about marriage at all. He must be chafing under Fulsom's demands.

"It wasn't our intention to try to trick you into marrying us."

"Wasn't it?" Nora asked. "Because it sure seems that way."

"We were testing the waters," Clay said. "I mean, if you had to find a husband in a short space of time, how would you go about it?"

"I'd be direct," Nora told him. "I'd state right up front what I was after and see who was interested."

"You'd go into a bar and randomly tell people that?" Jericho asked.

"Maybe not a bar."

"There are dating sites," Savannah pointed out.

"It won't work. What woman wants to join a sustainable community?" Clay asked.

"And be on TV for six months," Jericho added.

"What makes you want to do it?" Savannah retorted.

"I want a family," Clay said. "I've always wanted that. I want to help make this a better world for my kids."

"I just know that something has to change. I know that I'm good at seeing possibilities and trying them out," Jericho said. "I hadn't thought much about marriage until now. What I've realized is I need a wife who will put up with me." He shrugged. "I'm not a nine-to-five kind of guy. When I get into a project, I don't come up for air too often. Whoever becomes my wife will need her own passions, or she'll get... lonely." Jericho looked surprised at his own understanding.

"Anyway, we don't want you to feel uncomfortable," Clay said. "We know you're planning a wedding and want to make the most of your time with Riley. We'll stay out of your hair."

"We won't come near the manor at all," Jericho agreed. "But I was glad to get to know all of you." His gaze lingered on Savannah.

"Me, too," Clay said. He touched Nora's arm.

They turned to go and Riley shut the door behind them. "I'm glad they apologized, at least."

"I'm not glad about anything," Savannah said tartly. "I like Jericho. I don't want him to marry someone else.

And don't pretend you don't like Clay, Nora, because I know you do."

"Not enough to marry him." She shrugged. "Not yet."

Riley understood just how they felt. "I think they like you too, you know. It's not going to be easy for them to find women to marry, and it's not like they asked to be put in this situation."

"You're taking their side?" Savannah said.

"I'm not sure there has to be sides. I think there's just a bunch of unhappy people."

"She's right," Avery said. "You know what? I'm going to stay and see this through. I'm going to keep fighting to make it all work out."

"You're going to do the reality show?" Nora asked in disbelief.

"Why not? I was going insane when Riley invited us here. If I can't handle a little TV show, then I deserve to work in a cubicle all my life. Besides, no one asked me to marry them. I'll be an extra. How hard can that be? Meanwhile, I'll work on my screenplay, get tips from the film crew and hang out with one of my best friends." She hugged Riley.

"Two of your best friends," Savannah said. "Avery's right. There's no way it can be worse than my old job. I'll be an extra, too."

"And watch Jericho marry another woman?" Nora asked.

"Maybe. Or maybe not. Maybe I'll fall in love with him," Savannah said.

Riley's heart was beating so hard she thought everyone must be able to hear it. "Really?"

"Really." Savannah moved to stand by her. "And every time the film crew comes to the manor, I'll play my piano. Who knows? Maybe I'll get invited to play a concert or two when the show airs."

"That's a good point," Avery said. "It could be the making of your career—and mine."

"What about you, Nora?" Riley held her breath, knowing it was too much to ask.

"For God's sake." Nora threw her hands in the air. "Fine! I'll stay, but I'm going to hide every time the cameras come around. All I need is for that crazy student to figure out where I've gone and start harassing me again. And don't expect me to marry anyone."

"We won't," Riley promised her. "But are you guys serious? Are you really going to stay?"

"We're serious." Savannah gathered them all together. "We can stand anything for six months."

USUALLY RILEY WAITED for Boone to pick her up in the evening, but it was a beautiful night and she was too restless to stay in the house, so she left the manor at a quarter to eight and made her way down the dirt road to Base Camp. They'd spent most of the afternoon coordinating with Mia on the wedding. She'd only managed to spend an hour on her painting. She couldn't believe something could be so frustrating and compelling all at once. She missed the brief period of time when she'd had long afternoons to experiment. It was going to take time to figure out what she was doing.

"Ma'am," one of the new recruits said as she approached their encampment.

"Evening," she said.

The other men grouped around the fire stood up.

"Ma'am."

"Evening, ma'am."

Riley suppressed a smile. Now she really felt like she'd traveled back in time. "Has anyone seen Lieutenant Rudman?"

"Lieutenant? I thought he was an NCO," she heard one of them mutter.

"The Chief's in there." A man with a thick Scottish accent pointed to the bunkhouse.

Riley thanked him and went to knock on the door. Walker opened it, nodded in his enigmatic way and let her in. Riley nodded back, unsure of how she felt about the man. She'd always had a complicated relationship with him. Sometimes he'd watched out for her, other times he'd been the one to exclude her from her friends' exploits without a word of explanation. She'd never figured him out and when it counted, he'd stood back and let everyone else laugh at her.

As she entered the bunkhouse and looked for Boone, she knew Walker was watching her. "Well?" she finally asked.

"I should have spoken up for you," he said quietly.

"You drove me crazy back then. I never knew where I stood with you."

He nodded. "I bet I did. Thought I knew best. You

always rushed right in, no matter what was going on. Didn't want you to get hurt."

"Well, I got hurt."

Walker nodded again. "I should have done better."

She knew it was all the apology she'd get. Suddenly, it was all she needed. She was so tired of holding onto the sorrows of the past. There was plenty to worry about in the present. "Thank you."

He exited the building without another word, and when a door to one side of the bunkroom opened, Boone came out of the bathroom in his jeans and little else. His feet were bare. So was his torso. He was rubbing his hair dry with a towel.

He came to a halt when he spotted her. "Riley."

"I guess I'm early."

"No—well, yeah." He grinned and her heart did a funny flip. No matter how many times she saw him, he gave her butterflies. "I'll be ready in a minute."

"No rush."

As usual, they walked toward Pittance Creek, moving slowly once they made it past the gauntlet of recruits by the fire.

"I've got something to tell you," she said. His shoulders stiffened as if he was bracing for bad news and she was suddenly grateful she had something good to share. "Nora, Savannah and Avery are going to stay. They've agreed to be on the show."

"How'd you manage that?"

"I didn't do anything. I just have good friends."

He took her hand. "That is good news." He chuckled a little. "Did they agree to marry the guys, by any chance? I heard Clay and Jericho paid a call up at the manor."

"In a word? No. I think they made an impression, though."

"I guess that's something. It's funny, every man around that fire outside the bunkhouse is willing to marry, but like-minded women are impossible to come by. I guess I'll have to set them loose in Chance Creek to fend for themselves."

"I guess so."

"Clay, Jericho and Walker are disappointed, you know."

"Clay and Jericho I understand. But Walker?"

"You didn't see him when Avery came marching down here to tell me off?"

"No, I didn't."

Boone helped her navigate a deep rut in the dry road. "Walker's not too demonstrative. You have to know what to look for. I'd say he's a goner."

"For Avery?" She couldn't picture that.

"When the show's over we'll do anything we can to help you start your B&B."

She nodded.

"Riley. Can I…?" He reached for her.

She went willingly into his arms and when Boone kissed her she melted against him. She could tell by the way he held her he felt the same way.

"I can't wait until this is all over," he whispered into her hair.

"Me, too."

"Should we take this to the riverbank?" Boone asked.

"I've got a better idea. Let's take it to the manor. I've got a perfectly good bed there."

He held back. "What about your friends?"

"You're a SEAL right? Don't you know all about infiltrating enemy compounds?"

"You better believe it." Boone hurried her back the way they'd come and up the hill until they reached the back door of the manor. "Prepare to learn from a master." He took the lead with an exaggerated crouch. As he crept inside and took enormous tippy-toe steps, Riley bit back a laugh and followed him with equal exaggeration, grateful for Boone's sense of humor. They reached the opposite side of the kitchen without incident, but when they heard Avery's voice in the parlor, Boone flattened himself against the wall and pulled Riley with him. She knocked into a tall cabinet where their glasses and dishes were stored and set its contents rattling. Boone braced it with a steadying hand. "Watch it."

"You watch it," she hissed back. When Avery retreated to the far end of the parlor, Riley stepped away from the cabinet and quickly tiptoed across the hall to the base of the stairs. She slipped around the bannister and moved rapidly up the steps, but Boone, following her, was only halfway across the hall when Nora called out, "Riley? Is that you?"

"Just heading to bed," Riley called back. She prayed

her friend didn't come to investigate.

Boone scuttled back into the kitchen like a crab into its hole. Nora appeared in the doorway to the parlor. "Everything all right?"

"Yes. I'm just… tired. Do you mind?" Riley forced herself not to look toward Boone's hiding place. Nora studied her.

"Are you sure you're okay?"

"Positive. Do you need my help with anything?"

"No, we've got things under control. Sleep well."

"'Night." She waited until Nora went back into the room. She was just bending over the bannister to call softly to Boone when he appeared again, took the hall in two steps, vaulted the bannister and ran lightly up the stairs. He grabbed Riley by the waist, tossed her over his shoulder and dashed up the rest of the steps, his feet making no noise. Riley, jolted and bounced by his movements, could only hold on for dear life.

"Third floor, remember?" she hissed when he paused at the top of the steps.

Boone laughed. "Of course," he muttered. He took off up the second set of stairs and didn't stop until they reached the top.

"What room?"

Riley pointed. Boone turned around to see, and Riley yelped when he came perilously close to hitting her head against a doorframe.

"Sorry." Boone lowered her down.

"This one." Riley opened it, pulled him in and shut it again. Turning the lock, she faced him. "You're not very—"

Boone tossed her on the bed with a single, fluid movement and leaped up on top of her. Before she could say another word, he lowered himself down and kissed her.

Riley forgot all about talking. Making love to Boone in a bed was a revelation. No freezing water, no cold dirt, no ants or flies. Just soft covers, a comfortable mattress—and Boone.

He seemed to think he needed to take advantage of the situation to explore her body in a very intimate way. Riley had never been so kissed, caressed and teased and soon her veins were humming with desire. She ran her hands over his skin, touching every part of him she could reach, but all she really wanted was to feel him inside of her.

When he finally obliged, Riley gasped as he filled her. "Is that good?" he asked.

"So good." She rocked with his slow motions until the need in her built to a peak she couldn't withstand.

"Boone—"

"I'm here. I'll always be here."

Riley came with a cry she forgot to muffle. Boone covered her mouth with his, but all too soon he was grunting his release in time to their movements together. Riley sighed when they came to a stop, too wrapped up in pleasure to do anything else but lie there. Boone's weight on top of her felt perfect and she never wanted to let him go.

A quick rap on the door had them springing apart.

Riley scrambled for the covers and tossed them over Boone, crawling under them to hide herself.

"Yes?" she managed to say in a normal voice.

"Goodnight." It was Avery.

"'Night." She put a finger on Boone's lips to shush him. He snorted with laughter and she waved a desperate hand in his face. "Shh!"

She thought they were in the clear until Avery called out, "'Night, Boone!"

Riley gasped in mortification. She tried to block him, but Boone pushed her hand away. "Night, Avery!" he called back. He pulled Riley back into an embrace. "I guess we weren't quiet enough."

"You think?" But she couldn't stay mad. For one thing he felt so good, she had a feeling they would make more noise before the night was through.

For another, she was too happy to care what anyone else thought.

"I STILL THINK you should have taken that job I found you," Boone's father said the next night at dinner. "Makes a lot more sense than prancing around on television."

"I won't be prancing around, Dad. I'll be demonstrating techniques that people can use to cut their carbon footprint."

"You know I don't hold with that stuff and nonsense."

"I don't think climate change cares whether you hold with it or not. Besides, most of what I'm doing is good stewardship. It doesn't matter what you think about the long term. It's what you do today that counts. Isn't that what you always say? I'm going to take care of Westfield and the people who live on it the best way I know how."

"By ranching bison instead of good old-fashioned cattle?"

"Bison were here first, Dad. They're the ones who are old-fashioned."

"I heard Riley's back in town," his mother interrupted before his dad could wind up for a real argument.

"She's actually the reason I wanted to talk to you tonight." Boone scooped a spoonful of scalloped potatoes onto his plate and passed it to his father. "Riley and I are getting married."

His mother set the dish of broccoli she held down with a thump. "It's about time! I thought you'd never notice that poor girl! She's had her sights set on you since she was knee-high to a grasshopper."

"I guess it took a little distance for us to realize the nature of our feelings for each other."

His mother scoffed. "It didn't take distance for Riley. She knew a good thing when she saw one. You were the blind one."

"I'll grant you that." He didn't want to get into the past.

"Congratulations, son." His dad clapped him on the back, far more cheerful than he'd been just a moment ago. "So you're settling down at last."

Had his dad been afraid he'd leave town again? "I guess I am."

"And you'll live at Westfield?"

"As long as we meet Mr. Fulsom's conditions."

"I don't trust that man." His mother handed him the broccoli. "Take a big scoop. It's good for you."

"Yes, ma'am." Boone did as he was told. He was hungry tonight, anyway. "Fulsom's a showman. As long as you remember that, he's okay."

"He'll make an ass out of you," his father warned.

"You've got that right, so prepare yourselves. Not everything you'll see on TV will be pretty." He hoped his parents could take it.

"Why didn't you bring Riley to dinner?" his mother asked.

"I wanted the chance to talk to you about our plans first, but I'd love to bring her next time. Just so you know, we're hoping to have a baby soon."

"Not before the wedding, Boone Andrew Rudman!" His mother looked appalled.

Boone grinned. "Not before the wedding, Mom."

"I think I can put up with just about anything else. Except polygamy. I draw the line at polygamy."

Boone cocked his head. "Are you really worried I'll marry two women?"

"You're raising bison, aren't you?" his father said. "No telling what you'll do next."

Boone laughed out loud. His mother joined in. His father heaved a long-suffering sigh, but grinned. "All right. I'll admit it's good you're back, no matter what you get up to."

"I'll try not to embarrass you too much, Dad."

"We're very proud of you," Boone's mother told him.

His father snorted. But at a look from his wife, he nodded. "We are proud of you," he said. "But I've seen those reality shows. Try to keep your pants on, okay?"

"Roger that, Dad."

THE DAYS PASSED in a blur of preparations and before Riley knew it she stood on the elegant front stoop of Westfield Manor with her friends, watching as an airport shuttle van pulled up the long driveway. The bride and her bridesmaids would get special Regency treatment at Westfield for the whole weekend. The other guests would be accommodated around Chance Creek and other towns in the vicinity, their placement determined by how close they were to the bride. They were responsible for their own Regency garb and wouldn't arrive until Saturday. Riley thanked goodness for small miracles.

Between Mia, Alice, the Russells, and a host of other people, the wedding was on track. Still, there were so many things that could go wrong her mind was spinning.

"I've got butterflies," Avery said.

"Me, too," Savannah said softly.

"I know," Nora said. "I hope we don't screw anything up."

Riley had a stomach full of butterflies herself, but

she willed herself to be calm. "Everything is ready for our guests and they're going to be thrilled with the weekend we have to offer them," she declared, as if by saying it out loud, she could make it so.

She led the way down the stairs to greet Andrea and her friends. To her amusement, Mrs. Wood had arranged herself, her niece Marlena whom she'd brought with her, and Lyle Higgs, one of the coachmen James had sent over for the weekend, in a straight line in front of the manor. All of them wore period-appropriate costumes. It made her proud to see how seriously they were taking their work.

As the airport chauffeur climbed out and opened the doors of the shuttle van, a thin young woman with blond hair and luminous blue eyes spilled out. "Savvy!"

Savannah winced and Riley bit back a chuckle. Savannah had always gone by her full name.

"Andrea. Nice to see you again." Savannah allowed herself to be hugged, then made the introductions. Andrea, in turn, presented her friends as they exited the van.

"This is my maid of honor, Brook Wright, and my bridesmaids, Win Lisle, Belinda Huck, Fran Cotter and Ingrid Spiers. We're so happy to be here—when we landed I wasn't sure if we'd made a big mistake; the town is so tiny."

"This is the country," Riley said.

"Well, sure, but there's country and then there's *country*." Andrea widened her eyes as if the latter was something to be afraid of.

Riley decided not to pursue the topic. "Come on in. First we'll have light refreshments in the parlor while your things are brought up to your rooms. Savannah here will give you an overview of the weekend ahead and a quick guide to Regency dress and the particulars of getting into and out of it. Then Mrs. Wood will show you to your rooms. The seamstress will be along shortly to make any final adjustments to your outfits, and later we'll be ready for the first of our activities. Savannah, would you lead the way?"

As Savannah gestured for the women to follow her, Riley, Nora and Avery hung back to help Lyle, Marlena and Mrs. Wood gather up their luggage and bring it inside. Riley was dismayed to see how much they'd brought, given that they were supplying each woman with two gowns for the duration. They'd sent hints about appropriate footwear and undergarments, and Riley hoped the women had paid attention to them.

Inside, their guests identified their bags and Lyle carried the luggage to the proper rooms. Avery and Mrs. Wood served hors d'oeuvres and drinks in the parlor, while Savannah told their guests about their plans.

"We'll give you a little time to change and then we'll come knock on your door and ask if you need any help with your gowns," she concluded. "Later we'll go for a carriage ride to acquaint you with the property and its environs. Any questions?"

"Is it true there won't be a ball?" a tall, dark-haired woman asked. Riley thought she was Win Lisle, a sour-faced woman whose mahogany eyes seemed to judge everything and find it wanting. She wore a high ponytail and Riley could picture her at the country club asking, "Is it true you don't serve caviar?" Riley's dislike of her was immediate and visceral, and she sensed that Win had been chivvying Andrea since her wedding plans began. Riley knew her type, the poisonous frenemy who lived for the opportunity to show you up. "Andrea said there wouldn't be a ball," Win went on in her lazy, uppercrust drawl, "but I can't believe it. What's a Regency weekend without a ball?"

"There will be dancing at the wedding," Savannah said.

"But that's not the same as a ball, is it?"

"I'm not sure you understand just how big an undertaking it is to throw a ball," Avery said.

Win yawned delicately. "I understand—such a shame you're too small an operation to accommodate your guests' requests."

Riley read the exchange of glances around the room and sensed a rebellion forming. She was beginning to think that Andrea's friends might not really be so friendly. If they were looking for ways to mark down Andrea's efforts, then the lack of a ball would provide an easy target.

Andrea's face had clouded and Riley knew instinctively she was right. "Now, Win, you've gone and spoiled the surprise," she blurted, talking over Savannah. "Of course there'll be a ball, but it was supposed to be a secret. All of you will need to practice hard to learn the steps of the dances by Friday night."

"I'll be your teacher," Avery said into the sudden silence. They'd already planned some dancing lessons, even if a ball wasn't on the schedule.

Riley appreciated her fast thinking. She refused to let Savannah down.

Andrea broke into a huge smile. "What an incredible surprise. Savvy must have planned it." She nearly crushed Savannah with another hug.

"Up to your rooms," Nora said in her schoolteacher voice. Just in time, too. Savannah looked ready to snap. "Get changed and we'll be by to help shortly."

Mrs. Wood undertook to lead them up to their rooms, leaving Riley and her friends alone in the parlor when the chattering women were gone.

"A ball? The day before the wedding? Are you out of your mind?" Nora hissed as soon as the coast was clear.

"How are you going to pull it off?" Savannah demanded.

"I have no idea. But I know who might. Maud. I'll call her right now."

Savannah handed her the cell phone. When Maud picked up, Riley didn't waste time with pleasantries. "I need to throw a ball on Friday."

"I'm on it," Maud said gaily. "Leave everything to me."

CHAPTER FOURTEEN

⭐

W HEN BOONE PUSHED open the door to Thayer's Jewelers, he was pleased to see he was the only customer. He'd noticed a lot of changes since he'd been home and here was another one. Instead of the crusty old man who used to work here when he was a kid, a young woman he recognized stood behind the counter.

"Rose Bellingham? Is that you?"

"It's Rose Johnson now. I married Cab." She smiled and shook Boone's hand when he offered it. "Good to see you again. It's been a long time."

"It sure has." Rose was a few years younger than him. Boone couldn't believe she was grown up enough to be married. Or that Cab Johnson was the sheriff now. It used to be Cab's father.

"Can I help you with something?"

"I'm looking for a ring," he said. "Should have bought it weeks ago."

"Let's find you a good one, then." She came around the counter and led him to a glass case displaying engagement rings. Boone looked them over and quickly became discouraged. He wasn't sure how to pick the right one.

"Maybe I should bring her in."

"Some women like that. Others like to be surprised," Rose told him. "Tell me about your bride."

"I think you know her. Riley Eaton?"

Rose broke into a smile. "The Russells introduced us and Mia's helping her throw that wedding at Westfield. The one for her friend's cousin. Congratulations."

"Thanks. So do you know what kind of a ring she'd like?"

"Something old-fashioned, I'd say. If I remember correctly, engagement rings weren't really the thing during the actual Regency, but Riley will want one, I'm sure." She bent over the case. "Take a look at these." She pulled three rings out in quick succession.

One of them immediately caught Boone's attention and he picked it up. Like Rose said, it was old-fashioned and delicate. Its diamond wasn't large, but he knew without a doubt it was the one.

"I'll take it."

Rose smiled. "That was fast." She held it in her palm when he handed it to her and a faraway expression came over her face. After a moment she grew serious. "Boone, I know this is going to seem like a strange question, but is something going on between you two that you need to work out before you give her this?"

Boone laughed in disbelief. "What are you, psychic?"

Rose shrugged. "Kind of."

"Now that you mention it, there is something. Is Mia here? I hoped she could help me."

"Let me go get her."

Rose returned a minute later with Mia, who beamed when she spotted Boone. "Rose told me the good news. Congratulations!"

"Thank you. Here's the thing…" Boone explained the predicament he was in and the wedding they were supposed to have, as Fulsom had dictated it. "So how can we have a Regency wedding without having a Regency wedding? Riley will wear a fancy gown either way, right? So will her bridesmaids. Is there something I can wear that's modern but fits the bill?"

"I think so." Mia nodded.

"What about decorations?"

"We can walk the line between modern and old-fashioned. When is it?"

"June first."

To her credit, Mia didn't bat an eye. "At Westfield?"

"Yes. Outside, like I said."

"We'll get it done," she said.

"Just like that?"

"Just like that. One non-Regency Regency wedding coming right up. But I'll need something from you."

"Name it."

"I'm helping out with Savannah's cousin's wedding, too, and she's got so many guests they won't fit in the great room at Westfield."

"Hold it outside."

"She wants a roof over her head. I'm thinking about

the barn."

Boone made a face. "It's a mess. Hasn't been used in years."

"Better get cracking if it's going to be ready on time." She smiled sweetly at him. "I'll knock ten percent off my bill for your wedding if you get it done."

"Deal."

THEIR GUESTS SEEMED to enjoy the carriage ride Riley had arranged for them. Split between the Russells' barouche and the older town coach, they'd ridden around the countryside on a tour much like the one James and Maud had given her and her friends when they first arrived at Westfield. The two young men James had sent to drive them were enthusiastic and willing to go wherever Riley directed them.

When they arrived home, Riley was surprised to see James ride up on a handsome bay gelding. She ushered the guests inside, where Avery met them with more snacks, and ducked back outside to talk to him. "How's Maud holding up?" she asked him. "I shouldn't have dumped the preparations for a ball into her lap the way I did."

"Don't you worry about a thing; I haven't come to scold you. I came to check on you and the young bucks driving my carriages," James said. "Maud's already arranged for music and food and is hiring help to prepare the ballroom. She'll phone later to discuss dances, and she'll make sure the men can execute them perfectly. She said she'd send her dance instructor over to you ladies, too."

"Who did she—"

"I must go," James said. "Lots to be done, but I'll be back tomorrow. Try to enjoy your guests, my dear." He turned his horse and was off before she could voice the rest of her questions. She wondered who Maud had found to partner the women in the dances. She supposed they'd take whomever they could get. Back inside, she found their guests perched around the drawing room sampling the trays of snacks Avery had set out before them. Judging from their lively conversation, they were having a good time.

Riley caught up with Avery in the hallway outside the kitchen. "I think we might pull this off."

"Of course we will. Failure isn't an option."

"How's Savannah holding up?"

"I'm fine," Savannah said, coming up behind them, "but I could really use a glass of wine. Shoot me if I ever become as obsessed as those women with redecorating my master bedroom."

"Is that their latest topic?" Avery said. "Before that it was hiring good help." She disappeared into the kitchen.

"And before that it was how to know if your manicurist is judging you," Riley said.

"Savannah!" Andrea's plaintive trill betrayed her anxiety at being left alone with her friends.

"Time to save her from the piranhas," Savannah said. "Again."

"You're a good cousin," Riley told her.

"I keep telling myself that." She took the delicate wine glass Avery returned to give her, downed its contents and handed it back. "Wish me luck."

"Good luck," Riley and Avery echoed.

"Maybe Boone's got it right," Avery said. "Those wealthy women don't look all that happy. Maybe simplicity and sustainability really is the answer."

"Bite your tongue," Riley said.

EARLY THE NEXT morning, Boone stood with the rest of the men in the great room at the Russell's house, with Maud acting as hostess and her extremely beautiful niece, Angelina, standing beside her. Behind them stood several other women who ranged from a thirty-something soccer mom type to a crony of Maud's who wore a polyester pantsuit. Boone could tell the men were wondering why they had been brought to Cold-field. "Boys, this is Maud Russell. She'll explain today's assignment. But first, let me make it clear that this one is non-negotiable. If you fail, you're out. It's that simple."

The men exchanged curious glances as Maud stepped forward. As always, her clothing suited the early 1800s. "Gentlemen, thank you for coming today. I have a wonderful surprise for you." She paused dramatically and Boone braced himself. "You have been invited to a ball Friday night. A grand ball the likes of which hasn't been seen in decades in this part of the world."

"If ever," Jericho whispered to Boone.

"Excuse me, ma'am. A ball?" Greg asked.

"That's right. Surely you've heard of them."

"Um… yes, but—"

"Good. First things first. A seamstress will arrive in about an hour to measure you for your ball attire, but meanwhile, you gentlemen must learn to dance. I've been too long in the provinces to imagine you know anything about it."

More than one man shot Boone a confused and then pleading look, but Boone remained impassive as Maud paired the men up with female partners. Boone, Jericho, Clay and Walker joined them to make a long line. The women stood several feet away in a parallel one. He'd hoped the dances would be easy, but he quickly found out they weren't. He and Jericho crashed head-on during one particularly lively dance. They weren't the only ones. The men, who'd all mastered specialized equipment as well as scads of highly technical information and tactics during their service, were little accustomed to formal dancing, except for Harris Wentworth, who'd evidently taken lessons as a boy.

Once they saw how seriously Boone and his friends were treating the lesson, the recruits stopped complaining and buckled down to learn. There was some subtle vying for the chance to pair off with Angelina, but the dance instructor must have been used to that and allowed none of the men to get the upper hand.

As for the men, Boone was happy to see that apart from some consternation at the difficulty of mastering the formal steps, they betrayed no impatience with the activity. He'd judged his candidates well. They were professionals acting in a professional manner.

By the time they left the Russells' place, after a delicious dinner of roast lamb and duck a l'orange, however, the men couldn't contain their curiosity.

"Are you ever going to explain what that was all about?" Greg said as they milled around outside the bunkhouse.

"That was about tactics," Boone said, loudly enough for all the men to hear. "See that house?" He pointed to the warm lights emanating from the manor up on top of its rise of ground. "It's full of women. We're going to take it by storm, but we won't launch a direct assault. Instead, we'll lure its inhabitants out before we pounce."

"How are we going to do that?" Harris asked.

"And more importantly, why?" Greg added.

"By attending Maud Russell's ball and dancing with them. Look around. What's missing in this community?"

"Houses," Greg said.

"Food," Harris said.

"Women," Angus roared. The others laughed.

"That's right." Boone turned toward the manor again. "Our community needs women. Tomorrow we launch a successful campaign to win some."

Angus led a cheer that split the night. Boone wondered if Riley had heard and if she knew what was coming for her.

"I WOULD HAVE thought a ball gown would be more opulent," Win said, holding out the skirts of her new dress and craning her neck to see the full effect.

"This is an extremely opulent gown by Regency standards," Alice Reed said through a mouthful of pins.

"And we're extremely grateful you were able to find us all gowns at such short notice," Riley rushed to say to the seamstress. Thank goodness Regan had recommended her on their first visit to the Hall. The young woman had turned out to be very accomplished.

"I do look attractive in this," Win said. She turned around and looked back over her shoulder at the large pedestal mirror Riley had positioned in the parlor for their final fittings.

"I didn't have to look very far," Alice said. "I have a whole carriage house full of period dresses. Chance Creek doesn't host enough costume parties to keep up with me."

"I heard you design clothes for the re-enactments in the summer."

"I do. Luckily for you I have a score of British Redcoat costumes, too. I thought maybe the men in town would want to re-enact the revolution at some point, but apparently that wouldn't be historical. There wasn't even a Montana during Revolutionary times." Alice waved a hand. "I think that's silly. If they can travel in time, why can't they travel in location? They could pretend they're in Massachusetts for a day, couldn't they?"

"Since I've placed a Regency manor in Montana, I won't argue with your logic," Riley said. "You do such wonderful work. Why don't you sell your costumes on the Internet?"

"Oh, the Internet." Alice gave an expressive shrug. "Bah."

Win turned on her. "If you have the inventory you say you do, you could make a fortune."

Her sudden interest in the conversation animated her features, and for the first time Riley saw the woman Win could be. She'd learned from Andrea that Win was also supposed to get married soon. She'd quit her job recently to prepare for her wedding. "It's going to be five times more glamorous than mine will," Andrea had said with a sigh. "I don't know why I try to compete with her."

"I don't know, either," Riley had told her. "Friendship isn't a competition."

Andrea had merely sent her a puzzled look.

"I'm serious," Win went on. "All you need is to set up a storefront online. It's so simple these days. As you make your dresses, you post photos of them. And you can take special orders—you could charge a mint for those."

When Alice didn't respond, Win's impatience became all too clear. "I don't understand you at all."

Alice didn't take offense. "No one does," she said simply. Riley thought that would be the end of the conversation, but after another minute, Alice added, "I suppose it's because I have a fortune already."

That caught everyone's attention.

"If you have a fortune, why are you on your knees hemming my dress?" Andrea asked.

Alice sat back. "If you had a fortune, wouldn't you

do the one thing you love the most?"

Riley was impressed with Alice's wisdom. She hadn't known her when they were young. She suspected she was only three or four years older than Alice, but she didn't remember her hanging around with the other kids in town.

She quizzed the seamstress about that later while Alice packed up her sewing kit and was preparing to leave. Riley detained her by the front door. "How come I never met you all those summers I spent here in Chance Creek when I was younger?"

Alice gave a private smile. "My sisters and I had an unusual childhood. We didn't leave the ranch too much. We're more social now."

"I'm glad. And I understand completely what you said about sewing. If I had a fortune I'd do nothing but paint and ride." She glanced around her. "And invite people to my Regency B&B when it opens."

Alice gave her a sudden hug. "I'm glad you came back to Chance Creek."

"Me, too."

Five minutes later, Riley met up with Nora on the landing halfway up the stairs. "You look beautiful."

Nora did. Her updo was threaded with a chain of pearls and her gown was a dark wine red that set off her complexion. Its sleeves were short and her neckline plunging, but long white gloves covered her arms past her elbows.

Nora put a hand on Riley's arm. "You know, I haven't said thank you."

"For what?"

"For bringing us here—for insisting that I join you."

"You seemed pretty set on getting back to your old life just recently."

"I do intend to find a way back to teaching someday, but you offered me a haven here, and I'm better for it. Let's face it; I can't help anyone if I'm dead. I keep feeling like I should have stayed with my class, even if I did receive threats, but what if that student had followed through? My life would be over and so would his. That wouldn't help anyone."

"What made you finally change your mind?"

Nora looked sheepish. "Something felt different from the moment I got here, but it took me a long time to realize what it was. I was... lonely... in Baltimore after my mother passed away. I think whoever was stalking me fed on that loneliness along with my fear. I would never feel afraid like that here at Westfield. Being near you and Savannah and Avery makes me stronger."

For the second time in short succession Riley found herself in a warm embrace. She hugged Nora back. "I'm so glad you're here. I hope we find a way for you to stay for a long, long time."

"There's one more thing." When Nora pulled back, her eyes were shining. "I called my old school yesterday during my cell phone time and told them exactly why I had to walk away. I called the school board next and then the local papers. I hope that by bringing attention to the conditions teachers like me work in, the community and government will see something has to change.

Now that's done, I'm ready for a new challenge. There must be someone who needs me in Chance Creek."

Riley knew she meant children to teach, but her thoughts strayed to Clay. There certainly was someone in Chance Creek who needed Nora. If only Fulsom hadn't made things impossible between them.

"Meet you downstairs in fifteen minutes?"

"You bet."

"I LOOK LIKE a fool." Boone surveyed himself in a mirror he'd had set up in one corner of the bunkhouse and frowned. Knee breeches and hose were a horrible invention. No wonder they'd been consigned to the trash heap of time.

"You look like a dashing young officer," Jericho corrected. "The women will swoon all over you. Or so says Maud."

"Anyway, we're all in this together," Clay said, coming to stand next to them.

"Did we lose any recruits yet?" Boone asked him. He wouldn't be surprised if one or two had slipped away.

"None so far. They're being good sports about it all."

"Angus said it beats basic training," Jericho added.

"What about Walker? Did we lose him?" Boone hadn't seen the man in hours.

"I'm here." When Walker entered the bunkhouse, Boone had to grin. What would the women of Regency England have thought of their fearless leader? He cut an impressive figure, his dark, brooding looks set off by the scarlet uniform.

"I don't think I can remember any of those dances," Clay complained.

"The steps will come back to you." At least Boone hoped so. Otherwise he was screwed. "Ready?"

"Let's go," Walker said. "James is out front."

In an attempt to be true to the period, they'd accepted James' offer to convey them to Coldfield Cottage in his barouche, and the recruits were to ride in the town carriage. Boone suppressed a smile when he spotted the throng of Redcoats outside of the bunkhouse. Together they did a credible job representing one of Her Majesty's regiments.

"I'd get drummed out of my clan if they saw me in this gear," Angus called out as he boarded the cart. "No one better take any photographs."

"No worries; there weren't any cameras in Jane Austen's time. I think you're safe," Boone told him.

"Thank God," someone else muttered. "I'd never live this down."

They arrived at Coldfield to find Maud and James in the front hall waiting for them.

"Come in," Maud cried. "Right on time. I love punctuality in my guests. Go on into the ballroom and introduce yourselves. We don't stand on ceremony here."

Boone had thought they were to arrive before the women, so he was surprised by Maud's words, but the press of men behind him pushed him forward toward the ballroom. When he walked inside he was stunned to see that the Russells had drawn quite a crowd to their festivities.

The room was transformed with garlands and flowers, and the light of hundreds of candles cast a warm glow over the assembled guests. Men and women gathered in knots, greeting each other and chattering as if they knew each other well. Boone wondered where they'd all come from.

"The Regency Society," James boomed in his ear when he appeared suddenly by Boone's side. "It's a national group of like-minded people, don't you know. Montana and the Dakotas have a stronger membership than you might imagine. All too happy to come on a moment's notice for the chance to go to a ball. You should see upstairs; people pitching camp in every nook and cranny!"

James' happiness was palpable and Boone decided not to focus on the waste of fossil fuel. He hoped a few of the guests had carpooled, at least. "I think you and Maud are the most cheerful couple I know," he told James.

"Want to know our secret?" James leaned in closer. "We decided long ago to become each other's staunchest allies. There's no pride separating us. When one of us takes up a passion, so does the other one. You should see Maud shoot for all she pretends she doesn't. If we have a disagreement, we argue each other's side of it as well as our own. Our first thought we each have every morning is how to make the day wonderful for the other one. Works like a charm!"

Boone was impressed. "I'll remember that."

"I'm off to fetch the ladies. Meanwhile, enjoy yourself."

Boone decided to do just that. He turned to the men who had gathered behind him. "Circulate. Introduce yourselves. Remember you're part of a regiment newly stationed at Chance Creek."

"Is the quarry present, sir?" Angus asked, his Scottish burr as pronounced as ever.

"Not yet. But soon." They spread out. Boone approached an elderly couple and was grateful when they immediately began to ply him with questions. Far easier to answer them than come up with his own. Still, by the time a commotion near the door told him that Riley and her guests had arrived, he'd found out that they lived in Bozeman and attended every Regency event they could find.

All thoughts of conversation fled his mind when Riley entered the room.

She was luminous in a deep blue gown and matching earrings. Something sparkled in her hair and he longed to lead her straight from the room, get her alone, undress her and make love to her again. It had been too long. When their eyes met, she smiled and Boone's breath caught. No other woman had ever elicited such a strong physical reaction from him. He was drawn across the room as if she'd roped him and reeled him in.

When he approached she curtsied daintily. "Lieutenant Rudman." Her downturned look made her eyelashes sweep over her cheeks and the hunger within Boone intensified.

"May I have this dance, Miss Eaton?"

"Which one?" She looked up at him, her eyes alight with mischief. "At present the music hasn't even started."

He cursed his confusion. How could he think straight when her breasts strained at a neckline so low as to barely contain them? "All of them."

"That would be tantamount to announcing our engagement." She broke off, color staining her cheeks.

Boone forgot all about her breasts. "We'll announce it soon."

She bit her lip and Boone wanted to swoop down and kiss the lush mouth she was torturing. "You should tell your men to ask my women to dance." But when she looked around, she said, "Never mind. I guess you won't have to."

The recruits had already surrounded Riley's guests, much to the women's evident satisfaction. Judging by the smiles and laughter, they were already enjoying the evening. The buzz of voices in the room increased to a swell and Riley grinned at Boone suddenly.

"It's going to be a marvelous night, isn't it?"

He took her hand as the musicians began to play a piece that he immediately recognized from Angelina's practice sessions. "Damn straight it is."

AS BOONE LED her to her place in the newly formed line of women on the dance floor, Riley's heart beat triple time. She was at a ball. She was wearing the prettiest dress she'd ever owned. She was about to dance a quadrille with the man she'd loved since she was sixteen.

Could life get any sweeter?

When she'd told Maud she needed a ball, fast, she'd pictured a small get-together with her friends and guests and one or two men Maud might be able to assemble on short notice. This huge, sparkling gathering defied all of her expectations.

Maud and James must be her fairy godparents. They'd looked out for her every step of the way since she'd come home and they'd helped transform a drab, steadfast existence into something she'd hardly dared dream of. They'd stepped into the gap left by her grandparents' deaths—the gap her parents had never even tried to fill.

"You look happy," Boone said when the music changed tempo to signal the start of the dance. The two lines of men and women stepped forward to meet each other, then back again.

"I am," Riley said when they advanced again. "What about you?"

"I'm enjoying myself," he admitted when they clasped right hands and circled each other. "This is better than the stupid jumping around I usually do in bars."

"Our ancestors knew a thing or two."

"They sure knew something about women's cloth-ing." He nodded down at her cleavage.

"Behave yourself." They separated again.

"Kind of hard not to look." He did so as they crossed paths and separated again.

Riley laughed. She thought their ancestors understood something about flirting, too. The pace of the song and the steps that led them together and apart again provided the perfect pace for a romantic flirtation. The happy buzz of chatter around them added to the mix.

"You will marry me, won't you? You haven't changed your mind?" Boone asked the next time they were close.

"I don't go back on my word, Boone."

"I know," he said when the music brought them together again. "That's part of what I love so much about you."

"What else do you love?" She circled him and stepped back.

"I love your eyes. I love the way you care so passionately about people and places." They separated and came together again. "I love the way you move when I'm inside you."

Her whole body flooded with warmth and she nearly stumbled in the steps of the dance before she recovered and hurried to catch up to the beat.

"Is there anything you love about me?" Boone asked in a low voice when they were near again.

She realized she'd never given him any clue, except for allowing him access to her body. And yet he'd stood firm in his desire to marry her. With a rush of shame, she said, "Of course."

Boone smiled and Riley wondered why she'd never expressed her feelings clearly before. God knew she found it easy enough to tell him when she was angry. "I love your courage," she said when they met again. "I love the way you defend your ideas and the way you want to make the world a better place. I love that you learned to dance in order to make this a special night for me and my guests." Maud had told her all about the way Boone and his men had thrown themselves into their dancing lessons. That meant more to her than she could say. Riley lost the beat again as an inspiration for his wedding gift hit her. She'd have to work fast to pull it off, but it would be worth it.

"My pleasure."

This time the dance separated them for a longer span, as they each paired up with another partner for a series of steps. When she was faced with Boone again, she added. "I love the way you touch me."

"I could touch you forever." Boone snatched a kiss and spun away again. Heady with desire, Riley moved through the steps until they brought her to him again.

"I miss you at night."

"I miss you all the time," he growled. "Can we leave yet?"

"Not yet, Lieutenant." She moved away from him and circled back. "But we'll be together soon."

"NEVER THOUGHT I'D see you dancing, Walker." Boone lifted his glass of whiskey and polished it off in one shot.

"I'm a good dancer." Walker leaned against the archway leading from the hallway into the ballroom and surveyed the scene. It was an amazing sight, Boone thought. Beautiful, really, although frivolous as hell. Still, was it unsustainable? If the gowns and uniforms were worn again and again, and the candles were made from natural substances, and the food served would be eaten anyhow... he wasn't sure where the harm was.

On the other hand, if the ladies demanded a new gown for each ball and the gentlemen wiped out the beaver population as they'd nearly done once in their desire for fresh top hats made from beaver skin, then it would definitely not be environmentally friendly.

Still, Boone thought they had something to learn from their ancestors about homegrown fun. He liked the live music from local musicians and was glad Maud had employed local purveyors for the food and decorations. A dance didn't need to be anywhere near this fancy, either. Maybe most men would prefer the rough and rowdy atmosphere of a bar like the Dancing Boot in town, but to his surprise he was enjoying the gentility of this far more formal affair.

He spotted Clay partnering with Nora in the latest dance. Jericho stood near Savannah, chatting with her.

He was proud to see his recruits dancing gamely with Riley's guests. The tall, proud woman she'd mentioned once or twice—Win something—was laughing boisterously as she executed a complicated set of steps with Angus.

"Success," he said to Walker.

"Feels good helping her, doesn't it?" Walker asked in reply.

Boone looked to Riley, who had just emerged from the back of the house where she'd gone to freshen up. She was so lovely, her cheeks flushed with the exertion of the dancing and her eyes bright with the triumph of the night. "Sure does. I wish Fulsom wasn't so hard-headed. If he'd bend a little, those women would be on our side in a minute."

"Forget Fulsom. You keep waiting for them to come down that hill. You've got to give them a reason."

"Like what?"

"You'll figure it out, Chief." Walker moved off into the crowd.

Boone watched him go, puzzling over his words. He'd tried to get Riley interested in Base Camp, but she was too taken up with the wedding. If only her guests were interested in sustainable living—

Boone broke off that thought. Riley's guests...

A plan bloomed in his mind like a dandelion springing up overnight after a rain. It was so devious he nearly laughed out loud.

Riley's guests might be the key to everything.

EARLY THE NEXT morning, Riley was dreaming of Boone's arms around her, swirling her around a dance floor in time to the music of an orchestra when a rough pounding at the front door of the manor woke her up. She was alone in bed and she dimly remembered Boone leaving for Base Camp after undressing her and making love to her until she shattered in his arms. The whole night had been magical, and she wasn't ready to get up, but there were guests in the house, so when the knocking sounded again, she leaped out of bed, grabbed a robe, and rushed from her room, meeting Avery on the stairs.

"Who could it be this early?"

"I don't know." Riley hurried down the rest of the steps. When she unbolted the door and flung it open, she recognized Angus. He was dressed again in the redcoat uniform he'd worn the night before. Or perhaps he'd never taken it off, she thought. It had been very late when they'd trundled home from the festivities.

"An invitation, miss."

"To what?" She peered into the early morning mist, looking for some sort of explanation, but saw nothing other than the pale shapes of the outbuildings far in the distance.

"To breakfast. We figured you ladies would be hungry after all that exercise last night." Angus bowed. "We await you down at Base Camp."

"Breakfast?" Riley repeated, but Angus was already striding down the hill.

"Who was it?" Avery called down to her.

"Angus with an invitation to eat down at Base Camp. He didn't wait for an answer. I'll have to walk down there with our apologies; our guests won't be up for hours."

She hurried up the staircase to change into clothes,

but on the second floor, guests stuck their heads out of their doors.

"What is it?" Andrea asked sleepily.

"No cause for concern. The men invited us to breakfast but it's far too early."

"Breakfast sounds good, actually."

"I'm hungry," Win said from her room.

"We'll bring you up a tray," Riley said over her shoulder as she hurried to the next flight of stairs. "Go back to sleep. We'll have something for you before you know it."

"How can I sleep when a bunch of handsome men have cooked me breakfast?" Win exclaimed. "I'll be right there."

"Me, too," Andrea said. "I'll get everyone ready."

"But—" Riley hesitated on the stairs, then chuckled. "I guess we're eating at Base Camp," she said to Avery.

"Sounds good to me."

Back in her room, Riley quickly pulled on her clothes, then hurried downstairs to help their guests dress in their unfamiliar gowns. There was so much giggling among the bridesmaids, she felt like she was back in high school.

"Those men have made quite an impression," she whispered to Savannah as they passed in the hall.

"I can't say I blame them. I'm looking forward to breakfast, too."

"I thought you wanted to keep your distance from Jericho."

"I never said that." Savannah flashed her a smile.

"Don't worry about me, Riley. I'm a grown woman. You don't have to try to keep me safe."

Riley decided not to answer that.

They were a colorful group as they walked down the lane to the bunkhouse, their bonnets bobbing as they talked and laughed. Riley's heart soared as she breathed in the fresh scent of a new day. She felt a rush of love for everyone—even Win—and hoped Andrea's wedding went off without a hitch.

Boone met them near the fire, handsome in his old-fashioned uniform. "Riley. Thanks for coming."

"Thanks for having us. We didn't expect breakfast."

"Can't let you lassies go hungry," Angus said. "Come and eat."

Riley hung back, but gestured the others on. Avery led the way and soon there was a line of women by the cook fire. Clay and Walker labored over the flames. Jericho handed out mugs of coffee. She was surprised by how eager Andrea's pampered friends were to stand around in the chilly dawn when they could be fast asleep, but when she took in the way they were watching the men, she understood. The old-fashioned uniforms made them look earnest and dashing at the same time. It was too bad she wouldn't have more guests for months after this weekend. It had been fun to host them and she'd miss the extra women filling the house with chatter.

Still, she didn't dread the next six months so much anymore. Not since her friends had promised to stick by her, and not since she'd gotten to know Boone's recruits. They'd been such good sports at the ball. It would be fun to have such a lively group so close to hand.

Maybe it would be fun to live among them.

As Riley took her turn in the lineup, she caught snatches of conversation.

"...in charge of the hydroponics setup. We'll use conventional gardens for most things, but hydroponics allows for more sensitive crops and the ability to extend the growing season nearly year round..." Angus was saying. Win, sitting next to him on a blanket spread on the ground, nodded her head and leaned nearer.

"...so fascinated by solar technology," Belinda was saying to Greg. "I had an array installed on my summer cottage."

"My great-uncle patented some of the basic solar technology," Greg answered her.

"Can't wait to see the rest of it," Avery was saying to Walker.

"Happy to show you around," Walker said.

By the time she reached Boone, who'd taken over for Clay and Walker, she had reached a state of bemusement. She rested a hand on his shoulder. "What's there to eat?"

"Southwestern breakfast burritos." He took a spoonful of the beans and rice and held it up for her to taste. Riley blew on it a time or two and took a mouthful.

"Yum. That's good."

"Your guests seem to like it." He gestured at the

crowd surrounding them and Riley had to agree the women were far happier than she'd seen them yet, despite the primitive surroundings.

She found an empty corner of a blanket, sat down, balancing her plate on her lap, and studied Win and Angus surreptitiously. She was a little worried about the transformation in the woman as she chatted and laughed with the Scot. After all, she was due to be married soon.

Choose wisely, she willed toward Win. Marriage was a serious business.

She looked to Boone and was glad she'd found the man for her, even if they'd gotten off to a rocky start.

Savannah sat down beside her. She had a burrito on her plate, but she didn't take a bite of it.

"Something wrong?" Riley asked her.

"I can't believe I've been so silly. I acted like if we took a break from our Regency life we wouldn't be able to start it up again. I've been treating it like some gift from above, as if we didn't make it happen ourselves. That's not the case, is it? We managed to make it happen once. We can do it again. Meanwhile, we can be part of an interesting experiment."

"You think Base Camp is interesting?"

"I didn't realize how interesting until Jericho told me more about what they're going to do. He's really into alternative forms of energy and he's good at explaining the science behind them."

Riley smiled. "Nice."

"There's no piano down here."

"No, but there is at the manor. It's not going anywhere."

"I guess I can still practice even if I can't wear my gowns." Savannah took a tentative bite of her food.

Pleased to see her eating, Riley nodded. "I don't see why not."

"What about Nora? Do you think she'll be content while we wait?"

Riley turned to watch her chatting with Clay. "I hope so." It would be a shame if Fulsom's demands kept her from a man she could love.

"I still don't think I can marry someone I just met." Savannah's gaze rested on Jericho.

"You don't have to decide anything today," Riley told her.

"We're just a bunch of romantics, aren't we?" Savannah asked.

"I don't think that's such a bad thing."

When Boone came to find her, Savannah shifted away so he could sit beside Riley.

"This was a good idea," she said.

"I'm full of them. Wait until you see our new plans for the houses," he said.

"Will I like them?"

"You'll love them. But we can't start building them until we start filming the show."

"I guess I'll be part of the building crew, then."

"I'd like that." Boone took a bite of his burrito. "They're not the only plans I've been making."

"No? What else have you been working on?"

"It's a surprise." He shook his head at her. "Don't ask questions."

"Is it a good surprise?"

"Definitely. Think you can put up with all of this for the next six months or so?" He indicated Base Camp and the people around them.

"Yes. I think I can. The hard part is giving up our Regency experiment so soon. I'm afraid we'll never go back to it, even when the show is over."

"I've got that covered, too. The day filming ends, I'll burn all the modern clothes you've bought in the meantime. You'll have no choice but to pull out your Regency duds again."

"You'd do that for me?"

"I want you to be happy."

"Know what?" Riley said. "I think I already am."

WHEN THE WOMEN finally headed back up to the manor house to begin their preparations for the wedding, Boone asked Riley to stay behind.

"I've got so much to do," she protested as he took her hand and led her toward Pittance Creek.

"Fifteen minutes. They can last without you that long."

"Boone."

He kept going. As soon as they reached the creek he pulled her close and claimed the kiss he'd been wanting all morning.

"What was that for?" Riley asked when he finally let her go.

"I've missed you," he growled. "When are these women going home so I can have you all to myself?"

"You're greedy, you know that?" She wriggled in his arms, but Boone wasn't about to let her go.

"Yeah, I know that." He kissed her again and reached into his pocket. Drawing out the little velvet box Rose had handed to him in the jewelry store, he opened it and sank to one knee. "Riley, I love you. You know what you're getting if you marry me. A television show, a set of ridiculous goals, a whole lot of sustainability nonsense, and a scarred old Navy SEAL who should have been put out to pasture a long time ago. The only thing I can promise is that we'll have sex a lot."

Riley laughed. "That's your proposal?"

"I'm not done yet." He tugged her down to sit on his knee. "I promise to let you paint once in a while. I promise to cook for you over a fire whenever you've got a hankering for it. I promise I'll buy you a horse. And when you're ready, we'll work on that kid thing again. Probably sooner rather than later. We're kind of on the clock for that."

"I know." Riley made a face.

"I'm asking you to take a crazy ride with me these next six months. I promise after that it'll get better."

"Okay."

"Okay? Is that a yes?"

"That's a yes."

"You'll be my wife?"

"I'll be your wife."

"Well, hot damn!" He slid the ring on her finger. "I love you, you know."

"I love you, too." She sighed happily as she looked at the diamond sparkling on her hand. She loved the old-fashioned ring Boone had chosen. "Now I need to plan our wedding."

"No, you don't." He kissed her on the nose. "Leave it up to me. I've got it covered."

WHEN RILEY STOOD up, Boone knew she wanted to get back to help prepare for Andrea's wedding, but he wasn't done with her yet. "Uh-uh, not so fast."

"It's been fifteen minutes."

"It's been ten at the most."

"Boone."

He pulled her close. "It's been far too long since we've been together."

"It's been five hours."

"Seven. At least." He slid his hands to her waist and then lower still, curving them over her bottom.

"We don't have time for that."

"We still have five minutes."

"Even you couldn't be that fast."

"Ouch." He kneaded her skin through the layers of her clothing. "I can be fast. What about you?"

"For heaven's sake—"

He began to lift her skirts.

"I'm not taking off my clothes," she warned him.

"You don't have to. Except for this." He hooked his fingers in the waistband of her panties and tugged them down. When Riley stepped out of them he knew she wanted him as much as he wanted her. He stashed the bit of silk in his pocket and scanned the banks of the creek. Spotting what he was looking for, he directed her toward a birch tree that forked at about shoulder height. "Hold on." He lifted her hands above her head and she took hold of a wide branch. Boone shucked off his pants and boxer briefs, and lifted her dress again. "Can you keep this up?"

She let go with one hand, arranged the folds of her dress, shift and petticoat over her arm and took hold again. "No one better see us."

"They won't." Boone let his gaze trail over her body. She was a sight for sore eyes.

"Boone."

"Here I am." Coming up behind her, her ran his hands up her waist to her breasts, but they were still encased by her stays. He did his best to dip his fingers under the neckline of her dress and find her nipples, but it was difficult at best to gain the access he wanted. He'd have to try again tonight when the wedding was over. Meanwhile there were other parts of Riley's body he wanted to explore.

He pushed her legs apart with his, tugged her back so she was bent at the waist and ducked down between her legs. When his tongue found her core, Riley whimpered. "Oh, that's good."

"Yes, it is." Despite the need to hurry, Boone took his time, savoring Riley. He loved the way she tasted and the way he could elicit moans from her with the touch of his fingers and tongue.

"It's been more than five minutes," Riley gasped.

Her legs were trembling and she rocked her hips against him as he played with her. He knew she was ready.

So was he.

He stood up, sheathed himself in a condom, and pressed into her from behind, wrapping his arms around her and teasing her with his hand at the same time.

She sighed as he stroked in and out of her again. She felt so good he wished he could stay like this for hours.

"Boone," Riley breathed.

He knew what she wanted. Riley liked it fast and hard. He did, too. He sped up and Riley hung on to the branch for dear life. He kept his hand between her legs, knowing the added sensation would soon drive her over the edge. When Riley came, she cried out and slammed back against him. Boone bucked with his own release, spurred on by her cries. His orgasm was long and hard, and by the time he was done, Riley was clinging to the branch, her head hanging down.

"Are you okay?" Boone grew concerned.

"Better than okay. That was the best... ever. I just need to catch my breath."

Boone tightened his arms around her. "Lots more where that came from."

"Thank God." She straightened, let go of the branch and shook out her arms. "I don't suppose we could do that again now."

"No time." He kissed her. "But I'm at your service whenever you like. We can get it on while Andrea and her fiancé take care of all that nonsense up at the altar."

"No, we can't." Riley was scandalized. "We'll wait until they're cutting the cake."

"It's a date."

CHAPTER FIFTEEN

★

"How is Operation Regency Wedding going?" Jericho asked a couple of hours later when Boone joined him in the entryway to the biggest barn on the property. A few days ago it had been a dark, dank structure musty with the smell of old hay. Since then, under Mia's instructions, Boone had set the men to cleaning it up in preparation for the wedding. They'd even given the interior a whitewash. The building was fresh, clean, and strung with lights powered by solar panels on the roof; it made a perfect rustic wedding venue.

Hay bales, liberally topped with quilts they'd borrowed from all the farmhouses around, would act as benches during the short wedding ceremony, and then be lined up at the trestle tables they would use for the meal. Later they'd form overflow seating around the dance floor once the tables had been disassembled. Boone couldn't be happier with the plan that Riley had presented him. She and Mia had managed to combine Regency opulence with downhome sustainable practices for this wedding. The result would be unique.

"I think it'll do just fine for the reception. Once Riley and the women get through decorating, it'll look great."

"Can you believe we start shooting the show in a week?" Jericho said.

"No. I can't believe I'll be marrying Riley either."

"She's still not wearing your ring. I noticed at breakfast."

"That's where you're wrong. I proposed for real this morning. She's wearing my ring now." Boone glanced around. "I've got to go grab a ladder; Riley's coming with more garlands." He turned away, but Jericho whacked him on the arm to get his attention.

"Who's that?" He pointed to a limousine pulling into the driveway.

"Must be a wedding guest." It was hours early, though. The ceremony wasn't due to start until four and Boone had a feeling Riley would freak out if people came before it was time. A driver got out and opened the rear passenger door. Boone bit back a curse when he saw who emerged.

"That's Fulsom."

"It can't be—he's not coming until June."

"That's him all right."

A woman climbed out after him. Boone recognized Fulsom's secretary, Julie. Together they surveyed the ranch. Boone could only imagine how it looked to a stranger's eyes. His men were dressed in work clothes: jeans, boots, T-shirts, and work gloves. Riley and her friends had just approached carrying baskets overflowing with linens. The table runners, he surmised. The women looked fresh and pretty in their walking gowns—Boone had to chuckle that he now knew the designations for their various outfits—but to someone unfamiliar with them, they must seem a bizarre apparition.

"Boone? Boone Rudman? What the holy hell is going on here?" Fulsom's booming voice cut through all the activity.

"Fulsom!" Boone strode forward to meet him before the man could lose his cool. "We didn't expect you for another week."

"Obviously not or I wouldn't have interrupted this... tea party. Who the hell are they?" He gestured to the women, who had halted in their tracks at Fulsom's angry exclamations.

"That's my fiancée in the lead, so keep a civil tongue in your head."

"What's she doing in that getup?"

At least Fulsom had lowered his voice. Boone did the same. "Like I told you, my fiancée is a fan of Jane Austen. She's hosting a Regency wedding this weekend."

"I told you, no way in hell does that play with Middle America. Put a stop to it right now."

All conversation ceased around them as Fulsom's words rang out.

"We are putting a stop to it for the duration of the television show, which doesn't start filming for a week."

Boone hoped Fulsom caught the steel beneath his words.

"I don't think you understand what's happening here, Boone." Fulsom leaned closer. "I've invested millions of dollars to bring your community to life and televise the process around the world. If I show up a little early, we start filming a little early. If you can't take this seriously, let's cut the cord right now."

"I am taking it seriously," Boone growled. "We all are. We've worked our asses off to get ready for you—when you arrive in June."

"Doesn't look like it. What the hell have you done to this barn?" He stalked over to it and peered in.

"We're preparing for a wedding which is going to take place in about five hours. We can't film today." Boone wanted to drop kick Fulsom into the next week, but he tried to keep control of his temper. He sensed the rest of his men gathering around him. He knew they wouldn't be pleased with Fulsom's tirade, either.

"Whose wedding. Yours?"

"No." Boone struggled for control. "The bride and groom are my fiancée's guests."

Fulsom heaved a big sigh. "I don't expect this kind of incompetence from a Navy SEAL."

"And I don't expect this kind of rudeness from a billionaire."

Fulsom cocked his head—and then guffawed. "All right, all right. Jesus, Boone, learn to take a joke."

Boone bit back another angry answer. If Fulsom wanted to find a way out of the corner he'd backed himself into, he'd give him room to turn around.

As the man scanned the activity around him, Boone could practically hear the gears in his brain turning. "Okay—a wedding. This is good. We can use this," Fulsom said. "We'll film it; it'll be a before sequence to show how the ranch was used in the past."

"That sounds like a good idea," Boone said diplomatically.

"Of course it's a good idea." Fulsom clapped his hands together and men and women spilled out of a second vehicle that had just arrived. Within minutes they were unloading video equipment. "All right, folks," Fulsom shouted. "We've got a wedding to film. I want shots of the preparations, cameras capturing every angle. Let's get those waivers signed."

"Boone, make him stop." Riley, who'd so far hung back, rushed up to him. "He can't film Andrea's wedding."

Fulsom turned on her. "Why not?" he demanded.

"It's a private wedding. A Regency wedding. I'll be wearing a historical gown, as will the bride, all her bridesmaids and most of my female guests."

"And I'll be wearing a replica uniform, as will most of the men present," Boone added.

Fulsom paused, apparently taken aback. "We can change that," he said, clapping again. "Wardrobe!"

"We're not going to change it," Riley said.

"The lady's right. Nothing's going to change." Boone backed her up.

"Do I need to remind you who's footing the bill for

your experiment?" Fulsom stepped closer.

Boone didn't blink. "You know, at this moment I don't give a shit."

"I'd mind my tone if I were you."

Boone looked at the men and women who surrounded them and knew it wasn't fair for him to blow this chance for everyone. "Maybe I should step down and you can continue on with the others. I think I've had enough of this for now."

"No way, man. If you go, I go," Jericho said, falling in beside him.

"Me, too," Clay said.

Walker took his place beside them without a word. One by one the other men dropped their tools and came to stand with Boone as well.

"Well, isn't this touching? It's a mutiny." Fulsom crossed his arms. "I'll have you know—"

"Sir, if I could have a word?" Julie nudged her boss. She'd been dogging his steps, tapping on a tablet.

"Not now." Fulsom stepped closer to Boone. "I don't like my time wasted. I can call this whole thing off—"

"Sir, a word. I'd like to show you some ratings."

"For God's sake, Julie—"

The woman shoved her tablet in front of Fulsom's face. "Viewer numbers from the last time *Pride and Prejudice* aired on television. And here's *Sense and Sensibility*. And a documentary about a modern family recreating Regency life."

Fulsom frowned and peered more closely at the

screen. "Interesting." He took the tablet from Julie and thumbed the screen a few times. "Very interesting. That's the demographic we want." He looked up, took in the crowd gathered around him and shoved the tablet back into Julie's hands. "Well." He surveyed the barn, the workers, the sloping building site and the manor up the hill. Again Boone thought the man's mind was churning. Fulsom nodded once. "Boone, I'm all about framing simple messages with compelling stories. When you described your mix of sustainable living and Regency re-enactments, I'll be frank. I didn't get it."

"No shit."

"I thought it would cloud the picture until we lost our viewers. I made a mistake. More than a mistake. I was an idiot. Riley." He held out a hand. Riley slowly lifted hers to grasp it and he shook it up and down. "You are a lovely creature. I can see why Boone adores you. You and your wonderful friends add a whole new element to the narrative we're trying to share with the world. While Boone here will demonstrate the practicalities of sustainable living, you are living proof that sustainability can be fun. If we want to move toward sustainability, we have to attract women to our cause. They're the ones who make household decisions. You are the key to reaching them." He dropped her hand and turned to face the crowd. "We are all embarking on an adventure together. We will encounter hardships and misunderstandings along the way. Let us vow now to do whatever it takes to endure them." He turned back to Boone. "Are you sure you won't hold your wedding today? We could get the taping started early."

"Nope." He wouldn't budge on that. Riley deserved a wedding of her own.

"Then we'll work with what we've got. Where are those waivers?" he called out, sending his crew scrambling.

"Andrea's going to have a fit," Riley said to Savannah. "Boone, we really have to stop him."

Savannah put a restraining hand on her arm. "Are you kidding? Andrea will be thrilled. Getting her wedding televised is like winning the lottery to someone like her. There's no way Win will be able to top her now."

"Are you sure?"

"Positive."

Boone relaxed a little. "So, we're okay?"

"I don't know," Riley said frankly. "The idea of having that man around for the next six months scares the pants off of me."

Boone slipped an arm around her waist, took her basket and led her to the barn. "First of all, you're not wearing pants. Second, I doubt he'll be around that much; he's a busy man."

"Good." Together they took in the half-decorated barn. "I guess I'd better get busy," Riley said.

Before she could slip away, he caught her up and kissed her.

"Can't wait until it's our turn."

"Me, neither."

CHAPTER SIXTEEN

★

R ILEY WATCHED ANDREA walk down the aisle to meet her groom with a glow of pride in herself and her friends. They'd pulled off a miracle in two short weeks, and after the success of the ball last night, she had a feeling everything could go wrong today and it still wouldn't matter.

Andrea's groom, Steven, was a polite young man who obviously doted on his wife-to-be. The couple was so sweet together as they stood at the altar, Riley couldn't help but beam with happiness. Even with Fulsom's crew filming every moment of the festivities, they all managed to have a good time. During the course of the reception she overheard many of Andrea's guests gushing about the unique wedding, the beautiful gowns, the charming decorations and the wonderful food.

Well after midnight, when Andrea and Steven had left for their honeymoon and the guests had retreated to their accommodations, Riley, Avery, Savannah and Nora assembled in Westfield's kitchen for a private toast.

"To us," Savannah said, raising her glass of champagne.

"We did it," Avery said.

"We nailed it," Nora corrected.

"And as soon as that episode airs, I bet we'll be booked for a year," Riley said. She took a sip and nearly choked when the back door swung open and Fulsom entered the room.

"There you are, the ladies of the hour. You deserve to celebrate. Riley, well done. Well done." He shook her hand. She blinked at this intrusion into her kitchen so late at night, but there was no stopping Fulsom. "You were right. I was wrong. Regency living is where it's at. I want to invite all four of you to stick to your original plans; I'm sorry I doubted you."

"You mean we can—"

"Wear your gowns, run your B&B, put on your weddings… Boone told me about all of it. The four of you will add the kind of human interest we're looking for. I hope you're ready to be stars."

That sounded alarming, but Riley was too grateful for his change of heart to dwell on it. "Thank you!"

"Not at all. Goodnight." He slipped back outside again.

"That man is… ridiculous," Nora said.

"I think he's all right," Riley said. "I think you have to get to know him." She was willing to be magnanimous now that he'd changed his tune.

"I have a feeling we will get to know him whether or not we want to," Avery chimed in.

"It's already been a long, strange trip." Savannah raised her glass again. "To our future together at Westfield! It certainly won't be boring."

"Hear, hear!" The others toasted her back.

"Oops, we've got company," Savannah said, pointing behind Riley.

Riley turned to find Boone had come in from the front of the house. "Ladies."

"That's our cue," Nora said. She, Savannah and Avery headed for the parlor with enough giggling to make Riley roll her eyes.

"Ignore them."

"I intend to. Any chance we could take this upstairs?"

"I thought you'd never ask."

She came down late the following morning and found that Savannah and Nora had already packed most of the bridesmaids off to the airport. Riley was glad. After they cleaned up, she needed to get back to her painting. It was only a matter of days before her wedding, and the painting needed to be done by then so she could give it to Boone. She'd figured out exactly what to do to complete the image she was striving for. Instinct told her it would be the best work she'd ever done.

Now if she could get rid of Win.

Riley found her at the kitchen table nursing a cup of coffee.

"You don't have a plane to catch?" she asked, pouring one for herself. Boone had slipped away early in the morning to head down to Base Camp. She'd meant to get up then, too, but must have fallen back to sleep.

"I don't want to leave."

"Don't you want to see your fiancé?"

"No," Win said simply. "I'm a bitch, I know it, but there it is. I don't have the slightest urge to go back home."

"Could it be wedding jitters?" Riley joined her at the table.

"I don't think so." Win traced a finger around the rim of her cup. "He's not the right guy."

Riley considered her words. "I can tell you've connected to Angus, but—"

"See, that's the thing," Win said. "We have connected. I haven't touched Angus and he hasn't touched me, and I'm more turned on by him than I ever am by Leif in the sack."

"Forbidden fruit?"

"No. It's his mind I'm attracted to. His sense of humor—and his sense of honor. God, I'm in trouble." Win covered her face with her hands.

"I'm sorry."

"Don't be. I'm not. I'm going to throw it all away. Everything I thought I wanted. For a crazy Scotsman and a tiny house."

Riley reached out and took Win's hand.

Win looked up. "Am I insane?"

"Yes. Did Angus tell you the goals they have to reach by December?"

"He did." Win shook her head. "That's some crazy stuff."

"But you're willing to do it?"

"Aren't you?"

Riley nodded. "I guess I am."

"Me, too." Win straightened. Downed the dregs of her coffee. "Wish me luck. I'm going to head down to Base Camp and ask if they'll have me."

"Good luck," Riley said as Win stood up and took her coffee cup to the sink. She didn't think there was much chance the men would say no.

"IN TWENTY-FOUR HOURS, you'll be a married man," Jericho said as Boone surveyed the barn they'd just finished setting up for the wedding. "You ready for that?"

"Hell, yeah." He couldn't wait to have Riley in his bed every night. He was looking forward to his honeymoon, as short as it would be. He always felt he was competing with something else for Riley's time.

He glanced at his watch. "I'd better get going. Riley asked me up to the manor to sort out some last minute details."

"Sure, Chief."

Boone didn't rise to the bait. Riley actually had asked for his help, although he was hoping when they were done they could slip off for a little time alone.

He cleaned up and made his way to the manor, stopping to encourage the other men who were getting everything ready for the wedding. When he reached the house, he found Avery, Savannah and Nora on the back porch crafting garlands from flowers and greenery.

"Riley's in the kitchen," Avery said. "Go on in."

Boone did, but when he got inside, the kitchen was empty.

"I'm up here," Riley shouted down the stairs. Boone took them two at a time. Maybe they'd skip those details and get right to the good stuff.

When Riley let him into her bedroom, though, there was a large package lying on her bed. She shut the door behind her and led him over to it. "Open it. It's for you!"

Boone hesitated. He'd gone back to Thayer's and bought a necklace and bracelet set for Riley's wedding present, but he'd meant to give it to her tomorrow night.

"Go on," Riley urged him.

"Okay." He lifted the package carefully. Found a corner, and pulled off the wrapping paper. A framed painting lay beneath. Boone uncovered it—

And was nearly bowled over when he took it in.

"You painted this?"

"Yes," Riley said softly.

It was Westfield—a Westfield so alive he couldn't believe it was a painting. There were the pastures and rolling hills and the mountains in the background, but it was the way the manor house sat in the landscape that drew him in, until he noticed the outbuildings—

And the hobbit houses dug into the hillside nearby.

The neatly planted vegetable gardens he'd planned for Base Camp balanced the wildly untamed flower gardens near the manor. His tiny houses were humble and organic, while the manor stood brazen and unashamed on its hill.

The lines and brush strokes led his eye to a fire in a rustic outside fireplace left of center in the canvas. It seemed to dance and spark. But it was the man standing next to the fire with his arms folded that caught his eye. A man so at home in the scene he seemed to own it.

Him.

He didn't know how she'd conveyed so much with so few strokes of her brush, but he knew exactly what she was saying. That at Westfield, the natural world and man-made world came together in a beautiful whole.

And he was the one who was going to make it happen.

She was predicting the future and creating it at the same time with bold, powerful brushstrokes that resonated in Boone's soul.

"Do you like it?"

It took two tries for Boone to answer. "I love it."

"I'm glad."

"Riley—do you feel this way?" He gently put the painting back down on the bed and faced her.

"I do."

"I wish you'd put yourself in there with me." It was his only quibble with the work.

"I am in there. I'm Westfield, Boone. This ranch, this land is as much a part of me as I am of it."

Boone swallowed hard and looked at the painting again. If that was true, then the message in her painting was far more intimate—and powerful—than he'd guessed.

Riley waited for him to say something. In a flash he knew they'd come to another crossroads. She was standing in front of him at another dance, baring her soul. Asking him with her eyes to say yes.

Boone pulled her to him. "I love you. I. Love. You. And I will do whatever it takes to be worthy of you." He lifted her chin to kiss her.

"You already are."

CHAPTER SEVENTEEN

★

"I WISH YOU would have let me hold your wedding at my house," Maud said, interrupting Riley's thoughts. Savannah, Nora, Avery, Win and Alice had all helped her dress and were now attending to their own preparations. Her mother had fluttered in and out of the room but had gone to help her husband with his suit. Her father and his wife were already downstairs. Riley was grateful for Maud's company. She had no misgivings, but nerves were fluttering in her stomach and she didn't want to be alone.

"That would have been lovely, but it's important to hold it here. Boone and I are starting a new life together at Westfield. It seems right to hold the ceremony on the land where we'll live out the rest of our lives. Besides, Fulsom says we have to."

She didn't mind, though. Boone had put together a wonderful wedding, especially after Fulsom lifted his directive against Regency life. Once Fulsom changed his mind, Boone had shown her all the subversive tricks he'd concocted to slip a Regency wedding past Fulsom.

Freed from all constraints, he'd worked with Mia to make sure every one of Riley's dreams would come true.

"Have you resigned yourself to tiny-house living?" Maud fluffed out Riley's veil.

"You should see the plans for our house. I didn't think anything could entice me to try it, but Clay and Boone are going to build a masterpiece. It'll be like living in a piece of art."

"That sounds wonderful. It does my heart good to see you two happy together."

"One of the best parts about coming to Westfield was meeting you," Riley said truthfully.

"Oh, hush." But Maud looked pleased.

"Let's take a look at you." Alice came back into the bedroom to give her a final once-over. "That dress looks spectacular on you." It was made in the Regency manner, with a high waist and a long train. Riley loved it.

"It does," Savannah agreed, following her into the room. "You look lovely, Riley."

"So beautiful," Nora said.

"Stunning," Avery said, coming to join the circle around Riley. Their bridesmaid gowns echoed the style of her dress.

"I would never have come here if it weren't for you three," she said to her friends. "Thank you for coming on this adventure with me and for sticking with it when things got interesting."

"I wouldn't have missed it for the world," Avery said.

"But I can't believe you're going to spend your honeymoon in a tent," Nora added.

"With a film crew following you around, no less," Savannah said.

"No film crew. Boone made Fulsom sign a contract on that. We'll have two glorious nights to ourselves at the farthest end of the property. Then it's time to get to work."

"I can't wait to see what the next few months bring." Savannah stepped beside Riley to check out her own reflection in the big mirror that stood nearby.

"The possibilities scare me," Nora said dryly.

"It's certainly going to be interesting," Avery said.

She was right, Riley thought, turning to look out the window down at the encampment. There was no telling what would happen next.

BOONE DIDN'T THINK he'd ever been so nervous in his life as when he stood on the rise of ground where he and Riley had once picnicked and watched Riley's friends walk toward him one at a time on the arms of his groomsmen. They'd re-used the hay bales and quilts from Andrea's wedding to set up rows of seats. There were fewer guests than at Andrea's wedding, but despite the short notice, it was still well-attended by friends and family on both sides. They would be married with the Beartooth Mountains in the distance, then hold the reception on the manor's lawn where they'd set up tables and fairy lights.

Jericho escorted a pale but beautiful Savannah to

her place and came to stand next to Boone. Clay walked a beaming Nora down the aisle and left her with Savannah. Walker, his expression as serious as always, brought a beautifully blushing Avery to stand beside Nora. Boone took in Walker's solicitude with interest. Cupid had definitely hit his mark on the impassive man.

When Riley appeared on her father's arm at the head of the aisle, Boone forgot about all of that. He had eyes only for his wife-to-be, who looked more beautiful than he'd ever seen her. She moved with such grace, her gown giving her the look of a Grecian goddess as she stepped slowly down the aisle. His heart filled to bursting with pride that she would be his wife—this woman who'd matched him in passion, strength of mind and joy in life for as long as he could remember.

When she took her place by his side, Boone thought he'd never feel happier than he did in this moment, even if a camera crew was discreetly filming their every movement. He didn't care. He had two nights—two glorious nights—alone with Riley ahead of him. After that he'd throw himself into building her a home where they would begin to make each other's dreams come true.

"Dearly Beloved," the minister said, as the sun set to the west in a glorious show of pinks and purples. "We are gathered here today…"

Boone squeezed Riley's hand. He hoped she knew how much he loved her.

She squeezed back.

Boone couldn't help himself. He ducked down and

kissed her quickly. The crowd behind them gasped and then let out muted chuckles.

"Ahem." The minister cleared his throat with mock disapproval. "Wait to the end of the ceremony to kiss the bride."

"Just one more." Boone kissed her again. Riley leaned into him and returned his kiss eagerly. The congregation behind them began to clap and cheer. Boone finally pulled back. "Okay, I think I can hold out for a few more minutes. If you talk fast."

"Will do." The minister began again. "Dearly Beloved…"

Boone snatched another kiss.

The minister sighed.

"Behave," Walker said firmly.

"Yes, sir." Boone smiled down at Riley, who smiled mischievously back up at him as the minister continued with the ceremony.

He couldn't wait to start their sustainable Regency life.

To find out more about Boone, Riley, Clay, Jericho, Walker and the other inhabitants of Westfield, look for *A SEAL's Vow*, Volume 2 in the *SEALs of Chance Creek* series.

Be the first to know about Cora Seton's new releases! Sign up for her newsletter here!
www.coraseton.com/sign-up-for-my-newsletter

Other books in the SEALs of Chance Creek Series:

A SEAL's Vow
A SEAL's Pledge
A SEAL's Consent

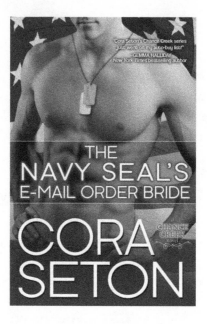

Read on for an excerpt of Volume 1 of **The Heroes of Chance Creek** series –

The Navy SEAL's E-Mail Order Bride.

"BOYS," LIEUTENANT COMMANDER Mason Hall said, "we're going home."

He sat back in his folding chair and waited for a reaction from his brothers. The recreation hall at Bagram Airfield was as busy as always with men hunched over laptops, watching the widescreen television, or lounging in groups of three or four shooting the breeze. His brothers—three tall, broad shouldered men in uniform—stared back at him from his computer screen, the feeds from their four-way video conversation all relaying a similar reaction to his words.

Utter confusion.

"Home?" Austin was the first to speak. A Special Forces officer just a year younger than Mason, he was currently in Kabul.

"Home," Mason confirmed. "I got a letter from Great Aunt Heloise. Uncle Zeke passed away over the weekend without designating an heir. That means the ranch reverts back to her. She thinks we'll do a better job running it than Darren will." Darren, their first cousin, wasn't known for his responsible behavior and he hated ranching. Mason, on the other hand, loved it. He had missed the ranch, the cattle, the Montana sky and his family's home ever since they'd left it twelve years ago.

"She's giving Crescent Hall to us?" That was Zane, Austin's twin, a Marine currently in Kandahar. The excitement in his tone told Mason all he needed to know—Zane stilled loved the old place as much as he did. When Mason had gotten Heloise's letter, he'd had to read it more than once before he believed it. The Hall would belong to them once more—when he'd thought they'd lost it for good. Suddenly he'd felt like he could breathe fully again after so many years of holding in his anger and frustration over his uncle's behavior. The timing was perfect, too. He was due to ship stateside any day now. By April he'd be a civilian again.

Except it wasn't as easy as all that. Mason took a deep breath. "There are a few conditions."

Colt, his youngest brother, snorted. "Of course—

we're talking about Heloise, aren't we? What's she up to this time?" He was an Air Force combat controller who had served both in Afghanistan and as part of the relief effort a few years back after the massive earthquake which devastated Haiti. He was currently back on United States soil in Florida, training with his unit.

Mason knew what he meant. Calling Heloise eccentric would be an understatement. In her eighties, she had definite opinions and brooked no opposition to her plans and schemes. She meant well, but as his father had always said, she was capable of leaving a swath of destruction in family affairs that rivaled Sherman's march to Atlanta.

"The first condition is that we have to stock the ranch with one hundred pair of cattle within twelve months of taking possession."

"We should be able to do that," Austin said.

"It's going to take some doing to get that ranch up and running again," Zane countered. "Zeke was already letting the place go years ago."

"You have something better to do than fix the place up when you get out?" Mason asked him. He hoped Zane understood the real question: was he in or out?

"I'm in; I'm just saying," Zane said.

Mason suppressed a smile. Zane always knew what he was thinking.

"Good luck with all that," Colt said.

"Thanks," Mason told him. He'd anticipated that inheriting the Hall wouldn't change Colt's mind about staying in the Air Force. He focused on the other two who were both already in the process of winding down their military careers. "If we're going to do this, it'll take a commitment. We're going to have to pool our funds and put our shoulders to the wheel for as long as it takes. Are you up for that?"

"I'll join you there as soon as I'm able to in June," Austin said. "It'll just be like another year in the service. I can handle that."

"I already said I'm in," Zane said. "I'll have boots on the ground in September."

Here's where it got tricky. "There's just one other thing," Mason said. "Aunt Heloise has one more requirement of each of us."

"What's that?" Austin asked when he didn't go on.

"She's worried about the lack of heirs on our side of the family. Darren has children. We don't."

"Plenty of time for that," Zane said. "We're still young, right?"

"Not according to Heloise." Mason decided to get it over and done with. "She's decided that in order for us to inherit the Hall free and clear, we each have to be married within the year. One of us has to have a child."

Stunned silence met this announcement until Colt started to laugh. "Staying in the Air Force doesn't look so bad now, does it?"

"That means you, too," Mason said.

"What? Hold up, now." Colt was startled into soberness. "I won't even live on the ranch. Why do I have to get hitched?"

"Because Heloise says it's time to stop screwing

around. And she controls the land. And you know Heloise."

"How are we going to get around that?" Austin asked.

"We're not." Mason got right to the point. "We're going to find ourselves some women and we're going to marry them."

"In Afghanistan?" Zane's tone made it clear what he thought about that idea.

Tension tightened Mason's jaw. He'd known this was going to be a messy conversation. "Online. I created an online personal ad for all of us. Each of us has a photo, a description and a reply address. A woman can get in touch with whichever of us she chooses and start a conversation. Just weed through your replies until you find the one you want."

"Are you out of your mind?" Zane peered at him through the video screen.

"I don't see what you're upset about. I'm the one who has to have a child. None of you will be out of the service in time."

"Wait a minute—I thought you just got the letter from Heloise." As usual, Austin zeroed in on the inconsistency.

"The letter came about a week ago. I didn't want to get anyone's hopes up until I checked a few things out." Mason shifted in his seat. "Heloise said the place is in rougher shape than we thought. Sounds like Zeke sold off the last of his cattle last year. We're going to have to start from scratch, and we're going to have to move fast to meet her deadline—on both counts. I did all the leg work on the online ad. All you need to do is read some e-mails, look at some photos and pick one. How hard can that be?"

"I'm beginning to think there's a reason you've been single all these years, Straightshot," Austin said. Mason winced at the use of his nickname. The men in his unit had christened him with it during his early days in the service, but as Colt said when his brothers had first heard about it, it made perfect sense. The name had little to do with his accuracy with a rifle, and everything to do with his tendency to find the shortest route from here to done on any mission he was tasked with. Regardless of what obstacles stood in his way.

Colt snickered. "Told you two it was safer to stay in the military. Mason's Matchmaking Service. It has a ring to it. I guess you've found yourself a new career, Mase."

"Stow it." Mason tapped a finger on the table. "Just because I've put the ad up doesn't mean that any of you have to make contact with the women who write you. If it doesn't work, it doesn't work. But you need to marry within the year. If you don't find a wife for yourself, I'll find one for you."

"He would, too," Austin said to the others. "You know he would."

"When does the ad go live?" Zane asked.

"It went live five days ago. You've each got several hundred responses so far. I'll forward them to you as soon as we break the call."

Austin must have leaned toward his webcam because suddenly he filled the screen. "Several hundred?"

"That's right."

Colt's laughter rang out over the line.

"Don't know what you're finding so funny, Colton," Mason said in his best imitation of their late father's voice. "You've got several hundred responses, too."

"What? I told you I was staying…"

"Read through them and answer all the likely ones. I'll be in touch in a few days to check your progress." Mason cut the call.

★   ★   ★

REGAN ANDERSON WANTED a baby. Right now. Not five years from now. Not even next year.

Right now.

And since she'd just quit her stuffy loan officer job, moved out of her overpriced one bedroom New York City apartment, and completed all her preliminary appointments, she was going to get one via the modern technology of artificial insemination.

As she raced up the three flights of steps to her tiny new studio, she took the pins out of her severe updo and let her thick, auburn hair swirl around her shoulders. By the time she reached the door, she was breathing hard. Inside, she shut and locked it behind her, tossed her briefcase and blazer on the bed which took up the lion's share of the living space, and kicked off her high heels. Her blouse and pencil skirt came next, and thirty seconds later she was down to her skivvies.

Thank God.

She was done with Town and Country Bank. Done with originating loans for people who would scrape and slave away for the next thirty years just to cling to a lousy flat near a subway stop. She was done, done, done being a cog in the wheel of a financial system she couldn't stand to be a part of anymore.

She was starting a new business. Starting a new life.

And she was starting a family, too.

Alone.

After years of looking for Mr. Right, she'd decided he simply didn't exist in New York City. So after several medical exams and consultations, she had scheduled her first round of artificial insemination for the end of April. She couldn't wait.

Meanwhile, she'd throw herself into the task of building her consulting business. She would make it her job to help non-profits assist regular people start new stores and services, buy homes that made sense, and manage their money so that they could get ahead. It might not be as lucrative as being a loan officer, but at least she'd be able to sleep at night.

She wasn't going to think about any of that right now, though. She'd survived her last day at work, survived her exit interview, survived her boss, Jack Richey, pretending to care that she was leaving. Now she was giving herself the weekend off. No work, no nothing—just forty-eight hours of rest and relaxation.

Having grabbed takeout from her favorite Thai restaurant on the way home, Regan spooned it out onto a plate and carried it to her bed. Lined with pillows, it doubled as her couch during waking hours. She sat cross-legged on top of the duvet and savored her food and her freedom. She had bought herself a nice bottle of wine to drink this weekend, figuring it might be her last for an awfully long time. She was all too aware her Chardonnay-sipping days were coming to an end. As soon as her weekend break from reality was over, she planned to spend the next ten months starting her business, while scrimping and saving every penny she could. She would have to move to a bigger apartment right before the baby was born, but given the cost of renting in the city, the temporary downgrade was worth it. She pushed all thoughts of business and the future out of her mind. Rest and relax—that was her job for now.

Two hours and two glasses of wine later, however, rest and relaxation was beginning to feel a lot like loneliness and boredom. In truth, she'd been fighting loneliness for months. She'd broken up with her last boyfriend before Christmas. Here it was March and she was still single. Two of her closest friends had gotten married and moved away in the past twelve months, Laurel to New Hampshire and Rita to New Jersey. They rarely saw each other now and when she'd jokingly mentioned the idea of going ahead and having a child without a husband the last time they'd gotten together, both women had scoffed.

"No way could I have gotten through this pregnancy without Ryan." Laurel ran a hand over her large belly.

"I've felt awful the whole time."

"No way I'm going back to work." Rita's baby was six weeks old. "Thank God Alan brings in enough cash to see us through."

Regan decided not to tell them about her plans until the pregnancy was a done deal. She knew what she was getting into—she didn't need them to tell her how hard it might be. If there'd been any way for her to have a baby normally—with a man she loved—she'd have chosen that path in a heartbeat. But there didn't seem to be a man for her to love in New York. Unfortunately, keeping her secret meant it was hard to call either Rita or Laurel just to chat, and she needed someone to chat with tonight. As dusk descended on the city, Regan felt fear for the first time since making her decision to go ahead with having a child.

What if she'd made a mistake? What if her consultancy business failed? What if she became a welfare mother? What if she had to move back home?

When the thoughts and worries circling her mind grew overwhelming, she topped up her wine, opened up her laptop and clicked on a YouTube video of a cat stuck headfirst in a cereal box. Thank goodness she'd hooked up wi-fi the minute she secured the studio. Simultaneously scanning her Facebook feed, she read an update from an acquaintance named Susan who was exhibiting her art in one of the local galleries. She'd have to stop by this weekend.

She watched a couple more videos—the latest installment in a travel series she loved, and one about over-the-top weddings that made her sad. Determined to cheer up, she hopped onto Pinterest and added more images to her nursery pinboard. Sipping her wine, she checked the news, posted a question on the single parents' forum she frequented, checked her e-mail again, and then tapped a finger on the keys, wondering what to do next. The evening stretched out before her, vacant even of the work she normally took home to do over the weekend. She hadn't felt at such loose ends in years.

Pacing her tiny apartment didn't help. Nor did an attempt at unpacking more of her things. She had finished moving in just last night and boxes still lined one wall. She opened one to reveal books, took a look at her limited shelf space and packed them up again. A second box revealed her collection of vintage fans. No room for them here, either.

She stuck her iTouch into a docking station and turned up some tunes, then drained her glass, poured herself another, and flopped onto her bed. The wine was beginning to take effect—giving her a nice, soft, fuzzy feeling. It hadn't done away with her loneliness, but when she turned back to Facebook on her laptop, the images and YouTube links seemed funnier this time.

Heartened, she scrolled further down her feed until she spotted another post one of her friends had shared. It was an image of a handsome man standing ramrod straight in combat fatigues. *Hello.* He was cute. In fact, he looked like exactly the kind of man she'd always hoped she'd meet. He wasn't thin and arrogant like the up-and-coming Wall Street crowd, or paunchy and cynical like the upper-management men who hung around the bars near work. Instead he looked healthy, muscle-bound, clear-sighted, and vital. What was the post about? She clicked the link underneath it. Maybe there'd be more fantasy-fodder like this man wherever it took her.

There *was* more fantasy fodder. Regan wriggled happily. She had landed on a page that showcased four men. Brothers, she saw, looking more closely—two of them identical twins. Each one seemed to represent a different branch of the United States military. Were they models? Was this some kind of recruitment ploy?

Practical Wives Wanted read the heading at the top. Regan nearly spit out a sip of her wine. Wives Wanted? Practical ones? She considered the men again, then read more.

Looking for a change? the text went on. *Ready for a real challenge? Join four hardworking, clean living men and help bring our family's ranch back to life.*

Skills required—any or all of the following: Riding, roping, construction, animal care, roofing, farming, market gardening, cooking, cleaning, metalworking, small motor repair...

The list went on and on. Regan bit back at a laugh which quickly dissolved into giggles. Small engine repair? How very romantic. Was this supposed to be satire or was it real? It was certainly one of the most intriguing things she'd seen online in a long, long time.

Must be willing to commit to a man and the project. No weekends/no holidays/no sick days. Weaklings need not apply.

Regan snorted. It was beginning to sound like an employment ad. Good luck finding a woman to fill those conditions. She'd tried to find a suitable man for years and came up with Erik—the perennial mooch who'd finally admitted just before Christmas that he liked her old Village apartment more than he liked her. That's why she planned to get pregnant all by herself. There wasn't anyone worth marrying in the whole city. Probably the whole state. And if the men were all worthless, the women probably were, too. She reached for her wine without turning from the screen, missed, and nearly knocked over her glass. She tried again, secured the wine, drained the glass a third time and set it down again.

What she would give to find a real partner. Someone strong, both physically and emotionally. An equal in intelligence and heart. A real man.

But those didn't exist.

If you're sick of wasting your time in a dead-end job, tired of tearing things down instead of building something up, or just ready to get your hands dirty with clean, honest work, write and tell us why you'd make a worthy wife for a man who has spent the last decade in uniform.

There wasn't much to laugh at in this paragraph. Regan read it again, then got up and wandered to the kitchen to top up her glass. She'd never seen a singles ad like this one. She could see why it was going viral. If it was real, these men were something special. Who wanted to do clean, honest work these days? What kind of man was selfless enough to serve in the military instead of sponging off their girlfriends? If she'd known there were guys like this in the world, she might not have been so quick to schedule the artificial insemination appointment.

She wouldn't cancel it, though, because these guys couldn't be for real, and she wasn't waiting another minute to start her family. She had dreamed of having children ever since she was a child herself and organized pretend schools in her backyard for the neighborhood little ones. Babies loved her. Toddlers thought she was the next best thing to teddy bears. Her co-workers at the bank had never appreciated her as much as the average five-year-old did.

Further down the page there were photographs of the ranch the brothers meant to bring back to life. The land was beautiful, if overgrown, but its toppled fences and sagging buildings were a testament to its neglect. The photograph of the main house caught her eye and kept her riveted, though. A large gothic structure, it could be beautiful with the proper care. She could see why these men would dedicate themselves to returning it to its former glory. She tried to imagine what it would be like to live on the ranch with one of them, and immediately her body craved an open sunny sky—the kind you were hard pressed to see in the city. She sunk into the daydream, picturing herself sitting on a back porch sipping lemonade while her cowboy worked and the baby napped. Her husband would have his shirt off while he chopped wood, or mended a fence or whatever it was ranchers did. At the end of the day they'd fall into bed and make love until morning.

Regan sighed. It was a wonderful daydream, but it had no bearing on her life. Disgruntled, she switched over to Netflix and set up a foreign film. She fetched the bottle of wine back to bed with her and leaned against her many pillows. She'd managed to hang her small flatscreen on the opposite wall. In an apartment this tiny, every piece of furniture needed to serve double-duty.

As the movie started, Regan found herself composing messages to the military men in the Wife Wanted ad, in which she described herself as trim and petite, or lithe and strong, or horny and good-enough-looking to do the trick.

An hour later, when the film failed to hold her attention, she grabbed her laptop again. She pulled up the Wife Wanted page and reread it, keeping an eye on the foreign couple on the television screen who alternately argued and kissed.

Crazy what some people did. What was wrong with these men that they needed to advertise for wives instead of going out and meeting them like normal people?

She thought of the online dating sites she'd tried in the past. She'd had some awkward experiences, some horrible first dates, and finally one relationship that lasted for a couple of months before the man was transferred to Tucson and it fizzled out. It hadn't worked for her, but she supposed lots of people found love online these days. They might not advertise directly for spouses, but that was their ultimate intention, right? So maybe this ad wasn't all that unusual.

Most men who posted singles ads weren't as hot as these men were, though. Definitely not the ones she'd met. She poured herself another glass. A small twinge of her conscience told her she'd already had far too much wine for a single night.

To hell with that, Regan thought. As soon as she got pregnant she'd have to stay sober and sane for the next eighteen years. She wouldn't have a husband to trade off with—she'd always be the designated driver, the adult in charge, the sober, wise mother who made sure nothing bad ever happened to her child. Just this one last time she was allowed to blow off steam.

But even as she thought it, a twinge of fear wormed through her belly.

What if she wasn't good enough?

She stood up, strode the two steps to the kitchenette and made herself a bowl of popcorn. She drowned it in butter and salt, returned to the bed in time for the ending credits of the movie, and lined up *Pride and Prejudice* with Colin Firth. Time for comfort food and a comfort movie. *Pride and Prejudice* always did the trick when she felt blue. She checked the Wife Wanted page again on her laptop. If she was going to pick one of the men—which she wasn't—who would she choose?

Mason, the oldest, due to leave the Navy in a matter of weeks, drew her eye first. With his dark crew cut, hard jaw and uncompromising blue eyes he looked like the epitome of a military man. He stated his interests as ranching—of course—history, natural sciences and tactical operations, whatever the hell that was. That left her little more informed than before she'd read it, and she wondered what the man was really like. Did he read the newspaper in bed on Sunday mornings? Did he prefer lasagna or spaghetti? Would he listen to country music in his truck or talk radio? She stared at his photo, willing him to answer.

The next two brothers, Austin and Zane, were less fierce, but looked no less intelligent and determined. Still, they didn't draw her eye the way the way Mason did. Colt, the youngest, was blond with a grin she bet drew women like flies. That one was trouble, and she didn't need trouble.

She read Mason's description again and decided he was the leader of this endeavor. If she was going to pick one, it would be him.

But she wasn't going to pick one. She had given up all that. She'd made a promise to her imaginary child that she would not allow any chaos into its life. No dating until her baby wore a graduation gown, at the very least. She felt another twinge. Was she ready to give up men for nearly two decades? That was a long time.

It's worth it, she told herself. She had no doubt about her desire to be a mother. She had no doubt she'd be a great mom. She was smart, capable and had a good head on her shoulders. She was funny, silly and patient, too. She loved children.

She was just lousy with men.

But that didn't matter anymore. She pushed the laptop aside and returned her attention to *Pride and Prejudice*, quickly falling into an old drinking game she and Laurel had devised one night that required taking a swig of wine each time one of the actresses lifted her eyebrows in polite surprise. When she finished the bottle, she headed to the tiny kitchenette to track down another one, trilling, "Jane! Elizabeth!" at the top of her voice along with Mrs. Bennett in the film. There was no more wine, so she switched to tequila.

By the time Elizabeth Bennett discovered the miracle of Mr. Darcy's palace-sized mansion, and decided she'd been too hasty in turning down his offer of marriage, Regan had decided she too needed to cast off her prejudices and find herself a man. A hot hunk of a military man. She grabbed the laptop, fumbled with the link that would let her leave Mason Hall a message and drafted a brilliant missive worthy of Jane Austen herself.

Dear Lt. Cmdr. Hall,

In her mind she pronounced lieutenant with an "f" like the Brits in the movie onscreen.

It is a truth universally acknowledged, that a single man in possession of a good ranch, must be in want of a wife. Furthermore, it must be self-evident that the wife in question should possess certain qualities numbering amongst them riding, roping, construction, roofing, farming, market gardening, cooking, cleaning, metalworking, animal care, and—most importantly, by Heaven—small motor repair.

Seeing as I am in possession of all these qualities,

not to mention many others you can only have left out through unavoidable oversight or sheer obtuseness—such as glassblowing, cheesemaking, towel origami, heraldry, hovercraft piloting, and an uncanny sense of what cats are thinking—I feel almost forced to catapult myself into your purview.

You will see from my photograph that I am most eminently and majestically suitable for your wife.

She inserted a digital photo of her foot.

In fact, one might wonder why such a paragon of virtue such as I should deign to answer such a peculiar advertisement. The truth is, sir, that I long for adventure. To get my hands dirty with clean, hard work. To build something up instead of tearing it down.

In short, you are really hot. I'd like to lick you.

Yours,
Regan Anderson

On screen, Elizabeth Bennett lifted an eyebrow. Regan knocked back another shot of Jose Cuervo and passed out.

End of Excerpt

The Cowboys of Chance Creek Series:

The Cowboy Inherits a Bride (Volume 0)
The Cowboy's E-Mail Order Bride (Volume 1)
The Cowboy Wins a Bride (Volume 2)
The Cowboy Imports a Bride (Volume 3)
The Cowgirl Ropes a Billionaire (Volume 4)
The Sheriff Catches a Bride (Volume 5)
The Cowboy Lassos a Bride (Volume 6)
The Cowboy Rescues a Bride (Volume 7)
The Cowboy Earns a Bride (Volume 8)
The Cowboy's Christmas Bride (Volume 9)

The Heroes of Chance Creek Series:

The Navy SEAL's E-Mail Order Bride (Volume 1)
The Soldier's E-Mail Order Bride (Volume 2)
The Marine's E-Mail Order Bride (Volume 3)
The Navy SEAL's Christmas Bride (Volume 4)
The Airman's E-Mail Order Bride (Volume 5)

The SEALs of Chance Creek Series:

A SEAL's Oath
A SEAL's Vow
A SEAL's Pledge
A SEAL's Consent

About the Author

With over one million books sold, NYT and USA Today bestselling author Cora Seton has created a world readers love in Chance Creek, Montana. She has twenty-eight novels and novellas currently set in her fictional town, with many more in the works. Like her characters, Cora loves cowboys, military heroes, country life, gardening, bike-riding, binge-watching Jane Austen movies, keeping up with the latest technology and indulging in old-fashioned pursuits. Visit **www.coraseton.com** to read about new releases, contests and other cool events!

Blog:

www.coraseton.com

Facebook:

www.facebook.com/coraseton

Twitter:

www.twitter.com/coraseton

Newsletter:

www.coraseton.com/sign-up-for-my-newsletter

CPSIA information can be obtained
at www.ICGtesting.com
Printed in the USA
LVHW031951240120
644729LV00002B/193